Wounds streaked
Slashed chest, arms pierced several times—hours of
fighting plunged him into weariness no human could
endure.

"So be it, I'm ready. One swift stroke of a silver
blade across my neck and I turn to dust and bone. My
soul will burn for all eternity." He pictured Alana. "My
Guardian… my love, from the first moment I saw you, I
was yours forever. I couldn't tell you. I couldn't put you
in danger again."

His fading mind turned to the motivation behind his
vengeance. "Lukas, my precious gift, I have always
loved you, little boy. I promised myself long ago that the
bastards would pay."

He could thrust and parry with the best swordsmen
of any dimension. He had centuries of practice. More
than ready, he raised his blade for what would be the last
time. Now so weary, a strange sensation rippled across
his unbeating heart.

"Is it finally over?" he shouted to the clouded
heavens. "I signed away any chance at salvation a year
ago to save my son! Have I at least made amends for
some small fraction of my past?" A resonant "no" echo
through his conscience. Because he'd done so much
damage as a vampire, during his long existence. He'd
never earn deliverance from damnation.

Yet, as much as he thumbed his nose at death, he
feared the finality of it. And he couldn't go on much
longer.

Praise for M. Flagg

"A fresh voice in paranormal has arrived."
~ N.N. Light's Book Haven

"Flagg's writing style varies from exquisite word choice and imagery in many descriptions to the simplistic in other situations."
~ Bitten by Books

His Soul to Keep - "This novel makes you want more and more. I highly recommend it if you love a wonderful sci-fi plot along with your romance!"
~ All Romance E-Books (5)

Night of the Crescent Moon – "I couldn't stop turning the page. I love vampires and M. Flagg delivered. Martine carried the story and never let go. Unrequited love buried so deep as to become unrecognizable and all too human emotions in this paranormal world make Night of the Crescent Moon a must read!"
~ Linda J. Parisi, Author of the Blood Rogue Series,
2022 HOLT Medallion Winner

The Vampire's Retribution

by

M. Flagg

The Champion Chronicles Book 1

The Vampire's Retribution

Cover Art by *Rae Monet, Inc.*

The Wild Rose Press, Inc.
PO Box 708
Adams Basin, NY 14410-0708
Visit us at www.thewildrosepress.com

Publishing History
First Edition, 2023
Trade Paperback ISBN 978-1-5092-4928-2
Digital ISBN 978-1-5092-4929-9
The Champion Chronicles Book 1

Previously Published 2008
Published in the United States of America

Dedication

This book is dedicated to my family and friends who encouraged me to believe I had more stories to tells after a long creative drought. I'd be nowhere without all of you.

Chapter 1

Son and Father

Lukas Malone ran as fast as the wind, following sense-memory to a section of New York City that had once been familiar territory. The sight of two old buildings brought back many uncomfortable feelings. *Everything in this world is not always what it appears*, he thought as he hung in the shadows. If he'd had an innocent's eye, this alley would look deserted with smoky fog swirling over rutted pavement. Only wide enough for a car, the passageway had debris strewn against its brick walls. Rusted garbage bins long ago chained with worn locks lining the other end's high fence. It had seen better days.

This wasn't the touristy side of the city. Rotted and abandoned except for rodents—and Hell-beasts visible at the far end. *I know what they are, and I know who they want.* They were in battle, engaging the tall, bloodied Champion with broadsword in hand, who stood before a flying creature's leathery hide—no doubt an ungodly assailant that had slipped through the inter-dimensional portal.

If Lukas were a normal teenager he'd be clueless. Just like the occasional human who staggered by, too drunk or drugged to know what was occurring in this, the final hour before dawn. His stomach churned and cramped because he knew the vampire, and every unnatural sense tingled. Somewhat startled by the reality of what he was witnessing, he didn't know why it was happening, but he knew the vampire was in the type of struggle that leads to the end of one's existence.

Disturbing memories from a year ago, mercilessly driven to sink a stake into this particular vampire's undead heart, flashed through his brain and his heart pumped wild as if jarred awake from a nightmare. The truth? He didn't want to face them, and he swiped at his eyes. His shoulders slammed against a rusted door on the alley's left side knowing the Hell-beasts didn't see him; didn't know who he was or why he was here.

"Just don't fuckin' lose, Michael," he muttered under his breath.

Grabbing the worn lock, and with a simple yank, Lukas ripped it off to slip into darkness. The air in the abandoned factory hung heavy with dust and a stench of rancid oil. Mold covered its walls. Rows of rusty hooks and greasy chains. Many smells assaulted his mystical senses—he could list each one. *Okay, so I'm different, but so is he...*

Hours ago, it had all come back, including what many others who knew of their world called the vampire. "Mystically enhanced...a Champion, a unique creature of the night," he whispered, almost too terrified to breathe. Tight against the inside wall, his chest heaved while he planned his next move. So many troubling memories hammered his brain that it refused to clear. Then he inched his way to a filmy window to watch. *The friggin' dreams* were *real. I'm not a normal kid, which makes this entire past year a lie. Fifteen for a day and it's all gone.*

His keen eyes scanned the action. Distance was inconsequential. Like his unnatural parent who fought the Hell-beasts, he possessed heightened senses far beyond human. After being rescued by Michael from three evil sorcerers on the eve of his thirteenth birthday, what followed was a year of stalking and viciously attacking his savior. Lukas couldn't recall why… but whatever the reasons? They were all wrong. Flat wrong, he now had to admit. Staking his unnatural parent had been like pure intuition. Back then, it consumed him dusk till dawn. How had his memories been changed? He had to know. Michael had the answer to that gnawing question. He studied the mayhem in the passageway and saw the proud vampire through a different lens. It wasn't the Hell-beast that frightened him. It was losing the Champion.

These things are programmed to kill you. Damn. You really pissed something off in a big-ass way. And Lukas doubted the final outcome. The mindless minions seemed to run on autopilot, a never-ending procession of death. With a turn, his fist clipped the wall, and just as quickly, his knuckles stopped bleeding. He wanted to fight the demons himself. One by one, he'd work his way through the Hell-beasts, slashing, gouging, disrupting their focus from the obvious target. A year ago, he would have been cheering them on. *Not now. And shame on me for trying to destroy you.*

Maybe it was the year of being just a normal kid that tempered the hate in his heart for the vampire. He'd never get the answer if the Hell-beasts succeeded in destroying the only connection he had to this world. Another thought came, which upped the guilt-factor. Was this fight because of him? Once again, only Michael had the answer.

He studied the action and the reality of the situation became surreal. Hell-beasts kept lunging through the portal. Blinking rapidly, he rubbed the moisture out of his eyes with his shirtsleeves. Emotions would only confuse him. Angry at himself for not knowing his next move made him antsy. He pressed against the window. Why had his life changed tonight? It was hard to think clearly, yet he knew the exact minute when reality shifted…May 20, 2005, at precisely 12:06 a.m. while standing at a payphone in Grand Central Station. In a panic, he had to call his parents after wandering the city streets in a fog. "The number doesn't exist," said a sympathetic operator. "Let me connect you with the police, okay? Hold the line for 9-1-1—"

His hand shook and his stomach soured as he hung up the phone. Both lives, real and unreal, collided in his mind blending horror with love and hate with happiness. Thinking took a nosedive, and he had raced back to the NWT building, where he'd been earlier. The way his curiosity peaked, entering the penthouse and how he recognized Michael's scent—something a normal kid could have never done. Then in a state of frenzied confusion, he found Michael's brownstone. Seeing it forced him to face other images—crazy ones. Finding the alleyway took full concentration, but he'd made it; craved a fight. And now the fact slammed into him like a shocking slap across the face: that vampire was his solitary link to life.

"This is fucking suicidal," he mumbled as he squinted through the dirty glass. "Even something like *you* won't survive this. They'll destroy you. I swear I'll get to you, and for the first time, not to shove a stake into your heart." Maybe a simple strategy was best. Shadow the alley inside the building and get closer to the action. Yeah. He knew what he had to do…with no room for error.

He took one step as every unnatural sense tingled. Like being caught in a spider's web, Lukas couldn't move forward and wasn't about to move back. But instead of another step, he found himself thrown face-down on the cracked, oily cement floor. He opened his mouth and sucked in stale sawdust.

Like a volcano ready to erupt his rage began to build and he yelled, "No! Not now. What the fuck? You won't keep me from him…whatever you are." Tears burned his eyes as he struggled against an unseen force. A heaviness thickened around him and he grit his teeth. And at that very moment, as if the space between heaven and earth had opened, he saw Helena in angel-form whispering, "*My dearest Lukas. You had to know.*"

Michael Malone met his punishment head on—the penalty for toying with immortal evil.

He had given NWT a bloody nose and he had just destroyed three ancient sorcerers. Arriving in the narrow passageway between two brick buildings, he had ripped off his shirt, flexed his muscles, and had readied his stance.

This was payback.

"Are you ready to end my undead existence and escort my soul home to Hell? Come and get me, you ugly sons of bitches," he sneered, proud to have duped the Triumvirate of Evil. His two-fisted grip on his trusted broadsword drove it clear through another Hell-beast's heart. With one booted foot on its leathery neck, he pulled his weapon out. Manipulating human or demon was child's play for immortal sorcerers. However, *this* creature of the night had planned…and he *had* gotten sweet revenge.

Double-cross executed smooth and simple. For one entire year, he kept his precious soul hidden to appear cruel and ruthless. The evil sorcerers never suspected his deceit. He enlisted two gutsy humans to accomplish tonight's treasonous act. Why had he enlisted humans to aid him in his revenge? They had mystical abilities, which they put to good use. But using them also triggered a purge of everything moral—perhaps confirming how even with a soul, evil still existed within him.

If they don't make it out alive, it's on me alone.

Nevertheless, Michael stood tall and proud as the portal spewed forth its macabre army intent on his destruction. Hell waited for him. He would suffer in eternity. For over a century, he controlled the beast within him. Mastering that which swallowed his soul on the night of his turning in 1690 allowed him to recognize right from wrong; to *choose* right over wrong. Even as he focused on this final battle in his own private war, the deplorable decision to involve two human beings in his vengeance clearly added to his guilt.

Centuries ago, when he was alive, he hadn't been particularly interested in following the moral highroad instilled in him by a very principled British father and mother. His own unethical brashness paved the way to his undeath. Once sired, he quickly gained a reputation in the vampire world. His aptitude for killing? Lethal. Legendary. He cleverly eluded the stake for more than two hundred years, unlike the majority of his kind.

Then came December of 1890—the last full moon of the year. His desire for human blood reached a lustful peak as never before. The holy women whom he drank to death never had a chance at survival. In the convent's chapel, he laid out their bodies as if to defy the wrath of a God who abandoned him the night he was sired. Drunk on the sweetness of the innocents' blood, dazed by the depths of his evil nature, he threw himself through a portal when it opened at the base of the altar.

Instead of bursting into a cloud of dust and bone, Michael landed at the feet of an angel, an Old One. She called herself Helena, and in her hands, she held what he had lost long ago on the night of his turning. The essence of the decent man he could have been was right before his eyes. In the inter-dimensional space, which exists between heaven and earth, he begged to own his soul once again.

Helena empowered him with mystical knowledge. Michael would learn to harness the beast-within as well as the desire to drink human blood.

Over a hundred years of wreaking havoc on demons instead of humanity led him here. To his final battle. There were some twists and turns along the way. He had been deceived by a dark seer in league with the sorcerers. It was because of her, what she gave him, that he was in this ungodly fight. But he had also experienced the love of a mystical woman, a Guardian of Souls. He would always love his Guardian. But the dark seer? How deep her deception ran. It was because of her that his child had been born and had suffered.

He waited. He planned. Now, fifteen years later to the day, he had done something about it. Slicing through another Hell-beast, he shouted, "This hocus-pocus voodoo screams of you, Clayton. Sorcerers' liaison, my ass. You're a sordid piece of human scum who brokered a deal with me."

A year ago, unable to get through to his brainwashed child, Michael Malone took Clayton Mails' quick-fix offer, authored, of course, by the continent's Triumvirate of Evil. The sadistic man presented an easy solution and one Michael couldn't refuse—to create an uncomplicated life for his raging boy. Lukas wouldn't remember being raised by Helena far away from Manhattan and he wouldn't remember hunting Michael Malone. His human son wouldn't remember Helena's brutal death, nor the following years of captivity in the sorcerers' realm. All his son's terror and suffering simply wiped away. Clayton swore the enchantment was permanent. Swore his son was finally safe. Swore his boy would have a happy, normal life. Knowing Lukas was safe, he threw caution aside and hacked his way through the next Hell-beasts with renewed purpose.

A father's vengeance laid its murderous claim on this passageway in the hour before dawn. The end of his undead existence was imminent. Michael steadied his resolve. He thought about his son. *Fifteen years ago… A sweltering May night.* Taking air into his dead lungs, he then breathed life into the newborn's tiny body and marveled at his baby's cries. The act held both fear and awe. A human child! The name Lukas came to him. He didn't know why, but immeasurable love filled his soul. And the desire to protect. But then a portal opened, and Helena appeared in human form. She vowed to raise his son where the child would remain undetected by any evil thing in this gritty city. Only a miracle could have allowed conception and birth— only a miracle with mystical consequences. To keep his son safe, he buried the knowledge of the boy's very existence deep, deep down in his soul.

Another Hell-beast charged, and he thought about Clayton Mails as he thrust his sword into it. *You're the bastard who knew the sorcerers had killed Helena and had taken Lukas. They turned an innocent child into one devoured by rage.* And yet, he had taken Clayton's deal.

Michael continued his final fight. "I gave him life, damn it! You made him crazy… and his enhanced abilities made him lethal. It's why I will end this." One brutal swipe of his broadsword severed the head of the next Hell-beast.

The synchronicity of multiple events is both mysterious and awesome. Michael Malone's plan to obliterate The Triumvirate would remain shielded from every dark seer throughout the mystical world. The Old Ones watched father and son from that place above the earth where angels hover in concern for humanity.

Helena was among them, no longer corporeal, no longer able to walk the earth.

The Old One sensed this Champion's anguish. Although the door to salvation was soon to open, he'd unwisely taken matters into his own hands. She whispered to his soul, *"How foolish of you, Champion. You may not alter your son's destiny. You may not alter yours. Vengeance consumes your soul, yet it is not your time. You cannot leave Lukas. You cannot leave Alana."*

The angel became Michael's mystical shield.

Chapter 2

Necessary Interventions

Over six years ago, a Servant of Souls had slipped into the human world to ensure Michael Malone, the mystically enhanced vampire, remained in control of his beast-within. This pure of heart individual sailed far beneath evil's radar. With curly red hair that appeared to have a mind of its own, Thorn's appearance was in stark contrast to Michael's head-turning good looks. Broad and barrel-chested, a huge man with thick arms and legs, the stylish vampire often remarked, "Push those thick glasses back up where they belong before they slide off your nose." Thorn's poor vision provided an ironic cover for his ability to read heart, head, and soul. Timid, but loyal, he was the vampire's day-time messenger in the city, his eyes and ears on its crowded streets.

Tonight, his burly shoulders slumped in defeat. Hours ago, he'd been yelled at, humiliated, and dismissed—by Michael Malone. Remembering the gruesome episode made the ground he focused on blur again.

"Walk away, Thorn...*right* now," Michael had loudly insisted as he held his office door wide open so everyone heard the arrogant, inaccurate accusation thunder off the walls. "You don't fit in at NWT—you never will. I gave you this assignment so I wouldn't have to hear you moan and groan, and you screwed it up good!" More heads turned their way. The rant loomed uncharacteristically cruel as if on purpose. "All you had to do was use that fucking, half-wit brain of yours to keep an eye on someone and report back to me. But what does this idiot do instead? Huh? You introduce yourself! You start a *conversation*!"

It was at this point in the outright lies that an office chair flew across the room, thrown, of course, by Michael. The last gulps of sweetened coffee he held in a paper cup, which, by the way, Michael had insisted upon fixing when he arrived, splattered across the beige carpet. This was followed by a string of curses never-before heard coming from the often-pensive vampire, who'd been Thorn's mystical mission for seven calm, quiet years. He pulled a wad of crumpled napkins from his pocket, crouched down to blot the dark stain. "It wasn't that way, Boss, I swear, I didn't—"

"What kind of jerk do you think I am, you idiot?" Michael slammed the door shut with a furious expression, and his voice sank into a hiss. "Lukas came *here* this afternoon! Unlike you, he's smart, and I did a whole lot of lying on the spot thanks to your stupidity. Clayton would stake me if he found out about this."

"What on earth are you talking about? I swear—"

As if on cue, Michael opened the door with a dramatic flair, his handsome angular features twisted tight. "Get out. You're fired. I'm finished with you. And don't come here anymore." Everyone on the thirteenth floor witnessed the rant of the commanding vampire. Thorn sensed collective curiosity as they scurried to prepare for some "special" twilight conference that would occur around midnight. Only Michael Malone and the Summoned Six, very powerful vampires, would greet three immortal sorcerers when they emerged into this dimension through the portal in the building's private penthouse.

Chastised so publicly for something he had *not* done; Thorn took the stairs to avoid the crowded elevators. Once on the busy city streets he shuffled aimlessly through the Friday night crowd—more confused with every step. Eventually, his legs felt like lead. Finding a bench in a secluded cluster of trees somewhere in Central Park, he sat down wanting only to rest for a while. But his heavy lids closed, and he fell asleep.

****

Celia Bookman sat in group meditation at the Georgian Estate in Hampton Hill, England. She was a long way from her home, her parents, and her friends. Paranormal occurrences were nothing out of the ordinary for her. Celia had a special talent, one so great that even as a teenager, her psychic ability was indisputable.

It all began with a mission. A sacred mission. A mystical mission accepted by Alana Ciminio, her best friend and adopted sister. Alana became a Guardian of Souls, imbued with the ability to identify and combat demons that slipped into this dimension. These evil entities brought mayhem to the human world. Few knew of their existence. But only Guardians of Souls could destroy them. When Alana accepted her mystical mission at age sixteen, Celia's psychic abilities reached new heights. That was over a decade ago.

During Alana's years of service, they made quite the team back in Manhattan. Celia sensed the demon and Alana destroyed it. Well over a year ago, Alana's mystical mission had come to an end. Her adopted sister was truly one of the lucky ones who made it out alive. Eventually, needing distance from the city, from her life as a Guardian of Souls, Alana relocated to Italy to live with her elderly great-aunt. Celia left the city as well. At her father's urging, she went to the one place where she could hone her sixth sense—the Georgian Estate outside London, England.

The crucial connection, the dynamic history between Alana and Michael sped through Celia's mind like a rocket racing toward its target. But once she saw the raging teen glued to the old factory's floor, worry filled every fiber of her being. "What did Michael get himself into?" she said to no one in particular. "And how the hell did Lukas get there?"

Her first instinct was to protect the boy. And that task would only be accomplished if others like her could assist Michael in this battle. In one sweeping motion, the meditation circle focused mindsight on the chaos in Manhattan, and Georgian psychics around the world heard the call at the speed of light. Like giant billboards in Times Square, messages flashed in mystical minds across every continent when she intoned a heart-felt plea, "They need us, sisters and brothers. Add your voice to mine."

Collective powers to me gather,
Save the Champion, make evil shatter.
City so far, passageway dark;
Turn them weary as they march.
Evil army, hundreds deep,
Return to Hell your wrath to sleep.
Your swords will wither as flesh turns to fire.
The Champion safe is our greatest desire.

Child so eager you must stay very still.
That would be your father's will.
Blessed be truth, blessed be right.
From darkness springs dawn. Dissolve in the light!

From the suburbs of London, across land and ocean the mantra lifted to the heavens, making its way to Manhattan. Her vision kept Michael's struggle in view. She called to the Guardians of Souls, a mystical army of innocents, pristine and powerful, warning them to be prepared for action. Her senses hummed as these demon hunters awakened in every corner of that far-away city. Just minutes before dawn, each one of them became aware of a significant event in the passageway.

At first, a proud smile appeared. "A little muscle for back-up is a good thing, but speaking of muscle, why can't I sense Dan and Rob? They're never too far from Michael these days. And where's Thorn. He's always…"

The smile faded as her heart began to flutter. *Oh God. Rob and Dan—they're dead. Oh God. Michael is alone. And his son is snooping around something he shouldn't be anywhere near. Does Ally sense this crazy chaos as well?* She felt the chant's potency roaring throughout the entire Georgian Circle as she entered the estate's budding garden with cell phone in hand. Her hand shook and her voice tremored connecting to her adopted sister saying two words: "My Guardian."

Chapter 3

His Guardian

Alana awoke from an unexpected nap gasping for breath because of an odd sensation… like someone was stomping on her chest. Amalfi Sun spilled through open windows, causing her to wince. She raised a hand to shade her eyes. Her long brown curly hair lay plastered to her sweaty cheeks and her skin felt clammy. Her leg muscles tensed as if she were still a Guardian ready to do battle, as if fully aware of some unearthly evil creature. Ironically, Michael was at her side—something that he hadn't been for the last six years of her mystical mission. And he looked awful!

Something's wrong—very wrong. I've never seen defeat on Michael's face—so lost, so weary. She peeled her back off sticky, wine-colored sheets and tried to pull herself out of the antique four-poster bed. She'd have to change the sheets if and when she could drag herself to her feet. She flopped back against the damp pillow, thoroughly spent.

Living in Italy proved to be exactly what she needed after ten years as a Guardian of Souls. The mountainous landscape of Portofino was beautiful, peaceful any time of the year… and the weather? Heavenly. She didn't miss messy Manhattan winters. She only missed him— Michael Malone. She stretched her arms wide and tried to shake the stiffness out of them. *The connection is always there. I'm convinced our souls are still linked, no matter how many miles separate us. And I know something's wrong.*

She had to pull herself together and got up to take the short walk to her private bathroom at the opposite end of her bedroom. It felt like a rugged mile. Turning on the shower brought on a frown and a groan. *Is it me or what? Haven't Italians ever heard of serious water pressure? It's like standing under a watering can. I'd kill for a hot tub, but I guess I shouldn't complain. Living in luxury and rent-free...this is all Michael, I'll bet.* The exquisite, fully furnished apartment upstairs from her great-aunt had been waiting for her when she left the states. The Georgian Council didn't support retired Guardians. And no one had a plausible explanation for generous cash deposits in a checking account that should have been meager. All instincts told her it was Michael Malone. And her instincts were usually right.

She was a city girl, born and raised. Her father owned a flower shop. Her mom taught music in a private school and gave piano lessons at home. She was an only child who basked in the love of two happy, but quirky parents.

On the night she turned sixteen, her life took an unusual turn. The September evening had been an all-out, happy celebration in her family's first-floor apartment on a quiet city side street. Homemade Fettuccini Alfredo, a decadent, chocolate-raspberry birthday cake, presents galore, and multiple good wishes topped off the Sweet-Sixteen Bash. She went to sleep with contented dreams. But shortly after midnight, those dreams became unusual night terrors.

Vampires, demons… Stakes and broadswords… She saw the world through a different reality. A legion of Old Ones presented this mystical mission to protect innocents, and she accepted destiny's call. Then she woke up, her life forever changed.

The new Guardian of Souls had extraordinary abilities. Many revelations followed. She sensed The Georgian Circle, a unique group of individuals with a never-ending commitment to defend the innocents of our world. The roots of Georgian beliefs, their common purpose traced back to followers of St. George the Dragon Slayer over a thousand years ago. Alana's best friend's father, Miles Bookman, who had always been a close family friend, proudly became her mentor for the next ten years of her life.

She was now a mystical warrior, possessing super-human strength, uncanny heightened senses, and the ability to heal quickly. No demon would be spared the wooden stake or silver sword. Like all who accepted the mystical mission, male or female, Alana vowed to remain untouched, pure in mind and body, during the decade of service, and her supernatural skills were contingent upon it. Some found this too difficult and walked away unscathed—also without memory of the soulless creatures that existed. Others met death long before the mission's end.

Alana had survived, even though she broke her vow before her ten years were up. Somehow, an exception had been made, a one-time only exception. But there were consequences that she paid, even to this day. Walking away from love continued to be an eternal punishment.

Tragically, some months into her mission, her

17

parents died, leaving her alone in the city. Miles and his wife Laura formally adopted her. Their daughter, Celia, was her best friend, and together they helped her adjust to living with such a loss.

Miles understood Alana's mystical mission. She was an enthusiastic learner, but often, and against Miles's warnings, the new Guardian went out alone. On one of those solo excursions, she came face to face with Michael Malone. Meeting the mystically enhanced vampire had given new definition to Alana's life.

As the showerhead trickled down lukewarm water, a smile began. Michael's dark-brown eyes had been stern yet amused. The look on his chiseled face at the end of their first encounter read serious concern. The recall flooded her with feeling she now kept hidden. "I was terrified that night. Surrounded by six hissing vampires, and yet, anxious for a solo kill," she whispered as she lathered her hair.

"She's fresh meat and very young," the menacing demon said to the others with a sneer. "She's pure. I can smell it. A filthy Guardian of Souls."

They moved closer.

I tripped over a stone; miscalculated a move. I should have listened to Daddy B. My short-sword lay far out of reach and my wooden stake tossed somewhere into the trees—a deadly position to be in. All I kept thinking was I'm gonna die!

The leader poised in front, with three minions behind him. All were merciless beasts. I looked to my left. Three more flanked him. Of course, I did the mental math and counted again.

Because something was wrong. There should only be six.

My senses took a dive into panic-mode. Then, a wooden stake sailed through the darkness, landing next to my hand. Was this a new player in town? I noted the leader's narrow-eyed look, and boldly asked, "Have you made other enemies in the city, demon?"

He snarled. "Perhaps someone wishes to die with you, Guardian?"

"Perhaps he doesn't, asshole," came out of nowhere. Then, the tall stranger staked two vampires with swift, incredible moves. When he turned their leader into dust and bits of bone, it presented the opening I needed to destroy the remaining three. I grabbed the stake and jumped to my feet, starting for them. But before I could attack, two more met their end. The last vampire looked stunned as the mysterious stranger grabbed it by the throat, lifting it high off the ground.

"Now why would you be menacing such a sweet, innocent thing, huh? What did this young Guardian do to deserve such a nasty ending? Didn't you pay attention in school, idiot? Six against one isn't playing fair." He let go and it landed at my feet. "Pay close attention. Now he's ready for you," he said as if he were my mentor and not Miles.

I shoved the piece of wood through its unbeating heart, watched it disintegrate into bits of dust and bone. Then I turned to face the drop-dead gorgeous man who saved my life. Before I could say "thanks," I caught his stern glare. His face was framed by wavy brown hair that brushed the collar of his shirt and his lips were as thin as a pencil. He came close enough to kiss me.

"The next time the researcher tells you not to go it alone," he said with more than a little irritation, "please listen—or else you'll never see eighteen and that would

be an incredible shame."

The tone of his voice was rich and low. He came off confident and arrogant. And he was so tall that looking up, my neck was fully exposed. His shoulders were very broad. High cheekbones made the angles of his face almost threatening in the moonlight.

I couldn't speak, nor look away.

"I'm only saying, my Guardian, that one so young should have someone to watch your back right now," he whispered, leaning in closer. Something about him seemed different, but I didn't yet know what it was. I happily drowned in his intense, masculine scent; swallowed, trying to remember how to breathe. I swear my very soul fluttered.

"Is that someone you?" I cautiously asked.

His thin lips curled into a smirk as if amused. "You never know, my Guardian, I just might be the one. Now get yourself home before I start to worry. Keep the stake, it might come in handy. And listen to the researcher."

The mysterious stranger stepped aside, pointing in the exact direction I would take to get home. He locked his arms across that broad chest and stood straight-shouldered with his feet slightly apart—waiting until I started to move.

Under a streetlamp seconds later, I finally found the nerve to turn around.

Michael was gone.

She rinsed shampoo from her hair. "When I described you to Daddy B, he knew who and what you were. He urged me to be careful around you. To keep my distance." As a Georgian researcher, Miles Bookman had extensive documentation on this particular vampire. He knew both sides of Michael Malone—the vampire who had terrified his victims for two hundred years, and the brave creature who had reclaimed his soul in 1890. She knew that *last* part was a first. Miles had studied every tidbit about Michael's undead life to chronicle his unprecedented transformation. Miles found him fascinating. So did she, but in a different way. As she became more attached to a centuries-old vampire, her adopted father's intuitive desire to protect her surged.

They argued about him constantly.

The researcher didn't trust the Champion. Alana loved him unconditionally.

Miles cautioned about the beast within Michael— itching to break free when his guard was fully down. But stubbornly starry-eyed and smitten, she challenged Miles time and again, doubting this dangerous side of Michael still existed. Of course, those warnings fell on deaf ears.

Turning off the water, she stepped out of the shower, refusing to look into the mirror while drying her tangled curls. The next memory of Michael shattered her life.

Fast-forward four years... I practically ran out of La Bella Cucina with Celia protesting, "I called but there's no answer, Ally. I mean, turning twenty-one is a big deal! Dad agreed to invite him because—"

"No, he didn't so don't lie to me," I replied totally hurt and angry. "Daddy B doesn't trust Michael, which means he doesn't trust me." I made it to Broadway with Celia still trying to keep up. "I love him. I know what he is, but I love him. Don't you get it?"

"Yes, I get it. I really do, but you don't seem to realize that he's not a man—at least not a living one. And Michael's been around since 1690!"

"For the past five years he's had my back. I've practically thrown myself at him. I've kissed him...that's

all. How can Dad be so unsure of me? I'm untouched. Virginity rules—no matter how much I want to... I honor my vow. I wouldn't be alive to see this birthday if it weren't for Michael. Maybe I've had enough of this. Maybe it doesn't matter anymore." I stopped at the intersection, waited for the red hand to disappear so I could cross. "I'm a senior in college, and I've upheld my end of this mission. But if Michael leaves me, I...I'll die." Tears blurred my vision and the red hand began to swim.

"Maybe you shouldn't have had all that champagne, Ally. You hardly touched your dinner, and you're not thinking straight." I pushed Celia's hand away and stepped off the curb. The theater crowd pushed onward. "Dad says he hasn't been seen in over a week. Michael's gone, Ally. Maybe it's time to move on."

"No. I won't move on. We're connected—deep down in my soul I can feel him." I left Celia B standing on that street. I just walked away, and a few blocks later I took a taxi to Central Park..

The September night chilled, and I shivered in my short black dress. As soon as I left the well-lit, paved pathway, I yanked off those tight black shoes and threw them into the trees. Rarely worn and uncomfortable though stylish, I hated walking in high heels.

Then I came to the spot where I first met Michael Malone. Sinking down to the damp leaves, I sobbed his name, over and over. Vulnerable and exposed, I didn't care. Memories of him hammered my mind.

Hours slipped past. The heavens rumbled above. It broke the reverie. Demons were near and I flailed my fists at the night sky. "I don't give a damn! Let them come. Let all the vampires come! I defy You. For the first time in my life, I turn my back on this mission. You made *him leave me. And I hate You," I screamed into the cold air. It would be over soon enough. I'd meet death after some vampire's fangs sank into my throat. I wouldn't fight it. Another dead Guardian. Another life lost. A sour taste filled my mouth and I threw up the contents of my churning stomach. Then I sat back on my heels, waited, and cried.*

You stepped out of the trees with fury etched on your handsome face. "What do you think you're doing? If a vampire finds you like this, it will mean your death!"

"Why would you care? You left me," the words choking out of me. I lunged at you with mystical strength and landed several blows. "Go away and stay away!"

It took several attempts before you finally grabbed my wrists.

"Stop this right now," came as a warning, but I continued my assault. A quick jab to my upset stomach was what finally did it. I was suddenly over a shoulder, with you running with vampire speed through the empty streets of the city, taking me to the safety of your brownstone. My anger revved again when you shut the door and I slid off your shoulder—landing on an uncarpeted floor with a thud. You pulled me to my feet, saying nothing. Nothing at all!

"You left me!" I hissed.

"Are you going to start that again?"

My fists clipped my hips, incensed by the calm reply. "You betcha, buddy."

"You look like a bad version of Kate in Taming of the Shrew." Your smirk was cutting.

"You left me!" I repeated, poking a finger at your chest.

"I merely stepped away for a while."

The simplicity of your arrogant tone took me off guard. "Why?"

With your arms locked across your chest, you answered a brisk, "Because."

"That's not an answer!"

"Well, it's the only one I'm going to give, so get over it."

My reply was to slap your face, and as I did, I knew I'd gotten to you. Your dark eyes closed... your nostrils flared. Still turned aside, you whispered, "I shouldn't have brought you here." Then my hands rested on your chest. Was it my touch? Did it drive you crazy? I know my heart began to race. "How could you even think I would leave you? I'll love you throughout eternity."

The kisses that followed were insatiable, hungry... My hands slid down in a greedy way. Your hand slipped under my dress, driving me wild. I could only gasp as you slid me up your body and my legs locked around your hips. The feel of you. Your tongue in a dance with mine—I went wild, throbbing with anticipation, excitement. I ran my hands through your thick, wavy hair, kissing you deeply, panting with need.

"Alana... I can't—"

"Don't say it," I sighed, the need building even higher.

I shivered against the pressure of you carrying me up the stairs to your bed. No. I didn't fight. I didn't say stop, either. Deep in my soul, I knew I belonged to you. Loving you was as natural as breathing. Although I'd never been with a man, instinct told me what would drive your desire. What would drive you insane. And only you could fill the emptiness within me.

Every experienced move you made had my body

quivering. I ripped at your shirt, and you pulled my dress over my head. When my fingers unnotched your belt, you unzipped your black jeans. By the time our bodies hit the bed we were naked in each other's arms.

Oh, the way you touched me. It made my breath hitch, coated my body with desire I had never known could exist. Every temptation led me to freedom, my mind lost in forbidden pleasures. Your masterful touch prepared me, eased the pain when you entered me.

What shot through me was pure bliss and I quivered as you began to move inside of me. When I felt you hesitate my eyes eased open. And I knew…

A deep growl sounded, raspy and threatening. Your eyes were a feral-yellow, and I came face to face with the beast-within. Its sharp fangs skimmed my breast and then slipped into my neck.

In that instant my mind cleared. My mystical strength emerged and I pushed the beast off my body. "You are not the man I love," I whispered, desperate to have you back.

But you weren't a man. You were a vampire. It was my blood on your fangs. You had tasted me. I had broken a solemn vow. I rose from the bed to study the lascivious beast-within, now fully exposed.

You threw back your head in an arrogant manner. An uncharacteristic sneer appeared as I pulled on my dress and backed away from the bed, stopping in the doorway once again. I watched with shock as the beast-within licked its lips. My blood. Guardian blood. It growled. Bared its fangs as I whispered your name.

"Such sweet blood, so hot, so strong," said in a different voice, one sinister and depraved. "My craving for you will never end."

25

When you lunged, one kick to the center of the chest sent you sprawling across the bed as you leered at me with lust in your feral eyes. Yet I turned and walked out of the room. I went down the stairs.

"I'll come for you, my guardian," you called out. "I'll take you again and again. You will ache for only me!"

I stepped through the threshold of your brownstone knowing full well that my only protection would now be daylight hours.

Alana studied her reflection in the bathroom mirror. "So young and headstrong…I didn't think, I didn't want to know." That one night had her heart full of regret. Although no one said it, everyone knew what she had done.

Weeks of terror ensued before Philip, Dan and Rob, all experienced Guardians, helped Alana lure Michael into the passageway. His beast-within continued to be obsessed with Alana. Celia, with her mystical mind inexplicably powerful, managed to open the portal in the passageway just as Michael took the bait, finally cornered her. Miles pushed him through the swirling mist, and Helena took him away. "I will always hate myself for pushing you so far that you lost control."

When the Georgian Sovereign Council convened to discuss her broken vow of purity, it was decided that because her mystical strength had not lessened, she could continue her mystical mission. Too many long, lonely years remained.

What happened that September night had changed her. Losing Michael brought her to a sad, empty place. She'd never allow her love for him to show, but it would always be there. Right under her skin. Branded on her soul.

When Michael reappeared in the city, Miles confirmed that he was, once again, in control of his beast-within. It didn't matter because he'd never touch her again. The few times they spoke it was brief and purposely distant. But was he watching out for her? Always from a distance? The Guardian in her knew it to be true.

Touching each other again was never going to happen—even after her mystical mission ended. The cost was too high. She'd have to drive a stake through Michael's heart to destroy the beast-within. She'd have to destroy *him*.

The depth of misery is often profound. And love can haunt one's heart forever. No one mentioned his name around her. Philip looked out for her. No other Guardians spoke to Michael except Dan and Rob.

The day Alana turned twenty-seven, after another uncomfortable full year of completely avoiding Michael, she left the city. Moving to Portofino meant beginning a new life, a healthy one that might include a "normal" relationship with a man she might learn to love.

Walking across her bedroom, she couldn't shake the weird sensation crawling through her mind and settling in her heart. She pulled on a pair of jeans. *You're in trouble, and I'm thousands of miles away. Oh God, I can't help you.* Her fingers shook as she buttoned her blouse. Sinking into the Queen Anne chair next to the bed, her elbows landed on her knees and her head dropped into her hands. "Michael, my love, what have you done?" When she heard the sound of the house phone's ring, she jumped up and literally ran into the living room to answer it.

****

Celia let out a loud sigh of relief when she heard her adopted sister's voice say, "Celia B, please... Tell me what's happening?"

"This is bad, Ally, really bad. Michael's in major trouble. Every right kind of good psychic in this dimension is chanting for his protection. I threw in some *'go into the light'* mojo for the Hell-beasts. I've warned the local Guardians in case they're needed." Celia stopped talking. Because she rambled, which she only did when extremely nervous.

"What's going on in Manhattan? I had this really strange dream. What did he get himself involved in?"

"Something very big and scary, I think. You had a yucky feeling, right? Mine was more like a vision—a mind picture while awake, you know? I'm getting the sinking feeling that Michael put a bee in someone's bonnet. My guess is NWT. Now that's *major* evil if you ask me."

"Philip told me he made some kind of deal with Clayton Mails. Has an office, locates and recruits wicked rich humans to work for the sorcerers. Do you think they finally hauled his evil vampire ass to Hell or something?"

"He's not evil, Ally, he still knows right from wrong," she said in Michael's defense. "And as for hauling away that gorgeous ass of his, I think they brought Hell to him." She didn't care for his cocky antics, but she was certain he still loved Alana deeply— very deeply.

"Come again? Brought Hell to Manhattan? Now that's new."

"Ally, I'm sensing you love him and don't love him

at the same time." Celia cleared her throat shifting from foot to foot. "No offense, but… You can get difficult, especially when it involves Michael. Uh… I don't think you're getting the big picture here. I mean, *right now* he's fighting a never-ending parade of demons. His son's glued to a really filthy floor, close to the action by some *mysterious* power. I can see those sandy curls. Lukas isn't too happy with the sticky thing, but if Hell-beasts get a whiff of him—"

"Did you say his son? Why would *he* be there? Did Lukas enlist inter-dimensional demons to finally put an end to dear old dad? I hear he's got rage that just—"

"Whoa, stop," she cautioned, hearing anxiety in her adopted sister's voice. "I'm not getting that. Really, I'd tell you if it were the case. I don't think Michael even knows Lukas is there." Her tone softened. She took in a breath to relax and stopped shifting from foot to foot. "Thorn's missing. I-I mean, I know he's all right, but I can't sense him anywhere. Anyway, that's not the only reason I'm calling." She had to approach this with care. "Look, I know you won't get to Michael in time. If our incantation works, and we incinerate the beastly things, he's going to need help, Ally. I'm getting another feeling, too. Don't ask me to explain, but I think something's going to like…bite him." She heard the gasp.

"Do you mean like a vampire—or a bug?"

"No, not like a—something a lot bigger, and it looks kind of, well, dirt brown. I caught a glimpse of it in my vision. The thing has three heads, all snapping and snarling. These mini-mind-messages can be vague sometimes."

"I've seen many a weird-looking creature, but the

idea of one flying around with three heads and taking a bite out of him is making me crazy. You've got to warn him."

Celia's free hand flew up, exasperated. "You know I can't do that. Whatever's going down in the city, your Michael is a major player. There are so many evil elements at work against him. Just keeping them safe is taking all our collective energy. Evil doesn't like to play by the rules, Ally." She paused to contemplate this convoluted mess.

"Celia... Are you still there?"

"Yeah... sorry but look. If Michael survives, he's going to need help. So will Lukas."

"Tell Dad to bring them here. They'll *both* be safe with me."

The line went dead and she whispered, "That's exactly what I hoped to hear." She ran up to her suite at the Georgian Estate to get her laptop and some personal items. There was no need to explain her return to Manhattan. The meditation group would understand. Her father would meet with the Georgian Council to approve an extraction plan. It was going to be necessary to get both father and son to Alana in Italy. As Celia reached the front door, a taxi pulled into the circular drive.

****

Alana had not waited for a response from Celia. She hung up the phone, lost in memories and holding on to hope. *I don't care what the Georgians think. I don't care what Dad thinks. I have to help him. I want him with me. We belong to each other, and we always will.*

She sank into the beige leather armchair in the living room, more on edge. *That demented child has resurfaced, and he's dangerous. Every Guardian in the city knows what Lukas is capable of doing. Where has he been for the past year, anyway?* Michael never told her about Lukas. Miles did. Her adopted father remained convinced that NWT had something to do with turning the angel-faced teen into an uncontrollable lunatic. Lurking around the brownstone, living on city streets, stalking Michael with one purpose in mind: torture and destroy.

I remember the day Daddy B told me he disappeared. It was months before I moved to Italy. Dan and Rob said drop it, and I did. Philip said it wasn't my concern. Now Celia says he's not crazy anymore. Well…I'll have to see for myself.

She twisted her hands, something she never did unless already beyond edgy.

Chapter 4

Father and Son

Michael Malone had had enough. It was payback time. He knew he couldn't win this final, self-imposed battle. He'd destroy as many Hell-beasts as possible before anyone dragged *his* soul to Hell. His foolhardy plan to kill all three sorcerers at once had *almost* worked. Then the last dead thing went and raised its burning hand just before it collapsed. That's when thunderous roars from Hell pierced his ears, and he knew the evil thing had opened the biggest portal in the city. In an instant, he accepted his last act on this good earth—one against many, a fight to the bitter end.

Both day and night had been long and complicated. It pushed him to his limits and beyond. Seeing his boy had made it worse, and drugging Thorn meant he had gone too far.

But this had to end.

Revenge took months of quiet preparation to bring all those soul-suckers down. Research had been meticulous. And he thought his strategy foolproof. Rob and Dan would stake the Summoned Six in the outer conference suite while he destroyed Hell's ambassadors in the penthouse's inner sanctum. Then, a quick bullet to the brain would put Clayton out of his misery as well—because Rob was good with a gun. The power-hungry liaison deserved no less for starting this. That sniveling bastard had led him to his brainwashed boy in the sorcerers' realm. Clayton knew that to keep Lukas from killing himself, Michael would sign away his soul to NWT…eventually. It took a year of his raging son hunting him, the child edging closer to being seriously injured or getting killed.

He swiped demon blood from both eyes and ran his hand down the leg of his jeans. As for the last part of his plan? Although he and the researcher despised one another, Miles was an honorable man. Michael had left instructions. Miles would watch out for his boy.

"Fuck it," he mumbled, aiming at another Hell-beast, "Evil gets as evil does." The sinister forces unleashed upon him were unrelenting. *My destruction is their purpose. Their destruction is mine.*

He raised the bloodied broadsword once again.

With every deathblow, another creature lunged. Implications of what he had done and whom he had lost weighed heavily upon his conscience. Survival meant putting everyone he cared about in harm's way. Only ending this existence would keep Lukas and Alana safe.

He sensed the hour. Sunlight would incinerate him along with these demons. In the long run, it didn't matter. *Either way, I lose.*

Ever watchful, with all senses heightened, he twisted to the left to skewer another Hell-beast. They kept staggering through the portal, and he readied his stance once again.

Never give up; never give in. This is one hell of a night.

****

Dripping with sweat, Lukas strained to claw his way

across the floor. Hands bloody and raw; his polo shirt stained with oil and sweat and blue jeans tore at the knees as flesh scraped along. He gagged on every breath. The force keeping him prone leaned heavier now. His eyes drew to the filthy windows lining the alleyway.

"This isn't starlight. And it isn't dawn. What the fuck is happening?" Intense nausea took hold as the area surrounding him brightened. Tiny beams, appearing out of nowhere, enveloped him. No matter how hard he tried not to look, these mysterious luminaries were mesmerizing.

"You are protected, Lukas," three voices echoed in his mind, much like a musical chord, harmonious and unbroken. *"Soon this will end."*

He fought the command to relax, insistent upon getting to Michael's side. "Why are you keeping me from him? I can help! Shit! Let me go!" Through no power of his own, his muscles weakened and again, he flopped to the floor. Desperate tears slipped down his flushed cheeks. One sob escaped before he bit down on his lower lip. "Please. I have to talk to him. I have to tell him I know." But one thing was certain. He wasn't going anywhere until this ended.

The stench in the humid alley turned nauseating after so many hours of fighting. A clammy mist still surrounded the Hell-beasts, swirling up from the bowels of the earth. Their blood formed a macabre pond, complete with odd-shaped steppingstones—severed limbs of demonic invaders.

These marauders, summoned like a last malicious whim of three dead sorcerers…no intelligence. Not an independent thinker among them. "You just spring forward to meet the same fate," he shouted as he fought.

"What…some kind of ancient enchantments propelling you idiots through the mystical hub? Hey, Clayton, are you standing in Hell watching me?" He sliced off a thick arm and winced at a Hell-beast's screech. "Does it give you a final perverted thrill, to play with this lesser being?" A shake of his head cleared his mind. That bastard Clayton thought he had him on a leash, like a pawn on a madman's chess board scoring another win for his gods. But tonight, Michael had leveled the playing field.

Wounds streaked his cheeks; blood matted his hair. Slashed chest, arms pierced several times—hours of fighting plunged him into weariness no human could endure. *So be it, I am ready. One swift stroke of a silver blade across my neck and I turn to dust and bone. My soul will burn for all eternity.* He thought about Alana. *My Guardian… my love, from the first moment I saw you, I was yours forever. I couldn't tell you about this. I couldn't put you in danger again.* His fading mind turned to the motivation behind his vengeance. *Lukas, my precious gift, I have always loved you, little boy. I promised myself long ago that the bastards would pay.*

He could thrust and parry with the best swordsmen of any dimension. He had centuries of practice. More than ready, he raised his blade for what would be the last time. So weary, he felt a strange sensation, as if an impermeable shield covered his vulnerable heart.

"Is it finally over?" Michael shouted to the clouded heavens. "I signed away any chance at salvation a year ago to save my son! Have I at least made amends for some small fraction of my past?"

A resonant *"no"* echo through his conscience. No matter how many good deeds he did, a special spot awaited him in Hell. Because he'd done so much damage as a vampire, during his long existence. He'd never earn deliverance from damnation.

Yet, as much as he thumbed his nose at death, he feared the finality of it. And he couldn't go on much longer. Hope slipped away. One last unsteady thrust, and his broadsword skewered the attacking demon. It fell into the blood pond as another appeared.

Then, he felt the blade before he saw it. It went through his right thigh, shattering bone from such force. Falling to his knees, he blinked several times, struggling through a strong desire to pass out.

In defiance, his gaze positively skewered this last dull assailant. The demon raised its weapon, about to sever his head. As the sword began its descent, scorching air around it brightened, and the Hell-beast burst into flames. Michael swiped away the blood dripping into his eyes and pushed his hair off his face. "Am I dreaming or am I already dead?" He grabbed his shattered leg and cringed with a hiss. "Aw…nope, not dead, but what the fuck just happened?"

Waves of weakness washed over him. He was bleeding out. Every inch of his body screamed. When he finally focused, he thought it a hallucination. Incredulous. Bright light sped up the alleyway. Luminescent specks of pale-blue flame hovered over another Hell-beast that charged through the mist. The closer it came, the denser the lights sparked. It raised its weapon—and burst into flames. He was too stunned to move as the unknown brightness steadily approached.

Sharp pains in his thigh snapped him back to attention. He dug the tip of his broadsword into the blood pond and leaned on it with all his weight to hoist himself to his feet.

"I choose to stand at my end," Michael shouted to the heavens, "not be on my knees like a coward. It's time. Make it quick; keep them safe—that's all I ask." He raised a shaky arm to his forehead to swipe more blood running down his face, but it streamed freely from multiple wounds. The brilliance turned into a sea of white light before him.

I am finished, he thought. His eyes slid to the three-headed creature sprawled lifeless against the fence. "You're the first thing I killed at midnight. I'm guessing you're the last thing I'll see in this world." Pride filled him. "Taking you down was an incredible high. Soulless beasts, flames emergent from within and above…and all of us meet our ultimate, fiery demise together."

Blistering hot air engulfed the dank passageway. The last Hell-beast let out pitiful yelps as it burned. The deadly portal swirled closed with a high-pitched roar.

He stood alone—no demons, no blood pond, no severed limbs, nothing except for him and the creature he leaned against. His throat was clogging up with blood, and he bent forward bracing his hands on his knees, coughing before choking out, "I didn't expect this—"

But as the last word left his lips, he heard it. Slight and steady thump-thumping. Had his senses *not* been so dull by the beating his body had taken, he might have understood.

One red eye opened as the flying-creature puffed out a breath of foul air.

Fight or flight took hold—flight winning out by a long stretch. Staggering off the beast, he ran, only to have his legs give out. A shattered bone protruded from his right thigh, and he landed hard, face down on the broken pavement.

Sharp talons raked his back, shredding the right side of his jeans. Screaming in agony, Michael tucked his head under one arm. Venomous teeth sank into his right shoulder, the shocking incision rendering him speechless.

It was done.

Then the vindictive voices of everlasting evil hammered his mind: *You want to scream, vampire, but there is no one to hear you in the darkness of this deed. You dare to destroy our earthly stronghold? Let dreams torture you throughout eternity. Impudent being, you have rewritten your own destiny!*

Venom slithered through his nervous system. Lying paralyzed he thought he saw Lukas staring at him, standing in the passageway. Shocked by the illusion, agony coursed like acid through his veins. Images of punishment and deliverance collided in his numbing brain. His next illusion was of Alana, so far away, so beautiful. *My Guardian...my love,* he thought with devotion. The possibility of putting everyone in danger gripped his unbeating heart like a vice as his mind slipped into infinite confusion.

Only a more powerful being could weave a way through the enchanted poison. Helena whispered to his soul, "*Son of my bloodline, I will not leave you. You must imagine your survival—how does it begin?*"

"*They will kill...*"

"*...Alana is safe. Lukas will soon be well hidden. Miles will find him. Now dream. Lukas is standing over you...*"

Was he strong enough to dream of redemption? Only time would tell.

Chapter 5

Repercussions

Lukas felt the spell lift. He sprinted to the door just as the mystical light descended on the passageway. Full of wonder, he stared out a dirty window. The last Hell-beast disappeared right before his eyes and the portal swirled counterclockwise, sucking thick gray mist back into it with a roar.

"This is awesome! How friggin cool! He won!" he anxiously gripped the rusted doorknob. In spite of his superhuman strength, it didn't budge. "No way, you fucking hear me?" He ran to the factory's other end. This door gave way.

Seconds later, he stood at the entrance to the alley, keenly aware of first daylight. He watched the air shimmer and spin above the screeching, three-headed creature with his eyes wide and his mouth hanging open. It disappeared through a small portal, writhing and angry.

His eyes slid down to his unnatural father and he took a tentative step, but then abruptly stopped. Had he seen recognition in Michael's eyes? He had to be certain. As he started to walk towards the bloodied vampire every heightened sense began to tingle. Chills ran up his spine and went off like fireworks in his brain. He leapt into the shadow of a rusted bin against the factory wall, instantly terrified.

A black van sped into the narrow passageway, screeched to a halt. Two men climbed out the back and ran to Michael. They grabbed him like he was a bag of garbage and threw him into the van, just as morning descended over the deserted city street. The doors slammed shut and it backed up straight and sped away.

Alone in the alley, he had to stop shaking and think. The sorcerers would come for him. They would capture him again. They would torture him again. He sat against the wall with his knees pulled to his chest and tried to think. "Somewhere safe. Where they would never look," he murmured. Then it came to him. Michael's brownstone. No one would think to look there.

****

Minutes before dawn, Thorn awoke with a tremendous headache. Woozy and confused, three faces entered his mind. Michael had introduced him to the Kendrick family, three generations of women who lived in Manhattan. Alone, these good witches were powerful. Together? The Kendrick witches created a magical force to be reckoned with.

"Not Georgians… Like Celia's father, but they'll help me figure this out."

Still dazed, Thorn struggled to get his bearings. "I may look a little slow, you pompous ass, but you know I'm not." He rubbed both temples, willing away the sharp ache. "These cobwebs in my head—*you* put them there. I'd *never* talk to the kid. No. You set up that show for a reason. What are you up to, Champ?"

Try as he might, the empath couldn't connect to the vampire's mind. With new resolve, he headed for the West 60s. "Damn it, Michael, how the hell did you do this to me?" he growled, unnaturally angry.

Fifteen minutes later, he was face to face with the youngest Kendrick witch. Martine, only seventeen-years old and dressed in purple paisley pajamas, grinned through an etched glass panel on the door. Raven-black hair piled on top of her head in a bushy bun and a series of thick, gold loops got larger as they reached the base of both earlobes. The teenager's eyes shone with witty intelligence as well as mischief when she opened the door.

"Thorn! Wow... Are we relieved to see *you,*" Martine said through a yawn. "You've gotta be able to fill in at least a couple of phrases in this weirdo crossword puzzle. What a wild night this has been." She grabbed his massive hand and pulled him into the kitchen.

Mary, her mother, and Martha, her grandmother, waited patiently for the coffee maker to stop dripping as he sank into a kitchen chair.

"The quizzical look on your face says it all, my friend. We were hoping you'd finally remember us. It seems our mutual friend is in trouble," Martha stated.

Although worried, drained of all energy, the soothing ring of her voice calmed him. "I-I was walking and then I had to sit down somewhere, apparently in a drug-induced sleep of some sort." He wasn't really sure....

"You must be starving, Empath, and you are just as confused as we are," Mary Kendrick observed. She handed him a hot cup of coffee as Martha prepared a plate of bread, cheese, nuts, and fruit.

"You, you don't understand. *He* did this to me. Something's wrong, ladies, very wrong." He shook his head while adding three heaping teaspoons of sugar before taking a large gulp of the fragrant blend. His mind sharpened a bit. "I think Michael did it on purpose. But why? Why send me to check on the kid and then twist the truth like that? I told him a year ago that this was a foolish deal. You can't trust Clayton and you can't trust evil sorcerers. I warned Rob and Dan to keep their distance, too. I can't interfere with a soul's destiny. And I don't think this kid has the slightest clue as to *who* he really is. No. Something's very, *very* wrong."

Martha touched his hand. "His very existence is now in jeopardy—the child's as well."

"I swear on my soul, Michael was a raving lunatic! Lukas doesn't remember. That was the trade. I do your evil bidding and the kid leads an uncomplicated life with no memory of demons or his unnatural father." Slowly, Thorn read Martha's fear. "My God, the kid knows, doesn't he?" His chin dropped and he shook his head slow. "Damnit. They're both gonna die." Martine stood behind, rubbing his shoulders. He reached up and patted her hand.

"Michael didn't want anyone to interfere with his plan," Martha stated.

Mary met his watery gaze. "Stay with us, Thorn. Martine got the downstairs' bedroom ready for you. You're safe here. Celia already knows about this. We heard her plea. We'll help keep Lukas hidden until we hear from Miles, but Michael has to fight his own battle." He watched Mary stand as Martine's hands slid off his shoulders. Both of them left the room.

The look of Martha's face would be easy for anyone to read. Her brow was knit, her eyes held sadness as they watered. Her lips turned down. He knew her bond with

Michael went back decades. "Eat," she whispered as she sat across from him. He reached out and she took his hand. After a pause, she added, "You will need your strength. When the time is right, you will go to him. He'll need you." Then she left him alone in the kitchen.

Eating was out of the question. Instead, he headed down to their finished basement bedroom, closed the door and stretched out on the bed. Closing his bloodshot eyes, he willed his mind into focus. Energy surged through him as if a connection had been made—a much deeper connection than just grabbing a thought here or there. This was intense. And he was ready.

"All right, you egotistical son of a bitch," he whispered. "Talk to me—and this better be good!" He swallowed unexpected anger… something he rarely felt. And let dogged resolve replace his natural tendency to worry.

****

Miles Bookman, Researcher for the Georgian Circle assigned to North America, always hated cell phones. They made irritating noises at the most inappropriate times.

He hadn't been able to sleep. After tossing and turning until the pre-dawn hour he decided to get dressed and go to the local all-night market near his home in downtown Manhattan. Entering the building's empty elevator, his arms were full of groceries. While thinking about having breakfast ready for his wife when she awoke, the irritating thing chimed again. He put one bag down and quickly patted every pocket. Celia, his daughter, insisted he carry the damned thing. Irritation turned to grave concern when he recognized the caller's number, bright blue and flashing across the screen. The elevator car flew to the top floor as if it knew the reason for the call. Placing the bags on the kitchen counter, he left once again.

The task before him along with a select group of Guardians was of paramount importance. Find the vampire's son. Keep Lukas Malone safe. Contact the Georgian Council to request extraction. As he ran out the door of his building, a small red sedan pulled flush with the curb, the driver a trusted ex-Guardian. "Something's gone down, Philip."

"I know. Miles. We all felt it."

"Get me to the passageway with the portal as quick as humanly possible. We'll start there and then comb the city because we have to find the boy before Clayton does. Lukas could be anywhere." Usually calm and steady, he didn't feel this way tonight. He was close to panic.

"You don't have to say it twice," Philip replied, pulling off the curb and speeding southeast through the deserted city streets.

****

The New World Technologies Building took up an entire city block in mid-town Manhattan. Just before dawn, two very different areas were ablaze with activity. As per the order put out by Clayton Mails, the vampire's office on the thirteenth floor was being scrubbed squeaky clean like he'd never been part of the company. Yeah— as if. All of Michael Malone's files hand-delivered to the upper echelon, whose offices were right below the private penthouse. They'd be gone through with a fine-tooth comb. Then, there was the matter of the penthouse. Left as is—mystically cloaked by dark seers; sealed off to all under penalty of torture and death.

Two human bodies had been removed. They would be found near the river, made to look like some kind of gun play gone wrong. But the most important activity was happening five floors below the ground.

Denny Kim slammed down the phone in the small office on Sub-Level Five. "Son of a fucking lard-ass bitch!" He threw down his poker hand, and Jamal Storm looked up. "That was the big guy, Clayton Mails. Says he has a delivery for us. No hose down, just immediate internment."

Jamal swept the deck of cards into the side drawer, and Denny locked it. He grabbed the code file. "5027, that's far enough away so we don't have to look at it."

They had heard something big was going down last night and had already bleached and prepped some units. He and Big J were ordered to stay an extra hour. That was fine with him. Overtime paid extremely well at NWT. Jamal strutted down the hall and unsealed the unit.

One of Clayton's men stepped off the elevator, dragging the creature by its feet. He didn't speak to either Denny or Jamal. They watched the big-ass minion grab the vampire's hair and belt, and then slam the bloody body on the cell's metal table. Pressing a side button, steel clamps gripped the thing across its neck, chest, waist, and legs. The hydraulic system hummed as the platform locked into position.

"That thing doesn't even look like it was ever human," Jamal whispered to him.

"Don't touch it," the man warned. "That's an order from upstairs. Just let it rot."

Already pissed off by the way he had been dismissed, Denny hollered, "Hey… does *it* have a name?" No answer came.

Then Jamal tapped his shoulder. "You know who this is? The tall exec in 1301… Look at the black jeans. It's all he ever wears. Damn! That's one damaged motherfucker," Jamal said with one of those rolling sways, a cool move Denny liked.

Denny pressed the activation code into the side panel. The glass door sealed itself. "Shit…he's a vamp!? We're gonna have to watch this one for worms. He's beaten to a friggin' pulp." He stared in awe at Michael Malone, Sub-Level Five's newest inhabitant.

It was as if a switch had been flipped in Michael's brain. Reality started to bend and warp. Memories twisted into distorted, fractured episodes. The ability to speak or think clearly was far out of his reach. Captured, shackled, and blood oozing out of every wound. Cold steel against his back. He knew where he was and why he'd been put here.

"*You must survive, Son of my Bloodline,*" echoed through him as if Helena was at his side and whispering. "*This battle. So foolish to attempt. This poison. So mystically insidious. Fight the poison. Walk the illusions with me. It begins with the child standing over you…*"

Chapter 6

The Dream of Survival Begins

Lukas stood over his father in the passageway, keen senses identifying the scent of animal blood oozing out of every wound. "Shit… What did they do to you?" His scraped knees hit the pavement to turn the vampire over. Michael's face was a mess with blood coating his skin like this was some horror movie. "I've got to get you out of here. I've got to get you out of—"

"The light of dawn… That's what you were going to say. Am I correct?" The tall, thin older man spoke calm and steady as he approached. His hair was more salt than pepper. Dressed in a tweed jacket and dark gray pants, he looked like one of those college professors in a movie. "I'm equally horrified by what I see." When he stood up, the man clasped a firm hand to his shoulder. Sensing no threat or any provocation, he didn't flinch. "My name is Miles Bookman. I know what your father is. I also know who you are. Come. We must move him to safety."

They both carried Michael into the deserted factory and lay the unconscious vampire on a soiled table. Earthly insects and spiders would do him no harm. He already knew this.

"You're British or something. You talk like one, anyway."

"Yes. But I've lived in Manhattan for thirty years. You have a good ear, young man," the older man replied with a slight smile but didn't take his eyes off Michael.

He ran his bloody hands down his jeans and sniffed the air. "There are others. Five beating hearts. Two are standing at each door."

The man gave a serious nod, looked as if he could mentally catalog each ugly wound.

"They're here to help."

The fifth beating heart approached, and Lukas glared into bright olive eyes. The girl had dark skin with black hair reaching down to her waist. He sensed mystical strength, yet she was petite and pretty with a round face. Latino. Not much older than he.

"Hi, it's Lukas, right? I'm Kayla—Kayla Gonzalez." She smiled at him but addressed the man. "Philip's bringing the van and the supplies, Mister B. Papa dropped me off at the corner. He said to tell you he's got clearance and everything's ready."

"Good," 'Mister B' replied. "Michael's skin has a pasty gray hue. He's going to need blood as soon as possible. We can transfuse him on the ride to Jersey. I don't think tunnel traffic will be heavy this early. Your father is in great danger in this city, Lukas. So are you. We have to get as far away from here as possible."

"Yeah, I get that," he answered in a flippant tone, even though he felt relieved someone was helping him. "So why New Jersey? It's not like there's some vampire hospital across the river, is there? I don't think they take the undead without Blue Cross."

The concerned look changed to something akin to parental. "I've known about you for many years. I also know what you did a year ago and I know what you are capable of doing. Keep your attitude in check. Your father has made a multitude of enemies tonight and there is no time to explain. You must cooperate, even if you don't understand. It is more important to get him *and you* out of danger, do you hear me?"

He tilted his head, sniffed the air again and stayed silent for a second, then gave a shrug. "We have company. Cargo van, smells like burning oil and the driver's male." A mischievous smirk began. "Is this, even though I don't understand, cooperative enough for you…uh, Mister B?" Boom, he thought, victorious! But the raised eyebrow didn't thrill him.

"I'm a parent myself, and for someone who just turned fifteen yesterday, angelic-face or not, smugness is not called for. Happy birthday, by the way."

"Yeah, right." *Some birthday present. What a shit-show this is.*

"Kayla, get the blood and the stretcher. We'll transfuse immediately. He's lost it all."

"She's one of those Guardians I've seen, right?"

"Yes."

Troubled memories flood his brain. One short year ago, Guardians had seen his multiple attacks on Michael, but not one had *ever* interfered. Which was strange. *Weren't these mystical warriors supposed to protect humans? But then again, he isn't human.*

Mister B stared at him briefly. Then the man traced a sunken vein down the vampire's arm, and worry lines appeared to deepen on his face. "This is worse than I thought."

His whole body stiffened as uncomfortable ramped up to I'm-very-much-fucking-afraid. "What do you mean? You've got to be friggin' kidding me. How could this get worse?"

Studying Michael's shoulder, the man murmured, "Oh, my Lord, what did they do to you?"

Lukas didn't know what to feel but seeing this amount of blood made him queasy as hell. He wanted to cry. He wanted to run away. Or really hurt someone or something *really* bad. He swallowed hard because of the lump in his throat and rubbed his bloodied palms down his jeans again. "He can't you know die, can he? You'll do something, right? I mean, anything you know how to do—you and these Guardians."

No immediate answer came, but Mister B attached a tube to the bag of blood like an expert. Or a doctor. "Let's try the jugular." Adding as he drove the needle directly in and secured the tube, "We must leave immediately."

Two Guardians lifted the injured vampire onto the gurney and covered him entirely to block the morning sun. Lukas followed, but stepping out of the building, he stared down at the broken asphalt. He sensed rumbling far below in the core of the earth, slithering its way up. *What if they take me back…now that I remember? What if they know I'm here?* Without thinking, he gripped the man's arm. "Something's happening. It knows we're here."

"Yes, I feel it too. But we are not sticking around to find out what it is. Get in the van."

He didn't argue, settling in next to Kayla. The other Guardians dispersed into the street, dropping out of sight in seconds.

Mister B turned to the driver. "Let's go, Philip. Get us out of here."

"You got it," the driver replied. As they sped

through the empty streets, the alleyway behind them crumbled deep into the earth, taking the dimensional portal with it.

****

Alana hated to clean. The third-floor apartment with a magnificent view of the harbor in Portofino began to sparkle—at least in her eyes. Just like a character in a fairytale, she'd gotten down on hands and knees, furiously scrubbing the floors with hot water and lemon oil. Her hands were rubbed raw now from the physical abuse of scouring, as opposed to staking vampires.

Everything gleams, the windows smudge-proof, and pillows fluffed against both beige leather armchairs. The kitchen sink is unusually empty and all appliances clean. Both tiled bathrooms positively sparkle. Mama Bookman would be properly impressed.

With every inch of her home now presentable, she thought about sleeping arrangements. *Miles and Lukas would share the guestroom. Celia B took over the cozy sunroom whenever she stayed here.* Michael would share her bed. She hurried to the master bedroom again, studied the exquisite antique furniture and a comfortable Queen Anne chair, which stood next to the nightstand.

She turned to the window, never imagining in her wildest dreams that she would use her aunt's heavy drapes for this particular reason. To shield a vampire, to shield her eternal love from the strong Portofino sun. *To see his handsome face again. To touch him, to hold him… I can protect you here.* New longings full of need and want filled her soul.

Convincing herself to leave Manhattan over a year ago had taken sheer determination. It was better this way. Safer. *Zia* Rosa knew very little about him. It was as if she now had a different life. Like loving Michael had never happened.

Alana left the master bedroom to check the other bedroom still lost in thought, looking at one of the twin beds, trying to picture Michael's son. Did Lukas look like his father? "His father," she whispered as she rubbed her forehead with her arm, "Why didn't you ever tell me about him, Michael? Why did I have to learn what was done to him by those evil things from Daddy B? And where did he go after a year of hunting you? There has to be more to this story." More than her adopted father let on. "Did your sudden, new 'position' at NWT have anything to do with Lukas's disappearance last year? You're going to tell me everything I want to know when you get here."

Unable to sit and relax, she moved through her spacious home two floors above a bookstore off the piazza. Then she stood at the dining room windows to check the busy street below. She remembered Celia B's rant, the confused look on her sister's usually happy face when saying how Michael had actually accepted a position with that totally disgusting company, NWT. Celia had said he flatly refused to discuss why he'd taken up with the well-known evil investment firm. "She said you knew exactly what had to be done." He'd been tight-lipped, almost brusque, and it hurt Celia's feelings. "I still find it puzzling—and I do not like puzzles. I didn't push her to tell me more… and I walked away from you with my dignity intact."

Checking the heavy drapes again, she knew the move to Italy had been good for her. "An ocean separating us is more than enough distance to mimic closure. The clean air and warm climate just enough to make me forget Manhattan, to forget everything that happened between us."

She walked over to the hutch and straightened her favorite vase that matched the exquisite dinnerware displayed, the way anyone expecting company would. And living upstairs from her great-aunt, doing normal everyday things, had a healing effect on her. One she was grateful for. "I'll see you though this…whatever it entails. There's nothing left for you in Manhattan. I have all the time in the world to devote to you. You'll be safe… And so will Lukas," she added with an anxious heart.

The ring from her cell phone broke this reverie, and she hoped to hear only good news. Pulling it from her pocket, she gave a bright and positive, "Hi, Daddy B."

"Hi to you, too. I've been calling the house line for hours. Is everything all right? I never put your cell phone number in my phone, so I had to call Celia."

Alana walked over to the secretary in the living room to replace the house phone on its cradle. "Oops," she said, a little less cheery, "I must have knocked it over while I was cleaning."

"I'm sorry, did you say cleaning?"

She gave a short laugh. "Very funny. But it isn't going to work. I hear it in your voice. Give it to me straight." She dropped to the couch.

"We arrive in three hours… Late afternoon your time. Prepare yourself. He isn't good. In fact, even I feel bad for the creature. Alana, did you hear me? Be prepared."

It took a moment for the warning to set in, and her 'bright' voice dissipated. "Yes, I hear you. Thanks." She flipped the cell phone off and put it on the coffee table.

Looking around the spacious room and through the wide arch to the formal dining room, she couldn't accept her adopted father's words. "Three more hours? Maybe he's a little worse than I thought. I've seen lots of ugly things during my ten years as a Guardian. How bad can he be?"

Just the thought of sitting around for another three hours made her edgy. She got off the couch and looked around again. Then she found a clean rag, soaked it in a fresh pail of hot water and lemon oil. "The floor could be cleaner."

She pushed fear from her heart.

Chapter 7

In The Air

"So, who is Kayla's father and why does he want to help," Lukas asked as he checked out the jet's magnificent interior. The trip to Teterboro Airport had been quick, only a few cars on Routes 3, 17, and 46. Already cleared for take-off, he was strapped in a plush leather chair that could recline.

"Cesar Gonzalez, Kayla's father is the owner of Medico Research Labs. He has a private facility in Florence, Italy. Also, he is a member of the Georgian Circle's Sovereign Council."

Not interested in any kind of council, he asked, "Was he ever a Guardian?"

"Yes, he served and survived his ten-year mission."

"So, he's sneaking us out of the country?"

Miles nodded as he checked his seatbelt for the third time. "He has no trouble accommodating a research team and us. In fact, the bedroom is now an emergency room for Michael."

"They know he's a vampire, right?"

"Yes. They are aware of your father and his history. A separate, secret segment of Medico Research is dedicated to the study of unnatural creatures. They document the ones we capture in the human world, study their physiology, and analyze the ancient chemical compounds used by sorcerers who control other deadly things."

"Are all these men part of your Georgian Circle thing?"

"Once again, correct, young man. Two of the very best of Cesar's people are working on your father now."

He needed to know more. "So, like, what are they doing?"

"Well, they have most probably cut off Michael's bloodied clothes, placed everything in sterile specimen bags. The clothing will later be catalogued by Arthur Chamberlain, the demon specialist assigned to your father's case. He is waiting for us in Italy."

"Okay. Then what," he asked, a little more curious.

"He will be covered with a hi-tech warming sheet with a portable examination board placed under him. It was created for the war arena in Iraq. It has an intricate web of sensors to detect even the slightest movement," Mister B answered in a clinical tone.

"Wow. You know a lot of things."

The man gave a slight smirk as one eyebrow raised. "It comes with the territory."

After take-off, Lukas stopped asking questions. He settled in, although still edgy. *One crazy night. Followed by an uncertain day.* He opened the bag of pretzels given to him before—practically inhaled them and downed a cold can of soda before putting it in the cupholder attached to the chair. He'd been up over twenty-four hours and he closed his eyes, even though he'd never flown before.

****

Lukas awoke with a start and his senses began to hum. He had no idea how long he'd slept as he gripped the seat, focusing his acute ability to hear. The hushed conversation between the two scientists in the flying ER had his full attention. His fingernails sunk deep into the leather seat as one said to the other, *"I've never seen something this injured. There isn't a spot on this body that isn't swollen, slashed, or bleeding, Baker."*

"This is a first for me too," Baker replied.

"Wait... Did you see it? Did you get a reading?"

"It's on the screen and I'm already noting the chart. Get Chamberlain on the phone."

"I call confirmation: 3 hours, 42 minutes into flight—REM begins."

"Well, what do you know... Our patient is dreaming."

Lukas closed his eyes, wondering if Michael was actually capable of dreaming. Because he was afraid to dream, afraid of what he would see in his mind.

The poison spiked, swift and furious in Michael's mind, vaguely aware of the two medics standing over him...

My body is so hot. A fire... seasoned wood gives off a fragrant, distinctive scent. Every breath hurts my lungs. The smoke-filled air is too dense to see through. I am suspended upside down, arms chained to my body, shackles around my ankles cutting deep into my flesh.

Fire crackles beneath, spitting flying embers to sting my face, to singe my hair, to burn my shoulders. In one quick plunge, I dip into the blazing bath of flames. It is beyond agony, but I do not die. My body flies up, into a holding position once again. I scream for it to stop; I beg for it to end.

"How long have you lived, demon? Did I hear someone whisper hundreds of years?"

I recognize the lyrical voice. My gentle mother, how I have wounded you in the heart. You, so full of life, so dear to me. Such remorse, such guilt. Her face appears. She glares at me through swollen eyes—then kisses my fevered brow. Her demeanor changes from contempt to compassion for one fleeting moment.

"I loved you, my son, so strong, so handsome. Why did you leave England? Why did you turn your back on me? This would never have happened if you had stayed at my side." Her fingers brush my burning cheek.

Blood tears cloud my eyes. I choke on my words— unable to speak.

"Hush. Save your anguished cries. You have many more trials 'till your soul is pure enough to stand with mine," she whispers.

Her prophecy is punctuated by the roar of flames as I plunge into the pit once again.

Lukas gripped the arms of his seat so tight that his knuckles turned white.

Miles unbuckled his seat belt and stood abruptly. "Please excuse me while I check on our patient." But Lukas's mind was already racing. Different scenarios. Different outcomes. What if his father suddenly woke up? He focused his hearing, sensing the man was now standing over Michael. "Can you hear me? We're taking you to Alana.. Lukas is with us, and he is safe. We're doing everything we can to ensure your survival."

"There's no response, Miles. We don't know if he can hear you."

"How much human blood have you given him, Baker?"

"This is the fifth bag."

"But his skin remains dull and gray. My God, he is

still unrecognizable."

"The slashes are sutured closed, *but* blood keeps oozing faster than we can—"

"Was there any response at all when I mentioned Alana and his son?"

"No," he heard Baker reply, "and you would think they'd be a reason for him to hold on."

****

Miles took his seat again and buckled his seatbelt. "How are your scrapes and bruises?"

Lukas was getting restless, but replied as if he didn't care, "Already healed."

"Well, that's good, but you know it was important to have them tended to by Doctor Baker even though you can obviously self-heal."

Lukas slid his eyes to the side. "So why did you take what I was wearing and give me these stupid blue scrubs to put on, which don't even friggin' fit? Are you going to analyze my clothes, too?" He repositioned himself in the chair and slammed his palms down on its cushioned arms.

"Everything about last night that we have access to must be analyzed and catalogued. Your bloody clothes included." Miles paused. "And why, may I ask, are you still so anxious? Please note, that I use anxious and not raging, which I know you are prone to—at the drop of a hat, I might add."

His eyes narrowed as he studied the bland facial expression. "You know about the rage, huh?"

"Indeed, I do. I have many, many episodes chronicled one short year ago—before the Georgian's lost track of you."

He quickly looked away. He wouldn't talk about the

year he hunted his own father. Not with anyone. Especially someone he'd just met. It was confusion that kept his attitude reserved, friendly at times. Even cooperative, for the moment. "I want to see him myself."

"I thought you'd like to know there has been rapid eye movement detected. Your father is dreaming."

"I know what REM means. That's a good sign, right?"

"It's a very good sign. It means he's in there somewhere. We'll be in Italy soon. You know, I don't particularly like to fly. Landings are torturous."

No wonder he kept his seatbelt on. He gave no reply at first but stood up with both fists ready if he didn't get his way. "I want to see him. You can't stop me."

Mister B let out a long sigh and turned his face toward the jet's window. "Very well, young man, of course… But just for a minute."

Triumph and trepidation battled within him as they took the short walk to the bedroom. His hands relaxed, but his heart raced. "You must remain calm, no matter what goes through your mind. Can you promise that?" Miles asked, almost in a fatherly tone.

"Yeah," Lukas mumbled, not at all threatened by the warning. "But you know I'm just as strong as one of your Guardians."

"Duly noted," the man replied.

When they entered the room, he studied the high-tech gadgetry on the opposite side of the bed. But he didn't expect to feel as queasy as he did when he looked at Michael. They had washed some of the blood off his face and arms. The blanket covered him up to the middle of his chest, which was dripping blood along with every other cut he saw. His nostrils took in the new scent, and he whispered, "This is human blood."

"It is *not* your father's regular diet, but it should speed up the healing process."

"Yeah. I get it... shit. I-I don't even recognize his face. It's so... so beaten...all sunken. His eyelids look like you painted black circles on a-a frickin' colorless corpse." The pretzels he'd eaten before felt like they were coming up his throat. He swallowed hard. Didn't want to puke.

What if Michael didn't wake up? What would he do then? Where would he go? He'd be in a foreign country alone without a connection to anyone or anything. He suddenly felt like the room was spinning. Mister B's arm shot around his shoulder. More than anxious and full of questions, he let himself lean against the itchy tweed jacket. But he didn't take his eyes off Michael's long, lean frame.

"Perhaps he senses you're here and it's a comfort to him," Mister B said in a gentle way.

Lukas sniffled back the drippy stuff clogging his nose. Felt a tug on his shoulder and didn't fight the walk back to his seat. Almost numb, he sank into the leather chair. Seconds later, he watched Mister B sitting across from him, fastening his seatbelt, and opening his laptop. He pulled a pair of round, silver-rimmed glasses from his breast pocket and settled them carefully on his face.

The sound of quick click-click-clicks on the keyboard amused him. "You type really fast." Mister B gave a slight smile, looked up, but didn't stop typing.

He locked his arms across his rolling stomach. "I'm different, you know. I've changed. I know Michael did this to me—for me—whichever way you want to put it in that report of yours. I remember all of it now," he added while showing nothing on his face. A warm grin came at him—instead of another attitude comment, and he relaxed. A little.

"Why are you so convinced I'm writing about you? Part of a researcher's job is to document everything seen and sensed, and I am more concerned about your father right now. If you are interested, I can fill you in on what I know. I've studied Michael Malone for most of my adult life. Perhaps when you trust me enough, you'll tell me about yourself."

Quickly, he quipped, "I trust you, Mister B. I came with you, didn't I? I can *see* they're taking care of him. It's not like he has all that many friends." Looking away, he mumbled, "Neither do I anymore."

Leaving behind a normal life, even if it wasn't real, hurt like hell. *There is no happy family to go home to... only a powerful vampire who triggered something close to murder in me for an entire year. I tried to stake him again and again. But then all the hate disappeared. Like magic. Wiped away. This past year of not remembering...* He glanced up. "You stopped typing."

Pulling off his glasses, he noticed the light-blue of Mister B's eyes, the wrinkles at their sides, the angles of his long, thin face. The man looked tired. Really tired.

He gave a nod with his thin lips tight. "This must be incredibly hard for you to figure out. You realize I wouldn't have left you there. You are very much in danger as well, and all of us will help you settle in. Besides, Michael's friend insists I bring *both* of you to her. If there's anything you don't understand—"

Before he could stop himself, he shot back, "Yeah, right... What if he doesn't come out of this? What if he stays, just like, in some undead coma or something?" He kicked his head back, deep into the leather seat, narrowing a glare at someone who had only been kind to him.

"Good. I'm relieved you are asking the right questions." The man closed the laptop, looking directly into his eyes. His voice was calm and reserved, soft and easy to listen to. "That will not happen. He will pull through. *His* Guardian wouldn't have it any other way." Slipping the laptop into a brown briefcase, he leaned in closer. "I represent an immensely powerful group. One could say evil has met its match in us. I know this is confusing. I know something's changed in you. But you are in good hands now, son."

"I'm not your son… I'm *his* son," he bit out, quick and sharp. He closed his eyes tight, told himself not to cry. He refused to drop his guard any further, breathing hard through his nose.

A long sigh came at him. Then he heard the seatbelt unclick. "We'll be landing shortly."

Lukas didn't respond, very aware of Mister B's unsteady walk to the bathroom. The door clicked shut, and he heard a cellphone on speaker. He zeroed in on the conversation listening with renewed interest.

"How close are you, honey?"

"I'm just leaving the airstrip, Dad. Thanks for the driver, by the way. There's traffic. I should be at Ally's place in about an hour. How's Michael?"

"He's very bad, Celia. I can't imagine Alana being prepared for this." A few details followed before there was silence once again.

Celia, he thought. I've seen her often in the city, specifically when I was hunting and stalking Michael. But Ally-Alana… whichever. Don't know her.

He heard water splashing in the bathroom basin, and then came a quick tongue click. "*I've not shaved in a day, nor slept in over twenty-four hours. I look like hell.*"

Wrong, Mister B, he thought. We are actually in Hell… With no way out.

Chapter 8

Arrival

Lukas sat next to Mister B in the back of an ordinary delivery van. Michael was on a stretcher, covered from head to toe. The two scientists sat in the cab. "So where are we going to stay? Is it, like, some villa or something?" he asked.

"Not at all. We will be in the middle of a sea-port town. Your father's friend lives on the third floor of a recently renovated building."

"It doesn't sound very big."

"But it is. Two apartments turned into one. It is very beautiful."

"Who lives on the second floor? How are we going to be safe?"

"Her great-aunt lives on the second floor, and the seaport's best bookstore is on street-level. As for safety, we will be mystically protected. Nothing evil will be able to enter."

"If it's a busy street, how are you gonna get him upstairs without anyone seeing?"

Mister B gave a short nod as he clutched his briefcase on his lap. "An old service elevator was restructured at the back of the building. We will pull into the garage, close the door and get the gurney into the elevator, which, by the way, and I'm sure you will ask, only opens in the foyer of Alana's home. 52 Via Amadeus is a corner building off the piazza, and all will be safe. Satisfied?" He gave a shrug. When the truck came to a halt, the garage door cranked open, and then it closed after the truck backed in. "See?" Mister B said to him, "all safe and secure."

As soon as Doctor Baker opened the back, Lukas jumped out of the van. Mister B stepped down more slowly. Standing at the elevator was a pretty woman dressed in blue jeans and a white sweater with short sleeves. Dark brown ringlets framed her serious expression, the rest of her hair pulled up high off her face. She had full lips—drawn down in a worried way. Her hazel eyes were shaped like almonds with long lashes framing them. Her complexion a different shade than his—like she had a deep tan. *So, this is Alana, his 'friend'. But the way she look says she's more, even though I never saw him talk to her in the city..*

"He's taken a vicious beating," Mister B said to her, holding her tight in a one-arm embrace. She was shorter than him, fitting under his chin with her face to the side.

"You look like hell," she replied in a soft voice yet full of emotion.

"I believe we've just come from there," Mister B said with a kiss to her forehead.

She pulled out of the hug and then her head tilted to the side as she looked at him. He stared back, showing nothing on his face, and then she flashed a cautious smile. His mouth curled into a small grin that didn't reach his eyes.

She was already at the gurney, but Mister B caught her arm. "This is Lukas— Michael's son." She didn't seem to see him. "Yes, well, we can save introductions for later. Please go with Doctor Baker, Lukas."

Lukas stopped gawking long enough to step inside the elevator with the scientist who held a large medical cooler. As the doors closed, he heard Mister B repeat, "He's taken a vicious beating, Alana."

Alana lifted the sheet from Michael's face. But then seeing his chest? Her hand flew to her mouth as she gasped. "Where is he *not* stabbed or cut? His skin is as white as this sheet! Jesus! Dark-purple, sunken eyelids, thin lips putrid gray— Oh my God." Her breath hitched as her eyes filled while brushing Michael's icy cheek. Did he know her scent, her touch? She took his limp hand. Fresh drips of crimson oozed out of the wounds covering his arm. *What did this to you? No way in Hell was I prepared to see this!*

"We need to get him upstairs, honey," she heard as he gently pried her hand off Michael, and the gurney rolled into the elevator as its doors opened again.

****

Standing at the foot of the four-poster bed, Alana couldn't believe how bad he looked. She'd never seen him with even a scratch. Now? There was barely a spot on his body that wasn't bruised, cut, or bleeding. The two scientists made quick work of settling him in. They had already covered the fitted sheet with a dense blanket that had a rubber back and laid a warming blanket over it before they put Michael in her bed. He was covered with another warming blanket and then they pulled the soft, satin sheet over it. Although she shored herself up, she only managed to whisper, "I want to know everything, Doctor Baker."

The young doctor gave a slow nod as he came over to her. "He's been out of it since we got him; not responding like a-a normal vampire." *Michael has never been a 'normal' anything.* "Whatever did this was pretty juiced, Alana. There's blood for him in the cooler. We had an IV drip of penicillin along with the blood. Doc Chamberlain also sent some vials of penicillin, sterile syringes, and wrap bandages. We don't know if antibiotics will help, but there's no harm in trying, right?" He cleared his throat. "Listen. He might be disoriented if he wakes up, and you'll want to be cautious. I mean, an injured vampire can be—"

"Thanks. We'll be fine. Tell Doctor Chamberlain I appreciate this."

"He'll check on Michael tomorrow morning." Doctor Baker paused. "Try to turn him on his side for a few hours. His back is pretty messed up. Look. I've been with Chamberlain for almost ten years. I've never seen any creature mauled so brutally actually pull...I'm sorry, Alana, I—"

"No. I understand. And thanks." She heard the door close, and it took a minute to gather her thoughts. Unwilling to take her eyes off him, she forced herself to switch off the recessed lights and then walked over to the other side to turn on the lamp on her nightstand. Even though the room was warm, she shivered. His beaten face, his bloody shoulder—carefully she lifted his arm to peel both sheets down to his waist.

Tears welled in Alana's eyes. If she let them fall, she'd be useless. She swiped them away with her palms. *Be calm, be patient and strong. It's necessary right now.* But what she saw... Sword slashes covered his torso. She eased the sheet down—multiple bruises covered his lower abdomen as if he'd been kicked by a herd of horses. One thigh had a gaping wound and blood oozed even though it was stitched.

Her heart pounded like a war drum. She took a deep breath and blew it out. Carefully turned him on his side. *Ugh… another horror show.* The back of his thigh confirmed a sword had gone straight through. *Three raw crevices down his right side from shoulder to knee. Muscles torn and exposed. His right shoulder gnawed and raw.*

Her hands shook as she rested him again on his back and covered him to mid-chest. She kissed his forehead and brushed his matted waves of hair away from his face. He'd always worn it a little too long, which only added to his singular good looks. "Come back to me, my love," she whispered, relieved he was finally here with her. She pulled the Queen Anne upholstered chair closer to the side of the bed. Leaning forward, she planted her elbows on her knees and rested her head in her hands. Her worst nightmare had just begun.

Michael could scent the woman he loved yet he could not react. His mind spun, full of distortions he could not control… *I am in my bed at the brownstone, and someone is with me… Soft satin sheets against my body. I am no longer alone. I smell the clean, soft scent of cherry blossoms and jasmine. Sweet breath lingers on my brow. She kneels beside me.*

"Michael," she softly calls, "No one knows I'm here with you—for you." Sensuous nibbles to my ear. Warm hands on my chest inch down. But the excitement is peppered with shame. She is innocent. Pure. Someone I cannot touch.

I peel her eager hands off me. Yet, she is determined and grips me tighter.

"This isn't right. Go home."

69

"You don't want me to leave," she purrs. "You want this as much as I do. Love me."

I can stop this. I know better. But what she does to me… caution is no longer within reach. Her beautiful breasts radiate heat, passion. A sinful sigh escapes her full lips. My body responds as if compelled by her touch. Hungry kisses lead me father away from reality, farther from rational thought. Her caresses are a tease.

And I want more.

My hands move down her body. Her hips rock in anticipation. She is warm, and I am cold. She is life and I am death. A moan escapes. Her back arches and my sanity slips father away. I cannot stop as she writhes beneath me.

Something awakens. Something I keep well-hidden, controlled.

My tongue longs to taste her. I will own her innocence. I will be her only desire. She thrashes beneath my weight, gasping, grasping for more in heated anticipation. Need thunders within, but I will ruthlessly tease until her body trembles. I am in ecstasy. The master of her desire. I bring her to climax, and then, only then, as no human man could, I possess her.

She tries to scream, but a growl slithers up my throat, and I thrust, brutal and quick. Do not deny the thirst for sweet nectar—for her innocent blood. It is a primal craving. When the beast-within awakens, it tears into her pulsing jugular to drink deeply, to assuage the craving for innocence once again.

Suddenly, she is still.

The beast-within is sated. It licks her sacred blood off my lips as it subsides, at rest once again. As it should be. Pulled out of passion, it is only then that I see the destruction. Her lifeless body. Panic swells within, cursing the beast that is and always will be a part of me.

"Control," I scream, "where is my control!"

Heavy footsteps approach the bed's edge. The Empath, a gentle soul, stares down at me. At her. No compassion in his demeanor. Eyes void of mercy... He fists my hair and with one, swift pull my body is off the bed and my face meets the floor.

I am paralyzed by guilt.

"You killed her. You slaughtered an innocent!" His foot presses down between on my shoulder blades. There is no escape. Every lick of the belt in his hand earns another wail from my throat. Raised, red welts from neck to knee mar my skin. The beating is as endless as the night. "You take what you want; do what you please. You stole her innocence. You stole her soul. Why must you destroy everything you profess to love?"

His accusations thunder through me. Left alone, I shiver. Blood tears cloud my eyes. Full of disgust, I curl into myself, quaking and sore.

Guilt engulfs my soul—endless guilt.

****

Alana awoke with a start. With her arms folded on the edge of the bed, she had rested her head never thinking she'd fall asleep. Sitting back, she glanced at the alarm clock on the nightstand. She scrubbed her face and then opened her eyes wide with a stretch. Hours had passed. Well after sunset now, as the soft sea air billowed against the window's heavy drapes.

She pushed the chair back into place, sat on the bed and leaned down to kiss Michael's pale lips. A chill ran down her spine. Blood tears glistened on his thick lashes. "Where are you, my love?" she whispered, wiping away the crimson beads with the tips of her fingers.

He flinched, and her heart skipped a beat. Gently she cupped his battered face in her warm hands. "Open your eyes. Please…" but he didn't, and her heart felt like it would shatter like a glass thrown against stone. "Oh God," she whispered, "please let him come back to me."

Chapter 9

Truth Time

Everyone in the living room had been busy since their arrival. Alana had not come out of the bedroom, and Lukas continued to take in his new surroundings. He learned that father and daughter had not seen each other for a year, Celia being "consumed with paranormal studies in England." Miles had announced that he needed to rest for an hour, which he did, "to renew his mind," whatever that meant.

Celia seemed awfully familiar with Portofino. She had been very talkative before saying how she had filled the fridge with healthy food. He preferred a bag of chocolate cookies or potato chips of any kind. Then she had looked directly at him with a bright smile. "I even bought you a pair of black sweats and a neat T-shirt so you can change after a shower. The water doesn't really ever get hot, so you don't have to worry about burning yourself."

That was an hour ago, and grudgingly, Lukas had complied with the shower taking.

Now he was back in the living room sprawled out in one of two oversized beige leather armchairs that must have cost a fortune. Celia sat with her legs tucked under her reading some book, and Miles had just come back to the living room wearing fresh clothes. His white shirt had the top button buttoned. The gray sweater had pockets and elbow patches and his trousers had sharp creases running down. *Yeah, I guess that's comfortable in a way. But very English-like.*

But *he* didn't feel comfortable. Not one bit. Didn't trust these people no matter how nice they were. Lukas fidgeted, on the verge of edgy. And he studied how they sat close together on the couch. Instead of a laptop, Miles had a handful of papers with writing on them.

Celia rolled her sparkling-green eyes, wrinkled her nose, and smiled at him. "You're a stubborn little guy, aren't you? We had one heck of time keeping you safe in that old factory. Your dad would have gone into a major frenzy if he'd seen you there."

Oh… so *she* was the one who kept him glued to that filthy floor. Good to know, but he had secrets, too. "I've…seen you before—a couple of times." Okay, so he'd had a stake mere inches away from Michael's unbeating heart. "You'd yell my name, and I would stop," he added under his breath and wondering if *she* was the reason he hadn't shoved the stake through.

"Yep. Right on both counts. Sorry about the crushing thing in the factory, but we had to keep you out of commission."

Whoa, he thought as his eyes widened. "I wasn't trying to kill him last night."

Miles looked up from the papers, snagging his attention and pulling off his wire-rimmed glasses. The leveled look was seriously parental as if to say he wasn't playing games. "Would you please tell us *why* you were there in the first place? We've got all night, and you've got our full attention, young man."

Lukas eyed them, blew out a slow breath. If he told

the truth, would they even believe him? "Why?"

"We hope to piece together last night's events."

Something said tell the truth, even if it feels weird to say out loud. "I went to see him yesterday. Relax," he quickly added with an slow roll of his eyes. "I didn't know who he was… Yet. This huge guy's been following me around, and when I left school Friday afternoon, I wanted answers."

"His name is Thorn. He works for your father. He's an empath," Mile offered.

"Yeah, whatever. A demon's a demon," he quipped. "The whole week I saw him everywhere. In the library, on the street—even at Tuesday's fence meet. I'm pretty good with a rapier. Kind of like a weird skill for a city kid." He shrugged his shoulders, keeping it loose because he had a hell of a lot to say. "So, Friday afternoon I decided to follow *him*. I'm awesome at tracking—another weird talent. He went into the NWT building. I watched elevator lights from the security desk. I made some lame excuse to the guard about needing a bathroom—really quick. The elevator light stayed on thirteen, so I snuck up the stairs, hid, and waited. Some lady was saying how this big exec…was in a meeting. The demon left. I didn't. Then this tall man dressed in black strides down the hall. I knew he had to be who the demon was looking for. So, I walked into his office and confronted him." He watched their reaction as a grin slid across his lips. "The look on Michael's face was, like, total surprise. He made some stupid excuse about studying teenagers and cell phones, threw some unintelligible technobabble at me—like I couldn't tell he didn't know what the hell he was talking about. I get the feeling he wants me gone—really fast. So, I left."

"What time was that?" Miles asked.

"About four."

"How did you know to go to the portal in the passageway?"

His fingers dug into the arms of the soft, leather chair. "OK, now it gets creepy. Something fuckin' twitched in me when I saw him, but I didn't remember anything—at first. I reached for my cell phone to call home, but I must have left it in my locker, so I went to the public library. The librarian knows me. She let me call home. Mom said we would all meet for dinner over by Juilliard…for my birthday. Me, her, Dad and my… my sister." Who doesn't really exist, he thought as he paused. "I hung with some friends and did some homework, and then headed uptown around seven. I get to Lincoln Center and start to feel like…really weird. I mean, I had to sit. My head's pounding, so I think I'd better go home." He sank deeper in the chair and closed his eyes.

"Tell me about the migraines."

He wondered how the man knew about them, and his voice grew soft. "Really bitchin' ones like my eyeballs are gonna pop. Sometimes I see crazy things… demons, blood, a hazy face. I didn't know it was Michael's face when I talked to him. Something stuck in the way, like it blocked me knowing what…who he was."

He looked at his hand gripping the leather. Saying it made him remember it, which was getting hard to do. "So now I'm walking, right? I mean, I know where I live and all, but I end up outside NWT again. I'm woozy. It's like really late, and I keep thinking Mom and Dad are worried. I walk back to the Met looking for them. I'm wiped out—can't recall how to get home." He bit his lip and paused. "Long after the opera lets out, I'm still all sweaty and my head's killing me. So I sit by the fountain, and BAM! These crazy-ass scenes explode in my brain. I want to hurl. It's stuck in my gut… But now I know there are…*other* things about me. I start running but I don't know where I'm going or where I've been. Then I see Michael in my head and I remember more."

Shooting out of the chair, Lukas walked through the dining room arch to a window before turning to them. "Jekyll and Hyde scenes play in my brain like I'm in some friggin comic book movie. I knew what I tried to do to him." Celia's pretty green eyes were wide. "I tried to torch him once or twice. You know what I can do."

Miles nodded. "You were always spry and quick, often ambushing him when he least expected it. Celia told me how Michael would finally grab hold—"

"Yeah and I'd kick, claw and punch until I was free." Not feeling proud, his stomach clenched.

"And you were thirteen at the time?"

"Yeah. I kept hunting him until my fourteenth birthday—when I didn't remember anymore."

"Nothing could stop you. Many Guardians confirmed this."

What could he say? He simply stared at them. Because it was true.

"Tell us what happened on your fourteenth birthday."

"Somehow Michael grabbed me. I cursed and kicked but he just kept saying he loved me, how he had to save me from myself. I spit in his eye when he kissed my forehead. The next thing I know, my mom's telling me to get up or I'd be late for school. I don't remember him anymore—" His voice trailed off. He crossed the room and flopped back into the chair, closed his eyes, and kept banging his head against its thick, leather back. "Last night, like around midnight, I knew I didn't have a family or great friends. It wasn't real."

"Lukas, look at me." When he did, the man shook his head slowly and rubbed his forehead. "How did you find the portal?"

"I went back to NWT. The whole place was deserted—not even guards. I tracked Michael's scent up to the penthouse. His two friends—the ones who knew about me—"

"That would be Rob and Dan," Celia whispered.

"Their throats were slit. I saw their bodies and six piles of dust and bone scattered around the room…but no Michael. The inner office was like Satan's sanctuary, with shriveled up corpses—three dead things. Their skeletons stank…all black and burnt to a crisp. Those things made me hate him." Bitterness edged up his throat. "I could smell Michael all over the room. The skylight was shattered—glass everywhere! That's where his scent ended. I ran out and headed straight for the alley, the portal." He was more uncomfortable now.

"You went to help your dad. You did a very brave thing." Celia said, adding, "It's all right. We understand—"

"No! You don't understand," he yelled as he shot out of the chair pointing a finger at her. He sniffed back tears ready to run. "I *remember* trying to fucking kill him! How many kids actually try to *kill* their fathers…and then try again and again? I wanted to *help* him this time, I swear, and then wham! I get glued to the fucking floor. Voices singing in my head, bright lights exploding the demons, the damned thing biting and clawing him—"

"What did you say?" Miles asked.

Celia stood quickly and stared at him. "It-it really *bit* him?"

"You heard me right! This fucking thing claws him and then takes a chunk of shoulder. I saw the flesh in one of its jaws. It had three damn heads! All the Hell-beasts were history. This creature didn't disappear until *after* it bit him. It friggin' took him down like he was some kind of cat toy!" Rage sizzled below his skin as his cheeks flushed. "I saw the fucking portal! I know *they* sent this thing to destroy him…then *they* took it back!"

"Of course!" Celia said to her father, "Wow. This really was one major slug-fest between good and evil. The incantation, the protection we sent Michael's way— it all worked!"

Lukas fully glared at her. His jaw tightened. His teeth grinding as his fists flexed wanting to grab her. "Did you see what they did to him? He's a vampire, and he's lying in there worse than undead. What friggin' planet are you on, lady?"

When he lurched forward, her father got between them, startling him in a way. "You have no reason to attack *anyone* in this house. The fact of the matter is your father is not gone. Now that we know what happened it is only a matter of time… he will heal. You saved him by—"

Lukas got in his face thinking how just one punch would do a whole lot of harm. *"Saved him?* I fucking *did* this to him! I'm responsible!"

"You were manipulated," was said with understanding, and it stopped him cold.

Talking about last night exhausted him. "I watched Michael sacrifice himself last night…because of me," he whispered. Even as his eyes welled, he told himself he wasn't going to cry. And he didn't pull away when Miles wrapped an arm around him. It felt like comfort, something he needed, especially after the last twenty-four hours.

"You are not seeing it all, young man. You must *never* feel guilt. You could not have known."

Miles held the boy tight. He rubbed his slender back as any father would. Lukas looked younger than his age, small of stature with the face of an angel. His deep-blue eyes were watery. His full lips were in a pout accentuating his deep-dimpled cheeks. His sandy blond hair was curly and soft when he pushed Lukas's hair away from his round face. The boy positively shook as he cried, and he understood much more about the boy now.

Now Miles was outraged by Michael's arrogance, being too self-assured to come to the Georgians for help with his troubled child. He had bartered Lukas. Bargained with the devil. His sworn allegiance to NWT was their thirty pieces of silver to keep his son safe.

This child was hurting. Lost somewhere between rage and guilt—over something he couldn't have understood. *Michael, on the other hand, should have known better.* His tone stayed soft, full of reassurance. "None of what happened is your fault. Your father will come out of this. I promise, and I never break a promise." Holding this lost little boy tight in his arms, Miles prayed he was right.

Chapter 10

Support

Celia's concern for everyone, including her adopted sister hit the stratosphere after the information Lukas just gave them. This whole situation was bad. Really bad. Ally had been alone with Michael for the first time in years. And Ally's love ran deep for Michael. His love ran deep for her. Her sixth sense said things had to start moving—like to jump-start his healing, and it had to happen soon. She tapped on the bedroom door before entering, and carefully closed it behind her. Turning to the elegant four-poster, she approached, focused on her sister, her best friend. Perched next to Michael and as close as possible, Ally looked like she was guarding him.

"Hey, sweetie, why don't you take a break?" Ally shook her head. Sinking down in the upholstered chair, she leaned in close and kept her voice low. "So, any movement?"

"They really did a number on him. I have to get him back. I don't care how long it takes or what I have to do."

"Why don't you let me take a look? I'll tell you what I sense."

Support, concern, and love filled her heart. Alana pulled the sheet down to his waist. She winced as a shiver ran up her spine. The huge gnaw red and swollen... Colorless strips of surgical tape held the shredded skin together, but the injuries appeared angrier. A queasy feeling hit her stomach. "Oh God. This looks infected. I know it's a long shot, Ally, and vampires aren't human and all—but Michael isn't your normal, run-of-the-mill, vacant vamp anyway. There's penicillin—"

"I don't know… What if it hurts him or something? I mean, what do we do? I don't think there's a Physician's Desk Reference for the undead."

"At this point, I'd give anything a try. These are nasty. They're deep, you know, to make sure the big bad flying beast did what it was supposed to do."

"What flying beast?"

"It had three heads! Dad got tons of info out of Lukas. If he hadn't opened up and told us what he saw, we'd still be in the deep dark. That dirt-brown thing bit and clawed him. I'm guessing its body juices were like poison."

"Jeez. I forgot about Lukas… God. Michael…is a-a father," Alana whispered, slowly shaking her head. "I didn't know. I had no idea—"

"I'll get Dad," Celia quickly said, "and Lukas, too. That boy's really hurting, Ally." She didn't wait for a reply. And on purpose, left the door ajar.

****

Alana didn't hear his approach but looked up to see Michael's son standing in the doorway. Funny. She couldn't stop staring. Sandy, uncombed curls hid his round face. When he finally looked at her, she marveled at the angelic features, his deep-blue eyes like the sea in a storm. Deep dimples that appeared even if he wasn't smiling. *No resemblance to his father, except the hint of high cheekbones and the intensity of his gaze. And his stance against the doorframe, with his arms locked across his slender chest, feet crossed in a casual way?* It was Michael's favorite pose.

"You can come all the way in. I'm not a biter," she said, hoping the invitation would shatter the awkwardness between them. It didn't, so she offered a slight smile. "When Michael stands like that, Celia B calls it lurking and looking. Do you think it's a genetic thing?"

Lukas barely broke a grin; gave a quick shrug. "Genetic? I don't know. Maybe. It's just kind of, you know, comfortable."

She watched his approach, his hands rubbing down his sweats. He sniffed the air, zeroing in on the shoulder wound. "It smells weird… It's infected, isn't it?"

Miles came in with a full syringe in one hand. "Yes, it is," he answered. With a definitive jab, he emptied the syringe into the festering wound.

Her flinch and wince were immediate. "I can stake vampires, but I hate needles. Being able to self-heal is so much better than going to a doctor. Don't you agree," she said to Lukas, catching the distant look he wore. *"He's really hurting, Ally." Celia's words ring true, and I have to trust her take on him. A boy needs his father. Michael would want him kept close.* "Do you think you can stay with him for a while? I have things to do," she lied, hoping he'd give a positive response.

"Yeah. I can do that," he mumbled, not looking at her.

Trust takes time, but it's a start. She stood, nodding to Miles and Celia, and then gently pat the boy's shoulder when he came farther into the room. *Lukas didn't stiffen. Didn't flinch. It is a good sign.* As they all left the bedroom, she stopped at the foot of the bed.

"We'll take good care of him."

Their eyes met again. Did his son feel a spectrum of emotions the way she did? Yes. He had to—pushing her own trepidations deep down.

Chapter 11

Awakening

The room was quiet and the light from the bedside lamp dim at his side, casting a soft glow. Lukas felt weird staring down at Michael. Maybe because of remembering everything. They both had mystical strength, but nowhere was the intimidating vampire he had hunted a year before his world had changed. This Michael lay helpless, vulnerable to everything. He brushed the large hand with curiosity; forced himself to relax, then settled his hand over Michael's bloodied one. No response. Not even a twitch. The last time they saw each other bitter rage had filled his heart. The desire to destroy had his brain locked in a vice. Tonight, however, nothing like hate entered his mind. This vampire was his father. "It's me. Lukas," he whispered with hesitation. "You're gonna be okay. You have to come out of this."

****

His son's touch, his son's scent. Both triggered a predictable nightmare. *So much to explain...* Lukas had been cagey. Murderous. Four years of captivity in the Second Realm did that to him. Shocked at the untethered rage in the child, he immediately began plotting a just revenge. *But now? In this state of forced inertia? No one was safe...*

"Help, Dad! I can't find you!" his son screams, a

piercing staccato in the solitude of a maze.

I am covered with sweat after hours of searching. Every time I think I am close his cries come from different directions. How could he be so lost? I call out to a stranger standing near, "Please, help me find my son. He's somewhere in the maze."

"You shouldn't have let him go in there alone. What a terrible father," he replies. One turns into many, a raging mob shouting barbs like "What the hell kind of father are you, anyway?" "Everyone knows no one comes out of this alive—it changes you—it feeds off the fear!" and then the mirage dissipates as if it had simply been a threatening cloud.

My son's screams fill my soul. I retrace my steps, only to find a bright light from above illuminating my path. I walk toward the light with courage in my soul. Helena appears, and a sense of hope is kindled.

"Thank God, you found me. Lukas needs me. He is lost—"

"So shall it be for eternity. Sons of our bloodline. The last, a miracle birth. All is lost. Because of you," she replies as if I repulse her, as if redemption was never in my reach.

"I love my son. I will keep him safe this time." When there is no response, rage builds within my soul. "I sought retribution for my son. I did this for him!"

"Now you are lost as well," is her reply. Helena turns away, disappears in the bright light from above.

The sudden sound of silence thunders in my brain. Silence is empty. So am I. Forever alone in this maze. I fall to the cold, cold ground. I cannot fight. I am not strong enough.

Lukas continued to hold his father's lifeless hand in

his own. Time kept ticking away. Confusion had him wavering between guilt and hope. Guilt over the year of his life when he tried time and again to kill Michael, and hope that his only connection to this world would somehow survive and suddenly wake up.

Then they could talk, and he wouldn't feel this way anymore. And then he just wanted to sleep, to let go. *Yeah, right, and there hasn't been any progress. He's fucking gone.* He blew out a long breath, resolved to get up and tell Alana. He made it half the way to standing when he froze. It was just the slightest squeeze of his hand.

"Shit," he whispered, "You've gotta wake up all the way." More insistent, his voice got louder. "Come on! Wake up! Open your eyes!" He looked up when Alana, Miles, and Celia burst into the bedroom. "H-he tried to squeeze my hand. I swear!"

When Alana came toward him, he lurched back, watching her roll Michael on his side. "Dad, look at the shoulder bite. Do you think it's the medicine? Is it doing something?"

He saw it for himself. The bite was pink, not an ugly deep-scarlet.

"Is this a good sign or what?" she asked.

"It's a strange one, but a good one," Miles answered. "I think the penicillin is counteracting the poison." And to him, "Perhaps your touch gives him more reason to fight."

"No way," he muttered, stopping behind the upholstered chair next to the bed, gripping its high back. His heart raced like a rabbit as his felt his cheeks get hot.

"But he's in a coma," Celia chimed in.

"He's not in a coma," Miles replied as he walked to

the foot of the four-poster. He began to pace with his hands clasped behind his back, as if it were a habit to help him think. "The poison must be a specifically prepared compound to induce a state of unconsciousness. There had to be something on the creature's teeth and claws."

"But why would antibiotics help?" asked Alana.

"That's the million-dollar question, isn't it? It's a long shot, but let's state some facts. Lukas sees the attack. The creature paralyzes Michael. Lukas gets to him in seconds. We arrive and begin a transfusion. The blood is Guardian blood, untainted—and it's *not* animal. His wounds are immediately cleaned. What can we deduce? One, he was not expected to survive. Two, if he did, the creature was their Plan B. Its purpose? To paralyze for capture."

Lukas's eyes darted back to Alana as she asked, "And you're saying the antidote is *penicillin*?"

"Think outside the box, honey, and just go with it. They couldn't know we'd arrive so quickly; that we'd transfuse Guardian blood, *human* blood—something they know Michael *will not* drink. Why can't an organic compound be an antidote? This isn't a synthetic antibiotic. It's the real deal." The pacing stopped. "Celia, you hit the nail on the head when you said we trumped them! We have diminished the effects of the poison considerably."

"And he's still as bad as this?" Celia blurted out.

"Give it to him," Alana said. The look on her face read pure determination. "Get the rest of the vials and use it all. We're not dealing with some mortal weakling who tripped and cut his knee. He is a mystically enhanced vampire who has a soul, and he's obviously trying to fight. You know he is! Besides, I've never heard of an undead creature of the night overdosing on penicillin, how about you?" The way they locked eyes was intense.

As if it were some silent signal, Celia ran out of the room. No one said a word while she was gone. And he stood glued to the back of the chair like it alone held him up. Coming back, she handed four small, glass bottles to Miles, who filled and injected syringe after syringe right into the gnawed wound on Michael's shoulder. Each jab appeared to change the look on Alana's face—from strength to worry. And each jab made him cringe, thinking he'd be sick right where he stood.

Celia was suddenly at his side. She had her hand over his. "You don't look so good. Maybe you need some sleep." He resisted as she tried to tug his grip off the chair.

"Go with Celia," Alana said softly.

"No. I stay," he stated, pulling his arm away.

"It's late, sweetie," Celia whispered, "You're tired. You need sleep."

Miles came over, adding, "Don't we all. You'll see him in the morning and every day after."

Fear flexed its ugly grip. His hands curled into fists. "You can't tell me what to do. I don't have to listen to any of you. I stay right here."

A tight glare came from Alana. "I know what you're thinking. I wouldn't try it. Too much happened yesterday… and today. I swear, I will not leave him. Go to bed." She paused, let out a long breath. "You should get some rest as well, Dad. What time is it, anyway?"

"Much too late for a talk about the hour, honey," he replied from the doorway.

Celia's brush of his shoulder made his brain tingle. His mind slid out of confrontation as his body screamed of exhaustion. His eyes felt dry when he blinked. He wanted to close them. "Come on, sweetie," she whispered as she led him out of the room by the hand. And just like that, he complied.

Alana shook her head, full of cautious relief. "That boy's gonna blow. His temper is something I can't deal with at this moment."

Miles shook his head as well. "He'll learn to listen. Give him time to adjust to us. Is there anything else you need?"

"For you to wake me up and tell me this is only a bad dream and none of this is happening?" She sank into the upholstered Queen Anne chair, tracing the floral pattern on its arms. "Michael's not one of your favorite creatures, Dad. Putting everything on the line to help him and his son couldn't have been too easy for you."

"Don't talk nonsense, honey." It was in his tone—a gentle scold. "Whatever I feel or don't feel about him… it's not the point. Taking on the evil powers behind NWT was incredibly brave and incredibly stupid. Two very brave, very capable ex-Guardians are dead. There will be consequences for him to face, from both the Georgian Council as well as whatever evil is left that he *didn't* destroy. You and I both know it." He paused before saying, "Look. You love him. You always have."

She refused to think about Dan and Rob. "But when I was twenty-one—"

"The Georgian Council dealt with it. You dealt with it. And you have stayed clear of him since then."

"I wanted to call him before I left the city last year," she confessed.

"It doesn't surprise me. After this mess, nothing does anymore." He gave a thin grin. "Now get some rest," he said as he left.

Alone with him, the room fell silent. She moved to the bed, stretching out beside him. She traced his eyebrows, cupped his bruised cheek, and kissed his pale lips. "Where are you, Michael, my love?" A worried sigh escaped before she closed her eyes.

Words. Many words. And their meaning. The poison is strong. The reality of two more deaths was on his soul alone. His mind slipped away as guilt took hold.

They sniff at my feet in a darkened tunnel. The rats are large, wild, and hungry. They've been on my heels, scenting ripped flesh on my back. The stench of the sewer fills my nose with nauseating odors that stick in my throat. Rotting garbage and waste from the city is not as tantalizing to vicious vermin as fresh meat. Once they pick up my scent, their evil little minds are made up. I will be a feast for them.

It is the pain in my thigh that first slows me down. Growling like rabid dogs, the rats stand still behind me. I hear snarls; imagine dripping saliva as their red eyes glower. Not yet ready to attack…this is to intimidate and eventually bring me to my knees.

Blood races up my throat like human bile, acidic and strong. Hugging the tunnel wall, I spit it out. I am cold, weak with exhaustion. My broadsword, a trusted friend for over a century, is lost—too heavy. My sharp eyesight is gone. The innate sense of direction, which always leads me home, is inaccessible.

Yet, I must keep moving. I must find home. If I choose the correct direction, Rob and Dan will assist. But which way is home? I cannot tell.

Rats jump, snap at my legs. Halfway down the tunnel, I see dim light. A door opens and I am determined to get to it. But the rats...

Frenzied, they sink their hungry teeth deeper into my skin. The added weight on my leg makes me stagger. I smell their acrid breath when they claw up my body. I reach my destination, and the rats hiss in protest, not wanting to give up their feast. I pull their angry jaws from my torn flesh, and I crush them against tunnel walls.

As I slip into safety, I close myself inside, hearing sharp scratches on the metal door.

As I lean against the lock my knees give out. I am home. It doesn't matter if I am hurt or in pain. Rob and Dan will keep me safe. They always do.

My eyes adjust to the darkness. I sense them across the room. "Wake up," I call out, "I need your help." But there is no response. No movement. "Come on, damn it! The rats are... the rats are..."

A scurry snags my attention. I crawl toward them, and the truth is exposed. Terror takes hold as I see their lifeless bodies. Two ex-Guardians who survived ten years of fighting demons... it jolts my mind. Rats cover them. Devour them. Suddenly, the crazed vermin stop feeding. They stare at me to inspect their next meal.

Oh God! I have killed them...

Alana felt him flinch. Her body stilled, her eyes opened, and immediately, her vision was more than 20/20. His bloodshot eyes wide open, his gaze fixed on something she could not see. She hooked his bruised chin and he flinched again. "Michael, fight like hell! You're strong. You can do this."

He gasped for breath he didn't need. "No, no, no,

no, no—"

"I have you. You're safe."

His body trembled as if he was trapped in a freezer. "Not safe. Never safe." The richness of his voice was gone. In its place a rasp, a gravel-like substitute. "A…la…na…"

"I'm right here," she replied. She smoothed his wavy brown hair and pulled herself up against the headboard to rest his beaten face against her breast. Brittle sobs escaped his lips. Cold scarlet tears spilled down her white sweater like tiny roses drawn on an empty canvas. "I'm right here," she repeated, hoping he could hear her, longing to reassure him.

How many times had she dreamt of being with him? None were like this. His confident stance, his commanding good looks, his fierce fighting skills. Those were some of his best qualities. Cradled in her arms, fear swept through her heart. He needed her now, and nothing, no one, would ever come for him again. It was as if her Guardian strength had renewed itself deep within.

When he drifted off and stilled in her arms, she whispered a much-needed prayer.

Chapter 12

Aid and Assist

Miles was the first awake, always an early riser and up before dawn. It didn't matter what time-zone he was in or what continent he lived on. His internal alarm clock never failed. Lukas still slept across the guestroom in the other twin bed.

Showered and dressed in pressed gray trousers and a white button-down shirt, he closed the guestroom door and headed for the kitchen admiring the renovations. The floor plan was open, creating a generous living room and dining area. All the woodwork was a dark, lush walnut to balance the crème walls. He specifically liked the detail on the main door to Alana's home, and much preferred it to the elevator set in the back of the rose-colored marble foyer.

A pot of strong coffee was called for. He fixed it, poured a cup, and sat in the sun-filled dining room to read days of e-mails. Philip, the ex-Guardian in Manhattan, had sent a brief message describing little to no demonic activity in the city.

"This is, truthfully, a first," he said to himself.

The second email was from Arthur Chamberlain, the demon specialist. Perhaps the poison is now identified, he thought. After another cup of coffee, it was time. He knocked softly on the master bedroom door, hoping to wake Alana. A quick "Come in" was the reply.

"I fell asleep in my clothes," she said through a yawn.

"How's he doing?" he asked in a hushed voice, noting, of course, tiny splotches of dried blood on her sweater. Michael was still and at her side.

"We were right. Penicillin had a definite effect. He woke for a few seconds. I think he recognized me."

"Very good," he said, more surprised than he let on. "Chamberlain will be here soon. You'd like some time to freshen up?"

"Definitely." She came off the bed, and immediately checked the heavy drapes to make sure they were secure. Even a sliver of the bright, Amalfi sunshine would destroy the injured vampire.

His attention stayed on Michael, the bedside lamp the only light. "His skin tone hasn't changed, but facial swelling is down, and the cuts look like they are, perhaps, starting to heal. We are making progress."

"You call this progress? It's disgusting! He's one of the strongest vampires the Georgians have *ever* documented. There *is* no healing. I think we're fighting the clock." He crossed the room, meeting her by the windows. "Michael needs to wake up. I don't care if we have to pump him full of every antibiotic known to modern science. He comes out of this today."

"I hear your determination, honey, but—"

"No buts, Dad. Today," she stated. He watched her walk over to the dresser. She laid a lilac-colored blouse and a pair of jeans over the back of the upholstered chair and met his eyes once again. "I don't know where his mind is, but I can bet you a two-week paid vacation in Paris it's a five-star rated horror hotel. These terror trips stop…*today*."

He cleared his throat. "Yes, well, I'll be in the dining room." Without another word, Alana went into her private bathroom and shut the door.

****

Entering the living room, Alana felt more determined than ever. Doctor Chamberlain and Doctor Baker were already there. She stood gripping the high back of a dining room chair hoping to hide her anxiety, to appear calm and composed. Her adopted father had often sung Chamberlain's praises, but she had never met him. A short and bald, muscular man, he had been in this line of work since the end of his military service, many years ago. Listening to the conversation, Chamberlain appeared kind but intense, with a no-nonsense attitude about him.

"Miles, I think it's time to meet our patient," the doctor said as the three men stood.

"Thanks for everything your team did on the plane," she said, leading them into her room. "Did Dad tell you what happened with the penicillin?"

"Certainly a stroke of good luck," he replied with a serious nod.

She switched on the recessed lights to brighten the room, stepped to the side. Baker set up the smart-board, which connected to his laptop on the dresser, and the exam began. Chamberlain checked Michael's reflexes. There were none. When Baker turned him over, the doctor's face became grave. Again, bite *and* claw marks were bright red. They looked much worse than last night. She bit her lip as her arms laced against her blouse.

"Clean these with straight peroxide and butterfly all open wounds one more time, Johnny," he ordered. "Set up an IV with pure penicillin. We'll flood his system with the good stuff."

Moving from the bed, Chamberlain led the two of them across the room to the windows. "Only the surface wounds are healing, not the deeper ones, nor his leg. Hopefully, another transfusion of human blood will lessen the grayness of his skin, but it's the infection on his back that's most worrisome. There's no radiant fever, which is odd. In fact, his body temperature is far too low for what we would consider a healthy specimen."

Alana's heart sank as her adopted father asked, "Have you identified the poison?"

"Tissue sample tests didn't identify it, Miles. It's nothing like anything in our database. That fact is crucial because certain compounds can cause a vampire's brain to mutate. I've seen cases where localized infections fester and spread through a creature's entire nervous system in days, virtually destroying the being. Most times, it's a good thing, but in this case—"

Immediately on alert, she cut him off with, "Are you saying you can't bring him back?"

Chamberlain leaned into her. "You need to be patient, Alana. I state what I think *can* happen. Flooding his system with penicillin should support Miles's theory about the antidote being chemical-simplistic. But, unless we match the specific poison to a specific antidote, this vampire, mystically enhanced or not, will never be what he once was. The poison was meant to cripple him into inertia. Most creatures would be lost forever, yet he's already fighting to come back and that's a positive."

Lost in all the description of what *could* happen, when Michael began to twitch and twist, she bolted to the bed. "Look at me! Fight with all your strength!"

"So…cold," he moaned.

"He can't sustain a body temperature, it's all over the place even with the warming blanket underneath him," Baker stated.

Panic took over, and she shouted, "Fight! Fight it! You have to open your eyes!"

His lids barely lifted, but it was enough for Chamberlain to further assess. "His pupils aren't demonic amber. His fingernails aren't thick and razor sharp, so there is no predatory weapon of defense."

"Pain should trigger these responses," she said because she'd seen vampires in pain.

"But it doesn't," he replied. Chamberlain checked his mouth. "His canines are not fully elongated. It's an automatic reflex, a split-second reaction and not something a vampire could control." He turned and looked at her. "I'd conclude the beast-within, that which defines his existence as a vampire, is not accessible. He can't produce the primal metamorphosis."

"What are you saying, Arthur," Miles asked in a cautious tone.

"I have *never* seen anything like this before. A deadly creature with hundreds of years of documentation is, more or less, defanged. He has no ability to tear into a vein to feed—no protection, either." He paused a moment before continuing to poke and prod.

But Alana had had enough. She moved behind the upholstered chair to hold on to something. When her adopted father put an arm around her, she melted into his chest. "Don't worry. He's almost finished," he said in a soothing voice, which made her shut her eyes tight, wanting this nightmare to end.

As the examination continued, pitiful sounds

assaulted her ears. Michael had always had great stamina when it came to pain. Now? Sharp shrieks punctuated with timid whimpers. Human expressions of agony accompanied unsuccessful attempts at a growl. "Baker, please assist," Chamberlain said, and then one long, loud shriek pierced her heart.

Suddenly, the door flew open, and as she turned toward the sound, both men were sailing through the air then landing on top of each other under the windows, a good ten feet away. Lukas stood guarding the bed with a threatening scowl on his face, flexing his hands. The look in his eye was pure menace. "What did you do to him?"

Her eyes narrowed. "I can't believe you just did that!"

As Baker helped Chamberlain to his feet, she walked over to Lukas and like an immovable vise, gripped his boney arm, not fazed by his wince and wiggle. A long, sharp yelp came out of him before she shoved him through the doorway. He landed hard on his butt close to the couch and many feet away. After Miles went to him, she took a slow, determined walk, to block the door to her bedroom. Her fists stayed glued to her waist. "If you don't know how *not* to behave, buddy, then let this be lesson one."

After slamming the door, she apologized to both men.

****

Lukas knew Mister B was staring down at him. "I am not an unsympathetic man, nor have I ever raised my voice to scold either Alana or Celia when they were your age."

Flushed and hurting, he looked up and caught the

very stern expression. "I-I-I thought—"

"No, you did *not* think!" the man bellowed, grabbing him by the arm in the exact same place, sitting him in the armchair.

Misery swept across his face, and his rear end ached. He didn't know what hurt more: his ego, his butt, or his arm.

"You ought to be ashamed of yourself. What on earth did you think you were doing in there?" With his hands clasped behind his back, Mister B looked close to losing it.

He opened his mouth, but nothing came out.

"Don't even *try* to justify what you did. Totally inappropriate, do you understand me? They're *helping* him, damn it… Not *torturing* him! You ought to know the difference between the two." Now his ears felt like they were on fire. "The next time you go ballistic, on *any* one of us, young man, for *any* reason whatsoever, you will be dealt with. Is this clear?"

His shoulders slumped and he replied very softly, "I hear you, Mister B."

"Good. You will sit here and think about your behavior. I have work to do." The man sat at the dining room table, put on his wire-rimmed glasses, and began to write in a thick leather-bound journal.

He did *not* move.

Chapter 13

A Much-Needed Break

A half-hour later, Alana walked the doctor out… ignoring Lukas, who sat in the living room as if he'd been given a much deserved "time out." She went to the fridge and took out a tall jar of human blood. Her adopted father followed her in. "How is he?"

"Well, he's awake, but he isn't saying much. He's doing a lot of staring and shivering, and I'm sure he's in pain. I'm going to try to get him to drink." She reached for a crystal mug from the kitchen cabinet. Twisting the lid off the container, she couldn't help but stare out the kitchen window. Sunlight flooded the room.

"You need to get out, honey. Why don't you take a break? You've been with him non-stop. Maybe you need fresh air. It will help clear your mind. I can sit with him. I'm convinced he'll drink if thirsty."

"He's so far away." She shook her head and sighed, adding in a quiet voice, "I'm not sure how he'll react to you. I know there's no chance of him hurting anyone, but did you notice how his fangs didn't, I mean…his canines didn't—?"

"What you're trying to say is he cannot bite, am I correct? Yes. I noticed."

"He's like…fragile. God, that's a word I'd *never* think of using to describe him."

"You need to step back, Alana, just for a little while."

"No. I can't—"

"Take Celia with you. Go get him pajamas, socks, and slippers."

"Dad, I—"

"Anything you think he'll need when he's himself again." He hooked her chin, searching her eyes. "Michael will have to get out of bed at some point. He can't walk around wrapped in a bed sheet, can he?"

The very image of such a proud creature wearing a satin sheet like a toga… "You've got a point there."

"Of course, I do, and it makes sense. Go. Spend a little girl-time with your sister."

"Wait. What about super-boy over there? I can't even look at him. Do you believe the temper on this kid? I thought it wasn't supposed to be there anymore? If he shows me even an *ounce* of attitude again, I swear—"

"I gave him a stern talking to. He's confused, caught between two very different lives."

"That doesn't excuse bratty behavior."

"Lukas knows he's done something wrong. Hasn't said a word since you *literally* threw him out on his backside," he added with a dry grin. "Get Celia, honey, and shop till you drop."

She hugged him, whispering, "Can you take care of this?"

"Of course," he replied.

"Half power for thirty seconds would make it more palatable."

"If you insist," he said, but she was already on her way to the sunroom, Celia's favorite room here.

****

Miles poured human blood into the mug on the counter and put it in the microwave. He didn't have to ask Lukas twice if he wanted to see his father. The boy looked anxious to help, and naturally, inquisitive about his parent's condition. Young Lukas Malone showed he could listen and be polite if he chose to. As soon as they walked into the bedroom, the researcher in him took mental note of Michael's condition. Faraway look…just as Alana said. Most superficial cuts closed, two black eyes, and cheeks gray and hollow. He set the crystal mug on the nightstand, saying, "Give me a hand?"

He piled pillows while Lukas, with his extraordinary strength, pulled the injured vampire up to a sitting position—without any effort. Michael knit his brow, staring at the boy. He noted a glimmer of recognition when he whispered, "Lukas," more of a question than a greeting. Nodding, the teen sat on the bed's edge and mumbled, "Yeah, it's me."

"My…son." The look of pride and wonder was noted as well. He handed Lukas the crystal mug.

The boy's face fully scrunched. "*Human* blood? I thought he only drinks animal?"

"It's what he needs. Keep him focused and get him to drink it." Lukas held the mug to his father's lips. Michael, eyes still trained on his son, drank a small amount.

"That's good," he stated, hoping to boost the boy's mood. But after another mouthful, Michael turned his face away. His purple eyelids fluttered, and then closed.

"Shit. He's out of it again." But then, Michael's hand inched over to rest on his son's. He noted how the boy examined the bruised and cut fingers. Then came the slightest whisper, "I'm here for you…Dad."

Michael looked at Miles, then lowered his gaze, as if it were a bow with respect. After a labored intake of air, a hoarse, "Thank…you," was heard.

Miles simply nodded. "I'll leave the two of you alone for a while."

With the door ajar, Miles walked over to the dining room table. Sitting with a sigh, as Researcher for the Georgian Circle, he was ready to journal everything. Every nuance. Every movement witnessed since the morning, including the first voluntary ingestion of nourishment. His archiving was exceptional. He had over thirty years of practice.

****

Hours later, when his daughters returned, Miles was still working on his laptop.

"And did you catch the look the salesgirl gave when you tried on that last pair of men's loafers." Celia giggled, a signature response. "I don't understand Italian, but I'll bet the frantic shouting match she had with the manager, hands flying in the air, sucking in on her teeth, were about you!"

Alana let out a laugh. She flopped into the armchair and set the shopping bags from *many* trendy boutiques on the floor.

He had been right; this trip lifted a dreary mood. "Will the stores survive?" he asked with a dry grin.

"I'd say barely, just barely," Alana replied. "You know, it isn't the easiest thing to shop for a man when you don't know his size. I had to measure every item against dozens of gorgeous Italian men. I think we were a hit!" Celia's infectious giggles filled the room as she kicked off her shoes and wiggled her toes. Alana shushed her and searched one of the many bags. "That wasn't the only mystery, Daddy B. We had to translate it into Italian. I still think in inches, you know."

"I thought you knew Michael's size, honey. You certainly spent enough time with him back then."

"That was almost seven years ago."

"Vampires don't tend to gain weight."

Alana gave him a sour look but followed it with a smile. "Very funny. But Italians don't use number numbers, they use kilo thingies. I just try on something before I buy it. And the shoe store better have a return policy, because I have no clue how big his feet *really* are. So, there you have it—Ally C's and Celia B's very own personal shopping disaster of the week in Pisa."

The two women exchanged mischievous grins, but he quickly asked, "You don't think you were followed by anything, do you?"

"Nothing detected—psychic radar was clean," Celia answered. "Although… There were quite a few hotties who begged for our cell phone numbers. We practically had to beat them off with those super-size Italian loafers. Oooh, the leather is so soft—"

"I don't recall ever seeing Michael in loafers. He's more of a boot man," he said.

"What's that tired cliché? If the shoe fits—" Alana's smile faded, but Celia giggled again. "How is he, Dad?"

"Lukas has been with him all afternoon."

"Good, then we move on to Phase Two," Alana announced.

"I don't follow you, honey." The pair of silk pajamas and black socks dangled from her hands. "What do you expect me to do with those?"

"I thought you and Lukas could, you know…dress

him," she casually replied with a shrug.

"That's one thing that will not happen in your lifetime. I will feed him, care for his wounds, and do what must be done to get him up and about. But I will *not* dress him. I believe you to be safe all on your own." She started to argue, but he held up a hand and went into the den. As he walked down the hall he heard, "A simple no would have done it for me."

Chapter 14

Alone-Together

Alana entered the bedroom, set down the bags at the foot of the four-poster bed. It didn't surprise her, feeling Michael's gaze lock on her. He appeared more lucid, yet still very weak. Her next thought went to Lukas with his super hearing skills, and whether or not he'd been listening to her conversation in the other room. There was only one way to find out. Putting the earlier encounter with Chamberlain and Baker aside, she kept her tone light, care-free.

"Did you have a nice visit with your dad?"

"Yeah, it was cool." A small smile complete with deep-set dimples came her way.

"Great! I did a little shopping and—"

"I know."

Her eyes narrowed. The way Lukas jumped off the bed and headed to the door spoke volumes. "Let me guess…It's the genetic thing again. So…you heard Daddy B refuse to—"

"Uh-huh… I'll leave so you two can, like, be alone," he said as he closed the door.

"Okay, fine. I can do this without any of you," she called after him while going through one particular shopping bag. She held up a set of expensive, black silk pajamas. "You like?"

107

His reply was an annoyed scowl.

She longed to sit close to him, but instead, settled into the upholstered Queen Anne chair. Angled next to the bedside table, only a few feet separated them, because touching him would be a temptation. Touching him would be her undoing. She folded the black silk pajamas on her lap as their gaze locked once again.

Was it the history, both bad and good between them? The temptation to only be a breath away? To reboot a romance, which ended years ago on such a terrifying note? Love for one another was a given. They both knew it to be true. But history is history. It doesn't change. Michael was vulnerable now. So was she. Maybe more than one type of healing had a second chance. She cleared her throat. "So, is it a yes or a no?" He shook his head stiffly, from side to side, but his finger tapped the mattress. "You want me to sit next to you?"

"Yes," came out of his pale lips, a whispered rasp. Was his rich baritone voice gone forever?

"You know why I can't do that."

His brows knit, turning the glare into a glower. "Say it, my Guardian."

She sighed, long and slow, as her body sank deeper into the chair. "Where do I begin? And why relive what can never be changed?"

"Say it."

"If this is a test of wills, I win this round."

"You held me… in your arms last night."

"You were unconscious, Michael."

"And now?"

"It's not right."

"Why?"

"Because you are awake," she stated, unwilling to

give anymore.

"I love you."

She closed her eyes, letting those three words sink deep into her soul. The memory of that terrible September night, almost seven years ago…

"Do not ignore me," he added, with an attempt to muster the old, peppered arrogance he often wore.

"Close your eyes," she said in a tender tone to deescalate the situation, "You need rest."

His hand brushed the bed covers. "No, Alana. I… want you…here."

"It's a dangerous demand, Michael. Those last years in the city, I controlled every deep, gnawing desire to talk to you, to come to you. To make things right between us."

Could she keep control now? His bloodshot eyes closed as if he had taken an arrow to the heart, and she sighed. Things *were* different now. He had nothing left. No strength, no ability to fend for himself.

"I'm sorry," she whispered, pulling herself out of the chair to settle on the edge of the bed. She studied his beaten face, recalling every handsome feature, every plane of his face that had often taken her very breath away. He was here. The immortal being she would always love.

A thin smile came at her. His features appeared to relax as if her nearness eased his pain. "So much… to tell you," he whispered with a rasp.

"Shhh…later."

Michael nodded once, and as if by divine intervention, she stretched out on the bed. They lay face to face. Even so wounded he was still the commanding being she fell in love with over a decade ago. A mystically enhanced vampire who saved her so many times in the field fighting demons. He had her heart.

She moved her face close enough to kiss him, and his dark, espresso eyes found hers. As if two magnets of opposing poles drew together, her body responded. She kissed his lips so gray and cool like a fine brush, slight of pressure. She eased back and traced his eye brows, ran a careful hand down his bruised cheek. God, she wanted him.

"Alana," he whispered, "Missed you…love you…need you."

His words called to her soul, awakened a hidden passion within. It always simmered just below her skin when she let herself remember… Her lips met his, and she wanted more. Instead, she whispered, "Sleep. I won't leave you." No, she thought, *never* again.

****

When his bruised eyelids finally fluttered down, Alana breathed a shaky sigh of relief. Smoothing the bed covers over his chest, her eyes drifted down his beaten arm laying at his side between them, close enough to brush against her. The sight of his hand right next to the top of her thigh forced a fantasy, a desire, which wouldn't be ignored. The way he had touched her so intimately that September night. The feel of his weight on her body… It all came back.

That ache within shot all the way to yearning. Made her heart race and her body react. Like a gentle wave lapping against a sandy shore, she let the sexual response take its course and then snapped back to reality. *Everyone remembers their first kiss. Only one kiss. All right. Two kisses.* How could she allow all these feeling to surface? But years ago, that first kiss imprinted on her soul. And it came from Michael Malone…

The young Guardian, barely two years into her mission, sensed Michael lurking, and had caught him leaning against a tree in Central Park. Rob and Dan, seasoned Guardians assigned to train her, had ordered her to go straight home. She didn't listen. Instead, veering off the path out of the park she made her way to Michael. And full of determination, she threw her arms around him and kissed him right on the lips. Locked in the stolen kiss, her stomach fluttered, and her senses sizzled. Seconds later, he had her by the shoulders, an arms-length away, his expression full of fury.

"What the hell do you think you're doing?"

Her eyes filled with tears. "I love you," she had confessed in a very dramatic tone.

But he locked his arms across his chest and glared. "Kissing me is something you shouldn't be doing!" A sound just short of a desperate sob escaped her lips. "Alana, we cannot be together. It's not… I will not—"

"How old were you when you died?"

"That has nothing to do with it!"

"I asked how old you were," she shouted as rage clouded reason.

He looked uneasy, plainly stating, "Twenty-seven, but I'm over three centuries old."

"Did you ever love anyone?"

He didn't answer right away, but then stated, "I loved my sisters."

"I don't mean family," she fired back, "You know what I mean."

Again, he took his time, eventually giving a curt, "No." He studied her as if she were a bug under a microscope, eventually gave a thin smirk. "My, my, my…

If looks could kill, I'd be dust and bone by now."

The insult stung. She walked away, calling over her shoulder, "Don't come near me again. I mean it."

"That's not going to happen, darlin'."

The word slipped off his tongue with the slightest lilt, like soft butter melting over warm bread. Darlin' — did that word make her his? The thought slowed her down…just a little.

"Stop being so sensitive. You're a talented fighter, but someone's got to watch your back," he said as he followed her. "Miles can't do what I can do. Neither can Rob and Dan." He caught up, blocked her path. "You need me, my Guardian."

On purpose, she fired off a spiteful glare. "So why are you always lurking in the shadows whenever I'm hunting creatures just like you?"

"That's not fair. I'm not like them and you know it."

"Yeah, right…you're just like them." She walked away again, but this time he grabbed her arm, spun her around with a merciless hold. The look in his eyes something she'd never seen… and would never forget. Then he kissed her. A kiss so unexpected. Possessive and sensual. Rough.

Desire clawed at her innocence. "Don't ever leave me," she whispered, tight to his chest.

"Never," he replied.

And it was that very moment, all those years ago, when she knew they were meant to be together. Forever.

****

Michael stirred. He slipped in and out of lucid thought, relieved Alana was still tight against him. Such enormous pain—yet he felt nothing. A sweep of a hand, a slight turn of his head… The fact that he could accomplish nothing else was infuriating. As for talking? Stringing words together came a bit easier now. He studied his beautiful Guardian lying beside him, the sweet comfort in her heart beating strong and steady. The scent of her as enticing as ever.

He loved her. *Always have. Always will. She is salvation. Soul imprinted upon soul.* Her life, her safety more precious than the rarest stone. But everything was different now. As sure as the sun rose and set, he had brought danger to her doorstep. This was what those bastards at NWT wanted. *To exist like this? Hell on earth. Dear God, how did I even survive?* It hadn't been his plan. And he alone would finish this fight.

He took in the master bedroom. The décor was perfect for Alana. The architects and decorators had done well. And he knew she was happy here.

His mind drifted to his son, whose scent lingered in the room. *If Miles had left Lukas in the city, God knows what the bastards at NWT would have done to him. That boy will never be out of my sight again. But what I orchestrated at NWT... The faces of two ex-Guardians who helped plan my revenge. Both gone.* His eyes shut tight against emotions he couldn't control.

His body shuttered, and Alana sat up, close at his side. A tear made its way down his left temple. She caught it, held it between her fingers with a look of confusion on her beautiful face.

"The color. The texture." He heard fascination in her soft voice. "It's... it's watery and pink, it isn't fully a blood tear," she whispered, studying his face. "Michael, please talk to me."

He struggled, looked aside, but Alana cupped his cheek, and he had no strength to pull away. "Rob...Dan, oh God... *I* killed them." Her kiss brushed his forehead. Her hand slid to his chest.

"No, you didn't kill them. They did what they had to. What they were trained to do. Heroes die. Don't do this to yourself."

Nothing would ever take away the guilt. Nothing, he realized as he closed his eyes.

Chapter 15

The Race Begins

Lukas's fingers thumped the chair's leather arms like he belonged in a heavy-metal rock band as Celia opened wide the dining area drapes. "We need some fresh, warm sea air drifting through the room," she said in a cheery voice as if he'd really give a response. "I can see the ships docked far beyond the tiny harbor. Portofino looks pretty spectacular in twilight."

He didn't answer. In fact, only listened to her with one ear.

"You know, Daddy B, I need some help here, of the major kind," she whispered, and he caught the look she gave her father—wide-eyed like they had a secret or something. And he studied the pretty smile that lit up her pretty face... just as a soft knock began on the door. "She's here, Lukas! Oooh... Wait till you meet *Zia* Rosa," she squealed, "and with arms full of food for the I-hate-to-cook-group!" She took off for the door, and then he heard a sweet, "*Zia*, it smells delicious! Thank you, thank you, thank you!"

Into the dining room they went. The older woman had a brisk step, a head of gray hair settled in a loose bun at the nape of her neck, and rosy cheeks. The dress she wore was simple, kind of old-fashioned with an apron around her ample waste. She looked at him, and her smile lit the room with a glimmer in her smokey-gray eyes.

Celia placed the platter on the table, and then hugged her as if she were someone very special. "How'd you know we were here?"

"I heard the elevator go up and down yesterday, but no one came to say hello. This tells me something worries you, no?" Miles and Celia both nodded. Oddly, he nodded as well. "Ah…*si*… I bring dinner. Too many skinny people here, *si*? *Mangia*! You need to eat."

As if on cue, Lukas's stomach growled, appetizing aromas suddenly filling his senses. *Zia* hugged Miles, speaking rapidly in Italian. Then, with a hearty laugh, she switched to English. Something about her drew him in. Like gentle strength, genuine caring, and pure love rolled into one. Celia pulled four dinner plates off the hutch and motioned him over. He complied, his empty stomach churning like a storm and his mouth already watering. Rosa came directly to him, clicked her tongue, and shook her head slowly. Holding his shoulders, she turned him around wearing a grave expression. "Oh my, my— *mamma mia*! This one is all skin and bones. I am very concerned."

Miles took a seat at the head of the table. "This is Lukas, the son of a-a dear friend of Alana's who's quite ill right now. We might discuss the details later…after dinner, perhaps?"

She gave a grave nod. "Yes. We should. I sense this is a complicated situation." Her smile reappeared. "Now come, Lukas. Sit next to me. You eat, *si*?" He let her take his hand, drawn in by her tender touch. A healing goodness filled him. "Your *papa* will have the finest care. I will pray for *papa* at Mass tomorrow morning, *si*?" She touched his cheek. "Ah, you worry too much for a little boy. It is difficult to push bad memories from your heart."

He looked from Miles to Celia. Had they been talking about him? "How do you know?"

"Oh, I sense many things, and I have many skills." She scooped some kind of pasta he'd never seen before onto his plate, sprinkled some sharp-smelling grated cheese on it, and placed two pieces of warm Italian bread on his plate. "You are safe with us. Now, please. Eat."

One forkful, and he was hooked. Suddenly starving, and totally willing to listen and eat instead of talk. Rosa smoothed his hair away from his face and watched him devour what was on his plate.

Celia picked up her fork. "I've missed you, *Zia*. Oooh, Ally's gonna melt when she smells this! Wait till you taste it, Dad. I love *Zia's* cooking. She makes everything from scratch."

"I remember Rosa's fine culinary skills from many years ago," her father replied. "Long before you were born, your mother and I were frequent visitors. Alana's parents spent summers here when we were in college. Fond memories," he added with a warm smile.

"Those were good years, Miles," she replied with a hearty laugh. "Ah, you will love Portofino, Lukas. I have lived my entire life on the Amalfi Coast. I was born in this building, and I took over the bookshop downstairs after my parents passed."

Lukas studied her. "You speak perfect English."

"And French as well. I went to college, which was rare for a woman of my generation from such a tiny village. That's where I met my husband. We raised three children here. I still live in the same apartment, one floor

117

down."

"Is he downstairs?" he asked with honest curiosity. A quick hush came over everyone.

"No. He passed last year. Alana's arrival helped me through the pain of loss."

"I'm…I'm sorry," he whispered, not really knowing what to say. "Do your children live here, too?"

"My two sons live in the states, but they visit four times a year. My daughter is a distance away. She's a doctor. Alana's coming to live with me was meant to be. We keep each other company." He noticed her glance at Miles. "Now to the situation at hand. A handful of Council members met last night at San Giorgio's Church. This is a critical time in the fight against evil."

"You are already aware of what happened in Manhattan," Miles stated.

"We are aware. My skills are at your service."

What does she mean, he wondered, sensing more to *Zia* Rosa than good cooking… *What kind of skills*? Obviously, she was a Georgian like Miles and Celia. Rosa locked eyes with Celia. He knew something was going on between the two women at the table. Were they communicating in a non-verbal way? Was Rosa a psychic like Celia? *Yep. Had to be.*

"Celia's vision of the Champion's battle entered my Saturday morning meditation." Then rubbing his back, she added, "Too skinny, indeed. Home cooking is filled with magical goodness."

Lukas swallowed first, then gave a guarded smile just as Celia cleared her throat and stood so fast that the cloth napkin landed in her food. "I'll…uh, just, uh, g-get Ally," she stammered like there was a sudden jolt to her system.

Celia's psychic senses tingled as she entered the bedroom closing the door quickly, leaning against it with her eyes wide. "Oh wow," she sighed.

Alana sat up. "Is something wrong? You look like you've seen a ghost, Celia B."

"*Huh?* Uh…no, but I don't, well maybe it's—"

"Do I smell food?" Alana whispered, running both palms down her face.

"Yep, of the home-made gnocchi variety, complete with fresh baked Italian bread!"

"*Zia?* Oh, wow, is she still here? Wait… Did she meet Lukas? What did Dad tell her?"

Celia's eyes narrowed. "Wait a minute. I'm picking something up and it's a *little* out of the ordinary." She took a sharp intake of air. "Whoa, Ally, back up the love vibes a little! But he's asleep. No, he couldn't. You didn't…So how did you…oooh…"

"I swear that sixth sense of yours has to go. Believe me, I didn't expect to react that way. Oh, Celia—"

Before Ally could explain, Celia had to change the subject because this was *really* important. "Listen, I got this strong mini-flash, kind of a preview when I looked at *Zia.* Don't ask me how, but she's going to bring Michael out of this."

"*Zia* doesn't even know about him," Alana whispered quickly.

"I think she knows more than she lets on."

"I-I never told her all the details about… I should have told her what we did; what put my name in front of the Sovereign Council when he turned on me."

"She's a Georgian, Ally. I think she knows."

The expression on her adopted sister's face as she looked down at Michael screamed apprehension. "Are you sure about this? Do you think she's willing to help him?"

Taking Alana's hand, Celia stared into those guilty hazel eyes. "As sure as I'm talking to you. Michael needs to start the journey back to you, whole and well, and very soon."

"God, I really want to believe you." As they opened the door, Alana added, "Why do I get the feeling this is going to be one hell of a night…again?"

****

Alone. Incapacitated. Bizarre images like hot daggers poked through Michael's hope of survival and twisting more truths. The Georgian Council could have expelled Alana from their protection. Wiped her mind clean of him. Or worse—she could have died a young Guardian because of what I did that September night, he thought as the poison held him in its grip…

Blood trickles though these withering veins as I enter the dark chapel. Caution slows me. "There's an old priest there," they had said. "He will exorcise your beast-within." I have wandered for days, searching for this sacred place tucked serenely in the mountains.

"Father died. He went directly to heaven," whispers a faceless nun.

"You should know better than to enter this House of God, vampire," says another.

"We've prayed for your immortal soul, dearest brother, but God doesn't need you anymore," says a third.

"I have come to ask you to pray for them, to pray for me."

I stare into the waters of baptism. Long for blessed redemption. Even if this basin stills, my reflection will not appear, taken away centuries ago. A solitary bead of blood drips to the basin. How it sizzles… And I lift my face to the magnificent crucifix above the altar. I kneel and grip the gilded rail to steady this weakened frame. A pungent smolder fills the air as the simple symbol of belief is branded on my palm.

"I no longer feed," is the admission to my Ultimate Judge. Yet it does not change the fact that I am an unholy creature of the night.

Over three hundred years ago, I found comfort when learning prayers, sitting at Mother's side. I recall every word. At last, I confess, "I crave absolution for the death and destruction I have caused, Oh God."

Victims' faces dirge before my eyes. Relentless shame forces me to bend low. "Forgive me, for I have sinned, and sinned again, Merciful Father."

When the nuns reveal themselves, they are my sisters. They look upon what I am—a tortured creature. One kneels to my left, one to my right, and each take a hand, resting these branded palms over their pure hearts. The coarse fabric of their habits prickle my skin, yet I crave their touch. My most beloved sister stands behind me, gently stroking my hair as she did so many times in my youth.

The Requiem is chanted, a litany of mourning in one voice lifting to the angels in Heaven.

God looks down upon my guilt-ridden soul summoning me to come to Him.

"Yes, Father," I reply.

My sisters bless their lost brother as I turn to dust and bone.

I am forever damned.

Chapter 16

Healer

Standing at the sink, Lukas scrubbed the dinner dishes. Alana could have told him about the dishwasher, but then she wouldn't have the enjoyment of seeing him work so hard. At least he hadn't been rude with *Zia*. That would have put him right back in a long time-out.

With the meal behind them, a lively conversation continued at the dining room table. Family news, familiar chatter about this or that. Lots of giggles from Celia and soft, thin grins from her adopted father. To have those she loved around her was an unexpected blessing in the midst of her worry—until a piercing scream jolted everyone at the table.

Shooting up, Alana's sandal snagged on the chair leg. She and Celia both toppled to the floor. When they finally untangled from each other, she sprinted into the bedroom and skidded to a stop. *Zia's* hand ran down Michael's bruised cheek, soothing him with soft Italian words. Then her fingers threaded through his brown wavy hair pushing it back and off his forehead.

Lukas tried to get past her, but with a firm grab to his arm, she walked him backward into Miles's waiting grip. "No way, buddy. You are not getting in the way. Stay in the living room." Her fingers hooked his chin, forcing him to look at her. "Listen to me. Stay with my father. *Please,* Dad." She added, "I don't care if you tie him to a chair."

Then her full attention was on Michael. She couldn't hide the fear that gripped her heart. Celia was rubbing his arm. *Zia* whispered, "He is why you left the city."

"Yes," she replied as guilt nudged at her.

"The poison is very powerful." Standing, her aunt added, "Stay and comfort him."

Michael shuddered violently as she sat next to him. She turned him on his side, and Celia peeled off the soaked gauze bandages. All three crevices oozed.

"Ally, this is not good." Celia gasped and coughed. "Oh my God. Ewww… the smell—this stuff is putrid. They're really infected now."

"Celia, tell Dad to get the penicillin and come in here."

Seconds later, Miles rushed in with a syringe and three small vials. "This is all Arthur left. Oh, my Lord, his back is… Not a good sign, honey."

"Use every last drop. I thought he was getting better. He even said a few words. I-I don't understand this!" More than frustrated, she watched him inject the antibiotic into Michael's shoulder until none remained. The only good sign was that Lukas hadn't followed him in to create another disastrous scene.

****

In the kitchen, Rosa picked out specific herbs and spices from the spice rack with Celia by her side. A pot of water came to a boil on the stove. Whispering ancient words, she added each ingredient. "My young psychic, you have a great gift. Great potential. Those are most unnatural wounds, *si*? Made by an unnatural creature with deadly magic to enhance its poison."

"*Zia*, I saw it claw him in my mind and I—"

"It is a dark magic spell impossible to decipher. It destroys him… mind *and* body. But he is unique. There is his conscience…a reclaimed soul. The Georgians believe him pivotal in our mission to fight the evil ones. Some choose to denounce it as impossible. Sadly, your father has been of that opinion, but in his heart, Miles knows there's more to him than meets the eye. Pure love for his child, pure devotion to my niece."

"I can help you," Celia stated softly.

"You have a good heart, Cecelia. I will guide you, and together we will let healing begin. The claw wounds must be cleansed immediately." She turned off the flame under the pot, blew on the boiling liquid, which cooled in mere seconds. Three times she blessed it, praying in an ancient tongue. "You will sense what you need to do. Now go to the linen closet in the hall and bring three white towels from the top shelf to the bedroom. Bring his son as well."

Celia left as her father came into the kitchen. Aware of his presence, Rosa reached above the refrigerator and found what she was looking for. The glass pitcher had a wide, silver lip. "Father Giovanni gave this to my great-niece as a housewarming gift," she told Miles. "How apt that something from the Sovereign Council's leader should be used to heal a vampire." Filling the pitcher with the blessed mixture, she left in the herbs and swirling spices. "It's been a long time since I have met someone as gifted as your daughter, Miles. She has the potential to eclipse all others of her generation." Rosa turned to face him. "It is time to begin."

In the bedroom, Rosa looked into Celia's wide green eyes. "May divine goodness guide our actions." Celia, kneeling on the other side of the bed and next to Michael, whispered, "Amen to that."

"Miles, pull back the drapes and open the windows." He did as she asked and brought Lukas to his side, far across the room and far away from Michael.

Lukas began to resist, and Rosa stated, "Do as you're told, child. Alana will turn on all the lights and lock the door, then she will stand with you. Miles, keep him close. No matter what happens, none of you may approach." Her tone softened as she added, "You cannot touch us, Lukas. The poison is mystically directed. You cannot help him, and we must not be disturbed during our ritual. What you did this afternoon with the good doctor must *not* happen now. Do you understand?"

"Yeah," he answered when Miles put a hand on his shoulder.

Celia settled Michael on his stomach with one white towel directly under his unbeating heart. Rosa whispered to her, "Now, open your mind and I will guide your actions. Drench a towel with the blessed mixture."

Words spilled into Celia; a chant whispered as one with Rosa. Together, they pressed the towel into the bite on Michael's shoulder.

He screamed pure agony, violently shaking as it absorbed into the exposed muscle.

Celia soaked the next towel with the remaining liquid, chanting with Rosa once again. Together they eased it down the length of the brutal claw marks, which ended behind his right knee. As she held it in place, another sharp scream exploded as thick black steam rose out of his wounds. Michael's terrifying cries jarred everyone, especially his son.

A rancid odor wafted through the room. All the

lights flickered, and when they dimmed, a hot, foul gust of air swept through the room and shot out the open windows. The heavy bedroom drapes billowed in, and then were instantly sucked out, flapping in the cool night air.

As Michael stilled, all remained quiet.

Sensing the question, Rosa looked at her niece and stepped to the foot of the bed. "It is safe for only you to approach." Alana walked to the Queen Anne chair and sank down into it. Her eyes were full of tears as she gripped her knees and leaned forward.

****

Rosa stood in the kitchen holding onto the granite counter. What had left the bedroom was pure evil, purposely planted in the Champion's body and mind. Celia had collected the rancid towels and the pitcher and brought them to her. Miles and Lukas came into the kitchen as she knew they should.

She let out a weary sigh. "The healing ritual is not yet complete. Now the two of *you* have an important task. Lukas, take off your shirt. Wrap the towels around the pitcher, and then wrap it all with your shirt." He complied without hesitation.

Then Rosa looked at Miles as Celia handed Lukas a clean sweatshirt to put on. "Now, this is where you come in, my dear researcher. Take his son and go to San Giorgio's Cemetery—behind the church on the north side. At the far wall facing the sea, dig down a full three feet. Lukas will place everything in the consecrated earth. *You* must not touch it, Miles. Pound it with the shovel's wooden end until it shatters. Fill the hole completely, *capisce*?" He nodded as did the child. "Go immediately. The sooner this is buried in hallowed

126

ground, the better it will be."

They left through the apartment door as she held on to the sink for a full minute. When she heard activity behind her, she straightened and walked to the master bedroom.

Alana had pulled up a clean satin sheet and the rest of the bed covers, which had been folded at the foot of the bed. She watched her tuck the covers down Michael's sides.

"*Zia*, we have to talk. I'll tell you everything—"

"It is not necessary tonight, *cara*. If the ritual worked, he will wake with the morning sun. This poison has done tremendous damage. Once his body heals, the Council will address his actions in the passageway." She turned out the overhead lights, leaving the bedroom door ajar. She let herself out of the apartment fully aware that the waiting game had begun.

****

Close to midnight, Alana heard the door to her home open and close. Lukas and Miles were back. The house went dark, and she left Michael's side to secure the heavy drapes. No bright rays of morning sun would filter through. Sunlight would not take him from her.

She locked the bedroom door, and with little energy left, changed into a comfortable nightgown. Settling next to him, she hoped to shed all the tension from another incredibly long day and night, which had somehow been filled with even more stress than the previous two days. She rubbed her brow, fully aware of raw, conflicting emotions—fear, revenge, fear, anxiety, fear, determination—fear.

Sleep didn't happen, even though exhaustion had set in. She carefully left the bed and sunk into the Queen

Anne chair. Hours passed as she studied him. Remembered him. Prayed for him. Dozing off, she'd suddenly snap back awake, hoping for some sign that he was healing.

But Michael had not moved. No groans or moans…no words…no breath, of course. In undeath he resembled a mannequin. Still… Simply here but not present. "You can't survive without me. I want you back whole and well. You have to come back to me," she whispered. And what would tomorrow bring?

Alana finally returned to the bed and came to rest on her side. She had to imagine his survival. How she would be in his strong arms, drowning in his touch. He would kiss her, his soul mate, her completion. He'd fill in all the blanks. About Lukas. About what led to the battle in the passageway. He would be honest, open, ready to explain his silence.

Then his kisses would tempt her, tease her awake, loving her as a man loves a woman. They'd take it slow, letting all the pent-up passion unravel like a thin silk scarf afloat in the warm breeze of the sea.

"I am yours," she would confess, "I have always been yours, my love."

He would know. He would sense her very soul, and her body would blossom with need. Her heart would flutter—blood racing and all inhibitions shed.

She smiled at the thought. Let out a soft sigh. They would love each other, reach a long-awaited climax together wrapped in each other's arms. Enchanted in each other's race to an ecstasy she so desperately wanted, so desperately needed. He would whisper, "I love you." And in reply, she'd whisper, "I love you more."

Lost in her fantasy, her eyes drifted closed.

He was the commanding, immortal being she would always love.

****

A familiar voice whispering her name threatened to pull her out of her dreams. She flatly refused to let it happen. This was where she wanted to be, hand above head, flat on her back, and lost in a reverie of love. A cool finger traced her lips.

The whisper of her name tickled her ear. Then "Alana, darlin'," followed, and her eyelids flipped open. *That one word...the soft lilt of his tone.*

His dark-espresso eyes came into focus. They were no longer blood-shot. His color was better, and the swelling on his face had gone down significantly. His lips were pale, and the weary expression he wore confirmed it had taken every bit of strength to roll onto his side and face her.

His head dropped onto her pillow, and he sighed. She kissed his hair and nuzzled his bruised jaw. Her heart pounded so hard in her chest that she thought it would burst.

"Alana," he said again. The tenor of his rich tone, low but less raspy.

"Michael, my love," she whispered, full of devotion.

"How long have I been out?"

"Three days," she replied. His brow tightened. She pulled away to study his face. Bruises covered every inch, but many cuts were closed. Her eyes began to glisten because fear had been a constant companion.

"I hurt everywhere."

"I've been right here with you."

"Christ, I'm in bad shape. Broken ribs, a shattered right femur—aches and pains too many to count." His voice was thicker than usual. "I cannot self-heal."

Worry filled her heart. "You know you're not in the city anymore."

"I'm in Portofino."

"Miles got you and Lukas out. Celia's here too…helping with things. The Georgians sent specialists and yesterday—"

A mischievous smirk appeared. "The two men my son sent sailing across the room?"

"Yeah… we need to talk about what happened. Lukas is itching for the control-yourself-or-else speech."

He groaned. "I killed the bastards who made him so crazy. He wasn't supposed to remember me."

She sat up, leaning against the headboard. "Michael, I need answers. Lukas is the reason you went along with NWT, isn't he? And those three sorcerers *actually believed* you'd give him up so easily—for an entire year?"

He looked away. "Not now, my Guardian."

"I'm not stopping, even if you don't want to hear me. But they were prepared, in the event you turned against them. A three-headed beastly thing waited in the wings to take a nip. I can't believe you missed that," she said, with a hint of sarcasm. "You don't get to play with big bad sorcerers, and then pick up your toys and go home."

"This is complicated, and I don't want to discuss it now. As long as he's safe, everything is fine." A devilish smile appeared. "I enjoyed watching you sleep."

She gave a grim smile. "Nice way to change the subject."

"My entire body feels as heavy as stone. Not a good grip in my hands. My senses are intact… but something feels different. Last night…What happened to me?"

"You were in bad shape; I mean really bad—"

"There was an old lady… a healer… Where did she come from?" She sucked in a breath, and he quipped as he stared at her, "I asked you a question. Answer it."

"An old lady—"

"If glares were stakes, Alana, I'd be dust and bone by now."

She blew out a breath as her eyes went wide. "Wow, that irritating arrogance is back with a vengeance! So, let's back up, buddy."

"Do not call me buddy." He eyed her comfortable, cotton nightgown and began to grin.

She sat up straighter, heading off the comment, which would probably include 'matronly' or something worse.

"First of all, you've been out of it for *three* days. I won't embarrass you with the crying and screams. Second, a lot—and I do mean *a lot* of people—have been trying to make you better. Third, that *old lady* who, by the way, took the infection out of you is my *Zia* Rosa."

"What's a "zeearosa"?"

And just like that, her Italian temper flared. "*Zia* means aunt in Italian and she's my mother's aunt, which makes her my great-aunt, or for your benefit, my *great* great-aunt who knew exactly how to get the poison out of your undead, ungrateful carcass. God, this is so unlike you! Try and show a *teeny* bit of appreciation, *buddy*."

Michael rolled his eyes, which kicked her into high gear. "She's also a member of the Georgian Sovereign Council. I knew *Zia* was a healer. I just didn't know she was powerful enough to remove the *undead* type of infection you got—after that *thing* took a bite of dead meat out of your shoulder, and then used your back as a scratching post!"

This verbal sparring, completely unexpected, had her fuming. She took a deep breath and sharply blew it out. It didn't help.

"When did you get so… cold? You're either a total ass—or you're not being straight with me." His bored frown floored her. "Okay. I've had enough. And you don't get to win the round," she announced, throwing the covers over his face and getting out of the bed. She rummaged through dresser drawers and with a bundle of clothes in hand, she walked into her bathroom and slammed the door.

****

"Well, that worked like a charm," he whispered.

Passion and vengeance spun like a coin on a table. Alana was his passion, his destiny. Waking up next to her made him all the more obsessive. "I'll drive you away for your own good. I'll live with the incessant ache in my soul. You aren't going to be the one way they can get to me." He calculated his new vengeance coldly, dangerously. If he was still on this earth, then someone or some*thing* would be coming to finish him off.

"I will walk into the sun and burn in the eternal fires of Hell rather than bring their wrath down upon you or any of these good people."

There were lots of ways he could cripple NWT… if there was anything left to the international company. But he wasn't about to include Alana. *He* was who they wanted. He had ripped the scab off a bloody wound, and they'd want their revenge.

Mulling over his options, he heard the water turn off in the master bedroom's ensuite.

Minutes later, the door opened. He shut his eyes, feigning sleep.

Without a word or a look, she left the bedroom dressed in blue jeans and a lilac billowy blouse, slamming the door behind her. Yep. It absolutely did the trick, he thought.

Chapter 17

Information

Still miffed by Michael's insensitivity, Alana added a little milk to her cup of coffee. "Oooh, it smells sooo good. Did you make the coffee, Celia B?" She got a nod and a cheery "yes" as she took a sip.

Dressed in whatever she had grabbed from her dresser, she kept her hair loose cascading over one shoulder. Although she grinned at Lukas, he just stared at her before digging into his bowl of cereal again. Grabbing a roll off the plate in the center of the table, the knife in her other hand could have been a lethal weapon. She slapped wads of sweet butter on the fresh, warm bread. She was so angry at him. How could he be so...

"Is something bothering you, honey? Are you aware of what you're doing to the roll? The amount of butter would send anyone's bad cholesterol off the chart."

Fire filled her eyes, anger crept up her cheeks, but she placed the knife down as she let out a sigh, not even aware she had been holding her breath. "I just don't get it, Dad. Everyone put themselves out for him, but all *he* does is act arrogant and rude."

"Is he awake, I mean like conscious?" Celia asked before anyone else.

"What did he say?" Lukas demanded, with a mouth full of crunchy cereal.

Obviously, the boy had no table manners. "Chew. Swallow. Then talk," she told him. Although still simmering, she had a bit more control. The strong coffee helped.

"Well," Celia said, "so how is he? Better?"

"He's conscious. Even speaking in full sentences. He remembers bits and pieces, including the fiasco with Chamberlain yesterday."

Almost choking, Lukas's round eyes were an incredible dark-blue and very intense. He dropped the spoon in the bowl and cleared his throat. "I tried to say I was sorry."

"And it's a good thing you did. Because I'd hate to think the attitude thing is genetic. And now the pout on your face as well." Turning to her adopted father, she said to him, "He had the audacity to get testy when I told him what *Zia* did last night."

A 'humph' came at her first. "I take it he's up and moving about. Perhaps showering?"

Oh. No. Of course. She put the coffee mug down carefully. It all clicked and feeling the fool, she shook her head slowly. How could she be so thick? "I think the infection is gone. But he is still... incapacitated. Did I get it right this time, Dad?"

He gave an austere nod followed by his typical thin smile. "Old habits die hard, honey. Michael has always been arrogant; also strong and independent. Not being able to protect or defend himself, not able to move or walk must be torture."

"Jeez, is there *anything* good about this?" She was beyond frustrated.

But Lukas leaned forward. The front legs of his chair hit the floor with a thud that made Celia jump.

"They can't see us here, can they? I mean, those sorcerers are dead, right?"

"Don't worry, I put one major protection whammy on the building," Celia stated with confidence. "We're hidden pretty well."

"Do you think we're in danger, Dad?" she asked as her stomach churned.

"No, I assure you, we are not. Perhaps the Council knows more about this. I'll talk to Rosa." But his concern showed. "Chamberlain will be here shortly to confirm he's on the road to healing. Try to eat something, honey. Perhaps I'll take nourishment to him and see his progress for myself. Agreed?"

His calmness was a trait she admired, and she gave a soft. "Agreed," while scraping gobs of sweet butter off the roll and onto her plate.

****

Miles had a mug of human blood in hand. He closed the door and turned on all the lights in the room, staring at Michael, fully satisfied watching the wince. The fatherly expression had already disappeared, being more than irritated with the vampire. Their history didn't include friendly chats, or for that matter, any type of assistance. After turning on the bedside lamp, he stood over Michael and simply held out the mug. The look of disgust coming at him only fueled his annoyance.

"Let me make an educated guess. You're totally helpless. And you're pissed as hell."

As expected, no response. Miles placed the crystal mug on the nightstand, then sat in the upholstered chair, crossing his leg at the knee with folded hands on his lap.

"I take your silence as a yes."

Minutes ticked away. Then came the muttered,

"Well obviously I can't move, and I can't feed myself…right now."

Analyzing his subject, the words acerbic, egotistical, and, of course, self-loathing came to mind. His next journal entry would be full of descriptive adjectives.

"Cut the attitude with me. I'm not the love of your life whom you're trying to push away, and you don't want me or any other Georgian too annoyed with you, *right now.*" He dug in deeper. "You have a truly confused child, who is troubled and raw, full of rage, *right now*. Celia worked a special kind of "good" magic in Manhattan to save you both. The Sovereign Council is standing with you, significantly impressed by your win. Rosa Bellini retrieved your sanity last night, and quite possibly, saved your miserable, undead ass." Like a bull ready to charge, he stood. "As for Alana, I recall a certain September night many years ago—"

"Don't go there, researcher—"

"Don't interrupt, please," he bit out in a very clipped, British tone. "If I recall correctly, you then went after her for *two entire weeks*. You *allowed* your beast-within to dictate every move, fully *unwilling* to control your demonic nature. *You* hunted her down, dragged her into the passageway. I fought you then, and I'll fight you now—if necessary. Celia, with many Georgians to assist, got the portal to open. Helena reached for you, but *I* was the one to shove you through." His voice sank lower. "How is it a *mortal* man had the strength to push an out-of-control vampire through a portal? A father's love is far stronger than *anything*. Perhaps what happened to Lukas allows you to understand *much* better now." He leaned in with a glare. "Hurt Alana again, and I swear before God, I'll stake you myself. Now, sit up."

Michael closed his eyes. It took many seconds before he whispered, "I can't."

"Precisely!" He gripped Michael's broad shoulders hard, ignored the gasp of pain and got his back against the headboard. Cupping his thick head of hair, he brought the scarlet sustenance to his lips with a curt, "Drink."

Small swallows. Small sips. It took a while. But when the primal need was quenched, the vampire turned his bruised face away. "My body screams in pain. My hands are numb. My arms feel like lead. I thought my time had come. I prayed you would find Lukas. And I never meant to bring danger to her. You're an honorable man, Miles, I...respect you. I don't want Alana to know—"

"How you paid Rosa triple what this building is worth? How you anonymously provide for Alana? The renovations alone must have cost a fortune. Let's add the fact that you employ an ex-Guardian to manage the bookshop who reports to you her every need. I know about the irrevocable trust for Lukas in my name, in the event you end up dust and bone. Plus, you've siphoned *millions* of dollars from NWT, filtered through highly creative bookkeeping, I must say, for The Georgian Council to train new Guardians. I've done my research."

Michael narrowed his eyes. "How did you know?"

Miles allowed a dry smirk as he clasped his hands behind his back. "It doesn't take a genius to figure out who connects all of us. You were hell-bent on making amends this past year, weren't you?"

"Does Alana know?"

"She's not as experienced with puzzles as I am." His

tone softened. A bit. "You and I shall call a truce for the sake of who we love. Agreed?" Michael nodded once. "Good. Chamberlain will arrive soon to examine you."

"No way in Hell. I don't need a demon quack."

"Demon *specialist,*" he curtly corrected. "You will cooperate and act civil. You will swallow every snide remark. And you are in no position to argue."

The look of disgust was priceless. "I have no say in this?"

"Positively none," Miles stated with authority.

****

Shortly after Chamberlain's arrival, the fireworks started. Alana's quiet home filled with outraged protests and more than a few threats from the obstinate patient. Anyone passing on the street below could hear the ugly rant. Hopefully, none of her neighbors would call the local police. The examination, punctuated with insults, didn't take long. Miles kept her updated. But Chamberlain's final request brought out a different kind of beast in Michael.

Sitting at the antique secretary in the corner of the living room, Alana sorted through days of mail. More thunderous threats echoed through the thick plaster walls. "Get your fucking hands off me!" "Miles… Make them stop! This isn't going to happen… I'll kill you, you bastard! Don't try it!" She heard the shower turn on and allowed herself a short but sinister chuckle.

Looking up, an idea came to mind and her attention turned to Lukas. With his legs dangling over the arm of a leather chair, he appeared bored.

"I can just imagine the look on your father's face."

"He'll kill them. I know he will," Lukas replied.

Engagement felt right. She motioned him over, and

he took the bait. "I won't tell if you don't, so give me the scoop. And I mean everything."

His head tilted toward the bedroom. "Baker has him in your bathroom. Man, he can curse up a storm. He's, like, beyond ballistic. Told Baker he'll hunt him down when he's walking again." They both chuckled this time. "Uh oh—Mister B says wash his hair. Man, he's way pissed." After another minute, Alana saw the cutest deep-dimpled smile ever. "Okay. He's out... Baker's drying him off. Uh...those pajamas are going on. He's still cursing." Lukas shook his head. "The score is one to nothing, in favor of the doctor."

****

Rage. Cold, calculated rage. And murder. Not to mention, the wretched humiliation of being soaped and scrubbed by this demon-doctor. Baker tucked the bedspread around his body. "And get your filthy hands off me, moron. You're enjoying this," he hissed shooting a nasty glare at Miles, who sat casually ensconced in the upholstered chair like a know-it-all.

"I'll bet you feel much better now," Chamberlain stated.

The short, bald man didn't know how lucky he was. Had he been able to move, the human's neck would be in his hands, because he was beyond angry.

"Go to hell, you fucking quack. I'm over three hundred years old."

"Compared to many of the evil things out there, three hundred is pretty damn young. I will admit, most vampires we study aren't as old as you. The ones we get to the lab are reckless—going for the quick kill and not too intelligent."

He poked Michael's hand with a pen and then ran it

up his arm. "Do you feel this. Yes, no?"

A low, long growl came before he replied, "Rot. In. Hell."

Chamberlain had the audacity to sit on the bed, studying him. Again... neck in hand came to mind. "I'll bet my last poker chip this is as scary as you get, vampire. You'd be a highly interesting specimen to study considering your history—both good and bad. This affliction of yours is one for the "unnatural" science books. Once again, you've proven to be unique."

"And foolishly arrogant," Miles added while slowly shaking his head.

"Your shoulder is healing, and the wounds are closing. But sorcerers are diabolical creatures. No one, not even egotistical vampires, can outsmart them. Forming an unholy alliance with that Triumvirate was the biggest mistake. You took the dangerous way out, and it came back to bite you in the ass...or should I be literal and say the shoulder? I hope you survive their retaliation, which you know will certainly come."

"Don't go there," he bit out with a tight sneer.

Chamberlain clicked his tongue. Many times. "Get over yourself, Michael. If Rosa hadn't helped last night, you'd have slipped into madness. The poison would soak up every lucid brain cell. The smell alone would be intolerable. Then you'd beg for a stake." He gripped the injured right thigh and didn't let go. Michael's eyes shot wide, and he let out a ragged gasp. "Note the chart, Baker: No metamorphosis. No long canines, feral pupils, or clawed finger. The subject does not howl. His response is that of a mortal man, not the fearless champion documented by Georgians for the last hundred-plus years." When he let go, Michael turned his face away. But the pain of the grab as he grit his teeth? He had certainly felt it. "So, now we move on."

"How so?" asked Miles, sitting so proper like an old English gentleman in the chair.

"Get him out of this bed. Forget about his *mystically* enhanced abilities. I want him out of bed."

"Force him back into the world of the living, so to speak?"

"My thoughts exactly," the demon quack stated. "You know I'm not a cruel man, Miles. But suffering his arrogance is something I won't tolerate." He stood and looked down with measured compassion. For once. "You couldn't kill me or anyone else in this condition. But there *are* certain perks. You have Lukas back. Neither Alana nor that complicated child should worry. As for the beast-within? I don't honestly know if it will ever resurface. I'll check him in another day or so, Miles. Baker will bring up the chair."

"What chair?" Michael asked, very confused.

"It will help you get around until you're walking again." Chamberlain didn't wait for a reply. He and the others left the bedroom, turning out the lights. Minutes later, the door opened. Baker parked the folded contraption at the foot of the antique four-poster bed.

"No fucking way," he hissed in the dark, empty room.

Chapter 18

Changes

Alana checked on Michael, who was once again asleep. She stood at the foot of the bed, lost in thoughts of him. The furrowed brow, the tense bruised jaw. He was handsome, a commanding creature. His six-foot three-inch frame almost dwarfed the bed. Was he lost in a dream? Would he continue to heal? Only time would tell.

She left the room, less worried but more anxious.

Miles had asked her to relay a somewhat cryptic message to Lukas. Silently, she approached the den. Lukas lounged in a comfortable sprawl on the den's denim loveseat, thoroughly engrossed in *X-Men II*. She studied him from the doorway.

What a strange mixture of conflicts. Rage and gentleness, frightened and brazen... So many contradictions rolled into one troubled fifteen-year-old.

There was no physical resemblance. Lukas was small for his age. Very wiry, just a bit over five-foot tall. His face reminded her of a Renaissance angel. *No. No physical resemblance at all...well, maybe the high cheekbones. But mannerisms? One could say: like father; like son.* Pulling out of her thoughts, she said in casual way, "When the movie is over, Miles has something he wants you to do."

Lukas jumped up. Then he rolled his shoulders loose.

"Sorry... I didn't mean to—"

"It's okay. Hey... Do you have the first *X-men* movie, too?"

"Sure. Look in the cabinet by the window. And I think *X-Men III* is coming out soon or maybe it's out already. I don't really follow these things too closely. Celia's the action-adventure aficionado in the family."

He hit pause on the remote and turned to her with a look of typical-teen curiosity. "Do you think we can get it?"

She had to smile. 'We' said he's comfortable here, getting comfortable with her. It was a good start. "Sure. Let's check the web together and buy the DVD. I'll even spring for super-speedy delivery," she called over her shoulder, heading back into the others.

****

"I gave him your message, Dad," Alana said as she entered the living room. He and Celia were in a hushed conversation on the sofa, which stopped as she sat in a leather chair across from them. Her senses tingled, a tense feeling she didn't ignore. "Give me a clue. What's next?"

"Dad has an idea, and I think it's worth considering." Celia appeared reserved, not her usual bubbly self. No playful way of speaking—not this time. "We're swimming against the tide here. I-I spent the morning downstairs with *Zia*. Both of us sense something big brewing. We have to be prepared...to take extraordinary measures."

Her adopted father cleared his throat. A grave expression settled on his face. "Doctor Chamberlain has helped tremendously, but your vampire is not cooperative, which exacerbates his current situation. But this must be voluntary—on everyone's part."

"Okay," Alana said, drawing out the word but open to what he had to say.

"Michael is genetically linked to his son, whose blood may increase his ability to heal. Likewise, volumes of Georgian documentation prove a Guardian's blood is like a pure shot of adrenaline to a vampire. It sends their senses into overdrive. If time is of the essence, simply put, I think he needs your blood. Lukas's as well."

"Then tap my veins today. I'm sure Lukas will be eager to give a pint or two."

"And of course, Dad and I will donate," Celia added.

"Michael's thirst is minimal We'll be able to sustain him for at least forty-eight hours."

Her lips settled in a half-smile. "From what I heard this morning, I don't think he'll miss the doctor's visits. I know Arthur Chamberlain's a good man, and I trust him completely. Doing this without anyone coming or going, in case we *are* being watched... We should start today."

"I agree," said Celia.

"Good. On to the next item, which may be more crucial. We must give everything we know about his battle in Manhattan to the Georgian Sovereign Council—and very soon. We are a world-wide network. Then, I'll ask them to share all the information they've collected, throughout three centuries, about Michael Malone."

"Why," Alana asked, very curious.

He nodded as if expecting the question. "Why did Helena allow him to regain his soul? What is their connection? Why choose him and not another vampire? I'd like to set up a formal conference with Father Giovanni as soon as possible."

"*Zia* will help. I asked her about a meeting this morning," Celia said. "And she's cooking something special for him. It didn't smell all that appetizing, but hey, I'm not into anything even *remotely* suggesting animal."

She stood, full of resolve. "Okay. How do we do this?"

He pulled off his reading glasses, laying his notes in his lap. "Talk with Rosa, Alana. She deserves to know your connection to him for the past decade. I'll get what we need from Chamberlain to begin the blood donations."

"What about Lukas," Celia asked, full of concern.

"You can keep Lukas occupied. Besides, you've always liked action movies. If and when the boy can pull himself away from the den, I want him to sit quietly at the dining room table and write down everything—and I do mean *everything* he remembers about being raised by Helena, his four years of captivity with the sorcerers, and his altered life as someone else for one short year. If you can persuade him to write about living on the city streets while he hunted his father, it would likewise be appreciated."

Celia blew out a long, slow breath. "You're talking days of writing, Dad."

"I have a notebook on the table waiting." He pointed to something leatherbound, the size of a steno pad.

"What if he, you know, gets too antsy, and—"

"You'll think of something, honey, perhaps guide his mind to focus."

Celia leaned in closer to him. "What if Michael wakes up?"

"After that childish tantrum this morning, I'd venture to say he will be out like a light for hours."

Alana gave her a bright smile. "I'll be one floor down, Celia B. Just send me one of those psychic mini-messages you're so good at. I'll be here in two-seconds flat."

If they could pull this off, it just might help.

****

Alana kissed her *zia* on both cheeks and stayed in her comfortable hug for a long minute. The gentle smile didn't leave *Zia's* face as she went back into the kitchen to bring a pitcher of homemade iced tea to the dining room table. She filled Alana's glass.

"How is he today, *cara*?"

"Doctor Chamberlain said the infection is completely out of his system. Thank you, thank you so very much." She sipped the sweet tea, refreshing and aromatic. Sitting down, her aunt patted her hand. "He's asleep. They, uh, got him showered and in pajamas—"

"*Oh, mamma mia*, so that's what we heard earlier?" *Zia* leaned back with a laugh. "Celia and I were in the middle of a very interesting conversation about the gift of healing."

"I'm curious, not to mention embarrassed. Why didn't you tell me you knew about him?"

"I know he is a legendary vampire. All Georgians do. The subject of his conscience, his ability to control the beast-within... It has been documented since the Georgians first sensed an angel's intervention with him well over a century ago. When I touched his son, I sensed something more." She shook her head, "Lukas is very troubled."

"I know. But our—"

"When I held Michael, his connection to you became crystal clear. I saw into his soul."

"He saved my life many times."

"Ah, but I read your heart. He hurt you. He hunted you."

Alana looked away. "I pushed. I forced him to face something beyond his control, and he couldn't stop. Neither could I, and to be honest, I didn't want to."

"What we do in life, the decisions we make, change us. But everything happens for a reason, *cara*, everything. Love is very real. The desire to protect and defend has taught him the difference between selfishness and selflessness. Perhaps his devotion to both of you will be his salvation. Only time will tell."

Her aunt stood. "Come with me to the kitchen." A large pot sat on the stove. She lifted the lid to stir it.

"Celia said you were making him something, but vampires don't—"

"Don't normally ingest food. Yes. I know. But this will nourish him."

Totally curious, Alana searched her eyes, a shade of gray so uncommon, hoping to know more. Her anxiety was rising by the second. "Will you assist Dad with the Council. Can a meeting happen soon?"

"Giovanni will call a special meeting." She shook her head as she tapped the wooden spoon against the rim of the pot. "Evil never rests, *cara*. None of us can see it clearly, but we feel it." Then her expression changed as she replaced the lid. "Now, tell me more about him."

Where do I begin... with how I knew I loved him? With how I avoided him after that September night? With the truth, she told herself, only with the truth.

****

One floor above, Michael stared into the darkness of Alana's bedroom. The doctor's accusations rang true. Two centuries of killing. His to own. What he'd done to Alana. His to own. Miles's accusations rang true as well. Turning to the sorcerers who had held his son captive instead of throwing himself at the mercy of the Georgian Council to beg *their* help?

His to own.

Pain pounded through every inch of his body, yet he couldn't move. Guilt choked his reclaimed soul, yet he still existed. So many truths, truth upon truth, is too hard to face.

He stared into nothingness…

The courtroom is packed. Hot sun streams through the windows and makes this place unbearable. Spectators line the walls, demanding justice. The guards remain unseen, but I know they're here, and I can't escape. I am shackled to guilt. Fear grips my gut, wishing the streaks of sunlight can inch towards me to end it all.

This is like a circus with accusations being shouted by one and all. Guilty. Merciless. Deadly. Immoral. Words strung together to form fractured sentences… Kill the killer! Let him burn! Give him the stake!

What I did cannot be undone… the drink and drain… violated innocents.

The dark seer appears in a mist before me. My blood is on her tongue. "You took him from my body in the passageway. He was born to be my gift to the sorcerers. Born from your dead seed. Born to destroy you!"

"I could not create a child, yet he took his first

breath in my arms. They will never take my son from me again," I reply.

"Wait and watch," she shrieks before disappearing in thin air.

I turn to the crowd behind me. My faceless victims are faceless no more. I recall each and every kill; each and every deadly pursuit.

I see my son behind them all, my reason to continue this existence... to save him.

But justice will be served. The rule of life is to accept one's death.

My beautiful Guardian appears, strong and serene. She stands before me with my love imprinted on her soul. Does she know how much I love her; treasure her? I do not see the stake before it sinks deep into my unbeating heart.

And I am dust and bone at her feet.

Drenched in sweat, gasping for an unnecessary breath, he closed his eyes. His conscience was a first-class author spinning tales of guilt and death.

"Dear God, what have I done?" he whispered.

Chapter 19

A Hard Night

Alana was close to exhaustion. It was late afternoon when she entered her home, put the heavy pot on the stove, and sank into the leather sofa in the living room. She closed her eyes thinking, how remembering it all drains you... and now Zia knew everything. Earlier, sitting with her aunt, memories had sputtered out of her like the changing tempos of a Classical sonata. Each memory like its own melody to be mastered.

The annoying sound of a tapping pen against paper continued to interrupt her rest. She rubbed her eyes, then forced them open. Lukas fidgeted next to her adopted father at the dining room table. Often punctuating his tap-tap-tapping with curses. When his fist pounded the table, she thought, oh no, please no, he wouldn't dare crank himself up again...

"I hate this! It's like friggin' busy work an old man substitute gives 'cause he can't teach! Fuck it," the teen spit out. She knew her adopted father's depth of patience. It would take more than curses and staccato taps to get a reaction.

"Please continue," he said without an ounce of annoyance.

"Fuck no! You just thought up this stupid shit because I wanted to watch another movie. Like there's

151

anything cool to do in this lame-ass place."

Looking for a reason to throw a punch? Not going to happen. But some action on her part was required. Pulling off the couch, she sauntered over to them to stand behind Miles with her arms folded across her chest. The boy *actually* had the nerve to rudely sneer.

"Great, a Guardian for backup. This friggin' sucks!"

And then it happened. Faster than the speed of light. Shooting through the air, the notebook missed her father's head by an inch. A beautiful favorite vase shattered on the hutch. A split second later, his good pen was imbedded deep in the table's exquisite wood. Instead of an apology, a snicker and another sneer lit Lukas's face as he pushed off the table just out of her reach. Miles sat back and pulled off his glasses, actually glaring at the kid. Her focus switched from the pen to the perpetrator. "There's barely an inch visible."

"Yeah. It's deep," he stated like he was proud of what he'd done.

"Celia and I gave Dad that pen for his fiftieth birthday. And that vase was my favorite." Seeing a twitch, she quickly added, "Don't even think about making a run for it."

"Yeah? Why? You think you can catch me?"

"Oh, I know I can, buddy."

"Yeah, right," he scoffed.

Her adopted father shook his head. "You will get yourself into trouble with this attitude, young man."

Lukas's blue eyes flashed defiant, his face scrunched and mean. "Get real. You can't do anything to me."

She stepped toward him, and as he backed away, Alana pulled the pen out of the wood and gave him a slight grin. "Maybe yes or maybe no. But your father's going to hear about this. And when he does, you'd better watch your bratty little butt." She slapped the pen down on the table, never taking her eyes off Lukas, whose cheeks began to redden. "I know Michael very well. My guess is you can forget about a time-out. Nope. I'm thinking more of a hands-on, old-fashioned approach to bad behavior. You should be getting that sinking feeling in the pit of your stomach right about now. Don't you agree, Daddy B?"

"I do, honey."

"And never forget. I'm just as strong as you." She picked up the notebook, brushed off the shards of the slain vase, and placed it on the dining room table.

Her adopted father wore a stern expression, one so rarely seen. "Sit down, Lukas." He complied…without attitude. "Pick up the pen and finish this paragraph. Or the Guardian may want to hold you down—while I paddle you myself." When Lukas started to write, he put his reading glasses back on and pulled his laptop closer. "Honey," he said, "come look at this."

She leaned over his shoulder. It was an email from Philip.

"GREETINGS and I hope you are enjoying this vacation. But it's best to stay out of the sun. Not much happening. May is turning out to be a peach of a month. Did you hear? A small fault line did some rumbling four days ago. No people injuries. One evil idiot still missing. Name sounds like dirt to me. Kisses to all. Keep an eye out for Mail from the city."

Her eyes opened as wide as quarters. Her heart raced. "Oh," she said matter-of-factly. "How interesting."

The laptop closed as Miles said to Lukas, "Put the pen down, please. Wash your hands and then go check on your father, and please close the door behind you." For once, he appeared to do as he was told.

She motioned Miles to follow her into the kitchen and turned on the faucet. They'd also keep their voices low as she reached behind and locked her hands to the edge of the counter.

"I've got to contact the Council immediately." He paced the limited space.

"This is a disaster waiting to happen."

"On many fronts."

"I didn't know if he was going to go into the bedroom or run." She blew out a breath. "Dad… the lines about dirt and mail from the city—"

"I know who's missing. It isn't good." She sucked in a quick breath as he added, "I must get to the church. Giovanni must be informed. Tell Celia, honey."

She turned off the faucet, heard the apartment door open and close.

Her head ached; her heart continued to race as she approached the sunroom.

****

Minutes before the bedroom door opened, Michael had studied the insulting thing at the foot of the bed. A renewed look of disgust crossed his face. Rage had him unable to focus for hours. "What a self-righteous quack. There was no way in Hell I'll roll around like some kind of human invalid. Demon specialist my ass—he's a fucking fool, and he can shove it where the sun doesn't shine. Just stake me now. I want this over. I want this finished." He closed his eyes and slowly, carefully shook his head. "I've screwed up my son's life. Now I'm in her home, in her bed, screwing up *her* life as well. She must hate me."

He had let out a groan when the door opened and then slammed shut. His son walked to the bedside table and turned on the lamp before flopping into the upholstered chair looking awkward and edgy. "No she doesn't."

"I'm sorry you heard that," he whispered, wondering if his son had heard more than just the last sentence. "My relationship with Alana is complicated. We have a history—"

"I don't like it here. When can we leave?"

The slight flush on his son's face, the bitter tone confused him. "Why? I'm sure Alana and Miles are—"

"They're making me write stuff down. Stuff like hunting you before I forgot. Mister B says I was programed."

You were, he thought. Memories haunt one's soul. He could relate. But his son looked ready to run, fidgeting in the chair and breathing hard. Michael patted the bed. "Come and sit next to me. It's hard to turn my head." Lukas blew out a breath but complied, staring at his flexing hands, and lost in thought. "Look at me, son." He didn't. Trying to engage further, he added with tenderness, "I'm truly sorry *all* of this happened. But we are safe here."

"I wasn't going to stake you in the passageway. I wanted to help you fight. I'm different now, you know?"

"I didn't think everything would come back to you. It's a lot to handle." His protected life with Helena. Taken by the sorcerers. A maniacal year, which led to a father's disastrous intervention to give his son a life less dangerous. Had it all been pointless? Had it further complicated matters?

"They killed Helena. They want you gone, too."

The lack of emotion was disturbing. "There's a lot to talk about. You have questions. I know. And we'll have time now because you're safe here. You're with me."

"Helena wasn't my mother."

"No…she wasn't—"

Lukas's head jerked, his eyes narrow and empty. "Who is she? My real mother. And why do I have these abilities? It is because of what you are… because you can see your soul?"

He ignored the first part. "I've controlled the beast within me since 1890. Why Helena allowed this, I have no idea. And a vampire cannot create life, but here you are—"

"Is my birth mother a witch with powers like Celia?"

"Who told you that?' His son just shrugged, and Michael gave a sigh. "She was a dark seer. Didn't use her powerful abilities to do good the way Celia does."

"*Was*? Is she dead?"

"Yes. She is," he offered, trying to shift, which caused irritating discomfort, yet only managing to move an inch. Pain etched his face, and his son studied him.

"Want help?"

"You can't move me—" Lukas already had his shoulders, pulling him up until his back hit the wooden headboard. Indeed, his son had enhanced abilities. His mouth quirked into a slight grin. His "thank you" was cut off by, "So who killed her?"

Rather stunned, he said, "Lukas, this is all very complicated."

"You said we have time to talk now."

"Right, but—"

"You did, didn't you?"

"In a way… and to save you, yes. I killed her." His son needed more. Deserved more because of all he'd been through in his short, troubled life. "I… I hadn't seen her for many months. I never knew she was pregnant. She found me in the passageway. Her skirt was streaked with blood, as was her face and hands, and she was in labor."

He vividly recalled the shock of her saying the child about to enter this world was his. The fact that she appeared no longer fully human, well, he kept that to himself. "She was skin and bone, except for her belly, and she looked beyond insane, threatening to cut you from her womb, swearing that she would give you to the sorcerers. I wouldn't let her." He paused, thinking of the right words to use. "She lunged at me with a knife in her hand but instead, she fell to the ground. I got down next to her, and she slashed at me until I wrenched the knife away. All this time she continued chanting words I didn't recognize, didn't know or care to know. The only thought I had was to save you. I pulled you out of her body and breathed life into you."

"Then you killed her," his son said in a whisper.

"You were alive. That's all that mattered." The dark seer, the hateful witch she was, had given up her humanity, given her soul to the sorcerers to create a child. To groom an innocent child to destroy him. His *own* child! It filled him—both then *and* now with incomparable rage. *May she burn in Hell for eternity.*

Lukas's slender shoulders slumped as if his body could collapse into himself. This unexpected confession grew harder by the minute, the chasm between them harder to bridge.

"You were *my child*…and that meant you weren't safe." Wrapping his fingers around Lukas's thin arm, he tugged with all his strength. To Michael's surprise, his son's head came to rest on his chest. And he was grateful to God that his son had not pulled away. He cleared his throat as raw emotions filled his words. "I wrapped you in my shirt, absolutely shaking with fear. The portal opened, and Helena reached for you, I placed you into the arms of an angel, but I didn't want to let go, son. My heart cracked into a million pieces as if I were a living, breathing man. Helena was a good mother to you, wasn't she?"

Lukas nodded against his chest. He couldn't feel it, but he saw it, and Michael's eyes clouded once again. "I never stopped worrying about you. I'd go back to that alleyway, hoping the portal would open and Helena would let me—"

"I was eight when I saw you," his son mumbled.

The math was simple. The same year when his beast-within resurfaced to hunt Alana. "How could—"

"I didn't tell Helena, but I found where she kept you. But you looked different…yellow demon eyes. Long fangs and growls that called to me, like in my head. You sniffed the air and howled like crazy when you saw me. But I couldn't look away."

It was as if someone had punched him square in the chest. After he tried to kill Alana, Helena had pulled him through the portal. To relearn how to control the beast-within. He had no idea where the portal had landed him. On the other side of the world? Or simply a few hours' drive from the city? How long had it taken him to regain control? Days? Months? And how could he *not* remember seeing his own son? *Another item to add to my own private guilt-list.*

"Oh God, Lukas."

"And I saw her take you back to the portal." His son's hand curled into a fist resting next to his hidden face. "Then this man came. I'd never seen him before. But he's the one who killed her. Deep cuts and strange words… He brought me to the sorcerers in the Second Realm. Said I belonged to them. But I kept seeing it in my head. Seeing *you* kill Helena…" His son's breathy voice, so very bitter, faded away.

His own anger choked him. This is what had lived in his boy's mind provoking hate and revenge. A cruel vision planted with a purpose. When Clayton Mails told him how and where to find his son, the brainwashing was already complete. What followed was the true nightmare. Dodging a cunning child. Trying to talk sense into someone who couldn't hear him. Then combing city streets every night until dawn for an entire year before a deal was made.

For his son's safety. For his son's sanity.

"I hated you. I wanted to kill you or to be killed by you. I wanted the pain inside my head to stop!"

He heard a sniffle and a sob. Lukas sat up, scrubbed his eyes with his palms and looked away. How he wanted to take this devastated child in his arms and hold him for an eternity. But he couldn't move. And he wanted to sniffle and sob himself.

"I *swear* I did not know."

"Yeah," his son whispered, unwilling to look at him, wiping his face on his sleeve.

"You came dangerously close to killing yourself during every reckless confrontation. I couldn't get through to you, so I bargained for your safety, and I planned—"

"Did you kill people for them?"

"No. Never. But I used my power of persuasion to grow their earthly fortunes." And quickly redirected millions out of their fat bank accounts, he thought but didn't say. "Look at me son," he whispered. Gratefully, this time Lukas did. His face was pale, but his eyes had been rubbed raw. "I would gladly give up my existence to take the hurt away. I'd stake myself if it would bring peace to your heart."

But his son's eyes welled again, and his lips quivered. "Yeah. I want this over. I want this finished… I heard you loud and clear." Totally stunned he whispered, "Lukas—"

"I won't stay here."

"Miles and Alana are good—"

"I won't. They can't stop me."

"You're safe with them."

"No," Lukas said as his voice hitched, "Not without you."

The sobs that followed were the saddest sounds he'd ever heard. Forcing his hand to hook Lukas's sleeve took Michael's last ounce of strength. His son's head slammed down on his other shoulder this time.

Michael closed his eyes and swallowed hard before he lost it. Kissing the mop of blond curls, the scent of his troubled child filled him with love and, at the same time, shattered his soul. "I have you, little boy. You're safe with me."

Of course, it was a lie. When, not if, they came for him, Lukas would die. His boy needed security, something he'd only find with Miles and Alana. Once he was gone.

They stayed quiet for a while with him loving the closeness of his child. The late afternoon ticked on in soothing silence until he sensed the tension leave his son's body. Yes. He absolutely loved the feel of him across his chest. How he wished he could wrap his boy in his arms and cradle him like a baby. He loved him that much. "I'll get better. You'll see. And very soon," he said, not knowing if he'd even be able to walk without a limp ever again.

"You have to get out of bed, Dad."

The last word filled him with hope. I have him, he thought, I have him back. Willing to lighten the mood, he gave a low groan. "I'll get back on my feet again, but that contraption—"

His son sat up, didn't leave his side, but gave a loose shrug. "Want to, maybe, suck it up and give it a try? You gotta take a look at this place. There's a huge TV in the den."

He scowled and sneered. "I can't even lift my head."

"I'll help. I'm really strong."

"I'm dead weight."

With that, Lukas stood up. He rolled the nasty thing to the bedside. The maneuvering was close to comical, but somehow Lukas managed to get him into it, although he listed like a piece of dead wood—a bit to the side.

"Ready," his son asked.

"Not at all," he quipped. "And no fancy moves, do you understand?"

"Got it, Dad."

"By the way, it wasn't nice to throw the demon doctors across the room." Lukas chuckled. "Not one of your better moments. Your temper will not show itself here, little boy." The rolling contraption stopped for a subtle second, which forced a stern tone. "You've been behaving yourself?"

"Yep."

"Good. Because you *will* end up over my knee crying like a baby." Of course, he'd never hit a child. Never had as a man or a vampire. "Until I'm back in action, you are to stay put at Alana's side and listen to her, is that understood?"

"Yeah, sure… Wow, you smell like flowers. What'd they use on you?"

The bristle was immediate. A low growl escaped. "Idiots. It'll be a cold, cold day in Hell before they get their miserable hands on me again. It's simply *not* going to happen anytime soon, rotten bastards," he grumbled, letting his son guide the chair out of the bedroom.

He already knew the layout of the apartment, but of course, he kept it to himself.

Chapter 20

Out of Bed

Alana stared in disbelief, amazed that Lukas *actually* got him into that wheelchair. She held a crystal mug of sustenance in her hands because she was heading for the master bedroom. When Michael met her gaze, all she could do was smile, easy and wide. His face was still badly bruised. He appeared listing to one side and weak. Her gaze left him for a quick second to focus on Lukas, whose eyes were red and puffy. Michael's look told her to let it go, which she did.

"I, uh, conned him into getting into this thing," Lukas mumbled.

"Well, *this* is some sight to see. I was just coming in." She lifted the mug a bit, then looked at his son. "Dad needs you in the sunroom."

"Sure," he replied with a shy smile.

The late afternoon sun wasn't strong, but setting the mug on the dining room table, she quickly drew all the drapes closed. Multiple lamps lit the room now, casting the spacious rooms in a golden glow.

"I'm not about to wheel myself into the sun, darlin'," he said in his usual soft voice, always sensual and tender with her. "You didn't have to close the drapes."

Oh, yeah. I most certainly did. With a relaxed smile,

she approached, picking up the mug, pulling a dining room chair next to him. She held the mug to his lips, and he drank it down as if he were beyond thirsty.

"This tasted—"

"You look much better."

"Alana, I'm sorry I—"

"Don't," she interrupted again. But when she pulled away from him, he sniffed the air and narrowed his eyes.

"There's fresh blood on you."

"I cut myself before. It's not a big deal, and I already have a bandage on it. Your sense of smell is already A-plus, isn't it?"

"Yeah, and so is my sense of hearing. What's going on in the other room?"

His handsome features settled into a familiar expression. Fierce eyes, dark as strong coffee, like they could penetrate her soul. Brows knit with a tilt of his head. With a condescending pat to his knee, she changed the subject. "Oooh… Wait till you taste the main course." Getting up, she steered the chair to the head of the table and then went into the kitchen. She knew he was watching her. When she placed the steaming bowl in front of him, he closed his eyes as if lost in the savory scent.

"*Zia* made it just for you. She said it'll speed up healing."

"What a magnificent aroma. What is this?" A slight smile slid across his bruised face. "But darlin', I don't eat." She had the spoon at his lips in a flash, and the strong potion appeared to slide down his throat with ease. He even licked his lips.

"*Zia* calls it something in Italian. I think a literal translation is, uh, Ox-blood soup." He raised an eyebrow but took the second mouthful eagerly. "And after what my aunt did for you last night, I wouldn't want to disrespect her by not finishing every last drop."

He swallowed and then said, "The nearness of you is an added bonus."

She ignored the charm, happy to feed him, anxious about what was surely happening in the sunroom. She brought another spoonful to his lips, meticulously working through the bowl of thick soup.

"You know, I wouldn't want to get her angry by not finishing ever last drop of goodness. Nope. You know, whammies work both ways. I'll bet she could put that infection right back." He gave a shocked look as if he believed her. She daubed at his kissable lips with a cloth napkin. Worry tap-danced up her spine. *Such a self-sufficient being so incapacitated. What if none of this helped him heal any faster?* Lost in thought, she leaned in to straighten his slumped body. He snuck a quick kiss to her cheek and then stared at the crook of her arm—right where a bandage covered her skin.

He raised an eyebrow. "What a strange place for a cut, darlin'."

"You're not playing fair, *darlin'*." She sank back into the dining room chair and folded her arms across her chest. "You and I need to talk. No interrupting. Agreed?"

He gave a gentlemanly nod. "Now, let's have the truth." He used the old you-better-come-clean-or-else tone, so she took a deep breath, and laid out their "new approach."

Anger sizzled in his dark eyes. "No. Not gonna happen. I'm not drinking you, and I'm not drinking Lukas—or Celia, *or* the researcher! Besides, you can't take blood from a fifteen-year-old without parental consent, and I am *not* giving it!" He turned his face away from her. "If I could sink my teeth into someone right about now, I'd feel much better."

"Just listen," she pleaded.

"No."

"Please listen to reason. We all agree. You'll heal faster."

"No, *damn* it!"

"Are you yelling at me? I'm shocked." Full on glare, she thought, nostrils flaring, lips as thin as a pen. Not to mention the sizzle in his eyes. Poking his chest on every word, she stated, "Because it is not going to change my mind!"

His voice grew louder, his look more furious. "You know I can't feel *anything* right now!"

"That's precisely my point, you obstinate ass!"

"Did you just call me an ass?"

And... her Italian temper flared, her hands flew up, responding both sassy and stubborn, "Get over it—And do it really quick."

Would he dare ask another question? Bickering was her secret weapon when he dropped a subject instead of pursuing it. He glared, speechless and seething, but as he opened his mouth to speak, she got out, "You pulled a fast one on me this morning." He closed his mouth because the guilt trip was working. "You did it purposely, with *intentional* cruelness. Just so I wouldn't know about the not-feeling me thing? How rude. If our blood helps, then you can shout and pout all you want. It. Won't. Matter. This is *my* house and you'll play by *my* rules, *capisce*?" *And now for the best jab ever.* "By the way, you drank eight ounces of Celia B as an appetizer!"

Before he could react, Alana stood and stormed out

of the room. A creative string of curse words began as she called over her shoulder at the door to the sunroom, "Stop cursing like a sailor. Not a good example to set for your son—Dad!"

Michael was livid. Outraged. Far past over the top, being forced to eat human food and then hoodwinked into drinking that tiny slip of a psychic's blood. And yet, for the first time in days, he was alert. The pain? Almost manageable. He rolled his shoulders, moved his neck from side to side. *Perhaps, just perhaps*—he lifted his arms, brought them down to connect with the wheels. Slowly, he was able to roll away from the table. Bending his sore arms at the elbow, he flexed his hands. It wasn't much. But it was a beginning.

He took in the fashionable living room and found himself curiously staring at the drawn drapes. Alana's blistering rant came to mind. "You always knew how to bring me down a notch," he whispered. This last exchange between them? No exception. Her fiery temper could turn him around in an instant.

The recall came so fast... *as if we were standing together in the Botanical Gardens, back in the city, what, close to eight years ago.* It was the first time he'd experienced that infamous Italian temper of hers...

Four demons, the color of earth-worms lay dead. Summoned by NWT's sorcerers to destroy plant life and vegetation for a specific purpose, the Botanical Gardens were now a disaster. And NWT's many subsidiaries would make a fiscal killing off the unsuspecting botanical board. Trees torn apart. Rare blooms uprooted. They'd have to pay hundreds of thousands of dollars to reopen. The press would get wind of a highly contagious, deadly bacterium to fuel panic in the borough's general population.

Alana had kicked the dirt cursing... Words he'd never heard her utter before.

"Whoa there, sailor, if Captain Miles heard your language, he'd keel-haul you!" An uncharacteristic chuckle turned her glare murderous, and she kicked him in the shin. "Aye, such a feisty little one you are," he added, collapsing into a rare fit of laughter.

"You know, you never could do accents very well. You should try watching more British programs on late night television," she said while he continued to snicker. "Damn it! This is my favorite jacket. Celia and I bought the last two from that little place off Bleeker. Now hers is like new and this—it's totally ruined. Look! Gluey demon goop's all over. And that stuff never comes out. Mamma B will throw a fit!" Close to tears, she wiggled out of it, careful to avoid the acidic, foul-smelling liquid.

"Well, I told you to hang back until I could kill the two on the end." He clicked his tongue. "But noooo... not my Guardian. You go full-steam ahead all by your lonesome. Serves you right, darlin'. Now apologize for running faster than me," he chided with a superior tone, leaning against a tree, and carefully flicking specks of green goop off both shoulders. The foul liquid clung to her knotted long hair as well. But he wasn't able to tell her without collapsing in another fit of laughter. "I told you these are a nasty species, but you don't listen." The dripping jacket sailed through the air with speed and landed on his face. Then she kicked both feet out from under him, eliciting a wince and a whiny "Owww."

"But you've got to admit—I have a really good arm," his Guardian replied, besting him. As if allergic, the demon ooze burned his pale skin like pin-points of *sunlight. Red welts bloomed on his smooth complexion. In a puddle of mud he sat, trying to scrape it off fast.*

Her pretty hazel eyes flashed wider. "What can I say? Twenty-year-old journalism major takes on three-hundred-year-old conceited vampire and wins." She brushed her hands together and strutted away saying, "Yep, it works for me."

Michael had a wide grin on his face, lost in the memory, when he heard movement.

"You're beginning to heal," the researcher stated as he walked into the kitchen with a freshly filled bag of blood.

He let out a low growl and kept his gaze averted, although curious at the strong citrus smell wafting his way.

"Can you wheel yourself into the sunroom, please?"

The cool, clipped request made him seethe. "Why? Do I get to watch and drool as you bleed each person, like in one of those macabre creature features, all for my benefit? I'm pissed off."

"I'm going to ignore your arrogant tone," the man dryly replied. "Donating blood can cause even an old pro like me to feel woozy. Imagine how nauseous a growing boy can feel, especially if he hasn't eaten in hours. I thought you might reciprocate the kindness and be there for him…just this once."

He spun the chair around. His skill with it suddenly uncanny, getting to his son's side quickly. Miles handed Lukas the orange juice. An odd shade of pale, his son sat on Celia's bed draining the glass. Brushing his sweaty curls aside, Alana wore a concerned expression. But Michael glared at her full-force and irritated.

"Wow, it's a good thing I'm between the two of you.

Talk about if looks could kill. Hey, earth to Dad," his son said. And to his surprise, he felt tapping on his shoulder. "Like I mean, I wanted to do it—'cause it'll help."

"You should have asked me," he said with sternness, and turning to Alana, he added in the same tone, "*You* should have told me."

The silent simmer grew thicker until they both turned to Celia. Her phone trumpeted the theme from *Indiana Jones* as she ran from the room. Plus, he knew the gentle psychic never liked to be around anything that resembled tension.

As Alana guided his son to his feet, she said in a sweet way, "How about I get you to your own bed? *Zia's* bringing dinner soon. That'll make you feel a whole lot better, I'm sure." She kept a strong arm around his son. Michael watched them leave together. The two most important people in all his very long existence on this earth.

****

Michael was able to slowly roll himself into the living room. He stared at the heavy drapes again, wondering why, even though it was well after sunset, no one seemed to want them open.

"I'd leave them that way, if I were you," Celia said in an odd tone he'd never heard before. Her teeth were clenched tight, and her hands were on her hips. She gave him a very uncharacteristic glare, which he studied along with her aggressive stance and unusual tone. In the next second, fully unexpected, the petite woman took a few steps toward him and slapped his face.

Shocked, he raised a shaky hand to an already bruised cheek. "I felt that!"

"How could you do it to Thorn?" she shouted, tears

dripping from her green eyes.

"Let me guess, it was Martine who called, the little tattletale."

"No, worse, you mean son of a bitch! It was Mary, her mom. *All three* Kendrick witches know what you did to him, Michael. I've been worried out of my mind for days!"

He sighed. The look Celia wore made him feel very, very guilty—for the moment. But the Kendricks adored the empath. He had hoped Thorn would go to them. At least one part of the plan worked like a charm.

"Hello—I'm talking to you, Mister I-don't-care-*who*-I-hurt-or-*how*-I-hurt-them! You *drugged* Thorn. You deliberately wounded a Servant of Souls. You yelled at him, embarrassed him, and sent him away!"

Celia positively shook with anger, and he shot her a furious look. "I didn't want him anywhere near me! The sorcerers would have destroyed him."

"He's been so devastated by what *you* did to him, that he… he hasn't eaten in days! Thorn's a loyal soul, Michael, a really sweet creature. What you did is a-a sin. He's been worried sick about you! There had to be another way."

But his expression stayed stone-cold. "You're wrong, Celia," he replied in a low rumble. "*They* would have read his empathic mind scrambling his brains in the process. I did what I had to do. I kept him off Clayton's radar. The demon wannabe would've killed Thorn and would've had a smile on his face while he twisted the knife in his ample belly. It was a decision I had to make—a hard decision. You know the kind, right?"

Celia stared at him. He knew about her secret visits to the brownstone, spending hours with the empath. Yes.

She kept him ever aware of Alana and where her mission led her. Had Celia sensed trouble for *his* Guardian, Celia would alert Thorn in a heartbeat.

But there was something else. The way Celia had looked at Miles when he mentioned NWT's brightest rising star. Only obnoxious Clayton stood between him and the sorcerers in their secret society of evil-doers. He hated the little weasel. He looked from father to daughter. Then his gaze slid to the drapes.

"What are the two of you *not* telling me? Why are we *not* letting the cool, fresh night air blow gently through the fucking tension in this room?" His gaze came to rest on Miles. "Give it up and give it to me straight."

Celia blurted out, "I'm so disgusted with how you treated Thorn—and now Clayton Mails is *MIA*! Wanna guess who's coming to end this little smackdown?"

Over on the leather sofa, Miles folded his hands in his lap. "Now do you understand the importance of our "macabre creature feature" as you most arrogantly put it?" The dry tone cut like a knife. "It should have dawned on me when Lukas told us he saw the ex-Guardian's bodies. He did not see a third, which means Clayton is alive. You exposed the liaison for the incompetent fool he is. This "treason" happened on his watch, Michael. He will want to minimize the damage to his ego. That we thwarted his plan to capture you? It appears to have bloodied his nose."

No. Oh dear God. No-no-no... "I've signed your death warrants. I'm so sorry," he whispered, unable to look at anyone in the room.

Alana came to his side. "Nobody's going to die. Not while I'm around." Her hazel eyes sparked with grit and purpose. "Your strength is in our blood. We'll step up the feeding schedule. We'll be ready for the little devil. You'll be ready—and I'll be standing right beside you, my love."

Michael turned inside himself. *No, there's no way in Hell I'll allow you to be anywhere near the devious man when he comes for me.* Fury gripped his unbeating heart.

Chapter 21

More Change

Michael sat quiet, stunned by the revelation and lost in the defeat of his current physical state. When the healer came to the table with an aromatic Italian feast, he studied her, now more interested in her familiar appearance, which shocked him once more. *Short and robust. Her eyes a shade of gray smoke, no doubt a mystical attribute, her silvery hair pulled back in a bun at the nape of her neck. She more than resembles Helena.* He was absolutely speechless and remained so throughout the meal listening to sporadic yet typical family table-talk.

Everyone appeared tired with a dose of tension to boot. Alana had served him a second bowl of the extraordinary soup, which he was grateful for. Each spasm and pang lessened while more sensation returned to his beaten and bruised limbs. Rosa sat beside his son, who had arrived ashen and visibly shaky for family dinner. Now he had healthy color.

"You can really cook," his son announced after devouring a second helping with Rosa's grand-motherly encouragement.

"This was delicious, *Zia*," Alana added as she rose from the table to pile the plates. He felt a sense of pride when Lukas suddenly sprang to his feet with an offer to help. He easily heard Alana preparing coffee in the kitchen, also aware of Lukas loading the dishwasher with some guidance. The distance was inconsequential, his astute hearing had returned.

"You look restless," she was saying to his son.

"Why are the shutters locked?"

"It's better this way. Safer. If you could go outside, what would you be doing after dinner?"

"I don't know. Probably shooting hoops with my friends who don't exist anymore."

The comment saddened him. His son was changed forever, in so many ways. "And what about doing homework," she was asking.

"Stuff comes easy for me. I was, like, on the Honor Roll this whole freshman year. Teachers always call on me. I think they like me. Can I go watch some movies in the den?"

He heard Alana's soft laugh. "Sure. If you can figure out the system, Celia has some video games."

"Cool. How do I, uh, turn this thing on?"

Michael heard the dishwasher start to cycle. His son came back in with a small smile on his face. They made eye contact. He gave a thin grin and a nod. Full of pride he watched his son walk down the hall to the den.

****

Coffee had been served and obviously enjoyed by all. Michael did not partake, although his one human pleasure of a strong, fragrant cup of black coffee remained a constant temptation. The mood around the dining room table changed without his son present. And tension bloomed.

"I've contacted Giovanni about an emergency meeting with members of the Sovereign Council," Rosa began softly. "He agrees. It is best to share all your information with them, Miles. I'm certain they will offer assistance." She folded her napkin carefully, laid it next to the saucer. Even her mannerisms reminded him of Helena. He looked up to see the healer focus on him as if they were the only two at the table. "Many council members believe this is to be my final existence on this good earth, but I'm not yet ready to take such a momentous journey."

It was uncanny, having more than one individual who could hijack his thoughts so quickly—without any effort. He felt the deepest gratitude for her abilities, which had initiated the healing in his seriously wounded body. Her expression exuded gentle warmth with the reply, "Ah, *prego, prego, campione.* I strongly suggest Miles takes your son on a short trip to Pisa tomorrow, Alana and Celia will accompany them. The child needs to be out and about during daylight while it's safe. There are many shops he might enjoy… and some of the finest stores in Italy. Casual clothes and a sturdy pair of boots for you, *Signore,* would be a wise investment at this time."

Careful and full of respect, he softly offered, "I don't think I'm ready to rumble yet."

As if she could probe his very guilty soul, she answered, "Love is a powerful healer, *Signore.* Savor it. Let it prepare you."

Locked to her gaze, Michael acquiesced with a slow nod, because if he could stand and bow to her, he certainly would. *Her strength is pure goodness. Just like Helena's…*

"Miles, l will call you with a meeting time. Once the Georgians decide how to proceed, we must do so very quickly." Conversation came to an end and Rosa stood, kissing Alana's cheek with the whisper, "Love heals, *cara*, and passion often accomplishes the impossible."

Of course, he heard every word. But instead of going to the apartment door, the healer slipped into Alana's kitchen. The refrigerator door opened for a brief second and then closed.

Of course, he heard her every word as she whispered a blessing. The connection came as if it were specifically telegraphed to his brain. Donations given by Miles, Celia; given by his son and the woman he would always love. *Blessed blood?*

****

Mary Kendrick pulled up to the International Departure Terminal at Newark Airport in New Jersey. Thorn had barely spoken during the drive in such heavy traffic. Her silent passenger got out of the rental SUV like a timid snail, lifted a travel bag out of the trunk.

"Okay, let's go through the list one more time." Her voice was full of worry. "Passport, driver's license, birth certificate, cash… All here?" He gave slow nods of confirmation producing each item except the wad of Euros. Her connections as an art gallery owner had its perks. The forged documents were exquisite. "Great job—let's hear the story."

"I'm Theo Thornwell, a thirty-five-year-old social studies teacher from Jersey who is going to the Amalfi Coast to study its architecture. I live with my mother and sister. I like soft music and shopping for antique books, but I can't afford to buy any of them on my salary even though I'm tenured, and whatever I do, don't read the people sitting next to me on the plane *or* talk about what I sense about them," he said with a gentle smile.

"And?"

He rolled his eyes on purpose as she brushed a lock of his curly red hair out of the way. "And I've been saving for this trip all year. Always wanted to fly first class… It's not *only* because I need more room."

"Hmm… I don't know how believable that *last* part is any more." Mary gave a nervous smile. He could no longer be considered *extra*-extra-large—losing at least ten pounds a day. She assumed concern for Michael lessened his enormous appetite.

Thorn had kept to himself in the basement bedroom, going up to the kitchen, but only for pitchers of spring water. In addition, the extra weight he retained had sculpted into healthy muscle. He was still quite large but gone were the double chin and flabby paunch. Most humans would kill for such a mystical ability. He decided to fly casual. And some travelers preferred comfortable, *really* loose clothing for long flights, although his T-shirt and elastic waist, bargain basement shorts had seen better days.

Reading the good witch's mind, he hugged her. "Don't worry, Mare. I promise to dress better when I go to Michael. I'll be fine. I know what I have to do. Thank you from the bottom of my heart, for everything the three of you have done."

Mary hugged him again, tighter than he expected. "Take care of yourself, Thorn. Remember, we're only a thought away. Stay close to Celia. She loves you; you know."

Keeping his gait lumbering and slow, he entered the terminal's sliding door. Helena wouldn't expect any less than a perfect performance. He had spent years with Michael, as per her orders. He'd fix things and the

Champion would be back on track.

Arriving at the boarding gate, he threw the thick glasses he'd always worn into the trash bin; his vision 20/20 or better. Another twelve hours and he'd be ready—mentally *and* physically.

****

It was after eleven. Celia checked all the windows, which were locked tight, while Alana prepared Michael's sustenance. Miles required Lukas's aid in getting him settled in bed. Although it appeared the vampire's legs were still unusable, he was able to steady himself with shaky arms and looser hands. He noted the new range of motion as well as less winces of pain. But healing wasn't happening fast enough. Not fast enough at all, he thought.

Miles waited until Lukas parked the wheelchair out of the way and left the bedroom to whisper low in Michael's ear, "Drink it all, and don't give my daughter any problems. Because more than just *your* life depends on it now."

But no reaction came to good advice, his arrogance in the way once again.

The living room was empty, so he met Alana in the kitchen. Worry came off her when she gave a small smile. A glass carafe was quite full. "I blended together all of our blood types, got the chill out of it in the microwave." She kissed his cheek with a soft "good night."

"I'll close the bedroom door behind you," he offered, to which she replied, "Thanks." He walked with her, carafe and crystal mug in her hands, across the quiet living room. After she entered her bedroom, he closed the door like he said he would.

Another long, hard day was behind them. It had been one of many changes.

But change wasn't enough. They needed help.

****

Michael pushed himself up to a better sitting position and watched Alana place two items on the nightstand—a glass carafe and a crystal mug. "Please," he asked, pointing to the heavy drapes, "Open them. I want to see the night sky."

Without hesitation, she crossed the room, lifted the two windows to unlock the outer wood shutters and push them to the bricks. Without a word, she went into her private bathroom. Seconds later, he heard the shower.

Awaiting her return, he focused on the bright moonlight, the clear night sky. Stars lit the darkness like flickering candles. The air was salty and warm, the breeze a graceful one. He breathed in and out wondering how close danger was to these good people this beautiful night.

The sound of running water stopped, and when she came into the bedroom, she wore a sleeveless white nightgown. It didn't resemble sexy, but looked functional, comfortable. Her long brown hair scented with lavender and jasmine glistened in its dampness. He couldn't take his eyes off her. She poured the scarlet liquid into the crystal mug; placed it firmly in his right hand. "Drink," she simply said.

"Alana—" he protested, knowing whose blood was offered.

"I don't want to hear it. Drink, I said." She tapped the mug, and then went back into the bathroom. The whir of her hair dryer faded away as he breathed in the mixture.

Like ambrosia and richly fragrant, his thirst heightened allowing the vampiric need to be in charge. He finished the unique blend of blood types quickly. It was warm. Went down easy, coursing through his veins. His body begged for more.

Alana was at his side, taking the mug from his hand, refilling it. His gaze slid to her as he drank. She brought the carafe to the mug for the refill. This time, he reached for it, trying to control his dependence on the heady elixir. A low growl began.. He drank deeply, the power of the blended blood a pure shot of adrenaline. He couldn't speak.

She filled it again, and then with the final mugful, holding the crystal mug tight, insatiable need hammered inside him. He drained it in his greed. He licked the tiny droplets on his lips letting them swirl over his tongue. He eased his head back and closed his eyes.

Keen vision along with all other senses heightened beyond his recall. Prickly points of pain tingled down his injured leg and then stopped as the throbbing wound through his thigh reduced to a dull ache. She was closer now, sitting on the bed's edge and taking the mug from his hand. Her scent was hypnotizing, and he opened his eyes to take in her beauty.

"Your bruises are fading. The dark-purple around your eyes is barely noticeable." Her stunning hazel eyes opened wider. "And your skin… it's not chalky white. My God, it's as if the waves in your hair are shimmering in the moonlight." She placed the mug on the nightstand and next to the empty carafe. But she looked hesitant, worried, when she faced him again.

"My Guardian. My love," he whispered, taking her wrist to pull her close to him. He kissed her palm, her scent echoing through his senses like never before.

"I...I hope I did the right thing. What if our blood awakens—" His answer was to place her lovely hand on his opposite shoulder, which brought her to his chest. Their lips were a mere inch apart. "We shouldn't do this," she whispered.

"I ache for you, my Guardian, body and soul," he answered, closing the gap between their lips. He kissed her deeply, and she responded as he hoped she would. His arm closed around her waist guiding her and settling her where he wanted her. Her breath hitched, as he nudged the night gown higher. His fingers ran up and down her thighs, and when this most alluring woman moaned, his need to love her grew stronger.

Emotions collided in his brain like fireworks against a darkened sky. "We'll take it slow," he whispered, knowing she would respond to his sensual tone. He'd show her his devotion, his eternal love, positive the beast-within was buried, perhaps never to be seen again.

He tugged at her nightgown. She sat up and straddled him. He pulled it up and over her head revealing a true vision of loveliness. Her full breasts, her soft as satin skin glowing in the moonlight. Her hands rubbed down his chest, unbuttoning the black silk pajama top. When she came off him, he thought to pull her back at once, then realizing why she'd left him. The bed covers slid down his legs. She flung her nightgown off the bed, and lay beside him kissing his chest, inching her hand lower to tug his pajama bottoms lower, lower until he managed to get them off his good leg and she peeled them off his wounded one.

Skin touched skin and he scented her arousal. His was already visible. He pulled her over his body, and she gasped. One hand cupped her left breast. The other sought the edge of her warmth. Her legs eased open, her back arched as he touched her, easing his fingers to the center of her core. He sucked at a swollen nipple, pleasuring her until she wriggled, capturing her gasp with a heated kiss, plunging his fingers in and out, building a rhythm of passion.

Her hands ran through his hair, then eased down, circling across his abdomen until she touched him. He groaned and their lips unlocked. Her gaze slid down, watching his response as her hand slid up and down the length of his erection. Her body radiated heat as her legs opened wider. It made him groan again, the moisture preparing her, inviting him. Gently guiding her hand off him, he slid his body lower down the bed kissing her flushed skin until he was where he wanted to be. When his hair brushed her thigh, she let out a small cry. His tongue traced her core and she gasped as he maneuvered her flat on the bed, all the while tasting her. One hand pressed her belly, holding her where he wanted her. She wriggled, then pushed against him, quivering against the pressure of his tongue as she orgasmed.

Her breath came hard and fast, and he guided himself up her body until the tip of his erection pressed against her coated core. Her legs locked across his back and with full control he entered her. Slow and careful he teased his way inside.

The rush. The sensations around his erection forced a long, low groan. Their bodies fell into the rhythm of love. Their lips locked in passionate kisses as they rode wave upon wave of erotic bliss. The bond of body and soul was undeniable. As if ordained by the stars they climaxed together.

And when he pulled out, she stayed tight to his chest. They talked. Opening up to each other as never before. At times, she became playful, temping him like a siren, sensually alluring. But one truth held. She had remained his. His alone.

Reality was so much better than any dream.

She loved him. There wasn't any doubt. Every erotic fantasy of being with her commanding lover paled in comparison to the reality of loving him, making love with him. It had been over seven years since she touched him. The feverish longing that she always kept hidden surfaced the day he was brought back to her beaten and broken.

Nights ago, alone with him for the first time, her body had responded immediately. Something she couldn't have stopped if she tried. Something primal and freeing.

Helplessly watching him scream in pain, seeing his brutal wounds, not knowing the effect of him drinking their blended blood—what was it her aunt had whispered, *"Love heals, cara, and passion often accomplishes impossible."*

Yes. Love was powerful enough to break through the wall she had built around her heart all those years ago. Love was truly powerful enough to heal.

Chapter 22

Evil and Good

New World Technologies' Italian office in Rome buzzed with frantic activity. Not only had the devious vampire taken out the Manhattan headquarters, but his surprising actions also devastated demonic activity throughout the entire United States and Canada. Days ago, Manhattan had been the satanic hub on North America. But now? Every portal there was closed.

In addition, minion companies, created and financed by NWT, met their demise at unprecedented speed. Humans who had signed the Oath of Allegiance in the North American Continent turned up dead at rapid rates—as if a sinister plague had plundered it with a vengeance. The suicide rate rose along with freak accidents among employees. Demons that used NWT to protect their earthly contracts scurried out of our dimension quicker than rats from a flooding sewer tunnel—using portals in Europe and Asia.

Michael Malone's well-planned attack had done such enormous damage to the balance of "Evil and Good" that day-to-day operations in Rome had to be suspended in order to devise a clever counter-attack. Guardians of Souls, in every part of the world, now raided demon hiding places day and night.

Dimensional portals outside of North America

opened without their sorcerers' mystical chants, swallowing massive numbers of antagonists who preyed on innocents. The glitch was that now they only opened one way. A demon could leave this world, but it couldn't return. North America was being purged, and the other continental offices wondered which one of them would be next.

Valetta Russo, earthly liaison to the European Triumvirate of Evil in Rome, was swamped with faxes, e-mails, and threatening blood-written pleas from clientele since the battle in the passageway. She would rendezvous with her American counterpart at a villa in Portofino tonight. He'd be a major player in putting the wayward vampire to rest—for good. But to Valetta, Clayton Mails resembled the worm dangling on the fishing pole. She'd be the one reeling him in, already swallowed by the big fish.

In the end, Michael Malone's ashes would be sealed in a cement vault until the end of time—along with that stupid ex-Guardian's decaying body. Alana Ciminio would die painfully while the groveling creature watched. Valetta let out a sinister snicker, thinking of the vampire's child. The fallen champion would witness his boy-child being dissected alive before she even started on his whore.

She smiled, clicking her tongue. How could such mayhem be caused by one deceitful idiot, and a vampire, no less? *I don't care if they say he's mystically enhanced, he's on my turf now, in the arms of his filthy ex-Guardian. Clayton's beastly back-up plan has worked.* "The champion is useless, nothing but a neutered creature," she hissed, "Love will do that to you. What a fool he is!"

The Italian Office was much better prepared for Michael Malone than the one in Manhattan. It had to be. Italy had the Vatican, over-flowing with countless saintly mortals. Seeds of goodness ran deep in this country. Then there was the mystical Order of St. George the Protector, with their obnoxiously sanctimonious Sovereign Council of the Georgian Circle.

They'll shield him, but only until realizing he's no longer useful. He won't be able to serve them when the beast-within resurfaces with a sinister bloodlust. After all, they're only human. Humans are expendable. Evil is immortal.

When she and Clayton were finished with Michael, that vampire would beg for the stake.

****

Sophia Vecchio had worked for Rossini's Cleaning Service in Portofino for over fifty years. In the 1960s, no one else would hire a disfigured girl of twenty who could no longer hear or speak. After surviving a fire, which took the life of her mother, the silent soon-to-be bride spent months recuperating with the Sisters of Saint Francis in Siena. Scarring made her once exquisite face hideous.

Her distraught father released his daughter's fiancé from the obligation to marry Sophia, and then paid Rossini a hefty bribe to employ her. Insisting she was meticulous when it came to dirt and grime, her eyesight made up for other senses lost in the accident.

Angelo Rossini, a cruel and ruthless man, put Sophia to work cleaning private villas in the hills of Portofino; specifically those owned by his more murderous clients.

She labored six nights a week, arriving after dark in

order to never expose any tourists to her disfigured features. Sophia's speechlessness and exceptional cleaning skills allowed her into those sacrosanct places where other employees were denied access. Angelo received generous bonuses from his villainous clients, but Sophia took home pitiful wages, and she never complained.

The driver dropped her off at the unfamiliar location hours after sunset. This rarely used villa belonged to an international company called NWT. Far up the mountain and tucked away at the end of a private road, it was protected by sinister dark magic. Giuseppe Scotto punched in the mysterious code, indicated to Sophia that he'd be back at dawn, and left as fast as the old car could get him away from this particular domicile.

Sophia entered the villa, sensing death written all over it. She toiled through the long night, memorizing every inch of the villa. There were three bedrooms upstairs. Each had its own bathroom. The main floor had a black marble foyer, a dining room, a living room, plus a huge kitchen that had a servant's quarter attached. Many rooms. Many windows—all shiny and clean.

She took an armful of rags to the basement and put them in the washer. Two more rooms needed attention, a wine cellar and a stone storage room. Sophia swept both earthen floors, pulled away spiders and cobwebs with a chewed broomstick found wedged between the wall and the staircase.

By dawn, she was finished. Giuseppe found her waiting outside, and he drove her to San Giorgio's for morning Mass, which was always a part of her daily routine.

Sophia took her spot in the last pew, body aching

and tired from the night's unrelenting work. This was a private purgatory for secretly setting the deadly blaze in her home so many, many years ago. But half a century of pain, penance, and punishment would be over soon enough. This peaceful church and the gentle sisters in Siena had been her salvation throughout her years of self-imposed suffering. Today, she took Communion. Something she had not done in decades. Sophia looked into Father Giovanni's eyes, letting him know she was ready to face her destiny. The old priest understood how truly invaluable she was. As morning worshippers left the church, Sophia, along with ten others, followed the holy man to a room underneath the altar.

The Georgian Sovereign Council was complete.

Steeped in devout religious beliefs and shrouded in secrecy, twelve members took their places. Each of them recited ancient prayers, specific to their individual missions in life. The thirteenth chair, placed under a wooden crucifix, remained empty—a reminder of St. George, the Patron Saint of Protection.

Father Giovanni began. "We come together to discuss a unique event—one set into motion by a creature we have known about for three centuries. Monks from the San Marco Abbey wrote *Leggende di San Giorgio* in the Sixteenth Century. Within the tome is mention of a dream the dragon-slayer had close to the end of his life. In it, *San Giorgio* speaks of "one who is not like us yet like unto us". The saint tells us this penitent warrior will take down a great beast whose evil has spread like gnarled roots of a giant tree across many nations."

All Council members knew the passage. It had been committed to memory many years ago, when they each took a place in this sacred organization.

"The Georgians have considered this to be about countries who bring our world to the brink of extinction. Theologians believe the dragon represents the Devil himself. Our researchers know those who assist Satan have called forth inhuman, soulless creatures to do his bidding. The creature who *Signora* Bellini tells us of today is in an inimitable position. Can he be the one who will slay our dragon? Is St. George's renowned dream, in reality, a premonition? Do we give him our assistance? My loyal Brothers and Sisters, I open the floor to discussion."

One by one, Council members added his or her knowledge, interpretation, and opinion. Rosa sat quietly listening to the lively discussion, to all pros and cons, and then described the events of the past days. She answered many questions. When Sophia Vecchio sent her thoughts to another, who verbalized her new critical information, the assembly voted unanimously to see Miles, Alana, and Celia later this evening.

Chapter 23

New Arrival

Alana's eyes flew open, her senses snapping awake and alert in Guardian-mode. With a quick turn, she examined Michael's face, which showed nothing. He was propped up on one arm simply staring at her. His mouth quirked to the side and a signature thin grin began.

But apprehension had her in its grip. "Michael?"

"Yes, darlin'," he answered softly, but she needed more.

"Are you okay? Are you—"

He tugged her body to his with a firm grip and planted a gentle kiss on her lips. "Were you not expecting it to be me?"

"No, but—" she blew out a long breath. Yes. She most certainly had been holding her breath. Pulling herself off his chest, she sat back on her heels and studied the bruised but handsome face of her soul mate, the love of her life. Last night was heavenly. He'd been a generous, skilled lover who still had her numb with pleasure.

"Go ahead. Ask the question, darlin'."

"The beast within you?"

"If it's still there it's buried pretty deep. Look." He opened his mouth for her to inspect his canines.

"They seem a little long," she said in a curious way.

"But they aren't *long* fangs, and no tiger-eyes. But there is this feeling…of loving you, needing you, and wanting you—always."

A blush crept up her cheeks. "And how do you feel, I mean… You know, physically?" His right eyebrow arched as his dark eyes sank to her breasts. "I don't mean *that* kind of physical… You know what I mean," she added trying to ignore the need kindling inside her as well. But there was much to be done today.

The smile he gave had her close to rethinking the day. "I'm weak, but I'm better. I'd like to shower. Of course, if you'd rather—"

"Can you stand by yourself?' she asked, because the sensual tone in his voice made her heart race. She wrapped the sheet around herself and stood. He swung his tall frame to the side and his feet hit the floor. When he didn't move, she offered a hand.

"Darlin', I've been on my back for days, and I'm considerably heavier than you."

"I can handle it," she replied, pulling him up, helping him stand. Together they took the few steps to the Queen Anne chair, and she held on, letting him sink down slow. He groaned, winced as if in pain. She sat on the bed, across from him. "How do you feel?"

"Like I just ran the New York City Marathon." He let out a sharp hiss, locking his elbows to his knees and dropping his head into his hands.

"What do you say to a shower. Together," she added. "I can help you get there. Then I might even, say, wash your back. Only if you say please," she teased.

A very broad smile appeared—a sight rarely seen. Totally unexpected and simply drop-dead incredible. "Now that, darlin', sounds like something I couldn't say no to."

****

Dressed in a fresh pair of black silk pajamas, Michael leaned heavily on Alana, limping haltingly into the dining room. Lukas smiled at him but didn't say anything, his mouth full of cereal crunching away. Miles pulled a chair out at the head of the table, and he held tight to Alana's arms to sit. Facing the draped windows, he thought, just great…another reminder of what is sure to come and me not able to protect or defend.

Then he studied Celia's tight expression as she sat at his right side and poured him a cup of coffee. There'd be time later today to speak privately with her. He was certain she'd forgive him and all would be well. After clearing his throat, he said in the humblest tone he owned, "I want to thank you all. I appreciate this— every incredible thing you've all done for me, for my son, and—"

The petite psychic suddenly jumped to her feet and rushed to the door, no doubt, interrupting the knocker. Prepared to continue his apology when she returned, he took a deep draw of his coffee, and then placed the mug back on the table. His grip was unsteady, and his leg hurt like hell, but he reveled in the sight of Lukas and Alana sitting next to each other on his left. Then powerful hands gripped his shoulders, and he landed heavily on the floor, struggling against new, blinding pain. He watched his son rush the huge man, only to meet a similar fate.

"Good, two birds… one stone, so to speak." Thorn stared at Michael first.

"I ought to punch your lights out, Malone. Do you see how annoyed you've made me?"

Then he stared at Lukas. "And you, kid. You might be pretty strong for a human, but I'll have you down for the count before daddy can stop me." He crossed his muscular arms across his toned chest and stared again at the object of his annoyance. "You put one nasty whammy on me, Michael," he said, shaking a thick finger at the stunned vampire. "Abusing my sacred trust has cut me to the core. That wasn't very nice."

He reached for Lukas first, felt the boy cringe when his hands wrapped around his skinny mid-section to put him firmly back in the chair. Michael sat up, inched back, but Thorn pulled the arrogant vampire to his feet, and then slammed him down in his chair as well, ignoring multiple grunts of pain.

After brushing his palms together, Thorn straightened his new and expensive designer golf shirt that went with his designer joggers. "Well, now that *that's* taken care of—" He extended a hand to Miles, who shook it immediately. "Hello, Mister B. Thorn here and at your service," he announced with confidence. "Ah, beautiful Alana, my charming Celia, good to see you both again." He gave Alana a warm smile, but a loving gaze lingered on Celia.

Taking the only empty chair at the table, he pulled Michael's mug away from him. Celia refilled it with fresh coffee, and he added three heaping teaspoons of sugar. "Until you're back in action, no caffeine for you, my wayward friend," he ordered, chugging the fragrant liquid down and then settling back in the chair.

A speechless, not to mention insulted Michael studied him with narrow, blazing eyes. And Lukas? The kid didn't move.

There was not even a hint of the sweet, somewhat

shy Servant of Souls. In his place? A much thinner, well-coordinated muscle machine. He purposely kept a fierceness looming in his eyes. But if you looked close enough, that old gentleness remained one and the same.

Alana cleared her throat. "You've, um, changed, Thorn, I… I mean your curly auburn hair is so… so … short and straight?"

He flashed her a winning grin. "I know, right? You'd think I look more like a wrestling coach in the prime of his career instead of a mystical being. Ah, the many facets of an empath demon. It's just awesome, isn't it? It took me a while to zero in on your need," he added in a tender way, but then shot Michael a punitive glare. "Seems someone's gotten himself into a pickle, didn't he?" He let that sink in and looked at Alana. "I thought you could use some help with tall, dark, and oh-I'm-so-achy here. My instincts say he still has a l-o-o-o-ng way to go, and no offense, but everyone at this table? Well…you're all a little wimpy when it comes to the hands-on, tough love he needs at the moment. Besides, he's been my sole responsibility in this world. He is my mission. It was someone greater than all of us put together who sent me—To keep him in line, that is. And for your information, boss, you *can't* fire me!"

The look of pure rage on Michael's face was priceless. Like his son, his arms were locked to his chest with an infuriated scowl.

"I'll whip him into shape, Miles. Let the Georgian Council know I'm here when you meet at the church tonight. Well, you all do what you have to do today." Ever respectful, he stopped Alana before she could speak. "I'll babysit him for you, dear Guardian, and I'll get him jump-started with a little, well, let's call it physical therapy." He eyed a pouting Lukas, saying with authority, "There's a travel bag in the hallway. Bring it in, kid."

The skinny teen sneered and ignored him. Thorn held the stern glare, his bushy brows almost touching. "Do what you're told, not what you're thinking. Daddy has no say in this matter. You've been getting away with a hell of a lot. I'd lose the attitude because now we all have to dig down deep and do the right thing for him. Believe me, kid, it's necessary. So, tuck away the bratty temper and do what I say—now!"

Close to rage, Lukas slammed his hands on the table and shoved against it to stand. He stomped out the door and brought in the heavy black bag—drop-kicked it with enough force to crash against Thorn's leg. With a slow shake of his head, Thorn leaned into Michael. "He'll learn, and so will you."

All further conversation ceased as Celia fixed his second cup of coffee, which he gulped down. When he finally stood, ready to begin the most critical part of his mystical mission, he read Alana's conflict like an open book. But she wouldn't protest or question him. Her instincts told her he was right. In fact, she could consider him a Godsend because emotion wouldn't get in his way.

As Alana left the table to prepare Michael's much-needed sustenance, the phone rang, and Miles left the table to answer it. Thorn sensed the researcher's curiosity upon his return. "The meeting's set for seven this evening at San Giorgio's." Thorn nodded as Celia cleared the table. "Lukas will be with us today," Miles said. "We will leave the two of you alone for a while."

Everyone saw the wild look in Lukas's eyes and the scowl as his face reddened. Alana quickly said to the kid,

"Pisa has lots of stores. We can get you some things you need… and a new video game."

"It'll be like a-a fieldtrip, because no one here has seen the leaning tower," Celia added, already in the boy's head calming him down. It was working.

Alana nodded. "Shopping, then a late lunch across the street from *Campo del Miracoli.* And since I don't have to be here, I'll keep you safe, in the event of any, you know…uh, any interference." She stood up, gave Thorn's massive shoulder a hearty pat before scooping up her car keys off the secretary in the living room. He grinned, aware of Miles's expression as he followed her. "Not to worry. I'm a good driver, Daddy B."

But Miles took the keys from her hand. "I'd rather get to Pisa in one piece, honey," he said in a kind tone. "I'm aware you passed the Italian road-test on your first attempt—after failing four times in Manhattan. Suppose you give directions and I drive this time?" Then the researcher paused just as Thorn knew he would. "Let's make a list of things you and your father will need. In the den, please," he said to Lukas.

The boy glared at Thorn, rolled his eyes, but followed Miles into the den. Alana placed a full carafe of sustenance in front of Michael, along with the crystal mug and then went with Celia into the sunroom, leaving them alone at the table.

The fury coming his way was significant, but Thorn stood and began to move the living room furniture around. It created an open space. The leather sofa and armchairs lined the walls, and he put the coffee table and lamps in the marble foyer. He left the thick Persian carpet on the floor. Afterwards, he sat next to Michael at the dining room table.

Michael drank the sustenance slowly with a simmering scowl on his face. But no bother. Thorn preferred to ignore the stubborn creature at the table— only until everyone left the apartment.

****

They were alone after saying all the 'be safe out theres' and 'good-byes'. Then the empath wrapped a hand around Michael's forearm. Michael growled, low and deadly, refusing to look at him, refusing to budge. He immediately tried to pry his arm loose, but it wasn't going to happen.

"Where'd this new persona come from? Don't tell me you've been a wolf in sheep's clothing all these years." Sarcasm dripped from every word. "Why did you come here, Thorn? I remember telling you we were finished."

"Yeah. No. Aren't you the narcissistic prince lording over no one, sitting at the head of an empty table in a spiffy pair of black silk PJ's—with killer good looks, I might add. It's a new day, Michael. You can thank me later," he added in a less than friendly tone. A pitiful growl came at him. "Now, now, don't get into a snit. You changed the mission, not me."

"Get your paw off me."

The pull-away was equally pitiful, and his grip tightened. "Is that the best you can do, Champ? Where's the scary Dracula mouth with those long fangs? Where's the yellow cat eyes? Where's the vim and verve?" he goaded; continued without sympathy. "All I see is one helluva cowardly lion. Wake up, Michael, we're not somewhere over the rainbow and this isn't Oz. But guess what, my pretty, I'm your wizard." Now it begins, he thought, standing and pulling the chair back to hoist the arrogant vampire over one cinder block of a shoulder.

"Put me down, you crazy son of a bitch or I swear I'll kill you with my bare hands!"

"Yeah, with the floor too many feet below your head. Look. Here's the thing.

I gave you *every* option to cooperate and do this nicely, but once again, here you are—going about things all wrong. And the language," Thorn added with a brisk smack to Michael's ass, "*that* needs correcting, too."

"That hurt, you bastard! What the fuck do you think you're doing, you crazy—"

"Use another nasty word and I'll do it again. Just accept it. You're no match for me." Thorn carried him and his gym bag into the master bedroom. He dropped Michael on the bed ignoring the muttered curses while searching the duffle bag, A pair of black sweats and a white cotton sleeveless undershirt landed on Michael's chest. "Put these on and then get your ass out there. You've got exactly three minutes—and that's demon time." At the doorway, he turned with the threat, "Trust me. You don't want to make me come back for you."

"No fucking way am I taking orders from you! What the hell… Is this another nightmare?"

An amused grin began as he studied the injured creature, who stared at the new clothes with murder on his bruised face. "I've never had to threaten you before. But after what you did back in Manhattan, maybe I should have." Allowing his softer nature to surface he added, "I'll not tolerate childish tantrums from you, my friend. There's very little time left. I'm prepared to do whatever I have to do—to get you ready."

****

Ten minutes later, Michael leaned dramatically on

the frame of the bedroom door. Trying to get into the clothes and walk across the room—without assistance—proved just how weak he really was. So, he chose the more honest approach. "I can't win against NWT, Thorn, it's not in me anymore. Just let them take me."

"Get off the soap box and save the pity party for your girlfriend. And lose the all-too-familiar brood. I want thirty laps around the room."

He didn't move, instead, locking his arms across his chest with his legs about to give way. "I can barely walk." He stared the empath down, until Thorn started to cross the room to him. *What will it be this time? Another smack? Maybe a punch to the gut?* A muscular arm came around his waist. His aching arm was placed with care over a beefy shoulder. His legs wobbled like jelly, but Thorn took all his weight.

"That's right—left foot, right foot... Keep moving to strengthen your sore muscles. I've got you." Kindness laced with determination was in his tone as they began to circle the empty living room. "We'll start slow, but I'm going to push hard. Thirty laps. You get ornery? I get more annoyed. Oh, and don't get your hopes up because this is only the beginning."

****

It was hours later when Thorn returned the living room furniture to its proper place. He sat in one of the soft leather armchairs thumbing through one of Alana's fashion magazines. Hearing the elevator's hum, he sensed everyone's exhaustion and relief upon returning to the protection of the building.

"Where's Michael?" Alana asked as they entered the living room, "Wow, it's so peaceful in here. Where is he?"

"Resting, my dear, dead to the world, and no pun intended. Hey, kid, did you have fun?" Giving him the finger, Lukas went into the guest bedroom with an armful of bags and slammed the door. Yeah… the kid's attitude issues would end and very soon, he thought.

"Any progress," Miles asked.

"We've made a start." But Alana's ripe worry had his attention. "Tell your aunt to keep that blood soup coming, and as for his liquid diet—there's only enough blood for tonight. He needs more."

Miles shook his head. "This is something I knew we would have to face. I don't have a clue as to how to handle it. It's too soon to tap our veins again, and with Clayton on the loose, I don't trust any blood that I do not take myself."

Heightened anxiety all around—it permeated the living room.

"Mention it at your meeting tonight. The Georgian Council members are trusted souls. They'll have a solution." He zeroed in on Alana once more, gave a hint of a smile. "I worked him mercilessly today. Ah, yes— you'd like to comfort him, so to speak. Not now, dear Guardian. Save it for later. He's got more to accomplish before resting in your embrace."

****

Alana needed to see him. The bathroom light was on, casting shadows across the room so she could see his face. She put the shopping bags down to unpack everything and then turning back to him she bit her lower lip.

He was snoring. Every day he seemed more man than creature of the night. Of course, his vampire legacy couldn't be changed. He would always need blood to survive. Even though his canines remained a bit long it appeared his beast-within was truly dormant. She kicked off her shoes and sat on her side of the bed. *His side. My side. How is this even possible?*

She loved him more than life itself.

He stirred with a moan. His jaw was tight as he turned on his side. Slowly she stood and tip-toed to the Queen Anne chair, sitting down without making a sound. How she wanted to run her fingers through his thick brown waves and run her hand down his bruised cheek.

She liked the look of him in a sleeveless undershirt. *What a handsome man. So masculine. Commanding even in rest.* Visions of last night's love making had her longing to be in his arms again. Yes… Tonight they'd talk about the day and hold each other tight.

Today was well on its way to being another long one. Thorn's timely arrival. The many changes in the Servant of Souls. Shopping. Giggling with Celia B. Keeping Lukas in line. She'd say nothing about his antics in Pisa unless Michael asked. But her mystical Guardian senses really got a workout today. And then there was the worry about Michael. It was always there.

Forcing her shoulders to relax in the comfortable chair, her head drifted back to the soft upholstery. The coolness of the room. The quietness of Michael asleep— her eyes drifted closed. Did he know that she was right beside him? Because she always would be.

Chapter 24

Truth

As if someone was tapping her shoulder, Alana woke with a start. Probably her psychic sister playing one of those mini-mind-games again. The alarm clock on the nightstand read six o'clock. Just enough time to freshen up and change. She pulled a pair of black dress pants and a modest blouse from her closet, went into her bathroom. It had only taken a few minutes, and as she put a pair of jeans and light sweater into the laundry basket in her closet, a knock sounded on the door. Michael didn't stir as she let Thorn in.

He stood in the doorway as if not comfortable enough to enter.

She stared into his dark-gray eyes flecked with green. "How'd he *really* do with you?"

"I'll take good care of him."

"You're avoiding my question," she said and touched his massive shoulder.

"Go to your meeting and take the kid with you. As for your soul mate, I know his immediate needs." His chin jerked toward the bed. "He can't have any loving looks shooting at him like Cupid's arrows. I know how to handle him. Try not to be so concerned." Loyalty was evident in his every whispered word.

They left the bedroom together as Miles and Celia

came into the living room. Lukas trailed behind looking like he was in a sulk. As they moved away from the closed bedroom door, Michael's son leaned against it with his arms folded across his chest, his feet crossed as well. He wore a dark-blue shirt, which matched his eyes, and the new pair of khaki's Celia forced on him at one of the shops in Pisa.

"I like the new look, especially the shirt," Alana said to engage him.

"I want to see to my father," came out in a nasty tone, complete with a glare aimed at Thorn as if Lukas were ready to fight.

"He's asleep."

"I said I want to see to my father."

Here we go again, she thought, recalling every stubborn scene during the shopping trip. Not only had she chased after Lukas for a few blocks, but more than once Celia had to cajole him into cooperation. And more often than not, her sweetness appeared not to work. And now, a truly ugly scene was about to unfold.

"Okay, come with me." She moved toward the door, but Thorn stepped in her path giving a firm "No", and in a flash Lukas's fists were tight, his face even tighter.

It was time to intervene, and Thorn stared Lukas down. "You can do something selfish like wake him, or you can go to church like a good little boy."

"Fuck off, demon. If you hurt him, I'll kill—" He had the kid by the arms, easily picking him up and plunking him down against the antique secretary, which was many feet away from the master bedroom. The feral look in Lukas's eyes was nothing short of shocking. And as if held in place by an unseen force, no one else in the room moved or spoke.

"Kid, you are way out of your league with me." He simply towered over Lukas, who didn't struggle against the immovable hold. "This attitude problem, which your father *won't* be happy about, will get you in big trouble and very soon. Look, Junior, let's get our facts straight— just for the record. I've never let anything happen to him in close to seven years. Helena sent me to him. The angel chose me, a tortured slave in Hell. She knew my heart." He let go but continued to stare into Lukas's drippy eyes. "Helena gave you pure, unadulterated love. Plain and simple."

The kid didn't know what every Georgian knew. Alana was certain, because an angel takes human form only once, and in this case, a horrific physical death followed.

"I am eternally loyal to her request of me. And I wouldn't hurt your father even if my life depended on it. That's a truth." When he let go, Lukas swiped his eyes with his shirtsleeves and looked away. "I see every single troubled thought. I see pieces of your memories like broken bits of a glass. The way you challenge everyone is wrong. Why aren't you getting this yet?" The question hung in the air. Thorn shook his head and moved away so Celia could take the kid's hand.

"Come on. Your dad will be fine," Celia softly whispered.

When everyone left, Thorn realized the kid was totally unpredictable. What he said had somehow deescalated the rage that simmered under the boy's skin—for the moment. But how long would it last?

He leaned against the wall, closed his eyes. "Come to my aid, Old Ones. I beg your strength."

Lukas would eventually come to understand the

depths of his father's love. Most likely the hard way. Michael, on the other hand, needed his attention now. He walked into the master bedroom with a mug full of blood in hand, placed it on the nightstand and poked a shoulder until the vampire's eyes opened. "Nap time's over. Sit up and drink."

Michael pulled himself up, his eyes barely focused. He took the mug from Thorn's hand and very thirsty, he drank it all.

"Take a moment to wake up and then meet me in the dining room," Thorn said as he left.

Unpleasant words tumbled from his mouth as he swung both legs around and set his feet on the carpet. Muscle aches plagued him and his hands braced the edge of the bed thinking about Alana. She had to have known Thorn was coming here. And she didn't tell him. Her scent was all over around the room. Absolutely miffed at the decision to leave him in Thorn's hands for a second time, he thought with resolve, oh you will definitely pay for this, my Guardian.

He muttered a few more choice curses, wondering why Alana hadn't awakened him when she got back from Pisa. *Why? Because Thorn asked her not to.* He cursed again before standing up.

The soup's fragrant aroma wafted his way as he left the bedroom. The way his stomach rumbled, a human response he hadn't had in centuries, fully shocked him. Stiff and with an uneven gait, he eased himself into the dining room chair. He refused to look at Thorn, who filled a bowl with the steaming soup. Of course, he ate in silence. But when Thorn began to pour a second serving, he briskly said, "I've had enough."

"Nope, finish another bowlful. Ah, what healing

goodness such a unique concoction has…down to the very last drop."

Grudgingly, he complied and then pushed the empty bowl away. On the rare occasions that he took a mouthful of food, he could take it or leave it. A vampire only craved the sweet taste of blood. But this soup was different. He could feel it loosening his sore muscles.

Crossing his thick arms, the empath leaned back in the chair at his side. "You've got a world of people pampering you here. You're getting spoiled."

The smug tone brought renewed annoyance. "Why are you riding me like this?"

"Because you need me to, and deep down, you know you want me to."

"No. I don't. I really don't. Your time with me is over. I'm not your mission anymore. I screwed this one up good, didn't I? When I'm strong enough, I'll walk away from all of them—on my own two feet. I will love Alana forever and always cherish the thought of her loving me back. I don't know how to raise a child. Miles is a good parent. My son will thrive under his care. Then I'll go to Clayton. No Guardian at my side, no kid to make me think twice this time. It'll be an eye for an eye. He can send me to Hell—and this nightmare will be over."

"In your dreams, cupcake." Thorn leaned forward and his hands slammed down on the table making the bowl jump and the spoon go clickity-clink. Their equally angry glares locked. "I'm not getting through, am I? You still think this is all about you? Well, let me fill you in on a secret: this stopped being all about you days ago when you ended up on *her* doorstep and you slept in *her* bed. Do you really think that after NWT chews you up and spits you out, in tiny undead pieces, they'll simply slink back to Hell with just one arrogant *vampire* in tow? You're the proverbial tip of the iceberg. Next on their death-list is that precious Guardian, then your cranky kid, and finally all the rest of the innocents who are helping you in this dimension. You opened up Pandora's Box and now you alone must close it. There's no other way out."

Now he was really pissed off. "I have *never* heard you speak an entire paragraph, not to mention such words dripping with drama. Now I can't shut you up! Where'd you learn to talk like this? Have you been secretly listening to talk-radio and watching soap operas? I mean, do you hear yourself?" He looked away fully content with his comeback.

"If you weren't so pathetic, I'd kick your ass right now because you're acting like a child."

A wicked smirk began. "I'm not a child, thickhead. I'm three hundred years old."

"Yeah... Well, I'm nearing a millennium—in *human* years, that is. So like it or not in my reality, you've got petulant punk down pat. You may have existed for three centuries, but from where I stand, you're in that pre-hormonal, defiant stage... Like your kid." Abruptly, Thorn stood and brought the pot and bowl to the kitchen, calling over his shoulder, "Get up— right now!"

Though tempted to continue arguing, he held the table's edge and stood unsteadily with a resentful growl. The empath paid no attention as he moved the furniture.

"Give me thirty push-ups for being so stupidly clueless."

"What are you? Out of your mind?" he hollered with

a scowl.

"You'd never admit it, but I frighten you, don't I?" A scene flashed through his mind, and Thorn wagged a thick finger. "You know I was never into those slash fictions all over the Internet, but if you push me hard enough, and you really want me to fulfill one of your punitive fantasies, just keep smart-mouthing me. I'll be glad to oblige. No one's here. It's just the two of us in a mystically protected building. It won't take too much effort for me to throw you down on the floor. I'm sure there's a thick belt somewhere around here. It'll do one hell of a nasty job on you. You'll wail in no time flat."

Michael narrowed another glare, hissing, "Stay out of my head, Thorn or—"

"Or what? You hobble after me like an old lady and slap my wrist? I don't think so. Alana agrees. I'm what you need right now, so move it. You're too weak to take me on. Isn't *that* the truth!"

Chapter 25

Meetings

The seaport overflowed with tourists as well as villagers out and about. San Giorgio's Church was up the mountain, a short distance away. Miles and the others stood in front of it. Although the outside was simple, the inside? Beautifully carved wood and ornate.

A white-haired priest waited at the altar. His face was lined with deep wrinkles, but his dark eyes gleamed with vitality and intelligence. Smiling, he motioned them forward. Brown robed, his beige ropes a belt cinched with three knots to signify the allegiance to vows of poverty, chastity, and obedience.

He shook Miles's hand in friendship. "*Buona sera*, Researcher, how good to see you again! It is the Council's pleasure to meet with the four of you." Giovanni introduced himself to Celia and Lukas, his rich voice warm with a heavy Italian accent. Meeting Alana's eyes, he took her hands in his saying, "It is always a pleasure to see you, Alana."

There was no disguising his considerable wisdom, nor his abilities. A hand came to rest on Lukas's shoulder. "I'm pleased to meet you, young man." After a blessing, he added, "You are welcome here anytime. San Giorgio is a place of refuge from the storm."

Motioning them to follow, Giovanni led them into

the sacristy and down a dozen stone steps. "This section of our church is very old. One of the dragon-slayer's swords is housed in the stones," he added, pointing to the north wall. He saw the troubled child's eyes widen.

Hidden and secure, the warmth of May didn't exist down here. Lit by small sconces and white candles, it felt as if one had stepped back in time. A long, oval table came into view with eleven people sitting around it. Four chairs were at its side.

They sat and Giovanni took his place. He sensed Lukas relax with a dimpled smile when he saw Rosa. But both healer and priest knew that after the discussion, the child wouldn't recall the other Council members who just nights ago had helped keep Lukas safe.

When Miles was appointed Researcher for the North American Continent, he'd been thoroughly vetted by this sacred congregation. Six others like him existed in the world, one for each continent. "Esteemed researcher," he said as the Council members opened thick files placed before them, "Since this event occurred in your territory, we would like a brief description of all that led to the vampire's current physical state."

"Of course," Miles said with a nod. The discussion began.

****

Valetta Russo stepped off a small launch and onto the harbor's gray stone. The liaison had spent the afternoon on a yacht, smoothing over the portal glitch with another unhappy client of NWT. She hurried up the steps and behind the crowded piazza to a waiting car where a hired driver held the door for her. The ride up the steep mountain to the villa was short, but treacherous. Valetta stared at the black pricey rented sports car in the circular driveway and rolled her eyes while cursing.

When she entered the foyer with a smile, Clayton Mails was waiting. "*Ciao bene*," she said, cheerfully, "I trust your drive from the airstrip was pleasant." The liaison sidled up to him, his black eyes gleaming. The short, wiry man kissed both her cheeks in proper European fashion and followed her into the living room. Clayton sat in the middle of the black brocade couch. Valetta poured a glass of dark red wine from the bar and sat across from him on a red silk chair.

A knowing smirk crept across his sinister face. "I like the digs, pretty lady," Clayton said with a leer and a pitiful attempt at an Irish brogue.

"We offer only the best for our liaisons, *Signore*. The team arrives from Rome tomorrow. They will assist you in any way necessary," she stated, as if deferring to his power. Only her confidence showed. "I will not rest until this is over. The European sorcerers wants a clean capture, c*apisce*? Our office in the Eternal City is equipped to handle them."

"So, what am I now, the bit of cheese that lures the mouse? *I* was the one who reanimated the poisonous creature! *I* was the one who knew the traitor would get to his skinny bitch the first chance he got! *I delivered*, lass. He's mine now."

Clayton's haughty nature had surfaced as well as bitterness in his tone. Valetta didn't flinch. Didn't like puny, whiny men, but she'd have to be careful with this one. He needed stroking.

"*Signore* Mails, you did a wonderful job in Manhattan," she cooed, took a sip of wine and then sensually licked her lips. "This continent's sorcerers are very impressed with you…as they are with me. It would be better if we worked together." A fake distressed smile began while she snapped her fingers to appear frustrated. "*Come si chiama questo…* I scratch your back and you scratch mine, *si*? Play with him, *Signore.* Make *il ragazzo* cry and the dirty *poutana* beg! Pfft… I do not care. But my masters want them *alive.* They have plans, *capisce*? We serve with loyalty but," she leaned forward, and his beady eyes sank to her ample cleavage, "There is nothing to stop us from having a little fun with our captives first, *si*?"

A secretive, albeit murderous smile stayed on her face. *Woo him into compliance.* Is he farther along than she was? Yes. Most of his humanity was gone. Keep the smile somewhat charming, she told herself, even though it is pure deception. He could think her a cunning bitch. She'd take care of him after she had the vampire.

With a facial expression as cold as ice, Clayton replied, "Very well, pretty lady, I'll do as you ask. Give me forty-eight hours, and I'll deliver them to you." He leered at her breasts. "But I want the demon. The empath is mine. Show me you agree."

It didn't take long.

She placed the wineglass down, rose and moved away so he could get the full view as she peeled off her dress. It fell to the floor, and she stood naked before him, except for high, spiked heels. Clayton grinned as the liaison slithered across the room to kneel in front of him. She licked her lips and unzipped his pants. One very experienced, manicured hand reached in slowly. "*Va bene, finito*," she said with a tempting grin, "Now we seal the deal with a kiss."

Two soulless liaisons competing for the same prize. Who was going to win?

****

Michael stretched out on the carpet, totally spent. He was dripping and baffled by it. A vampire didn't need breath, but he couldn't stop gasping for oxygen like a man. A vampire doesn't sweat, but his clothes clung to every stiff muscle. He really needed a shower.

"You did good tonight. And I got here in the nick of time."

Too tired to hide exhaustion or bicker, he huffed between breaths, "Yeah? How's that?"

"Another day of self-pity and Alana's many "oh my God, I won't let them hurt him ever again" thoughts and you'd be twice as difficult. Yep, got here right in the nick of time. How the truth does hurt."

"Don't flatter yourself, Empath. I would have worked out with her."

"Now that makes me chuckle. I can see it as we speak. Three limping laps around the room, two sad glances from those big, brown, puppy-dog eyes, and one slow stroll into the bedroom for another round of tender kisses and erotic pleasures. Get your brain off the sex-fests and focus on healing. Don't kid yourself. I got here in the nick of time." Thorn stared down at him. "It's hot shower hour because you are truly sweating like a—"

"Do *not* say it," Michael bit out. Taking the huge hand extended down, he let the mystical being pull him to his feet. His legs felt like bendable twigs, and if not for Thorn, he'd have collapsed like a ragdoll. Standing by himself wasn't happening, and unable to hold on to the little dignity he had left, he quipped, "Jeez, if I had known you could change like this, I never would have sent you away. Think of the mayhem we could have created in that alleyway."

"Oh, I think you did enough damage all by your lonesome." Thorn grinned with a shake of his head. "No, my friend, an empath is a servant, not a warrior. You did what you had to do then, and I'm doing what I have to do now." A supporting arm tightened around his waist. "I'll get you into the shower because your legs are about to give out. I'll even set the water temperature, but you have to wash yourself. There's a limit to this new relationship of ours.".

"You're still a gentle soul."

"Flattery will get you nowhere. You're still washing yourself."

****

They all sat in the last pew of the church. Celia leaned down to Lukas, who looked lost in thought. "You okay? Those questions didn't scare you, did they?"

He shrugged but met her gaze. "I've never been in a church before. It feels, I don't know, safe."

His tone was soft and open, which made her smile. "Why don't you walk around and look at all the wonderful wood carvings?"

"Yeah. I think I will."

Then she focused on her adopted sister's nerves. "What if they say no, Celia B? What if they don't help him because of what he is—or because of what we did last night?"

She knew what came next. *When Ally starts with the "what ifs", one just listens.*

"Did you hear all those questions? What if they didn't like our answers? Thank God Dad did most of the talking. But the fact that Michael has a-a-a human child, and he loves Lukas—it works in his favor, but they also know what we did almost seven years ago." Alana blew out a long breath as her fingernails drummed on the wooden pew. "They *know* I cursed God when I thought Michael had left me. What about how he found Lukas? But only after making a deal with Clayton at NWT? Then there's the vengeance thing. Well, *that's* never really popular with the religious crowd. I mean, did Michael ever just turn the other cheek? No. He goes after anything standing in his way! And then... Letting the sorcerers use evil hocus-pocus to make Lukas forget. How absurd... placing trust in the ultimate evil on earth! I could go on and on but that last one's the capper. I can feel it."

Alana's eyes began to glisten. Tears would follow because her hope was sinking into despair. But she wasn't finished yet.

"And the whole drink our blood thing to heal *without* asking the Council's permission first. And all those Georgian psychics chanting for his protection how many night ago...is chanting like praying? Nope. Not gonna help him. Oh, God," she moaned.

"Okay, stop, Ally, because "Just listen" time's over. You've got it all figured out. I get it. Michael is condemned to Hell for eternity. You end up there, too. That scared little sweetie over there lingers in purgatory and earth is forever overrun with demons. No way. Have a little faith."

Alana shrugged and closed her eyes, tears about to drip onto her lap as she continued.

"Put the brakes on doubt, and see what Michael *really* did. He accomplished in *one night* what the Georgians have been preaching about for a *thousand* years. Don't you think closing the portals all over the North American Continent counts for something?

Humanity doesn't need the "Devils for Dummies" kind of assistance, which NWT offers. People have managed very well with no help from sorcerers to create top-of-the-line chaos!"

"He's *not* a human being, Celia B. Michael's got a beast-within, a-a demonic nature that makes him a part of what he fights!"

Keeping her church-voice was getting harder. "Hello? Where exactly do you think I've been for the past five days—living in La-La-Land? I've seen his tears go from scarlet to pink to clear. I haven't seen any fangs, nor have I seen those gorgeous brown eyes turn yellow," she stated in a logical but sweet way. "You've made mad, passionate love to him, but I haven't seen hide or hair of the beast-within. Michael is changing, Ally. Yeah, he can still smell us in the other room and hear every whisper—I'll give you that, and he's stronger than any guy you'd meet in the piazza for a glass of Chianti. But he's more human and less vampire every day. He's never been your average creature of the night. And now, he's loving his son, loving you—like a man, not a de…man." She put her arm around her sister and hugged her with a caring smile.

Ally smiled slightly, palmed away a tear. "I like your play on words."

"Say a prayer. Make peace with the Big Guy and think positive. Besides, I think *Zia* would've kicked him into the street and rolled him out to sea if she thought he could turn evil again."

"What would I ever do without you, Celia B?"

Her sister's soft sigh warmed her heart. "You'd have figured it out—eventually."

Father Giovanni and Miles were coming toward

them with Lukas following behind. Her sister stood graciously as if ready to accept the council's position on her soul mate. They had certainly taken enough time to make a decision, her sister was thinking. But she knew the real reason because she was like her father—wordy but thorough.

The priest smiled. "We made a decision an hour ago, however, the details of our part in assisting the Champion needs to be specific and carefully documented by the Researcher." He raised his hand in a blessing. "May the courage of *San Giorgio* sustain you." Father Giovanni turned to Lukas, blessing him separately. "Love is stronger than fear. Always remember that."

"Thanks," Lukas whispered. Giovanni clasped his shoulder, and to everyone's surprise, Lukas hugged him.

Chapter 26

Obsession

They returned to the security of the apartment close to midnight. Thorn stood when they came into the living room. Celia smiled at him and went into the sunroom, exhausted from the day and Alana's emotions. Lukas mumbled a quick goodnight and went into the guest room. Miles gave the empath a steady nod and took his laptop into the den.

"He's asleep," Thorn said to Alana. "I'll be down in the basement—if that's all right with you. It has an earthen floor, you know?"

She smiled. "Celia told me once how you liked to sleep in the backyard of Michael's brownstone, preferring the garden over a mattress. Can I offer a warm blanket and a pillow maybe?" Not waiting for a reply, she went to the hall closet and pulled them out.

"I don't need—" He was suddenly holding them.

"Nonsense, it's the least I can offer. You can have the den if you want."

"No, but thanks… The good earth calls—reminds me of home. I'll see ya in the morning." He lowered his gaze and started for the old wooden door.

Alana touched his arm. "I don't have the words, Thorn. What you did today for Michael, for me, it's appreciated."

He put a finger to her lips. "You don't have to say anything, not at all. It's the least I could do for you, dear Guardian. It's the least I could do for him, although I'm sure he's cursing me in his dreams. Go to him. Ease his mind. You're the only one who can do it. He truly loves you. I should have seen it, sensed it as well. Bring him your blood, mix it with the kid's and let this play out." When he left, she turned the deadbolt.

Once in the kitchen Alana took the last of her and Lukas's blood out of the fridge and blended it in the glass carafe. Waiting for it to warm in the microwave, she noticed that Thorn had washed and dried Michael's mug. The pot and soup bowl as well.

A smile began. *What a thoughtful, kind being. It was hard being away from Michael today. Most likely, he's furious with Celia for getting Thorn to come all the way to Italy.* The empath had been tough on him. Of this, she was certain. "Deal with it," she whispered, "I care about you too much to lose you now."

****

Alana turned on the bedside lamp and set the carafe and mug on the nightstand. Michael looked peacefully asleep, and she'd wake him after her shower. Grabbing something just bought from a shopping bag, she tiptoed into the bathroom and locked the door. After undressing, she stood under the tepid drizzle with a moan. How she longed for serious water pressure.

As soon as she stepped out, her reflection in the mirror captured her interest. Almost twenty-eight, she had survived her mystical mission without a scar. How many times had he shielded her body from punches and claws? How many vampires had he staked when she found herself in over her head? How had she gone those ten years without a scratch?

Michael was the reason.

Sometimes they'd talk till dawn. Long winter nights meant slow walks through Central Park in the snow. Those memories were from years ago. Would they make new memories now?

She brushed her teeth and ripped the string and paper off what she had purchased in a trendy, upscale store—a silk nightgown. The saleswoman had already snipped off the tags. It was the color of French lilacs, flowing and soft. The tiny buttons on the bodice had the thinnest loops she'd ever seen. Simple yet elegant, and the shade accented her tanned skin in a sensual way.

Tonight, she'd be sexy. But Michael was comfortable with every facet of her personality. Sassy or tender, enticing or stubborn. Even through the solitude and sadness, the regret and remorse of those long years apart, love was always there. And on the rare occasions when they came face to face, Michael always turned away first, unable to shield his affection for her.

She came into the bedroom and stopped midway to the bed. It was empty. So was the carafe on the nightstand. Her heart skipped a beat, seeing him sitting tall and proud in the Queen Anne chair. He was bare-chested, which made her begin to blush.

"I didn't know you were awake," she whispered at his side.

"Surprise, surprise," he answered in an even tone.

Without another word, he stood. His signature strides took him out of the bedroom. Those black silk pajama bottoms hung low on his hips, which had an egotistical sway, his gait always so distinctive.

She sank into the Queen Anne chair as if she'd just

been punched in the stomach.

****

Michael entered the guest room in silence. Miles was deep asleep and snoring loud. Lukas looked peaceful in the dim light that formed a slim path from the hallway lamp.

He sat on the bed and brushed his son's warm cheek. Delicate features, but his cheekbones were high as if there was more than a trace of Slavic blood in his ancestry. The innocence on his face was pure relaxation. Very different than mine, he thought. The vivid recall shocked him. *Mother always said that as a little boy, my sleep-time expressions were angry, fierce as if lost in dreams of courageous knights and daring swordfights.*

Curled on his side, his son hugged a pillow tight to his slender chest. In life, he had preferred sleeping on his side as well. How many other similar traits did they share? He wanted to find out. And knew he never would.

The father in him tried to envision all the missed years, the exciting "firsts" a child accomplishes. His first steps. His Christmas mornings. His first tooth or his first day of school. *Three evil things took those treasures from me. Forced to give him up to Helena to keep him from their wrath. But they found him anyway.*

No recorded history of Lukas Malone existed and there would never be one.

He placed one hand over his son's heart. The strong muscle pumped evenly against his cool palm. Ours is a strong bloodline, he thought. Leaning down, he placed a tender kiss on his son's forehead. The boy didn't flinch, didn't startle.

With Miles, he'd truly be safe for the first time in his troubled life. "I will always love you, little boy," he whispered with the confidence of a caring father. He left the room in silence. As he strode down the hall toward the master bedroom his mood changed, thinking, now—it's time to deal with Alana.

****

Michael entered the master bedroom and locked the door. Without a word he crossed the room to the two windows, hitched the heavy drapes behind their brass holders. With determination he opened the windows and flung back the shutter to the bricks. Moonlight flooded the room, the fresh May air warm and balmy from the sea. Alana remained in the Queen Anne chair. He could hear her heart beating fast. And he knew she was looking at him.

He kept his stance impressive, the silk pajama bottoms slightly billowing with the gentle breeze, his arms locked against his bare chest. Evil was close. But the blood mixture had worked its magic once again. *Not an ache or a pain. Full use of legs and arms. Heightened senses and eagle-like vision.* He was ready when they came for him.

He still hasn't said a word. Of course, it would annoy her. Made sure his "I'm in charge, and I'll deal with you when I'm good and ready" attitude came through loud and clear. He could tick off the minutes knowing how this would eventually play out between them.

He sensed her shiver before she cleared her throat. "Hello—I'm waiting, Michael. Aren't you going to talk to me?"

In a low, cold tone he gave an abrupt, "No."

"Why?" she asked softly.

"I am absolutely furious with you." The glare he

223

gave when turning in her direction appeared to startle her. And he heard the skip of a heartbeat as proof. "You knew Celia sent for him. Yet you said *nothing*. You thoroughly enjoyed giving me over to that sadist today. Yet you did *nothing*," Alana opened her mouth to speak, which he quickly put a stop to with a low, "Do. Not. Dare." He took a few steps forward in a menacing way. "I needed you here *with me*. Instead, I got thrown over that thing's shoulder, taken down more than a few pegs, and forced to circle your living room like a toddler in a fucking playpen. It's payback time, darlin'. You do not make decisions for me. Do you understand?" Another few steps and he stood over her. "You will never do that again."

The expression on his face was purposely murderous, while she had a familiar "here we go again" expression on her face, just as she often had years ago when they bickered. And just like he had years ago, his voice sank in a stern warning, "Do not roll your eyes at me, little girl."

Her captivating hazel eyes shot wide. "Oh, please… you know you needed this."

"Don't tell me what I need. You *will* suffer this decision."

"Why? Because a *little* truthfulness hurts, and you're acting a *little* touchy?"

"What did you just say to me?"

"Do you want me to repeat it for you?"

He leaned down to her. "You had better stop right now."

She glared back, and he locked his hands on the chair's arms, effectively pinning her in.

Her heart raced wildly. He saw her swallow before

saying, "Or what? You'll keep intimidating me with low growls? You'll brood and act hurt? Insulted because I left you in the extremely capable hands of your very loyal empath? It worked, didn't it?"

It was multiple question time. Which meant he was getting to her. Roughly, he grabbed her shoulders and ignored her wince. When he had her out of the chair and at eye-level he wanted to ravage her full lips, but instead kept her far enough away. "Perhaps your previous comments were unnecessary. Perhaps you need to rethink those remarks."

She blinked and whispered, "Okay, okay, you win— you're at full power and then some. Now let me go."

Not a chance, he thought as he slowly lowered her. When her feet hit the carpet, he didn't release her, eyeing the way the dark silk clung to her body, noticing the delicate buttons at her breasts. She looked stunning in it. Ready to be ravished, so it was time to edge up the heat. Perhaps, more than a little.

"My God," she whispered as if out of breath, "You are powerful."

If he waited any longer, he'd take her right on the carpet. Right here. Right now. His erection throbbed as his hands slid up the sides of her thighs. Her breath hitched. Her eyes closed. His finger flicked across her breasts and her head fell back. With one very calculated move, he ripped the nightgown right down the center. Buttons popped off in rapid succession and the soft silk slid down and off her lovely shoulders.

She gasped as his hand palmed her core, her arousal sweet and fragrant.

Her arms flew around his neck. The kiss he gave her was deep, his tongue penetrating her lips to dance with hers. He grabbed her thigh, lifted it to his waist as her leg hooked around him. His erection pressed against her through the black silk pajama bottoms, but he held her there, sliding his hand until it was splayed across her bottom.

She wriggled as the lurid kiss continued. He broke from her parted lips as her body bucked, and then he bent his head to take a nipple between his teeth. She sank her fingers into his hair, breathing hard.

But the erotic tease was not close to over. Two fingers slid into her, and she whispered his name in a shaky voice. He used his thumb in a most sensual stimulating manner. She gyrated and moaned. She was coated, slick with moisture. He wanted her so badly that he lifted her off the ground still keeping his hand in a most pleasurable spot and strolled to the bed knowing each move of his hips had her panting and bucking with her arms tight around his neck.

He laid her across the four-poster bed reaching down deep to keep himself under control. The way she writhed with her arms above her head as he stepped out of the pajamas to free his erection was a sight to behold. God, how he wanted her. Pushing her legs wide, he knelt on the bed directly between them and grabbed her luscious bottom. Craving her as never before, he brought her core to his mouth. Her arms flung wide. She fisted the sheets. The sounds she made revved his passion. His tongue took quick possession of her need. She squirmed against every slow lick. And when he grabbed her bottom tighter, she orgasmed.

Now she was ready, whimpering, breathing hard as her breasts heaved and her back arched. He angled his body over her hips and plunged his erection in deep.

Quick and rough he thrust. Her legs came around him as he nipped at her breasts, and then lingered at her neck to graze her skin. He found her mouth while still rocking rough within her. She orgasmed again, her body quaking as she rode another wave of ecstasy. As she rode his release.

When her breathing slowed and her heartrate came down, he lay at her side.

She started to speak, but his finger came to rest on her full lips. "No words tonight, my Guardian," he whispered low. "Your mystical strength is of no consequence right now. You will stay exactly where I put you." When she tried to pull away, he held her firmly to his body with one hand splayed low at the heated edge of her sex. She was the one temptation he could not refuse. He adored her, but he would make sure she understood that he alone controlled his destiny. "I have told you before. I know what I need. I know what I want. There is no discussion."

His finger inched down and just touching her had him hard again. He guided her knee up as she began to pant. And then he took her again.

His immense strength. The commanding way he possessed her. Every new erotic pleasure had her speechless. Alana lay in his tight embrace fully ready, willing, and able to submit again and again to his every desire. She belonged to him for all eternity.

Moonlight spilled through the open curtains. Warm sea air caressed her naked body. Every fiber of her body continued to quiver, yearning for his touch. If the heat of passion continued throughout the night, he could possess her over and over again in stubborn silence because in a way he was right. Their love needed no words.

Chapter 27

Apologies

The urgent siren of a police car startled Alana awake. Her eyes shot open. She was still tight in her immortal lover's arms. Vivid recall of unrestrained passion…so many sensual pleasures. An erotic night heightened by his sexy aggression. The memory alone made her damp again. His raw power. The urgency of her need. His obsession took her to new, never imagined heights. When his body stirred behind her, she had to wonder what his first words to her would be.

His arm eased off, prompting her to softly call his name. No response came.

Edging away, she grabbed for the bedspread covering herself, clutching it tight. Sitting back on her heels, she studied his expressionless face. He couldn't still be mad at her, could he??

Rolling onto his back, Michael supported his head with an arm. He waited for the aches and pains to begin. There were none. He felt more than strong—completely healed. As for his Guardian, he knew the expression she wore. Shallow breaths, hands clutched to the bedspread. The curious quirk to her lovely mouth. "Dear God, I love you so much," he whispered. It was an absolute truth. His passion for her, his obsession with pleasuring her, protecting her, positively dominated his soul. She came into his arms resting her head on his chest.

"About last night—"

"I meant every word." He grinned at the way she now clung to his chest. "I hope you've learned a lesson."

Looking up at him, she grinned as well. "Which lesson would that be?"

"I'm the master of my own destiny. Plus, I'm back and I'm strong."

Her lips came to his, and the kiss was deeply aggressive. He loved it. Although it was very difficult, he changed his focus to the bright streaks of sunlight cutting through the room, not yet reaching the bed.

"I'd race you to the shower, but you'd win…only because I'd burn up on entry."

"What if you gave me a head start?"

He let out a laugh, which was a rare sound. She sat up and stretched. The bedspread slipped off. Her beautiful body, supple yet firm—the physical sensation stirring a particular part of him. He groaned, and she reached for the bed cover again, but he quickly got it out of her hand.

The way her eyebrow arched produced a sensual growl and he said low and lusty, "I dare you to give those nosy neighbors across the street such a delectable eyeful." She stood, a vision of loveliness. Her bend down caused his hips to jerk. She was that enticing. The ripped silk nightgown against her tanned skin hid very little, and she smiled sassy, sexy. "It conceals nothing, darlin'."

Her slow sashay to the open window was bold. She unhooked the heavy drapes and secured them against the strong Amalfi sun. Then she dropped the ripped silk and stared at him.

"Are you going to bend down and pick it up again?"

"In your fantasies, buddy, in your fantasies," she replied, a crooked finger over her lovely shoulder beckoning him. Of course, he followed her into the bathroom. He'd taste her and then take her again in the shower.

****

Alana's unhurried steps to the dining room table didn't reflect her mood. If she were a dancer it would have been pirouettes. She was beyond elated. The sundress, so soft and flowy accented her figure. The color of a sunflower against her skin was perfect. Her long curly hair spilled across one shoulder.

"Oooh…I totally like," Celia said with admiration.

"Thanks, Celia B," she said with a bright smile. "We both fell in love with it in Pisa, but I grabbed it first."

"Ally knew it'd look great with her tan, Dad, and without a second thought, she put it on her credit card."

Her adopted father gave a thin frown as he cleared a spot for her. Files, notepads, two laptops, and an assortment of empty breakfast plates littered the space. On her way to the kitchen, she closed the apartment door, which was ajar, happily lost in thoughts of last night and then headed to the kitchen. A fresh pot of coffee stood waiting. She filled a mug from the mug-rack, added a little cream because she liked it on the dark-side, and went back to join her family.

All eyes shot to Michael when he came out of the bedroom and walked into the kitchen. He wore the clothes Alana picked out with style. Snug black jeans and the black cotton shirt looked as if they'd been designed with him in mind. He had rolled the cuffs up the way he normally would. The classic Italian loafers—something he'd normally never wear—fit perfectly.

His gait was steady. The sure, characteristic strides so natural and familiar. He poured coffee instead of sustenance and joined them at the table, keeping silent and looking aloof.

Celia B's jaw dropped as her green eyes shot wide. "You look amazing,"

A bland expression and a dismissive wave were all she'd get. "I'm not speaking to you. You brought Rambo here without asking me first." Her guilt-ridden gaze slid back to a laptop in front of her.

"Are you threatening my daughter?" Miles asked, looking up from a worn, old manila file. "Because if you are, I will withhold the blood Father Giovanni delivered earlier. And I doubt you would want me to. You do look good, by the way," he said in his dry way of speaking, "and I don't mean the clothes."

The researcher resumed reading, which was fine with him. He'd ignore the researcher as well. Although his need was not overbearing, he went back to the kitchen, opened the fridge, and reached for a glass container. Breaking the seal, he stood there and drained it. At first swallow, he knew it to be a blend of blood types. And it was enormously powerful as it absorbed into his system.

Returning to the table, he sipped at his coffee, scanning the clutter, and then focused on two things, which were disturbing. "Is something missing from the hutch? And why is there a hole over here on the table, my love?" His finger rimmed the wood. It looked as if it had been drilled. Both women simply stared at him, but Miles stopped reading. To Alana, he gave a slightly sarcastic smirk. "Were you, maybe, practicing a new cross-bow technique and missed the target—for once?"

But her gaze locked on Miles instead who said, "It's best you tell him, honey."

"Lukas can get very… uhm, angry."

He leaned forward. "My *son*... did this to the table?"

"With a pen."

"What? When?"

"A few days ago. You're just back on your feet. Maybe you want to…let it go for now."

Michael raised an eyebrow. "I don't think so."

"He has quite a temper," Miles said as he continued reading.

"I specifically warned him about his temper, and I told him to behave." He sat back, locking his arms across his chest. "Let me guess—it hasn't been happening."

"Lukas was very polite last night at the church," Celia chimed in.

"You and I… Later," he said with narrow eyes. He ran a hand over the marred antique. It looked horrible. But the silence in the room told him there was more. "He's been giving all of you a hard time, hasn't he? First the doctors and—the vase?" Alana gave a slow nod. "The table will be repaired." Although he didn't want to, he had to ask, "So what else has Lukas done?"

Again, both women stared at Miles, who pulled off his reading glasses and met his eyes. "There have been quite a few incidences of concern. As a parent, you have the right to know."

The candor with which Miles detailed incident after incident was appreciated. They took Lukas in with open arms, he thought, and after a stern reprimand it will stop. "I warned him not to step out of line. What else?"

Many minutes later, after another round of his son's transgressions, Miles ended with, "Yesterday he wandered off in Pisa."

"I caught him, though, blocks away," Alana added. "He can have a very fresh mouth."

After a shake of his head, he whispered, "I can imagine."

"He was talked out of another explosive scene last evening…by Thorn," Miles added.

Just hearing that name irked him, and for a brief second he switched gears to say, "I'll take care of *him*, too." He met Celia's tight eyes with a frown, but his focus remained on one out-of-control little boy. "I asked him if he was behaving himself."

"And his answer," the researcher asked.

"He lied." Running his fingers through his hair, he said, "Temper tantrums. Rudeness, cursing… not to mention throwing grown men across the room."

"You may have to be a bit firm with him, Michael."

"Just a bit, Miles?" He stood. "Where is he now?"

Celia quickly said, "Probably the den because Ally brought him some video games yesterday to, you know, to keep him happy. But—he's been a perfect angel with me, honestly, *really*."

"My dearest Celia B, the sweetest woman on the planet, who wouldn't be a perfect angel with you? You know I love you." He kissed her cheek full of deep affection. She blushed as he whispered in her ear, "But I'm still mad at you." She grimaced, bobbed her head continually as he walked away.

First, he checked the guest room, and then the den, the main bathroom, and even the sunroom and foyer. With determined strides, he came back to the table. "He isn't here."

"That's impossible," Miles said as he stood.

Alana shot up out of the chair. "Wait… the door was open before."

He stared at the dark, drawn drapes, and his panic grew. "No one's gotten in. I'd pick up a scent, human *or* demon. *Damn it*! My son knows he's supposed to stay put."

"He had breakfast a while ago," Miles stated. "But I didn't hear the door—"

"Did he say *anything* about leaving?"

Celia stood up, quickly spewing, "N-no, nothing except, you know, good morning, what are you doing and I'm hungry a-and then what's there to eat in this place. Just like any other normal kid, antsy for something to do." Her green eyes seemed to sparkle, and she ran to the door, flung it open with a shrieked, "Lukas is gone!"

Thorn's ample fist was up, ready to knock. She pulled him into the living room as he said, "Well, I'd sense it if he were in trouble, so—"

"He's going to be in a hell of a lot of trouble when I get my hands on him. And you—" A ferocious scowl locked on Thorn as Alana sprinted past him and out the door. His irritation soared as he flew at the empath pinning him to the floor with his left fist raised. "You son of a bitch! Give me one good reason *not* to knock your teeth out. Go ahead—just try to think of one. I'll give you five seconds…in *demon* time!"

About to pummel the man's face, Alana shouting his name snagged his attention. Michael looked up fully pissed-off. What he saw stopped him cold. Her hand was on Lukas's shoulder. Thorn slipped out of his hold, and he stood up to face his son.

"I was with *Zia*," his son said with a shrug.

He looked at Alana, who stated as if she were

holding in her own irritation, "The truth is, *Zia* found him *outside* when she came home from the market a few minutes ago." Every pat to his son's back brought the boy closer.

He positively locked his arms across his chest and approached his son, stopping with less than a foot between them as his eyes slid down. "Didn't I tell you to behave?" Lukas gave a shrug and turned his face away while shoving his hands into the back pockets of his jeans. "I warned you what would happen if you didn't."

"It's no big deal."

"Let's try this again. I want the truth."

Lukas's chin jerked toward the others with a mumbled, "They were reading things."

Everyone stood under the dining room arch except for Thorn who appeared comfortably ensconced in one of the plush leather chairs.

"You will not lie to me. Take your hands out of your pockets and relax your fists."

The roll of his son's eyes irked him as well as the muttered, "Fuck."

There were so many issues here, he didn't know which to address first and cleared his throat. "You went outside even though you were told to stay put. What were you thinking? A short hike up the mountain? A quick dip in the sea?" He caught Thorn shaking his head and a whispered, "I warned him."

Grabbing an arm behind his back, Lukas's lips twisted into a scowl. "Okay, so I lied. Don't get so parental."

"What did you say? You will *feel* me get parental, little boy, because I told you what happens if you misbehave. And I specifically told you to stay put."

"So what? I can take care of myself," his son bit out.

The next eye-roll absolutely pressed a button he didn't even know he had. "Your behavior is horrible. And your attitude? Worse. Now let's address your temper. A broken vase? A pen drilled into expensive wood? Shall I go on?"

A sneer snagged Alana of all people. "Betcha couldn't wait to tell him. Fuckin' tattletale," his son muttered, as his fists flexed in plain sight.

"Watch your mouth."

"He's back on his feet and you want to see me get my ass kicked."

"Oh, I promise I'm not thinking about kicking it. Apologize to Alana right now. Then go to your room. You're punished."

With a step back, his son's hands flew up. "Why?"

Oh, where to start, he thought. Those fists were tight and twitching again as Lukas shifted from foot to foot. "Apologize and go."

"No."

"Do not dare to challenge me, Lukas."

"Or what?"

"You know what happens." He didn't dare unlock his arms because he was faced with a decision. Either he followed through on his warning or he let it go.

"I'd apologize, kid, and fast," Thorn warned.

"Nobody's talking to you, demon."

"Lukas," he said and took a step forward. Before his other foot hit the floor his son turned and ran only to be snagged around the waist and lifted before he got to the door.

"Fucking put me down!"

"Absolutely not, little boy. This ends right now."

Twisting and flailing, he carried Lukas into the guestroom. He kicked the door closed, put a foot on the bed holding his raging child across his knee. Even *this* didn't stop his son from cursing. It took smacking his son's backside until he heard hitched breaths and sniffles, and then he released him.

The way Lukas flung himself across the bed and buried his face in the pillow said lesson learned, albeit the hard way. Michael kept his tone low and even. "You do not leave this room until I say so, little boy." He eyed the window and silently said a prayer before he left the room and closed the door.

****

Miles was in conversation with Thorn as Michael sank into the other leather chair with a sigh. The responsibility of raising a son shook him to the core of his soul. Facing Hell-beasts was simple compared to this. His head fell back to the cushion as his hands gripped the chair's thick arms. "I really didn't want to do that."

"But you needed to," Thorn said.

"I didn't hit him hard."

"But hard enough, I hope. God only knows what could've happened outside the protection of this building," Thorn replied.

"You're absolutely right, but maybe I should have tried to reason with him." Rarely did he lack self-confidence; however this was new territory.

Celia sank down on the sofa and Alana came behind him, rubbing his shoulders while Miles simply shook his head. "Although I'm sympathetic to the fatherly feelings you're experiencing, the truth of the matter is, you did what was called for. You didn't beat him within an inch of his life. You disciplined him out of love, not anger. I agree with Thorn. Lukas could have been easily taken. I would imagine he'll think twice before misbehaving again."

"He's upset," Celia said, "I could go to him and—"

"No, dearest," Thorn interjected, "The kid will be all right. Better he's sore than taken from us."

"I also owe you an apology," he said to Thorn, "I'm sorry for wanting to rearrange your cheerful grin."

Thorn shrugged and thumped the arms of the chair. "Aw, Boss, I've missed the champion in you. I'm glad you're back."

But he didn't feel like a champion right now. He looked over his shoulder at Alana. "Thank you for finding him. Thank *Zia,* too. If it weren't for her, he might have found danger."

"Not a problem, my love. So, what do we do now?"

"I've got to talk to my son. I take it those files are filled with information, Researcher?" Miles nodded in the affirmative. He squeezed Alana's hand. "Help your dad out. See if there's anything that jumps off the page. Thorn, you were sent by Helena, and I get the impression you've been around much longer than I have. Why were the sorcerers hellbent on destroying me? Check out those dusty folders with the researcher." They all stood and moved into the dining room while he sat in the chair and took a few minutes to clear his head.

****

His son was on his bed facing the wall when he entered the room. "Lukas," he whispered with a light touch to his son's sandy hair. There was no pull-away, which was a good sign. He stretched out on the bed, slipped an arm under his son, who turned and buried his face in his chest. The sobs and hitches continued, and

Michael gave him time to cry it out tight in his arms. Emotions swelling up from his soul were like none other. He would hold his boy like this for hours if that's what it took.

When the crying stopped, Lukas whispered, "I-I'm sorry. I'll apologize. I swear."

"I believe you. That's the right thing to do."

"You're stronger than me now, aren't you?"

"You already know the answer."

"It still stings," his son whispered, which made him smirk. *So much for self-healing.*

"Only because it came from my hand, little boy. Now you have to learn to listen and do as you are told. All bad boy behavior goes. Lose your temper or you will give me no choice the way you did today. If I see it or hear about it, you'll be over my knee staring at the floor and crying again. Do you understand?" His son's head bobbed against his chest. Of course, he felt guilty as hell. Parenting was no walk in the park after sunset. But his son's safety was all that mattered. "With things the way they are, you cannot do what you want."

"I can take care of myself, Dad, you know I can."

"Not against *this* man, you can't. Clayton is devious. I meant what I said. And things are different between us now. That's good, isn't it?"

"Yeah—and we're good, right?"

His son's reply made him smile. "Absolutely, my boy." Lukas pulled off his chest and stared at him. Michael pushed his sandy, shaggy locks away from his face. "Tell me about video games—I hear they're *very* cool." He flexed his hands. "My fingers could use a workout."

"I'm pretty quick, Dad." Lukas ran his sleeves over

his eyes. "You look good, like, better than good. My blood helped you heal?"

"It most certainly did. Yours, Alana's—and what Thorn put me through yesterday. Believe me. I didn't know the empath had it in him."

"I promise I'll apologize to him, too... I swear I will."

Love for this child grew with every new minute they spent together. "That would make me very proud."

"Was Thorn, like, really tough?"

"Amazingly enough, but even an empath wouldn't be as good as me at video games. All right, up," he said. "Teach me how to play." His son came off his chest and they both stood. But his son didn't move and he stopped at the door.

"Am I still punished?"

"No. So let's get a move on." Lukas walked through, and he followed. In over three centuries of existence, Michael had never felt like this...a loving man, a loving father.

Chapter 28

Research

Alana counted thirty file folders, each very thick. The two piles in front of Miles indicated those he'd read and those he hadn't yet opened. She could tell he'd been at this since dawn, and it was now well past noon.

Of course, Celia and Miles had each perfected their own method of work-mode. Miles had said he pulled up Council entries that had been electronically archived. Some went as far back as the 1800s. He also had the foresight to bring a series of discs for cross-reference. Celia's job was to search data bases of Georgian psychics. Some had chronicles and links to web sites which included paranormal events dating back to the 1500s. She used *Malone* and *Helena* to key into her laptop, finding an array of interesting entries. Like her father, Celia took meticulous notes. As much as she was part of the technology age, she preferred long-hand as well. Sitting across from Miles, Thorn's job was to read the files the researcher had already finished, looking for anything peculiar. *We are like some well-oiled machine—all of us working together for my eternal love.*

She pulled her chair closer to Celia deciphering her print-script, which was an unusual cross between the two ways of writing. Celia B prided herself on this perplexing method of note-taking, invented back when they were kids. To everyone else it just looked like some blocky gibberish. Alana, however, read it with ease. Although she hated puzzles and did very poorly at figuring them out, this cryptic script was forever intriguing. In fact, she, the one who didn't like puzzles, was the fastest de-coder. On the ninth page, she gave a curious look, and couldn't seem to pull her eyes away from it.

"Wow, this is odd. Three sisters from England, all healers, end of the Seventeenth Century. Wasn't that when he was sired, Dad?"

Although focused on reading from his laptop, he replied, "Yes. He was turned in 1690, I believe, but not in his native England. Michael had settled in the new world. America… Manhattan, to be precise."

"Turned in the new world, huh?" She held the page, still unable to let go. "Add the word tech and we have a winner… NWT. How's that for a little irony?"

"Didn't Michael come from London?" Celia asked. "His father was a merchant or something."

Miles looked up. "Yes, owner of Martin Malone Imports, specializing in printed silks and other cloth goods. It was established in 1655 by Martin and his brother Lucien, who died shortly afterward. Their father had been a respected tailor of the royal court." He clicked and another file opened. "Ah, yes… Here it is. I created a lineage document years ago. Lucien Malone died of consumption in his thirties. Never married, no children, legitimate or otherwise. He was deeply religious and quite good looking if I recall the family portrait."

Alana's eyes went wide as she leaned forward. "There's a family portrait—since when? Is it here in Italy, with the Council? You didn't tell me? You really have a picture of Michael and his family?" The pro at multiple questions never realized one might exist.

"Oh, yes, of course I do—well, the Georgians do, that is. And there's more than one. They're kept at the Hampton Hill Estate. When it comes to the ancestry of a creature such as Michael, we prefer thorough research. All the Malone family members were upstanding citizens and very involved with their faith. Oddly enough, they weren't Church of England, but Roman Catholic. They somehow managed to prosper no matter what the religious trend was at the time."

Her eyes stayed wide. "I never thought about his family history. What about the others? I mean, are there any descendants somewhere in England?"

"None." He took off his glasses and leaned back. "His father married the same year he started the business, which took off rather well. The man was never a debtor and quite prosperous for the time. He married Rebecca Croydon on May 5, 1655. Rebecca's father was a printer, an engraver. Rebecca, an only child, was quite beautiful. Soon after they married, she had three girls, each a year apart. Anne is born first, followed by Rosalind and Priscilla. Five years later, in 1663, Michael is born. Rebecca had many servants, and the children had a private tutor."

"Wow. He never told me. Well, I never actually asked him about his human life. But vampires don't remember their mortal existence."

"No, not much… Soon after being sired, all life-memory fades except for the last moments before they meet undeath." He took a moment. "The Malone family was very upstanding. Martin sponsored many charity cases and gave generously to the church." Thumbing through an ancient-looking folder, he added. "Did you know Michael was an altar boy?" His dry smile appeared. She smiled back, but all she could think about was last night's erotic romp. "Yes," he continued reading down the file, "ironic, isn't it? And all three sisters entered a religious order together. Ah.. Here it is. August 19, 1678, the day they left the family home. Michael was fifteen at the time and had become quite a handful, it seems. I would imagine that was *after* his altar boy days."

She was stunned and kept staring at the same page. "Does the entry say more?"

"Well, his tutor kept extensive notes, which is how we know the date of their departure. He was, apparently, very bright, exceptionally good in mathematics and science. This other file stated how, upon his father's death, he inherited Martin's business, which continued to prosper under his guidance. By that time, he was quite popular with the ladies. His mother died after he left England. And there's nothing at all about his sisters."

"Oh yes there is," said Celia, with a look of surprise.

"Ditto," added Thorn, holding up a file Miles hadn't yet read. "We have a connection to the Georgians."

You could see excitement building in Celia. "And it says here in this website entry I'm looking at… they were seers, the early version of psychics. Oh my God, Dad, do you think we have triangulation?"

"Wait—back up a little here. I'm confused. Are you saying there's information about Michael's sisters on websites, in Georgian files, and in old journals, Dad? How is it we didn't know all this before?"

Looking at Celia's screen, Miles then took the folder from Thorn's hand, and became very quiet. He leaned forward and pointed with his reading glasses. "There's something more here. Can it be possible there is a Georgian connection? Humph… The thought never crossed my mind." Sifting through the files his expression became more intense. After carefully turning many yellowed pages, a stunned look appeared. "Oh, good Lord," he softly said, throwing down his reading glasses. "All these years of studying him… how could I have missed it? All the journals I filled. I never thought to look back farther than his parents *or* into his sisters." He sat back and rubbed his temples.

They all were a captive audience, until Thorn and Celia both closed their eyes. She saw it happening…The conversation-switch to non-verbal, and she shook a finger at them. "Okay, cut the telepathic telephone game, both of you."

Her adopted father reexamined each piece of information, and then uttered a labored sigh. "It's in the female lineage. At first, it wouldn't make any sense to trace his ancestry back before Rebecca, but it's here. When we cross-reference Rebecca Croydon, we find one common name shared by all the females of her mother's line—like a pre-ordained baptismal name. I'll lay odds this dates back to the first recordings made by Georgian researchers at the turn of the millennium, in 1001." He had a hand on his brow, pensive.

Thorn pulled another a piece of parchment from the file, more brittle with age and her senses tingled. "I've got to know, Dad. What common name?"

Celia shuffled through pages of notes to the very first page of today's hieroglyphics. She scanned down, stopping on one word, and showed it to Alana, saying, "All their middle names are variations of Helena."

"And let me guess, the *original* Helena was one of

the very first Georgian Sovereign Council members, and she's the angel who…" her voice trailed off. This was shocking!

Thorn leaned in, his massive hands firm on the table. "Now we connect some dots. Our Michael gets his conscience tweaked, wrestles his very soul back in 1890. That's no random act of kindness on the Old One's part. Let's say this is an ancient and mystical matriarchal lineage. His sisters and Lucien are out of the picture, and so the line can only continue through Michael. No one expected him to be turned into a vampire, which, of course, ends that possibility. So, Helena finds Michael. The Old One knows he's strong enough and pulls off a mystical intervention. He's made different, which is why we tag him a *mystically enhanced* vampire, a one-of-a-kind creature of the night. Except, no one realizes just how unique he is."

Always a brilliant thinker, her adopted father continued, "Perhaps the Old One intervened again… Allows him to father a child, but why with a dark seer?"

"To push him over the edge?" Celia said with a tentative look.

"It could work. Lukas is not only human, but he inherits his father's mystical abilities. Knowing he has a child; Michael is forced onto the only path a true Champion such as he would take. Then he falls deeply in love with someone who should be shoving a long piece of wood into his heart, as if devotion to you, honey, creates a pre-destined path of honor."

Thorn gave one slow nod. "It's getting clearer. Under my nose, he comes up with a deadly plan to get even with those who ordered Helena's death and took Lukas. Portals close and evil takes a nosedive. That's some fancy footwork for one vampire if you ask me." He leaned back with a sigh. "They've already figured this out. Clayton is going to make everyone suffer."

Miles stood and started to pace. "I'm worried, Thorn. Michael cannot know this. The concept of an ancient bloodline being renewed through him must not be *anywhere* in his mind for them to siphon out—in the event they come for him."

"Oh, they're coming for him, Miles; you can bet the farm on that fact," Thorn said with a certainty that made a shiver run down Alana's spine. "Clayton's getting closer every minute. You know, I serve Helena without question. The purity of an angel's soul is legendary, and it's as if her soul is closer to God than most. She lets Michael see the beast-within and teaches him to control it. Maybe he's stronger than *he* even realizes. And no creature could've taken on what he did in Manhattan and actually survive."

"It does make sense, honey. Loving you forced him to take a clear look at himself. That love made him the Champion he's become."

Celia squeezed her hand. "Oh, sweetie, I told you he has a good soul."

Thorn's gentle smile rested on Celia while saying to Alana, "It must have been torture for him…to find his destiny in you, dearest Guardian, knowing he couldn't touch you."

"Then there's Lukas." Her adopted father barely whispered, "He is the direct continuance of Helena's lineage. This child's safety became Michael's critical diversion, which is why he used NWT to his ultimate advantage—and this leads us here. Helena set this in motion…all of it. I'm now convinced. Each piece falls into place."

Alana leaned forward, elbows on the table and palms supporting her face. "All of you, just back up a minute. With *mystical* women in this lineage, why'd they ever *allow* him to be turned into a vampire in the first place? Where was Helena when he was sired? What about the humanity *he* was unleashed upon? Nope. It doesn't add up. There has to be a catch."

"There are always casualties in a war, Alana, there are sacrifices and deaths," Thorn stated. "It's called the greater good. You should know all about that, dearest Guardian."

"Yes, but a Guardian doesn't have a choice—"

"Neither did Michael, apparently," Thorn stated. "He did what a vampire is supposed to do and stayed smart enough to do it without getting a stake shoved through his heart. After 1890, he didn't drink and drain humans anymore. Think of all the vampires you've staked. They're not the brightest bulbs in the demon world. They aren't jacked up like The Summoned Six or those who sire. You find them and stake them. It's easy because they have only one thing on their minds...like teenagers when they discover sex."

Everyone saw him turn very red, very quickly.

"That's an accurate analogy," Celia said in his defense.

After clearing his throat, Miles whispered, "In any event, what Thorn's trying to say is Helena created his path to redemption. We know of his sire. Cyril continues to elude Guardians. He chooses specific individuals. He was drawn to masculinity, arrogance, and strength. Suppose the 1600s were too soon for a showdown between good and evil? My point is, Michael's feeding pattern was specifically lust-driven, not megalomaniacal. Yet he's clever enough to survive. After being safe, throughout hundreds of years of historical events, perhaps now it's time to regenerate the bloodline."

Celia said, "The world's changed since 1690, Dad. Could Cyril have been in league with the sorcerers?"

Miles didn't seem to have to leaf through a file to answer the question. "New World Trading assumed Malone Imports profit after the young Englishman went missing. It's not a far reach to believe sorcerers were raiding companies as far back as then."

"He was set up—from the very beginning," Alana stated with coldness in her voice.

Thorn shook his head and took her hand, "No. All this was his destiny." The empath closed his eyes. "Your aunt wants him to pick up the pot of soup—alone."

****

Hours had passed. Alana watched from the doorway and smiled. *They look like a normal father and son at play.* The quick laughs sitting next to each other... Just seeing him like this made her love him more. Instead of going over, she remained in the doorway. "Thorn wants you to go downstairs to *Zia's,*" she said to him. "And Daddy B wants you to continue journaling, Lukas."

"Why? My dad's fine. I don't feel like writing any more of it," Lukas insisted.

Michael leaned into him. "Are we having a short-term memory problem? Miles asked you to do this, and you will." Softer, he added, "I know some things are hard to face, but it's all in the past, far behind you now."

"Can I do it in here?"

Alana handed over the notebook. "I thought you'd

ask me that. But keep the television off." The teen gave her a guilty grin and sprawled out on the couch.

Once in the hallway and out of sight from everyone, Michael stopped her. After a passionate kiss, he lifted her. Held her in a tight embrace, against the wall. "There's something about you in a dress," he whispered as more kisses fluttered down her neck. "My mind goes to one particular place every time I touch you."

Although she didn't want him to stop, she finally replied in a breathy whisper, "You have to go to *Zia's,* and I've got work to do."

The slide down his body was very sensual. Determined hands wandered to her breasts, then gripped her waist, and then cupped her bottom, inching the soft fabric up. Thumbs feathered the thin elastic lace low on her hips. The brush of his hand against her produced a visible quiver. "There's always later," he whispered. After another heated kiss, he walked away.

She stayed flat against the wall watching him, fanning her face. His arrogant stride was more than a pleasing sight. She took a deep breath and let it out slow. After straightening the soft yellow sundress, she went back to the dining room, which, at the moment, felt more than a few degrees hotter.

Chapter 29

Important Conversations

Upon closing the third-floor door, Michael stood in the hall with a little bit of trepidation before walking down the stairs. At Rosa's door, he glanced at the padlocked apartment across the hall and then gave a soft knock to her door.

When Rosa appeared, she craned her neck up and a smile lit her gentle face. "You are very tall, *Signore*." And he was suddenly very conscious of his six-foot-three height, a little unsure of what to reply. She stepped aside with a soft, "Please, come in," and his gaze came to rest on the crucifix in the living room.

With his right hand over his unbeating heart, he bowed slightly... a human habit. A human remembrance. Yet he couldn't find his voice as he took in her home's charming, old-fashioned décor. Against the closed shutter, he could imagine how the handmade lace curtains gracefully deflected the strong Amalfi sun. Priceless Florentine-glass lamps lit the small living room, and each piece of hand-carved furniture took him back to another era. Peering through the wide wooden arch that separated the dining area, he said, respectful, "Your home is very lovely, *Signora*."

She gave a simple nod. "Won't you sit?" She indicated a chair at the head of the dining room table, a place of honor in an Italian household. He obliged with a gentlemanly incline of his head. A floral-patterned coffee service was already set with lace and linen napkins. The spoons were pure silver.

"*Signora*, I'm sure you're busy."

"Nonsense, we must talk." She poured aromatic espresso and then sat to his left. The first sip was delicious. Another remembrance of his human life. "Ah, that was a long time ago."

"*Si, Signora,* a very long time ago."

Her head crooked ever so slightly. "Your conscience is full of sadness and regret. The desire to do what is right fuels your decision to leave as soon as possible." As a stunned expression crossed his face, she added, "It doesn't matter how much of a private man you are. This is truth."

"You know I must leave them."

"The eyes are windows to the soul, but I can read yours without looking into them." Rosa clicked her tongue. "Leaving will not help. All it does is delay the inevitable. Without you, Alana and Lukas will die horrible deaths. And the world remains exactly as you left it. You will not have affected anything. Evil wins. Humanity suffers. Is this what you want?"

"If I give myself to him, he will leave them be." There was no other way out. He was positive. Only his survival stood in the way of their safety.

"We have helped you, *Signore*, even when you had no knowledge of it. Many Georgians kept your child safe in the passageway and we sent protection your way during your battle. We cleansed you of the poison and I have blessed every ounce of your sustenance."

"How is it that I haven't burned from the inside out?

I cannot touch a crucifix without sizzling. Holy Water melts my skin. I'm a still a vampire. Reclaiming my soul does not change the facts."

"Perhaps it is no longer true." Stunned, he sat back, and Rosa's warm hand came to rest on his cool one. "There is a much-studied legend about a dream St. George had—toward the end of his courageous life. In it, the saint fights a powerful demon. Its swordlike tentacles slash at him and George grows weary. He prays for deliverance, aware that death is close. It is impossible for one to win against an evil such as this. But then, an unholy beast happens upon this battle. Instead of killing saintly George, it takes up his cause and slays the demon. Mortally wounded, it reaches out to the holy man, and George blesses it. He prays for it to be spared, knowing the creature is as it was made, through no desire of its own. George presses its paw to his heart and asks the angels above to intercede, to change this creature, to make it worthy of God's mercy. The good Lord complies."

Michael stared into the aromatic espresso. "It is a legend, *Signora*, and legends are half-truths."

"Ah, but the greater question is which half is the truth?" Without hesitation she reached over and made the Sign of the Cross on his forehead. He winced, waiting for the burn. It didn't happen. "When the time is right, *Campione*, you will come to us. Only after will you be able to slay your own dragon." She left his side, going into the kitchen and coming back with a pot of the healing soup. She blessed it in front of him. He stood and looked into her smoke-gray eyes feeling unsettled. So much weighed on his soul alone. "We are aware of all the beast-within had led you to do before the angel intervened." He was speechless. And when he inclined his head, she took his face in her hands.

"*Signora*, I'm not worthy."

A tender kiss met his cheek with the reply, "Who among us on this good earth ever is?"

She held the apartment door open, and as he walked through, hope nudged his soul. *This nightmare would end soon. Sacrificing myself is still the only way.* He climbed the stairs slowly.

****

Michael placed the pot on the stove, lifted the lid and stared inside. Blessed sustenance, blessed soup. Unexpected memories of his sisters flooded his mind as if a swollen river had spilled over its bank. He skimmed the soup gingerly with one finger ready for the sizzle. And then raised an eyebrow in wonder.

Thorn leaned down next to him. "Now isn't this an odd sight to see. Stealing a snack between meals... How unlike you, Champ." The empath reached into the refrigerator coming back with a bottle of water, which was gone in a few hearty gulps. Then he crushed the plastic with one hand. "Are you up for training or is it feeding time for a babe lost in the woods?"

He met the empath's wide grin with his mouth turned down. "Why? You think I'm lost?" He didn't wait for an answer. He didn't want to hear one, either. "Damn it, Thorn, these metaphors and the visuals they force me to see—I'm impressed. Are you finished with the researcher because I'm itching to take you on and get even for yesterday."

A snort and a smirk came at him full-force. "Yeah, I'm through with the files and ready to let you try." The empath cracked his neck and folded his beefy arms across his broad chest. Michael mimicked his stance with arrogance. "Take another lick of that yummy animal blood concoction on the stove because the next time you taste it, every muscle will ache again. It just might make your Guardian go all teary-eyed wanting to kiss the boo-boos, so they'll go away."

"Sarcasm too," Michael replied breaking the stand-off and heading to the master bedroom to change. "I liked it better when you were mono-syllabic."

Thorn walked back to the dining room. He stared at Celia, basking in her beautiful smile. "Michael and I are, well, we'll train through supper. Can you spare me, Miles?"

The researcher wore an amused expression as he looked up. "Thorn, I have to know—which is the real you?"

Alana started to smile, but then leveled a disapproving look at Miles. Celia sparkling green eyes flew wide and nudged her father's leg under the table.

"It's okay, my love. I guess you'd all like an honest answer. Well, you see… Certain aspects of who I am can't be changed. I read thought whether I want to or not. I can't lie—even to save my own life. My mission is Michael's needs whatever they might be. A Servant of Souls is a mystical creature, so reading heart, head, and soul comes with the territory. I can't take a life…can't change a life. I simply feel—and then do what's necessary for the greater good." His heart melted when he looked at Celia. His eyes burned with respect. "Now they both know how much I treasure you." She blushed deeply and met his gaze with love in her eyes.

Thorn gave a shy smile and then left Alana's home. It was an unexpected revelation, but Celia was secretly happy her love for Thorn was out in the open.

"Honey, I never knew," her father said as he pulled off his reading glasses.

"I can't explain it, Dad. There's a very intense psychic link between us. I feel it deep in my soul."

Unlike the shock in her father, hurt came off Ally and slammed against her heart. "Why didn't you ever tell me? Do you love him? I mean, I knew you were always at the brownstone, but I didn't think—"

"I, well, I—Ally, please don't ask me to try to explain right now." She sat back flustered and a little guilty over how she'd kept it a secret.

Her father touched her shoulder. "I'll go check on Lukas and leave the two of you for a short while."

She'd tell him everything later and waited until he was out of sight. After taking in a deep breath and letting it out slow, she looked at Ally. "All right, I guess now it is. I've loved Thorn since the first time we spoke, right after Michael came back with his soul once again intact. I felt like I'd always known him. He's such a sweet soul and so very important to me that... Plus, I had to be sure Michael was in good hands. I mean, you couldn't be anywhere near the brownstone."

Ally sighed as Celia sensed the hurt waft away like a blown-out flame from a tiny candle. "Maybe I've had my own Guardians. One unbelievable psychic sister always at my side and one unique vampire just a whisper away—it's probably a first in Guardian history."

She gave a definitive nod. "Yep, I totally agree. I think it sounds like a movie of the week. Oooh! I know. Let's write a script. How about it? We'll cast it with big Hollywood stars. A young Sofia Loren look-alike as you and someone like Uma Thurman plays me," she added, which made her sister laugh. "So, who do we cast as Michael?"

A secretive smirk appeared. "Dark eyes…handsome and commanding," A face flashed in her mind. "Nope… I'm too fast for you, Celia B! Got that thought shielded like a pro."

"Oh, come on, sis—"

"Nope. It should keep you guessing for a while."

****

When Miles came into the den, Lukas looked up. "I'm really sorry about my, uh, bad behavior. It won't happen again."

Miles had to smile at the serious expression. "Apology accepted. Now, to your writing."

He handed over the notebook. "I could give you a play by play, you know, about what Alana and Celia B are saying because I can even hear whispers when—" Miles gave a stern glare before scanning the latest entry.

Lukas shrugged with a guilty grin. "Oh. Sorry again."

"You really can be quite mischievous sometimes, which I sense to be genetic as well." It didn't take long as an astute researcher to notice certain aspects of the boy's writing skills. A clear cursive script, advanced vocabulary, and correct sentence structure. These were ingrained habits that didn't come from only one short year in a private high school. Lukas was bright just as his father had been centuries ago. But the foundations of this child's education came from Helena. And it hadn't left him during the years he'd been held hostage by the three sorcerers in the Second Realm, nor during the year of hunting his father. But Lukas came off edgy, perhaps anxious over what he'd written in the leather notebook.

"This is very good writing," he stated.

"Do you really think I'm like my dad?"

Miles gave a rare, full smile. "I would say yes, you really are very much your father's son. May I sit with you and read more?"

"Yeah, sure."

As Miles read, Lukas appeared more relaxed, even moved closer to him on the denim sofa. As they discussed some well-written passages, a deep sense of pride lit Lukas's angelic face. Experience as a parent recognized the change in him. *Yes, he feels safe. But he also feels his father's love. That alone is priceless.*

Chapter 30

Many Facets of Love

The long busy day turned into a quiet night. Celia had told her father about the love of her life before dinner. Rosa had come up, preparing last night's leftovers as only a true gourmet could. It tasted like a freshly cooked meal. As she finished drying the coffee cups, the way Lukas had pulled her and Ally aside to apologize for the way he had been behaving warmed her heart. The little cutie was easy to love, and she sensed his sincerity straight from the heart.

A smile began recalling Lukas's introduction to Italian pastries from the bakery one block over. He had a sweet tooth, a taste very evident to everyone at the table. Now, Lukas and Ally were getting to know one another, talking quietly in the den.

And all was well.

She had watched her father leave with the Rosa, and with everything washed and dried she wanted to make a special plate for Thorn. Reading her father's thoughts as he waited for the deadbolt's click on Rosa's door, she whispered with a sense of pride, "You know the lock is useless, Daddy B. No earthly deterrent can stop the evil NWT employs. Only this mystical shield is our protection. And Georgian strength is super powerful."

With a sweet smile spreading across her face, she

covered a platter of vegetables and fruit and then placed it in the refrigerator. She had written Thorn's name with a bold marker on a large piece of paper and taped it to the top. Every day, her beloved would find one just like this. "With love from Celia to my Thorn," she whispered. In fact, she'd grab a few more sheets of paper from the secretary and make the love notes in the guest room before going to bed.

But a big weight had come off her today. At least now she could tell Ally how much she'd missed him this past year and be totally honest. Thorn was her soul mate. Plain and simple. Often, with the others unaware, they spoke to each other without words.

Now there's no reason to hide my devotion. Thorn's new muscular frame may have shocked everyone, but to me? Physical appearance doesn't matter. It was his pure, courageous soul that had her heart. She saw his spirit—it's all she needed to keep on going.

****

In the basement, Michael had Thorn pinned to the earthen floor. "That's better, but if I do this," he said, and flipped Michael over, who was suddenly face down, kissing dirt.

One powerful jerk of his opponent's body sent Thorn suddenly careening into wooden barrels lining the wall.

"Then I get to do that," Michael said as he spit out dirt, swiped his mouth and then brushed his hands off.

Thorn laughed, rubbed his chest. "Good move; real good move. Wow, what a difference a day makes—or should I say a night?" Michael's expression changed, and the immediate decision to block last night's sexual exploits didn't happen fast enough. He caught the whole scene in a split-second. "Yep, I'd say it was a little of both. You're quick, but I'm quicker." He hopped onto an old barrel and wiped streaks of sweat off his brow. "Your full strength is back. Our hard work and the healing powers of consecrated blood paid off…in more ways than one."

"I told you before, stay out of my mind."

"Yeah, yeah, but I've got to admit this last stroll was in color and far better than those worn, spicy novels I found in the brownstone. I guess a man's gotta do what a man's gotta do." He cracked his neck and then his hands gripped his knees as he took in a few deep breaths.

Already on his feet, Michael leaned against the wall and glared. "I found them in the basement of the brownstone in a box. I've no clue who put them there, and I never read them. My bookshelves are lined with classic literature. But let me guess, a natural curiosity for all things human got the better of you."

"Nah, I'm only teasing." He stood and stretched his arms. "The sun's been set a while already and you need nourishment. Heading upstairs?" Michael nodded while dusting off his shirt. "By the way, will you be telling Alana about your new residence any time soon? You know—the apartment across from Rosa's?"

The look of shock came with a narrow glare. "Is there *anything* you don't know? Just keep it to yourself and far away from Celia." A dour smirk came at him. "And I catch the looks you give her.. Did I hear the ever popular "my love" and "dearest" leave your lips? You're getting as red as an apple, empath. All those nights at the brownstone when she came over with the excuse of keeping me updated on Alana. I'd go watch my Guardian and leave the two of you alone…*never* giving it a second thought. That green-eyed little slip of a psychic was really there to see you."

"She's a very pure soul with a big heart and soon to be one of the most acclaimed psychics the Georgians will ever know. My Celia's a very special lady."

Michael leaned against the wall with his arms crossed against his chest and his feet crossed at the ankles. "I knew I'd get it out of you down here. So, what is your intention?"

"Not what you're thinking. A Servant of Souls can't partake in physical pleasure. But I'll always love her, deeper than I can ever express. Meeting such a beautiful soul and getting to know her has been the most precious experience I've had in this world."

"Loving Alana, being able to make love to her is something I will always treasure. And it's more than just physical. I swear I can feel my soul quiver when we are one. It's not fair, Thorn, because you're the best man I've ever met—in my very long existence. That's the truth, my good friend."

He watched Michael go up the basement stairs. Then he sat on the earthen floor. He took a fistful of red dirt into his hand letting it fall back to the ground as if it spilled out of a broken hourglass. "You're ready," he whispered, "and my mission comes to its end. I don't regret these years on this earth; what I've been asked to accomplish. The only regret is leaving my loving soulmate behind."

****

When Michael came out of the shower Alana was sitting in the upholstered chair. "It's very late," she whispered. A full pitcher of sustenance stood waiting upon the nightstand; alongside the crystal mug he had been using since the first day he'd been brought to her.

Alana said softly, "I like the look."

The dusty-rose towel was wrapped low on his waist, his chest still beaded with water from the trickle of a shower. Standing in front of the draped windows, he studied her. A vibrant vision of loveliness—and she was his. Her head tilted to the side, her long chestnut hair resting across one shoulder. Like a Mediterranean princess framed by the Queen Anne chair. The hue of the dress against its floral pattern completed the portrait. Her legs were crossed at the knee, one foot kicking the air ever so slightly, her back straight and her breasts rising and falling with each breath. Her flawless, tanned skin meant she'd spent many days in the bright Amalfi sun.

"Have I mentioned how much I like you in this dress? Yellow becomes you, darlin'. Especially that shade. You didn't wear sundresses too often back in the city. I guess they weren't practical in your line of work."

"I had one similar to this back in New York. Don't you remember it?"

"Ah, but that one was quite a few shades lighter, and it didn't have such thin straps."

"Now that's odd. I bought it long after graduating from college. Give it up, you sneak, because Celia confirmed what I always suspected—you were always only a heartbeat away."

"I thought psychics were good at keeping secrets. Guilty as charged, my love." His mischievous smile not a bit contrite. "Now how shall I make this up to you?"

Alana stood, approaching slowly, and locked to his gaze. The sway of her hips? Very sexy. A tug to the towel and it dropped to the floor. "That wasn't very nice," he whispered, leaning into her and gently edging the sundress's hem higher.

"Are you hungry?"

An earthy ring to her question, a sassy look that said she planned the double entendre. He growled low. His arousal, of course, highly visible. "Always," he managed to say.

"I like you naked," she whispered in a sensual way.

He expected a kiss, but instead, Alana sauntered slow and sexy to the door in silence, where she turned to him. Her pose seductive, her hazel eyes, heavy and hooded. And focused on his erection. "You said you were hungry."

But as the last syllable slipped from her inviting lips, he was already in front of her. His hands planted firm on the door framed her face, his mind drowning in her tease. "Do you wish to tempt me?" She was so alluring, so provocative in her boldness. He wanted her. Now. Her fingers ran through his damp wavy hair, and she stood on her tip-toes to nibble his ear whispering, "Uh huh, so what're you gonna do about it?"

And he went right over the edge. Pressing against her, he reached under her dress expecting to rip her delicate lace panties off. But they weren't there.

"A Guardian always comes prepared."

"Does she, now." Her hand slid up and down his erection. He ravaged her lips; his tongue danced with hers. More than desirous, he lifted her with one hand around her waist. Her legs saddled his hips. The scent of her arousal made him groan, and she rested her forehead against his. He positioned his erection and she looked down to see him enter her. Her whimper excited him even more. She threw her head back, her arms tight around his neck. He held her bottom, pulling out slow and then thrust deep. The slick, tight wetness of her revved his passion. Her body bucked in orgasm and then she rested in his arms, soft and supple. His fingers found her core and she gasped in a quick breath.

"I find myself ravenous tonight," he whispered in her ear as he walked her to the four-poster. He put her down so that her back rested against a bedpost. Slow as sin he undressed her. When her hands reached up and gripped the post he sank to his knees. The look of pure ecstasy was on her lovely face, eyes closed, lips partially open. He ran his hands up her legs and when her thighs parted his mouth took over. She whimpered and wriggled against his tongue. Yes, he thought, I am truly ravenous for you.

****

They spooned together in the middle of the bed. To say the past hours had been passionate would be an understatement. Alana was pleasantly spent. Years of dreaming about making love with him had unlocked a primal need. The ways he used his tongue drove her wild, unlocked a hot urgency within. "This is what it feels like, isn't it? Loving each other—in a-a *normal* relationship." she said.

His arm covered hers, their fingers laced together. With a kiss to her shoulder, he replied, "Yes."

"These days, Michael, caring for you, not sure if you'd ever come back whole and well, watching you grow stronger, Oh God, there are so many emotions I can't sort through them."

He pulled her closer, held her tighter as tears glistened in her eyes. "Shhh, don't." He kissed her shoulder. "This is what it feels like but we're pretty far from normal." His cool lips brushed her neck. "I adore you, my Guardian. I treasure this private time together; I'd walk through the fires of Hell to keep you safe."

She took his hand in hers, kissed his palm and pressed it to her heart. "I belong to you, Michael. I've yearned to feel you inside me for so many years. Remember the night we met? I had just turned seventeen."

"I'd already been watching you. Please don't ask why. Something about you called to me."

"Tell me, my love," she whispered coming out of his embrace to see his handsome face.

"I will have to take a leap of faith hoping you will understand, my Guardian."

"Of course," she whispered, curious as to what he would say.

"The first time you were with your father. You were a couple of years younger than Lukas is now. I spent many nights lurking near the passageway where the portal is. After he was born, I'd just stand there hoping somehow Helena would show him to me. One night, dawn was minutes away, and as I headed to the security of the brownstone, there you were. In the flower district with your father, coming out of a flower wholesale store with tiny red sweetheart roses clutched to your sweater. You held your father's arm like you were royalty."

"I went with him often before school. I loved leaving in darkness, returning after dawn."

He nodded. "April through October, every Thursday in the last minutes of darkness. I knew Alfonso's shop…I knew where you lived and often listened to Stefania giving piano lessons. Even then, I suppose I protected you should anything try to bring you harm. When you turned sixteen and accepted this mission, I sensed the mystical gift. I saw Miles take you on your first mission. I watched you sharpen such fascinating skills. I've dodged many Guardians in my long, undead existence, but you were perfection, darlin'. I made a silent vow to keep you safe no matter what the cost. Then the first time we talked…I knew I loved you." He paused but she wanted, no, needed to hear more. "I saw you bury both your parents. The day was overcast. No sun at all. How I longed to take that ungodly pain away. You were safe when the researcher brought you into his family, but I was always a breath away when you left the penthouse after sunset, my Guardian." He paused and closed his eyes. "Those deadly weeks, when the beast-within me raged—"

"Michael, don't."

"I thank God I didn't kill you." Raw emotion came at her, his voice low and rough. "The punishment was well deserved. When I came back, I vowed to never touch you again. But I'd be damned for all of eternity if anything ever dared to lay a hand on you. As you often said, I lurked in the shadows."

She kissed his lips in a tender fashion, closed her eyes, and molded her body to his once again. He kissed her hair. "I don't know how or why I'm able to be with you like this. May it never end." Her eyes filled with tears and her heart quickened. "I am yours, Michael, forever and always."

Chapter 31

Humanity

Perhaps it was the power of blessed blood—along with the fact that a distance now existed between Michael and those he loved. No longer drinking the life force of Lukas or Alana, the blended blood was Georgian. He had clarity.

His eyes shot open at dawn, not needing to look at the alarm clock beside the bed. Alana still slept curled to him, safe and secure. As if he willed it, she turned with a sigh. He slipped out of the bed on the other side. No sound. No disturbance to the love of his life still fast asleep.

After a quick shower, he pulled on the sweats and shrugged on the undershirt still hanging behind the bathroom door from last night. Standing at the sink, picking up the toothbrush she'd bought him in Pisa, it was only natural to lift his eyes. The habit? An absentminded glance in an empty mirror, as always, when he ran the brush over his teeth.

But this time, he stared in disbelief.

A cloudy image peered back—one that hadn't been seen in centuries. High cheekbones, straight nose, and an angular face…unmistakably his. Leaning into the mirror, he couldn't see his eyes. But it *was* his reflection, something lost the night he'd been sired. It was one thing that set a vampire apart from humanity. As much as it fascinated him, it frightened him as well.

He walked through the bedroom, closed the door, and then strode across the dining room. He hooked every set of brocade drapes and opened every window pushing the shutters to the bricks, studying the quiet street below.

"It's overcast today, researcher. There's no sunlight."

He heard Miles set down his cup of morning coffee. "That may not be wise."

"Who are you kidding? They know I'm here. It's only a matter of time. I know you're still staring at me. You and I must talk."

His walk to the kitchen was slow. Opening the fridge, he reached for a glass container and quickly draining the blessed blood. He took a mug off the rack, and with a cup of black coffee in hand, he sat across from the researcher and began in a low voice.

"First, tell the Georgians how much I appreciate their support, no matter what happens to me. Second, I am truly sorry for dragging you and everyone in this building into it—for putting you in those evil bastards' line of fire—my son, the woman I love… It's gonna get messy." His brow tightened feeling deep respect for the man across from him. Folding his hands on the table, he leaned in to close the distance between them. "Please forgive me. I honestly regret this. I feel it coming, and I want everyone at San Giorgio's by sunset. Take Thorn with you."

The researcher ripped off his reading glasses and threw them on the table, shooting him a glare. "We will not comply. You're not going to upset my daughter or your son, or our routines, for that matter, until we know for certain there is no *other avenue.* Look, we have three among us who can sense danger. You cannot second-guess the next move. What utter foolishness! Try forcing Alana and Lukas to leave tonight, and you'll have World War Three to contend with. No. Let it play out, or one of them will get hurt trying to be at your side—*again.*"

The curt reply hung heavy in the air. Finally, Michael leaned back. "I'll accept your words for now, but I want a promise. When the time comes, you will get everyone to the church without hesitation—without questions."

He kept a fierce expression on his face until Miles gave a quick "Of course."

"Good. Now I need your cell phone." He held out his hand as the researcher reached into his trouser pocket and produced the phone with a curious expression. When he got to the door, Miles stood in full panic. "You cannot go out there! It's daylight, hazy daylight, but the sun—"

"I'm not leaving the building. Relax. I'll be back soon."

****

Michael yanked off the padlock on the empty second-floor apartment. Closing the door behind him, he stared at the dark space. Rooms empty, shutters locked, and wood floors hardly dusty. He punched a series of numbers into the cell phone and expected the groggy "hello."

"I know it's the middle of the night in Manhattan, Patrick, but this can't wait. Get out of bed, don't wake your wife, and find someplace where you can talk. I'm calling in your debt."

Patrick Christenson owed the vampire his life. On the night Lukas was conceived he had saved this hopeless human already in the clutches of the dark seer. The accountant would've made the deadliest mistake of all… going with her. Of course, he had intervened. One night of sex with a mystically enhanced vampire was the trade-off—and the human on the edge of despair got to keep his soul. The accountant turned out to be a valuable asset. He had set up the trust funds for Alana and Lukas. And he kept Michael's finances squeaky clean, legal, and above all, untraceable.

"Okay, I'm downstairs," Christenson finally said. "After I saw the hole in Manhattan where your office used to be, I thought you were dust and bone. Where are you anyway?"

"I'm in Italy—Portofino to be exact. I need you to do a couple of things for me very far under the radar, understand?"

"I'm a wizard when it comes to money—the good kind of wizard. And I'm always discreet when it comes to you. What do you need?"

"Move half of my funds to *Banco Italia* in Portofino. The rest is to be placed in a Swiss account under the name of Lukas Malone, with an access code sent to Miles Bookman and a copy of it to Miss Cecelia Bookman at the Georgian Estate in Hampton Hill, England. Mary Kendrick, owner of the Kendrick Art Gallery on the upper west side, can help you with what comes next. Tell her I need a birth certificate, social security number, and a list of phony medical and dental records for a fifteen-year-old boy. Lukas was born May 19, 1990. Place of birth should be listed as St. Francis Hospital in Manhattan. She'll know what to do. Everything has to arrive in less than twenty-four hours, understand? The address is 52 Via Amadeus in Portofino. Send them to

271

Rosa Bellini." He paused. "Mary must go to my brownstone and remove all artworks. Some pieces are hundreds of years old…all originals. My books are first editions, worth a fortune. Have her sell everything and keep the proceeds from the sales. If she starts to argue, just enlist Martha Kendrick to persuade her. Have Mary take anything else of value. But it must be done immediately." He didn't want any loose ends dangling for those bastards to chew on. "When all is completed, you are to burn any information that connects you and me including the phone in your hand. Computer flash drives, paper files … everything and then bury the ashes in consecrated ground. As for your usual fee? Double it."

"Look, you're worth millions after twelve months of aggressive and strategic management. Are you sure about this? I mean, I can work fast, but are you sure you *want* me to? How about leaving one account open—"

"No. Not necessary, Patrick. You won't be hearing from me again. Take care of that beautiful family of yours. One last thing… Leave Manhattan. Take an extended cruise to Alaska or Hawaii. Book it today—and get your family the hell out of there. Enjoy every minute with them. Those you love are those who matter." He ended the call.

He studied each room lost in thought. *Lukas could never return to the city. Thorn will keep him in line. Miles will see to a proper education. Alana and Rosa will help raise him. My boy will have a good life… without me.*

****

Once upstairs, Michael placed the cell phone on the dining room table and begrudgingly resumed his place across the table from Miles. It was still early and they were the only ones awake.

Miles stopped typing on his laptop, pulled off his reading glasses. and sat back.

Curiosity and dread competed in Michael's brain. He folded his arms, leaned his elbows on the table knowing dread was the winner. "What exactly do the Georgians know about me?"

"Is something bothering you?"

Shifting back in the chair, he kept his arms locked across his chest, crossed his legs as his eyes shifted to the open windows. "I was never a religious man. I find it ironic how your group is willing to get so involved with something like me. I mean, they got me here, they healed me, and they tapped their veins for me—all those holy people."

"You look uncomfortable."

"Wouldn't you be? I spent two-thirds of my undead existence feeding off people just like them. The holier they were—" He shook his head and looked down running a hand through his hair then locking his arms once again.

"It's no secret you had a penchant for nuns," the researcher stated in a casual tone, sounding more like an off-the-cuff statement rather than the serious indictment it was. "I would surmise the creature you *were* found this particular type of kill exhilarating—the most innocent of the innocent—like your sisters."

He leveled a cold but curious gaze at Miles. "What would you know about my sisters?"

"Do you remember them?"

"Oddly, yes… and for some unknown reason very vividly, even in my dreams. I'm a vampire. Even mystically enhanced, I shouldn't be able to recall human life."

Miles moved his laptop aside, picking up his pen. "Since you've brought it up, I'd like you to journal what you experienced... the pain, the nightmares."

"Not on your life, researcher... Those little snip-its of agony stay with me."

"Then tell me about your sisters."

"I-I loved them and they loved me. Being the youngest, they doted on me."

"And your parents?"

He shifted uneasy. "Father said I was a spoiled little boy. He was strict, but he was a fair man. When my sisters left, I became a handful. The year 1678... I was Lukas's age. God how I missed them. I got into quite a bit of mischief in the months that followed. I knew exactly what to do to make Mother cry. She was a gentle soul. Father overlooked my antics once or twice. Then he took a strap to my backside."

"You had no other family."

"No. Not a cousin, aunt or uncle. I rebelled against Father's very ethical ways as I matured. He was an honorable man, like you, and well respected. He had a moral demeanor. I was very head-strong, very ambitious... And I never saw my sisters again. There was no discussion of them, like they had never existed. I didn't even know the name of the convent they went to, but I knew it wasn't in England... Some Catholic country, I presumed."

"That must have frustrated you—not knowing where they were."

"Try resentment and rage. And I can't believe how much I remember my humanity." He shook his head as if to clear it. Rarely talkative, he found himself almost wanting to share what he now recalled. "By the time I turned twenty there wasn't a pretty rich girl in London who didn't sigh with pleasure *if* she caught my eye. Father's death completely devastated Mother, who now lived in a silent daze. Months later, I placed her in the care of a trusted servant and moved the business to America. I'm not proud of leaving her. That alone should have me burning in Hell." Like in my first terrifying dream, he thought. "How she pleaded with me to stay. Without Father tweaking my conscience on a daily basis, I didn't care anymore. I left the servant money, enough to last through the end of Mother's life. It was cruel…I am aware. I never sent word of my whereabouts. If you thought me extremely self-absorbed, you wouldn't be wrong, Researcher. A short year later in Manhattan, Malone Imports was once again a thriving business. That success allowed me to have my way with all the pretty ladies in a new city. With no intentions of being duped into marriage, I stayed far away from the single ones. Then at the age of twenty-seven, a jealous husband paid handsomely to have me taken care of…for good. Instead of killing me, Cyril turned me into what I am. I can still see the aristocrat's ice-blue eyes turn amber before he bit me." He swallowed hard. "Shortly after I was sired, I saw an old friend from London who had immigrated to America. He said Mother had passed. Vicious beast that I was, I made sure his death came slow with many screams of agony." Keeping his voice low and his gaze averted as he thought, which is why I deserve Hell.

"And your sisters?"

"Anne, Rosalind, and Priscilla. They owned my heart." So many emotions thickened his tone, and he narrowed his eyes. "I know what you're trying to do.

You want me to say it, even though you know all about me." He leaned forward first in anger, which instantly slid to shame. "Many sins and many, many more will haunt my soul in Hell forever. I never drank from a child. I never killed a Guardian of Souls. I preferred women over men. Their blood tasted like honey—and I was driven by lust. Virgins… The sweetest nectar I—" He paused. "Let's just say there were more than a few convents on the North American continent where I left my signature. The last one was a turning point, so to speak." He scrubbed his face and sighed. "1890… They called it an outbreak of consumption, but the Mother Superior knew the truth. I violated their bodies. I drank from them—and I slaughtered them all. That was my last foul act when Helena found me."

Pushing off the table, he stood and walked to a window with his face turned toward the sunless sky.

"I'm not a fool, Miles. There's no way I could *ever* make up for what I've done. It wouldn't make a damned bit of difference if I spent a thousand years on my knees in penance. Nothing will bring my victims back. I'm going to Hell, and that lousy little inhuman Irishman is waiting for the right moment to make his move…to send me there. You should have left me in that passageway. I have had enough."

He wished he could walk away from this. He didn't continue—couldn't say any more as if he were on an emotional rollercoaster, not knowing what awaited the next climb, the next terrifying dip. Intense nausea gripped his stomach as if he were human again.

Bracing his hands on the window frame, he whispered, "Why did I tell you this? Why did I say it out loud?" He swiped at the corner of his eye fearfully aware of the clear liquid on his fingertip. "Tell me what I am now, Researcher. My tears are clear, my stomach aches with human hunger and I saw my cloudy reflection in the mirror. My unbeating heart is so full of love for Alana and my son that I swear I feel it ache. What kind of twisted, cosmic joke…showing me everything I want but can *never* have?" He turned back to the window not sure if he wanted to sob or punch the wooden frame.

"Yours is a predestined path. I can only state what I know in my heart. As God as my witness, you will be victorious, having already accomplished the impossible."

The soft, calm reply forced him to shut his eyes. He didn't move yet he wanted to run. Lost in solitude, he stood there many minutes. Then he went to the kitchen, and fixed Alana's breakfast. All he wanted was to hold her. All he wanted was what was best for his son. Their safety was all that mattered.

Miles watched him walk through the room in silence. He was stunned by this conversation that could almost be classified a confession. Bringing his laptop front and center, he stared at a blank page trying to digest every nuance of what he'd just heard. Repositioning his reading glasses he began this entry with the truth. *Michael isn't only suffering… he is frightened.*

These insights were crucial pieces of information about the unusual transformation taking place within a tortured being. *Vivid human recall, unguarded emotions, an expression of hunger, clear tears, a reflection— significantly unique characteristics.*

Typing the words on the blank page forced him to wonder about their meaning as well.

Chapter 32

Preparations

As the sun rose, Valetta Russo limped into her penthouse in Rome. Floors above the office, the liaison locked the door with a look of disgust. Clothes trailed to the bathroom suite. She stood under a hot shower, scrubbing her skin raw. She brushed her teeth until her gums bled, and gargled with peroxide, spitting it out into the sink all the while cursing.

Rage swelled when studying her naked body in the smoky wall of mirrors. Bruises and bite marks covered inner thighs, breasts, neck, and arms. *Clayton Mails is a pig—a vile, nasty animal.* He'd pay what he did to her. Red marks marred her throat and wrists. A high-neck, long-sleeved sweater would conceal his fetish from her office staff.

The red silk robe settled over her tender skin, and Valetta picked up the phone, pressed 6 to connect with her assistant. "*Ciao bene*, Ricardo, send the team to Portofino. Make sure they have the drugs with them. Carlo must call when they arrive. Cancel my meetings this morning. I'll be in at noon." She left the phone off the hook and snuggled between black satin sheets.

The pig would surely pay for every single abuse.

Small tears lingered in the corners of her eyes. So many illegal contracts, hundreds of unholy kills, and acts

278

of perverse loyalty to the sorcerers she had racked up over the years. Of all the things she had done to get ahead, being a willing participant in Clayton's sadistic fantasies last night was, by far, the vilest request ever asked of her. The liaison ran back to the bathroom toilet, stuck her fingers down her throat and threw up until there was nothing of Clayton left in her stomach.

****

Siena was many miles away from Portofino. Mother Aurea stood wearily after Morning Devotions. Thin and bent, the nun's dark-gray eyes watered with age. The last sixty-five years of her life had been spent the exact, same way—Mass at dawn, meditation, and busy hours tending vegetables and fruits in the garden. As Prioress of her Order, Aurea's spiritual mission took precedence, leading cloistered sisters through their vocations in the mystical sect. Sister Rosalinda assisted the healer into the fragrant promenade surrounding their convent. "The day is hazy and dull, so unusual for Siena this time of year." She glanced to up to Heaven and said in her calm way, "It is time, Rosalinda."

Other remarkable women dedicated to prayer, healing, and protection prepared themselves in the chapel. All pure of heart and spirit, each had been individually called by the angels to lend strength to those whose hour of need had been thrust upon them.

A long white passenger van idled where the garden path ended. Sister Rosalinda guided the holy woman to it. "Gabriella is driving," she whispered to the Prioress, "I thought it best, since time is now of the essence."

She agreed. "So young and full of energy, Gabby's need for speed is uncanny for someone called to our way of life. But who are we to judge?"

279

Sister Rosalinda settled her into the middle row of seats, making sure she was safely belted between herself and another. The rest took their places while two sisters filled the back of the van with fruits and vegetables from the garden for the pastor at the ancient church of San Giorgio—in Portofino.

****

Everybody's busy except me, Lukas thought, looking at Celia and Thorn in quiet conversation on the living room couch. He was at the dining room table with his dad and Miles. Sitting next to Miles, he kept glancing across the table watching his father read a pile of worn, yellowed files and oblivious to everyone, including him.

Miles looked up from his notebook with a fatherly grin. He eagerly awaited another positive response. "I always, kind of, liked language arts class. I had this really neat teacher. She let us dissect all these different poems, you know, for the rhythm of the words. It was cool."

"It shows, young man. As much as you may complain about doing this, I have to say, your skill is impressive. Perhaps I'm in the presence of a budding novelist or a future researcher for the Georgian Circle. May I show this to Father Giovanni?"

"Yeah, okay." He gave a shrug because his dad hadn't reacted to the compliment. "There's nothing in there that would shock a priest, right? Who knows? It might help." Bursting with pride, he itched to tell him all the normal things he'd learned in school.

A wider smile appeared on the researcher's usually staid face. "I highly doubt anything would shock him, and quite possibly, you are correct. This might help the Georgians better understand your father... better understand you." Miles patted his back and added, "On second thought, why don't we deliver it together? He may have a question or two for you. Perhaps, you and I can take a walk later on."

His eyes lit up, and he looked at his dad, who was squinting over weird, purple lettering. "Celia's Notes" stood out in bold block letters across the top. Lukas could see it through the page. Then his dad put the Celia papers down and gave Miles a murderous glare. "We'll see how the day goes, all right?"

Lukas sat back stunned but didn't get angry. Maybe his disappointment showed because Miles gave him a pretty positive nod.

****

Fresh Italian bread and an array of fresh-cut fruit and cheeses were brought to the table by the woman he loved. "Okay, everyone, lose the books. The boy's gotta eat, Daddy B."

Michael caught the smiles passing between her and his son. Knowing that they'd become comfortable with each other pleased him. He handed Miles Celia's nine pages of notes, which were indecipherable to him. The ease of his son's comfort with everyone became more evident as they shared a mid-day meal together. Although the savory smells made his stomach rumble, he slipped into the kitchen and drank his sustenance in private, returning to the table with a fresh cup of coffee, which he brewed himself.

After the table was cleared, he leaned back and studied the empath. "You know, Thorn," he said with a devilish smirk, "I've gotta hand it to you... Last night those same clothes were covered with red dirt."

"It's Mother Nature at her very best. I waited till

midnight and took a walk down the coast. I took a dip in the sea. It was very refreshing. The water was clean and warm. I've got to admit, there's nothing like that back in Manhattan."

"You left? After sunset? What about the mystical protection on the building? How the hell did you pull that one off?"

"Not a problem for an empath. If you touch the doorknob and feel the right words, the lock opens all by itself. Right, Celia?" She nodded in agreement. Thorn shot Lukas a semi-stern glare. "But you shouldn't try it. Just in case you get any bright ideas. First, it'll backfire completely and then you get spanked."

Seeing his son's dark-blue eyes widen, he glared. "Change the subject, Thorn."

"Why don't we workout as a foursome today? I'd like to see what you've got to offer, kid, and I know our Guardian here is a gifted fighter. Any suggestions where we can do that; where there isn't a dirt floor and doesn't involve moving furniture, Boss?"

Michael wanted to wipe the innocent grin off Thorn's face, but instead, casually answered, "Why don't we use the empty apartment downstairs? I'm sure the owner won't mind."

"Gee, ya think? How about I ask him?" Alana poked his shoulder. "Can we use your place, my love?" A sweet grin followed. "The shock on your face is priceless. What? Did you think I'd *never* guess? A flare for expensive antique furniture, original masterpieces, dark luscious colors, soft beige leather couches, I could continue the list, but you get the picture. I just can't imagine why you didn't put in a hot tub."

"Believe me, I thought about it. But Portofino's

zoning board wouldn't budge. I know. The water pressure leaves a lot to be desired. I should have offered a bribe," he added with typical arrogance.

His son's eyes were wide again. "You mean you *own* this place? That's way cool! So, when I got you out of the bedroom… You already knew what everything looked like—"

"I never saw the drapes before that moment." He stood and strode to the door motioning the empath to follow, saying to his son, "Change into sweats and meet us down there."

As they started down the steps, he hissed, "Nice going, big mouth." Thorn started to chuckle while he bristled with annoyance.

****

Sitting in her kitchen for a late lunch, Sophia Vecchio watched the light on a specially equipped telephone go off flashing red at three-second intervals. She walked to it, pressed "read" and a message scrolled across its screen:

Rossini wants you sleep at villa you cleaned. Three days double pay. I bring groceries. You cook/clean for client. Meet you outside 6:30 pm. Be ready. G. Scotto.

She blessed herself, sat in the single chair at the table and looked at the food on her plate. She ate slowly and then scraped what remained into the garbage pail. After washing the dish, she replaced it in the kitchen cabinet and preceded to empty out an old, humming refrigerator throwing everything into the pail as well. Tying its plastic liner, she'd throw it out when she left.

At the kitchen table, she wrote a short note to Father Giovanni, which she would hand to a downstairs neighbor's daughter on the way out. The young Guardian would deliver it late in the evening.

With clean white sheets from a drawer in the bedroom dresser in hand, she covered the worn furniture in the living room. One chair and an old sofa. Stripping the bed, she bundled the sheets tying them together and placing them at the door. They would be thrown out as well. Sitting on the threadbare mattress her gaze came to rest on her mother's crucifix hanging on the wall above the headboard, and she began meditation.

Hours later, she pulled an old cardboard suitcase from under the bed. Two black dresses and toiletries were placed in it with care. Other personal items went in it as well. The last item, the crucifix, lay on top of her housecoat before it was closed, and its rusty hinges secured. Lamps were unplugged, shutters and windows locked. At the appropriate time with tied trash bag and bundled sheets in one hand, and her suitcase in the other, she left her home. At the old bin behind building, she lifted its lid and placed the two items inside and then, suitcase in hand, she went to the front of the building to wait.

Giuseppe was five minutes late.

****

Thorn's reason behind suggesting this workout became clear to Michael as soon as he said it. They were into their second hour, and he now had a very good picture of what his son was capable of. While Alana and the empath sparred with each other, he studied his son's every move.

Pulling Lukas off the floor, he added an approving pat to the shoulder with the compliment, "Good. Swift engagement and precise."

Lukas shrugged off the bruise to his elbow. "I heal

really quick, like Alana does."

"No doubt you withstand more physical abuse than any other person your age." Again, his son beamed, with a proud fist pump in the air and a triumphant "Yes!"

They switched partners, and an hour later, Alana stated, "Wow...I'm impressed with the smoothness of your counters and quick footwork."

Lukas swiped sweat dripping in his eyes. "Like a Guardian, right?"

"Definitely," she replied with a serious face, "and not a newbie either. Those are some seasoned moves, Lukas." He dodged another well-placed strike and managed to pin Alana down.

His son's ego soared, and he was careful not to show a deepening worry. *Although strong and quick, the only victim of his assaults that troubled year was me. And I tempered my attacks with him. Spryness and speed are in his favor, and yes, he moves like a Guardian.* He couldn't deny his child possessed unique talents, a perfect blend of human and mystical abilities.

But Lukas was an innocent and demons were devious.

The workout had been intense. He saw his son tiring, grabbed a shoulder and pulled him into a tight hug before kissing the top of his damp blond hair. "How about heading up and hitting the shower?"

"But, Dad, I can keep going," Lukas said in protest, to which he adamantly ordered, "Upstairs. Shower. Now."

"I'll go with him," Thorn offered. "I need to put my feet up a while."

He nodded, waited until they left to let out a sigh of relief. Then he studied Alana as he leaned against the apartment's locked door. "Now my Guardian, let's see what you've got." Her sassy smile began, and he readied his stance once again.

They sparred with ease. Alana, one of the fiercest Guardians in Georgian history, was now positive. Michael was, in fact, different. Much stronger, quicker than ever before. As the session was coming to an end, her grip to his neck slipped, very aware he was sweating like a human.

But in the next instant his move stunned her. He had her high off the floor. It was a lethal position for anyone, even with mystical abilities. The possibility of hitting the floor head-first could sever her spinal cord. She didn't even realize she was holding her breath, too shocked to scream. She gasped in a long, deep breath and then coughed.

His cold hands cinched her waist like steel clamps. "Don't worry, darlin'. I've got you."

Breathing normal again, she let herself go limp. Slow and careful, he brought her down. "I couldn't... I wouldn't have...survived!" Relax, she thought, get more oxygen to your muscles.

They both stretched out on the floor. He lay on his side gently pulling off stray tendrils stuck to her flushed face. "I never would have hurt you," he whispered.

She rolled onto her back and propped herself up on both elbows, studying him. "I felt how super-strong you were two nights ago. But I didn't say anything. I thought it was because you were so furious with me. My God, you're such an enigma."

"That's a-a good choice of words, I'll admit." But he offered no explanation, saying instead, "Still love me?"

"Forever and always," she whispered. And as if on cue, her body switched gears. He looked sexy as hell. Her body was already flushed and yet her temperature rose even higher. Her heartbeat, which had slowed, suddenly raced again.

As if he knew her desire, a hand cupped her left breast. She sighed.

Between kisses to her neck, he whispered, "Did I lock the door?"

Her "Yes—" came with a tug to his undershirt, which flew off in a flash. He made quick work of removing her clinging T-shirt and sports bra to nuzzle her breasts and then lick her taut nipples. Playing with the waistband of his sweats, she bit her lip and he leaned away landing on his back and pulling her on top. He was already hard.

With a perfectly placed sensual squirm and a naughty grin, she got the response she wanted. When his hands slapped against the floor, she sidled down his legs pulling his sweats with her. He kicked them off the rest of the way with ease. His erection was so inviting. She leaned down and took him into her mouth as her core coated. Her lips worked in a way that made him groan. Again and again, she teased him, loving the sound of every quick hiss. His handsome face had ecstasy written across it. With her hands splayed across his chest, she kept up the erotic tease.

Her anticipation heightened when he slid her up his body. She whimpered and ground hips her into his. In one swift move he rolled on his side and suddenly she was face down on the floor. He made quick work of pulling off her sweatpants. His fingers danced up the back of her legs, which moved apart as if by command.

Her arms stretched wide as sensual kisses fluttered at the small of her back. When his palm met her core, it created a friction that made her hips rock. Her bottom came off the floor to welcome further exploration. She breathed hard in anticipation.

"Enjoying something new, my Guardian?" he asked in a low, sensual tone.

"Uh huh…" was all she could get out.

"You will climax in my hand," he whispered. Her breath hitched at the command, and the explosion of pure pleasure had her gasping for breath. Her hips rode the motion as his mouth came to her ear. "You are so damp with desire. I like you this way. I could take you just like this."

She wriggled against his palm with a whimper. It was her way of saying 'yes, yes, yes'. His hand slid slowly up her thigh, lingered on her bottom, and then held her hip. Leaning into him they rolled on the floor, His cool fingers explored the wet heat of her, which made her buck. She was bathed in new sensations. Splayed on the floor, she was ready to try something new and with determination she brought herself up and over his waist. With her head thrown back, his hands repositioned her and his long erection became an even more inviting tease. Poised at her core, she cried out when he took her.

As if by some primal command they joined together, the rhythm building once again. Slow then hard, she wanted more. She positively quivered. His eyes were closed and the expression on his face read bliss. Thrusting harder and faster, when his hand swept across the tip of her core pleasure shot through her like a rocket. This orgasm was powerful, deep. It sizzled through every part of her body. Holding him tight within her, she wanted to stay like this forever.

It took time for her breathing to go back to normal. After he pulled out slowly, he peeled her off and brought her into his arms. A gentle kiss brushed her cheek. She bit her lip and nestled against him. The sight of him. The feel of him. He was her rapture. He was need and desire. She looked up to see his sensual grin. "Ah, my love, your passion captivates me," he whispered.

He was hers. And he was perfection.

Chapter 33

Family

After sunset, everyone made their way downstairs to Rosa's home. The change of scenery would be good. The clothes his Guardian had purchased in Pisa fit him like a dream. A plum-colored shirt and tight black jeans as if they'd been tailored to fit his frame perfectly. She knew his style. The loafers felt like an exotic massage on his feet.

Holding Alana's hand, looking at her hair, still damp from their shower together and pinned in a high bun, made Michael feel like Prince Charming escorting his fairy-tale beauty. Yet the eyelet lace on Alana's flowing, white summer dress gave the impression of a gypsy queen, washed free of color except for his soulmate's soft, sunbathed skin.

Luscious aromas lured his senses as it did everyone else's, no doubt. His stomach actually rumbled. Rosa had prepared another culinary feast—fettuccine with crispy bacon in a creamy sauce. A zucchini stew void of meat for Celia and Thorn, and a fresh pot of the mysterious, healing sustenance for him. They ate with gusto. They laughed at family banter and chatted about this and that. The mood was light as if everyone's worries had been buried deep or didn't even exist.

The after-dinner wine mellowed everyone. "An old

family friend made it," Rosa told them. "It was waiting on the doorstep when I came home from Mass."

Even he enjoyed a glass. Lukas took a sip of his wine, made a face as if he'd just bit into a lemon, and admitted how he preferred Rosa's homemade iced tea.

By ten p.m., Rosa appeared far too tired for a houseful of guests. "Maybe all this cooking is finally getting to you, *Zia*," Alana said. He saw the concern in her eyes. "I'm thinking it's time for me to learn, huh?" Both of them caught the loving smile as her aunt leaned unsteady against the kitchen doorway. "Ah, *cara*, what a pleasure it would be! I'll teach you to make red sauce first, and then we'll move on to the art of the pasta." But her words almost slurred as she swayed.

In a split-second Michael was at her side. "Let me help you to the couch. I insist, *Signora.* Lukas will clean up." A flurry of movement began as Thorn and Celia pitched in. Sensing her about to protest, he calmly whispered, "All will be done in no time flat. I'm not taking any chances. You need rest."

He lifted her with care, carried her to the sofa and placed her down gently. Alana placed a beautiful muted-green afghan over her. The crocheted wool fine, almost delicate, and the intricate stitch matched the pattern of the sofa it had been draped over.

"*O mamma mia*, I didn't mean to cause any worry," she protested with an embarrassed smile. "I'm fine. I'll be myself again in the morning, you'll see."

Alana came over to her. "You are important to me beyond words. Maybe I'll stay with you tonight."

He nodded once. "That's a good idea. Everyone's concerned. You shouldn't be alone. You are important to me as well, *Signora.*" With a lean down he took her hand

and kissed it. "Miles and I will stay while Alana goes up to get her things."

After everyone said good night, Thorn and Celia left with Lukas. When Alana came back with her nightgown in hand, he gave her a chaste kiss good night. He waited by the closed apartment door until he heard the deadbolt click.

"You never cease to amaze me," Miles stated as they climbed the stairs together.

"Rosa's a special lady. I owe her my sanity and much, much more. Besides, Alana needs to focus on someone other than me for a while."

Together, they entered Alana's home. Celia and Thorn were engaged in a discussion by the closed drapes, and Lukas was sprawled in an armchair. Thorn kissed Celia's forehead with tenderness and came over to Michael. "Well, the sea is calling once again."

He gave a fierce shake of his head. "No, not tonight—take a shower like the rest of us. I insist." Thorn started to speak, but he held up both hands. "I don't want to hear it. Something's wrong with Rosa and you're needed here, just in case."

"Honestly, Champ, she's fine. I'd know it if anything was seriously wrong. Besides, I need to inhale the salty air and feel the warmth of the sea on these weary bones." Michael walked away. "Come on; don't go all broody. I'll be back before you know it. One quick dip and a light scrub for these clothes. Nothing's on the radar."

Celia looked back and forth between the two men. "If it'll make you feel any better, Thorn can take my phone. Ally's number is programmed in. All he has to do is hit one key." She ran to the sunroom and was back in a few seconds later to show Thorn what to press.

Michael glared at the empath who, in turn, smirked, knowing full well he'd won. One firm finger poked repeatedly at Thorn's massive chest. "If anything—any little thing even *smells* funny, I want a call. I am absolutely serious. I've got nothing to do but sit right here and wait for you to return Celia's phone. Do you understand me?"

Thorn grabbed his hand and shook it firmly. "Gee, thanks. See ya later."

Michael shot him a look as he walked out the door.

"Maybe it was that scrumptious zucchini, but I'm so relaxed…and really beat," said Celia through a long, uncontrollable yawn. "I swear my eyes just want to close. I have to lay down for a couple of minutes. Wake me when Thorn gets back?" She leaned her head onto her father's shoulder as Miles nodded a "yes". "That wine was to die for—and the bouquet!"

"It was very fragrant, aged just right," Miles replied. "I don't think I've tasted such a delicious wine in all my life." He put an arm around her. "I'm going to be totally spoiled when I get back home to your mother. All this fine Italian food will be just another dream. I love her dearly, honey, but British cooking is not the finest cuisine on the planet. Thank God for take-out." He kissed Celia's red hair. "Go rest. I've got writing to do."

Once in the sunroom, she stretched out on the bed. A warm breeze brushed over her. A last thought came… Of the gentle empath. Of the sweet kiss he planted on her forehead.

She was loved.

****

Shifting in the other armchair, Lukas thought his

father looked annoyed. Everything seemed too quiet, and a bored expression lit his face. "Can I open the drapes?"

"No," his father barked. Whoa, he thought, definitely annoyed. *No way am I asking again.* So he went over to Mister B who was seated at the dining room table opening up his laptop. Zeroing in on the piles of files, his notebook stuck out, resting between two faded ones. Like it was divine inspiration, he formed a plan.

"Did you know there's a festival in the village tonight? *Zia* told me. It's for some patron saint of fishermen. Can you hear the music?"

Mister B leaned back with a tilt of his head. "Yes, I can."

"There are lots of people on the street, I mean, like probably police and maybe even kids my age. Tourists too, right?" Mister B shook his head in a slow, grave way. But he really wanted to be outside and leaning down close, he whispered low, "The church is probably open when they have saint festivals. Do you think Father Giovanni is walking around? I mean, it's only what, like, ten o'clock, right? If you say he's expecting us, Dad might let us go. Maybe he'd even come with us?"

"You're just antsy, young man, it will pass," he replied in a hushed but parental manner. "Your father is already worried about Thorn and Mrs. Bellini. Worrying about you… if pushed too far you know how he'll react."

He sank down in a dining room chair right next to him, not willing to hide a pout. "Please, Mister B? Just ask him. He'll listen to you."

And it worked. Mister B stood and walked over to his dad in the living room chair. Just in case he didn't get the right answer, he quickly inched the notebook free of the files and shoved it in the back of his jeans, pulling out the shirttails of his new shirt to conceal it.

He almost jumped out of his skin when his dad stood, but all he did was move the leather armchair next to the house phone on the secretary and then settled back with a rub to his forehead. Ready and eager, he walked over, stood front and center as Mister B said, "Your son wants to ask you something. Lukas, the stage is yours."

"Can we go to San Giorgio's so I can give Father Giovanni my journal? I swear we'll come right back…" his voice faded as his father leaned forward with his eyes narrow. He caught the glance to Mister B and swallowed hard before he found the courage to add, "I'm a good writer, Dad. Maybe it's a talent, but like a "normal kid" one. Maybe I wrote something really important!"

Lukas heard the low grumble of "I should have just said no at lunch."

But he was too lit to back down. Plus, he had asked in a polite tone. But he wanted to be outside something awful. He locked his arms across his chest and said, "Wait—before you *totally* shut down. It's no way fair. He's probably right outside the church. You can walk us. Come on… Everyone knows that friggin' demons don't party until after midnight!"

His father stood very quickly. "If I were you, I'd stop right now, little boy."

The parental tone along with the look he got clearly explained what "if pushed too far" meant, and he took an almost two-foot step backward. "No, wait… I-I'm sorry. I'm so sorry."

His hands shot straight out as his eyes filled, a reaction he couldn't stop. And when his father stepped forward, his stomach did flips. As if he'd been doing it all his life, he put his arms around him and held on tight, resting his head against his father's chest. The absence of a heartbeat didn't bother him at all. Strong arms wrapped around his shoulders holding him secure and safe. "I love you," he whispered, "I really do." And he meant it with all his heart.

"I love you too, more than you'll ever know."

Tender yet powerful words. Lukas would never forget this moment. Never. And he stayed there clinging to his father for a long minute before saying, "I'm gonna watch a movie, okay?"

"Sure," was the reply. Leaving the embrace, he walked down the hall to the den and shuffled through the shelf until he found one he liked.

Even though Michael's head throbbed like a jackhammer, he didn't relax until he heard some thunderous theme song coming from the den. He leaned his head back with a groan.

"I'd say you handled that very well. You should be proud."

"I love him with every fiber of my being, but I'm lousy at this parenting business."

"Children don't come with a handbook. Sometimes it's a shot in the dark. And your love for him is evident. I once told you a father's love is very powerful." Miles yawned and immediately apologized. "That caught me off-guard. I'm exhausted," he said as he turned out the light in the dining room. But then as he came back into the living room and said, "Are *you* all right?"

Massaging both temples, Michael groaned, "I think I have a-a headache. Believe me when I say this is one mortal feeling I do *not* care to experience. I swear it's making my vision blur, and I'm nauseous to boot." He couldn't stop the moan. "If that empath doesn't walk through the door to return Celia's phone soon I will wring his neck."

"After Thorn arrives, be sure to get some rest." Miles said as he left the room.

Maybe if I close my eyes, Michael thought. He did. And fell fast asleep.

Chapter 34

Capture

Thorn waited at the bottom of the stairs and looked at the large wooden door that opened onto the street. He touched the sturdy frame with reverence. It was of the earth, just like him. Thorn saw the tree, which had become this door, standing majestically in the forested hills over a century ago in 1890. This house had been built the same year the Champion reclaimed his soul. Helena planned every detail extremely well. The woodsman was a Georgian, a carpenter. He cut the tree, and with his two sons, molded this door.

The tree gave up its life for protection. Its mission was complete, yet it lived on.

His fingers ran against the grain, and he closed his eyes as profound sadness took hold. At first, the lock refused to yield. Perhaps to stop him from facing his destiny. Blood tears began to drip when his heart opened to dearest Celia one last time. He envisioned holding her tight, easing her worries. The purity of his soul enveloped her, goodness and healing permeating his soulmate's very essence as she slept two floors above.

Sobbing aloud, he whispered her name. An empath's love is beyond the depths of most human imaginings. But Celia would know. She would understand. The last tender kiss would prepare the gentle psychic for his gift once it was released from his soul. He'd always be with Celia—throughout eternity.

The lock slid open; the knob turned in his hand. He walked out into the warmth of night, the sea calling one last time. He said a silent prayer for the Champion, for the boy, for the Guardian.

When finally at the edge of the sea, warm waves lapped at his legs. He stripped and laid his clothes on the rocks. *This is a beautiful world. Even though the night is dark, it's like a million stars in the heavens and the full, round moon has cast a path of light, just for me.* It reflected off the water as if to show him the way home.

Water is life. It ebbs, and it flows. It could create, and it would destroy. He splashed his chest and arms, letting it refresh, letting it cleanse after the task of preparing the Champion, his sacred mission in this life.

Fear suddenly gripped him and the human body, given by Helena, wanted to run. But the demon steadied itself. Strong, muscular arms wanted to punch and kill, ready to rip its attacker limb from limb. But the demon, a gentle old soul, forced it to relax.

His mouth dried with terror, fight or flight programmed in the oldest part of a brain. But he was prepared to leave corporeal form. He stood naked on the shore, turning to acknowledge a short, scrawny man. *Michael may have been right. The liaison isn't fully human anymore.*

Clayton leered with disgust on his evil face. "We own that pitiful soul of his. The vampire pledged it to the sorcerers as payment for the boy's safety." His nasal voice had lost the lilting Irish accent. Besides a high-pitched whininess, it sounded like a hiss.

"*Buona sera*, Mister Mails, and by the way, it wasn't

his *own* life-blood used to sign your clever document. I think he chose rat that night. Gotta love the poetry, don't ya? I mean, he knew why he was meeting you. Drinking rats to play with rats—definitely a hint of poetic justice there." He reached for his pants, another human reflex, but stopped just as Clayton came closer.

"Satan has missed you, Thorn. That old, meddling angel paid for her transgressions... taking you away. Rescuing your very essence from the fires of Hell. The master will let you keep this neat, toned body... if you want to stay in the game, but on the other team—the winning team. Evil pays a hell of a lot better. Plus, there are all sorts of perks."

Thorn laughed in his face. "Are you making me an offer, you slimy bastard? Do you mistake me for a moron, like yourself? This would be a big score for you—tons of extra points with the sorcerers. Why, they might even forgive your bungling failure with the three-headed flying beast! I'm telling you, Clayton, let Michael go. Look the other way. It's not going to work out too well for you. Trust me, I see things, remember?"

The evil creature snickered and sneered. "This is my last offer, Thorn."

He saw the glistening ancient blade in Clayton's left hand, curved and covered with primeval icons that would destroy the ability to ever walk this good earth again, the same as it had for Helena. He steadied himself, waiting for the first cut.

It came swiftly, and more pain shot through the mortal body when the liaison twisted it in his stomach. Clayton moved it higher to dig beneath his rib cage. The strong body quivered as the blade progressed downward, to the left and then right, carving an ancient Christian symbol revered by many around the world.

Thorn's lifeblood formed a pool around him as he fell to the stony beach.

The liaison pulled out the blade. He severed the head but left the heart on a stone for the animals to eat. The heavens rolled with thunder. Lightning flashed over the tranquil seaport.

"Score one for us and none for You," he hissed to the storm clouds above. He searched through the pants pockets and found Celia's phone. It would come in handy in a few hours. After dropping Thorn's head into a thick garbage bag so as not to destroy the expensive leather interior of the high-end sports car he put it on the seat beside him and drove back to the village.

His moment in the sun had arrived.

****

"Hey Carlo, wasn't that the ugliest old bitch you've ever seen?" asked the youngest member of Valetta's team with a snort. They all laughed as the van careened down the treacherous mountain road. "Deaf and dumb, too! We could call her a cow to her face, and she'd never know it." He cursed as the driver hit a rut in the road.

After an ample supper, each man had taken his post. Dressed in dark shirts and trousers, the team looked like typical tourists on the prowl for a good time. Around their waists, each had a leather pouch with a forged passport, one hundred dollars, a couple of Euros, and two syringes filled with a tranquillizing agent.

"The church festival's a perfect cover. Who knew the "other side" could be so cooperative?" Carlo laughed as they all agreed with him. Soon, they'd all be in position and the van would be parked outside 52 Via Amadeus. State of the art communication-gear kept the team members in constant contact.

Evil will win tonight. Carlo was certain. *How the puny American liaison bragged about a stroke of luck earlier in the day, intercepting a bottle of wine. Using a blend of narcotics obtained from a local druggist was ingenious. Just what my Valetta would do.*

Plus, the liaison was very clever. The pharmacist's body would never be found. He had bragged how dark seers would make sure *everyone* drank that wine tonight. The sorcerers' legion of loyalty ran deep in Italy and Carlo knew everyone wanted a piece of this win.

Fifteen minutes later, he had confirmation. The empath was spotted walking toward the sea. They were warned to only target the Guardian and the boy tonight. He recalled how the short American emphasized extreme caution around the vampire. But if this team didn't come back with who they had been sent to retrieve, an agonizing death awaited each of them.

Then, after eleven everything fell into place like a dream. Carlo aimed an electronic device, which could pick up thermal images. Seeing a change in patterns, the plan altered to his team's advantage. He pointed to the second floor, whispering, "Ten less feet to climb. Look at the fire escape." Nothing moved anywhere. "Wait…One's missing." Carlo radioed two team members a short distance away. "Check the festival. You see the boy, take him down immediately. Do not hesitate."

****

Wow, what a stroke of luck it had been, Lukas said to himself as he walked around the festival. And the way he had calculated his every move… He had gone to the kitchen for a glass of water and saw his father fast asleep, actually snoring really loud in the living room chair. Didn't even stir when he tip-toed right past.

In his mind, it was meant to be. With his speed, he'd be back quick. But there was so much to see. He'd tell his dad the truth tomorrow, probably end up over his knee and pretty sore afterward, but this was exciting. *Yep. I'll take my punishment and then apologize—and all will be forgiven.*

Proud of himself, he sauntered along, recalling how he had opened the window in the den. The distance to the second-floor fire escape—only ten feet. Down to the awning over the bookshop's side window? Another ten feet or so and then he had been on the sidewalk. He had made safe jumps landing without a sound on the narrow side street.

As he got close to the church, his enhanced vision caught sight of the stone steps. The crowd was thick, but he saw Father Giovanni standing by the wide-open doors and a girl was handing him a piece of paper, which he quickly slipped into the pocket of his robe.

Curiosity had him almost mesmerized by the festivities. People singing; old folks dancing to an accordion. Tourists clapped to the music's steady beat, adding percussion to the song. He took a deep whiff, enticed by all the incredibly aromatic Italian foods on tables lining his way. Minutes passed before he remembered why he'd come in the first place.

With a turn toward the crowd, he watched Father Giovanni scan the tourists who were laughing and singing along with the villagers. Although the priest's gaze came to rest on him, he sauntered half-heartedly to take it all in. But he reached around and quickly had the notebook tight in his right hand. Then the priest's expression changed. Some tourist came rushing toward him. Only inches separated them, and his heightened senses went on full alert. With a strong arm, he flung the notebook, which flew like a Frisbee sliding into San Giorgio's church.

Someone shoved. He raised a fist in defense. A sharp prick to his shoulder. A brutal punch to his stomach. It knocked the breath out of him, and he felt as if time slowed. His arms were twisted from behind. The tight crowd pushed and shoved in their merriment, singing an Italian melody about the sea and the night as numbness spread up his arms and down his legs.

"Hey, *ragazzo, quella cosa?*"

He couldn't call out, couldn't move his mouth.

"Ah-hah, *molto, molto vino. Vieni qua*, we take you home— *andiamo!*"

His couldn't feel his feet. Then everything went dark.

Fear gripped Father Giovanni as he ushered out the last of the visitors to San Giorgio's Church. He appeared jovial until he closed both doors. Seven holy women were kneeling at the altar in prayerful preparation. He picked up the child's journal and knelt in the last pew to read the note from a young Guardian before joining the sisters in meditation.

****

Carlo and his partner pulled down the fire escape's wrought-iron stairs. He pried off the worn shutter and cut a hole in the thin glass to unlock the second-floor bedroom window. Sliding the window up without a sound, he entered through and began to smile knowing he'd hit the jackpot on the first go-round!

The woman was out like a light, but he didn't

hesitate to plunge the syringe into her neck. The paralyzing liquid would ensure she stayed out of commission. He knew all about Guardian strength, but she wasn't moving. He lifted her out to his partner, who swung her over his shoulder. The climb down was easy and the van with its motor running awaited them. His fellow team member put her next to the boy in the back and they jumped in the van before it slowly rolled away.

Sitting in the front with the driver, he hit a series of numbers on his cell phone. "*Signore* Mails, we have them both," Carlo said, easy and proud. Halfway up the mountain road, he text-messaged the only woman he'd ever admired. His darling Valetta would reward his loyalty.

Chapter 35

Dazed

At first, Michael thought it another twisted dream. Agonizing moans. Pathetic screams to punctuate the night's silence. His eyes snapped opened and pain as sharp as knives shot through his skull. Sleep held on tight as he winced, his vision wonky, cloudy.

Then recognition. The voice was Celia's. As hard as it was to stand and steady himself, he did. The living room spun like an out-of-control top, and his run to the sunroom felt as if he were treading water. But the sounds were beyond sorrowful and what he saw turned his stomach. Celia lay on the bed, writhing and crying from a cross carved from her breasts to her waist. Deep gulps of sobs shook her body. The smell of her blood seeped through his dulled senses. He covered her with a sheet, but the crucifix oozed tiny scarlet droplets as if it were a brand for all to see.

He sat on the bed easing an unsteady hand down her cheek. "Oh God," he whispered as his eyes misted, "Please, talk to me, talk to me—"

"He's dead, he's dead," she repeated through sobs. Her sparkling eyes were dull, staring at nothing. No. Staring at something that terrified her beyond reason.

"Who did this to you?"

"No-no, they did it to *him*!" A horrified scream

followed. He swallowed a sob himself. Didn't want to ask but had to. "Who's dead? Tell me who's dead."

"They took his soul and sent it to hell." Her sobs broke him, and he fought back tears. "I love him! I love him!" She broke apart, and he pulled her up into his arms and cradled her, rocked her—wished to God he could soothe her.

A sob hitched in his throat. "His soul is pure. He's not in Hell."

She cried, and his own clear tears dripped to her hair.

In the doorway, Miles stood disoriented and holding on to the wooden frame. As if slow to pull out of a fog, he said in something just above a whisper, "What's wrong? What… what has happened?"

Michael shook his head, unable to speak as he watched Miles hold on to the furniture until he reached the bed and saw his daughter's wounds. The researcher turned away to vomit, bent at the waist and gripping his knees.

"I've got her, Miles," he managed to say, "Please wake my son."

Miles stumbled out of room and a second later, began shouting Lukas's name, his voice full of undeniable panic. He laid the sobbing woman down. Still unsteady, he ran to the guestroom.

"No, no, no," he yelled, backing out into the hall. And as clarity returned so did his strength.

He ripped the deadbolt from the apartment door, jumped the flight of stairs. One kick to Rosa's door and it flew off its hinges. He followed Alana's scent to the second bedroom and slammed a palm near the knob. It cracked the lock off and he stood in silent rage staring at the open window.

A syringe on the floor by the empty bed. He smelled the narcotic. The scent of a man. No. Two. He sank to his knees. An unearthly scream of rage came from the depths of his soul. His shoulders slumped and his arms hugged his chest. He rocked and trembled.

How? Why? They wanted *him. How had this happened? The wine? No. If it were the wine, then how did they get my son? And why? Why take the two of them?*

But that answer came easy. To make him suffer. He sat back on his heels paralyzed with fear. What would Clayton do to Alana? To Lukas? He hid his face in his hands and couldn't stop the sob because he alone had brought death to them.

Rosa approached slowly. Michael's screams of rage had pulled her from a drugged haze. Her body felt heavy from the narcotics, and she had to hold on to various pieces of wall or furniture to keep herself upright. She stood in the doorway and her heart broke at the sight of him; at the state he was in.

She came behind to fold her arms around his shoulders. He shuddered against her, but nothing would soothe what she sensed within him. *Guilt. Fear for those he loved with all his soul. Terror. Worry. Contempt for those who dare to take from him.* He turned into her as if to hold on to sanity itself. She smoothed his hair, whispered a prayer.

"It is time, *Signore*. Focus on what you must do." He trembled. Such turmoil within. He couldn't think; couldn't move. "Stand, *Campione,* we will give you all you need to bring them home."

"I want to end this existence," he said, barely able to

control the emotion in his voice, "It is the only way to save them."

She unwrapped his arms and held his shoulders. "Michael, you must stand." Reluctant at first, he then palmed his eyes and, as if on command from a much higher power, got to his feet. She cupped his cheek and then took his hand.

It was as if a bolt of electricity coursed through Michael. A healing touch. A touch of wisdom and compassion. Other people's lives depended on his next step. Each and every one of them meant the world to him. They had his love. He had to act. Moving as if in a dream, he followed her to the apartment door and up the stairs.

Each step brought him closer to ending this nightmare. They walked through the living room and down the hall to the sunroom where Miles held his sobbing daughter. Her wound still oozed through the sheet. Relieved that Rosa was at his side, he looked at her noticing for the first time that she was still in the clothes she wore last night.

"Yes. I was affected by the wine as well and fell fast asleep." Her voice stayed at a whisper. "And now here we are. All of us horrified by the depths of evil's wrath upon such a gentle soul." The healer closed her eyes as if in prayer, and Celia's cries ceased.

She stilled in her father's arms.

Miles laid her back on the bed, stood up. Both looked at each other with swollen eyes.

"You're going to the church with Rosa and Celia. Get dressed."

Miles didn't reply, nor did he challenge the statement. The mystical seal had been broken. They were all no longer safe. He left his daughter in most capable hands and did as asked and as fast as he could, still struggling through the brain haze and loose limbs.

Coming back to the sunroom, he took in everything about his precious daughter. Although looking as if she were at rest he could only imagine what pain must be coursing through her, both body and soul.

"Take Alana's car to the church. I'll get Celia down for you. Help Rosa. She's still weak from whatever they used on us."

"What about you? Michael, I'm so very sorry. Lukas was—"

"Lukas may have left of his own accord. He didn't have enough of the wine. I pray he got away… at least, I hope," his voice broke, " I-I have to know the three of you are safe."

Still groggy, he scrubbed his face. "Where is Alana?" Fresh tears dripped down Michael's face, the expression of defeat. His own eyes watered as rage took hold. "Clayton? I'll kill him! I'm staying!"

"No. Go to the church. If he could do all this— Kill Thorn and… Clayton's become too powerful." Defiance simmered. Rational thinking couldn't get a foothold in his brain. "Celia needs you right now, Miles. You have to be with her. Look… Alana and my son… They'll need you *alive*. I can't go into this unless I know you'll be there for them, waiting safe at the church."

"I cannot… Will not stand around while—"

"Clayton doesn't want *them*, Miles, he wants *me*!" exploded out of Michael. A trembling hand gripped his shoulder. "I'll get Alana and Lukas back. You know I will."

He took in a deep breath and blew it out slow. His vision blurred again, but it was the right move. The only move. "Should anything happen to you. I will raise him as if he were my own."

Michael gave a slow nod, moved to the bed and carefully picked Celia up. Miles took Rosa's arm to steady her. They went down the elevator in silence. As soon as the doors opened, the garage light came on. Michael watched Miles settle Rosa into the front seat. Carefully, he placed Celia in the back seat of Alana's car and Miles got behind the wheel. The engine started; the garage door went up with a high-pitched hum.

Rosa quickly grabbed his arm. "Focus, *Campione.* Then you must come to us, *capisce?*"

Michael inclined his head. Miles backed out and the car seemed to vanish into the darkness. When the garage door came down, he felt sealed off from the world and alone in this nightmare. He didn't know how long he stood by the elevator. A minute…an hour. Staring into the blackness of an empty space, his only thought was how no life existed here anymore.

****

Michael didn't remember stepping off the elevator and into Alana's foyer. A scent penetrated his daze, though, and he scanned the hall as he sniffed the air. His gait was again unsteady as he followed the scent, one he already knew. Clayton Mails.

His stomach cramped and he bent forward. Weak, he thought, need sustenance. But he was also eerily aware that there was more to face. The vile liaison's odor was strongest in the kitchen. He stood paralyzed in front of the fridge. *Had Celia's injury destroyed the protection spell? Had he gotten into this protected home and had he done that to Celia? Or was it a dark magic spell?* The filthy man's odor was so strong in the kitchen, but why?

Plus, he desperately needed blood. And he needed to open the refrigerator door.

When he did, he gagged, rushed to sink and wretched. He had to grip the edge of the counter to pull himself back to a hideous revelation. The empath's severed head was on the plate Celia had made for him. His gray lifeless eyes were wide. A steel spike was driven through his forehead holding Celia's note, now folded. His rage reached an ungodly height. He ripped the spike out and grabbed the last jars of blood, broke each seal, and drained them.

Murder stayed in his eyes as he read what had been written in the empath's blood. He recognized the numbers…Celia's cell phone. Staggering into the living room he all but fell into the chair by the phone. His eyes were wet again damnit, and he angrily brushed his palms across them. "Crafty bastard," he hissed, "using a narcotic with no scent…no taste."

And consecrated blood coursed through his hungry veins. It had worked its magic once again. He shot out of the chair and ripped all the drapes off rod by rod, opening windows and thrusting back wooden shutters. He went room by room.

Once in the den, he knew how Lukas escaped. Thank God, he thought. A window was open. He prayed his boy was hiding somewhere. Somewhere safe. His strides back to the living room were even and sure. Standing at the open window in the dining room, he took in a full breath of fresh air. "Portofino is peaceful in sleep. The full moon, the smell of the sea, fresh and clean… And hours until the dawn," he whispered full of bitterness.

Not able to turn away from destiny, there was only

one direction left to take. His hand trembled as he reached for the phone, his palm slick with sweat and tears. He punched Celia's number into the landline, sank into the chair again, and seethed.

On the third ring, he heard Clayton's voice.

Chapter 36

Evil

"Top o' the evening to you, boy-o! I knew you'd be waking up from your debauchery, sooner or later. Found my note, did ya'?" The cheery snake continued, "Ya got over your empath's death very quickly, eh? This world's no place for a gentle soul, now is it, laddie? Shame on you, vampire," came with a click of his tongue. "Now why would ya be lettin' the poor demon out of your manly sights to go skinny dipping in the sea?" Then a raucous laugh.

"You loquacious jerk," he snarled through clenched teeth.

"Ah, Michael, you slay me! You didn't think I'd forget about that annoying earthquake you caused in Manhattan, now did ya? I've come to take ya home, but I'm thinking I have the two people ya really want to see before the final good-bye." His ego soared as he slipped in and out of his phony Irish accent. "Would I be right there, lad?"

Two people? Oh dear God! No longer composed, he hissed, "You son of a bitch—" He knew how to get to Clayton, if he could only control the desire to kill him.

"Now, now, laddie boy, there'll be no name callin' allowed. I've got to hand it to you though; she sure is a pretty lass. Who'd have guessed you'd go for such a classic Italian beauty?"

He was speechless yet he wanted to scream. Then he heard Alana moan.

"Ay, I'll bet she's a real spit-fire when she's awake, erotic and sassy. I'm startin' to feel all tingly in my crotch just thinkin' about it. Ya see, though, that's where we're different. I like 'em rough and raw, but every once in a while I could get a yen for a pretty little thing who's a wee bit sleepy and loose," Clayton cackled. He kissed Alana loudly, and Michael heard him move away, then one door close and another open.

"And the boy, merciful Mother Hell, he's *still* a feisty runt! Looks just like his mother. When the tranquilizer wore off, he gave my men a real run for their money! Your daddy's on the phone. Want to say hello?"

His son's sobs made his eyes glisten with new tears ready to spill. *He* did this—another frightening memory for his child to contend with. Clayton would pay.

"Nah, truth be told—he's kind of hung up, if ya catch my drift. I've got to ask, what kind of a father are ya—letting the boy out when ya knew wolves were closin' in? He almost made it to the church, but my men just picked your puppy up like a rabid stray. And what a filthy mouth! Cursing like a pro when I stripped him down to his under shorts. The brat didn't give me a choice, I *had* to tie his feet, or he'd have kept kicking me," the liaison added with a chuckle. "But don't worry, I'll be teachin' him a proper lesson." He held the phone near Lukas's mouth so that Michael could hear his cries.

A fist clenched, imagining his son's terror. "You want me, Clayton, not them." Then he yelled, "Release them and I won't send you to the Hell that's waiting for you."

"Let's get one thing straight, you horse's ass," Clayton shouted back, "I'm the liaison, and I make the deals!"

Then, silence.

"What do you want," he barely got out.

"What I've always wanted—*you*! Well, as dust and bone, that is," Clayton said casually. "I think we're gonna make a deal, me and daddy." His son's uneven whimpers cut through his soul. "Sorry, *vampire,* it was getting a bit noisy. So, are we gonna dance or not?"

"I need to know they are safe first," he quickly said.

"Now, you're not listening there, boy-o, I said *I* make the deals," Clayton shrieked, and then a pause. "Wanna hear my terms?"

Biting down on his lower lip, he tasted blood. "I'm holding my breath."

"That's the vampire I know and love!" His jaw tightened hearing the lunatic laugh. "First, ya come alone. How's that for starters? Is it simple enough, vampire?"

"Yes," Michael replied in a dry tone.

"Second, ya bring no weapons—*Capisce, paizano*?"

"I understand."

"Third, say your Act of Contrition before arriving, because you'll not be leaving." The pause seemed endless, and the phony Irish brogue had vanished. "Did you get that last part, vampire! The sorcerers want you with them in Hell! Make your peace with *whatever* before you get here. You'll have thirteen seconds with each of them, and then I end your fucked up existence!"

"How will I know they're safe?" Michael asked in a flat tone, giving him nothing.

"Now I'm wounded. After all the years we've

316

known each other, working on the same team—oh, wait—we weren't! What's the matter, hero, don't you trust me?"

Terror crept back into his voice when he said, "Clayton *please*—"

"Don't fuck with me anymore, you egotistical bastard! These are my terms. Accept them or I kill both pitiful humans right now. I'll even let you listen—because I respect you." His fevered pitch was rife with delirious hate.

Yet Michael knew he was beaten. "Where do you want me to go?"

"Ah, we're not ready for you yet, and since sunlight isn't too healthy for someone with your, uh, affliction, you have *many* hours to quake and shake, wondering what I'm doing to your woman and child. I like that, hero." Clayton snickered. "My, my, my, that gives you hours to make your thousand-page confession, to cry those dark eyes bloody, to beat your muscular chest, sobbing *mea culpa, mea maxima culpa.* Every torturous minute will feel like a day. Tell ya what—let's play. I'll be merciful, seeing how much sorrow this must be causin' that poor, guilt-written conscience. Smell out the spot where we took your naughty little boy as the sun sets. I'll gather a few drops of blood from both of them, maybe a piece or two of the lass's panties, which she doesn't need with me keeping her warm—you know what I'm talkin' about? I'll mark the way for ya—a righteous path to my door. And don't ya go worryin' about your brat either, lad. I'll keep both of them *properly* entertained." The line went dead mid-cackle.

The maniac was feeling very full of himself and his newly acquired satanical power. Managing to place the phone gently on its cradle, Michael scanned the empty room. He slumped forward to rest his head in his hands.

Pushed beyond his limits, so many emotions assaulted him as he broke down.

They were as good as dead.

Chapter 37

Captivity

Alana's eyes fluttered, fighting artificially induced sleep. Blinking to pull her mind from unconsciousness, even this slight movement caused sharp hammering in her head. Both eyelids were like sandpaper scraping up and down. Her limbs were outstretched, and fighting panic she thought, *I'm tied with my head against a stone surface. Where am I? How did I get here?*

Focus came all too slow as the realization took hold …someone stood over her. The light was dim, and his features were caught in the shadows. Questions were plentiful. *Where am I and how did I get here? Who is he? What is he?* Her mouth was grainy as if she had swallowed dirt.

A dry cough erupted, causing more needle-like spasms in her throbbing head. Only then did she realize that ropes bound her waist, not allowing her ribcage to expand. But when her vision cleared, she recognized the shadowy figure squatting at her feet…painting her toenails?

"Clayton," she whispered.

"Ay, lass, you've had one helluva nap, haven't ya now? My little narcotic cocktail works like a charm. So, you remember me, you delicious lady. It's been years— a fiendish length of time."

"Get away from me, Clayton," she warned, watching his hand creep up her thigh, though not feeling it.

"Now is this any way to treat a man when you come to visit? Did you feel that lass?" Alana saw him pinch her inner thigh again. "I'm thinkin' no. I gave you an extra dose in your lower spine. That's so you'll be fully awake and alert—from the waist up. But this tempting lower half—Well, that's different."

Perverted glee lit his face and she tried to disguise the growing panic because she couldn't access her mystical strength. "That handsome, brooding hunk thinks he's coming for a trade, but I'll let you in on my secret. I'm getting more than just one disintegrating vampire. I tell ya, that vamp's got good timing. We're gonna create our own destiny with you all fertile." He blew on her toenails. "I think they're dried. I'd love to stay and chat, but I've got his boy in the other room, and the brat's tested my nerves. I could have kept him drugged, but it makes me hard just hearing the sobs. He'll scream his way out of this world."

The short, evil man appeared to tap-dance his way out the room.

****

Lukas shivered at the touch as Clayton patted the side of his leg. Swollen welts ran down his body, all crusted with blood. His lip bled from biting it. He was hanging in the center of a cellar. The smell of old, rancid wine like acid in his nose. The only light came from hurricane lamps near the door. A meat hook, dangling from a chain in the ceiling beam, kept his bound wrists high. It had been rigged so only his toes could scrape the stone floor and only his straining arms would hold all of his weight. His body screamed with pain. His brain fought mind-numbing fear.

"Oooh… You've been like this since midnight, poor baby. Those welts are gonna fester for days—assuming ya have any left. Have you died already?" Fingers dug into a bleeding welt, and Lukas screamed. "Now that's more like it. What would Daddy say if you were already gone?" The evil man sniffled back a mocking sob. "Oh, my precious son, I've just gotten you back, but I've killed you!"

Lukas shut his eyes, holding back tears and swallowing hate. He sucked what little saliva was left in his mouth and waited. As soon as his attacker leaned in again, he aimed and spit.

Almost crazed, Clayton wiped his eye with a finger. A sinister smile appeared and then a punch to the center of his chest made it hard to suck in a breath. "You miserable little bastard. You should have clung to Daddy instead of going off to visit a filthy priest! Ya know, many years ago, I might have felt…I don't know…compassion? But Michael Malone's gonna pay for what he did, and then he'll watch you die."

A jagged breath hitched. Searching for comfort, he remembered standing in the church, a place of sanctuary the priest had said. He thought about his father. How it felt to be in his arms. Being tight to his broad chest… Lukas knew he'd never see him again. Sobs cut through every uneven gasp.

And he cried.

****

"Get up, Cow, we're hungry," snickered the team leader poking her shoulder as she slept in the narrow bed off the kitchen. The wind-up clock Sofia brought with her read 5 a.m., but she sat up and read Carlo's lips, watching the not-so-intelligent man point to his open mouth and his belly.

Giving a nod she stood and wrapped herself in an old housecoat. She shuffled to the villa's kitchen to make a pot of coffee. Bringing leftovers to the counter, she slowly gathered pots and pans to reheat it. Four men lounged around the kitchen table, laughing, agreeing it'd been an easy job. Like tribal hunters from thousands of years ago, they told the story over and over to celebrate success.

Eying their neanderthal gestures and reading their lips, she pieced together events. One hanging on a meat hook. One tied spread-eagle to the floor. They were both in the basement—two separate rooms. Pure evil dwelt within the liaison, within the villa itself.

Her heart broke imagining the terror both of them must be feeling. But her mission was a most important one. She whispered prayers of deliverance as she poured the coffee—and opened her mind to the spiritual leader of the Georgian Sovereign Council in Portofino.

****

Michael felt nothing, numb as if lost in inertia because they were both suffering. *Lukas and Alana. Dawn minutes away.* He had walked this earth for over 300 years, and he was never a creature, good or not good, to run from a fight. As a Champion, he always raced toward the action, taking matters into his own deadly hands every time.

Yet he couldn't seem to pull himself up and out of the living room chair.

The house phone rang again, which it had been doing regularly since he'd hung up with Clayton. Full of abject misery he lifted the landline's handset to his ear. The Researcher's familiar but frantic voice continually shouting, "Do you hear me? Michael—you are running out of time, damnit! It's almost dawn! They will die!"

"I-I cannot, I—"

"Listen to me. You *must* come to the church! You *must*! Pull yourself together *right now*. Come to the church—*now*!" The line went dead. The sobering brusque tone. One last demand filled with a roughness he'd never heard in the researcher's voice.

"Oh please God. They cannot die," he whispered as if any prayer said by one so unclean could reach the heavens. As if one so unclean could have a prayer answered... But slowly he stood. If there was a chance, he had to take it.

He made his way to the master bedroom. How he wished his Guardian was lying across the four-poster bed, safe and sound. How he wished his son was fast asleep in the other room. Kicking off the loafers, he went to the closet and took out the boots Alana purchased for him. Her scent filled his senses. He saw a brown leather suit jacket hanging beside her sundress dress. She must have purchased it as well. The tags still hung from a sleeve. He pulled them off and put it on, thinking another perfect fit made of the softest leather he'd ever felt.

If he had to wait in the church until sunset, then so be it. He'd spend the day on his knees beneath the crucifix and then at sunset, he'd search out their scents.

Glancing at the dresser he caught his reflection in the mirror. Milky, yet sharper than this morning. It brought back a flash of a memory. A twenty-seven-year-old, arrogant Englishman who'd been turned into a vampire. Another memory caught him, and his attention slid back to the closet.

He needed one specific weapon. More clear-headed, he searched through Alana's trunk on the closet floor. He rummaged through it and nestled at the very bottom, he found it—the pearl-handled knife, which he tucked into his boot. It had been his gift to Alana on her eighteenth birthday, just as it had been a gift to him... on his. How proudly it was presented to him. It had been tooled by his grandfather. Alana lovingly called it her "good luck charm" because it was always on her person when she fought.

His astute senses confirmed the sky would turn pink in minutes and he picked up his pace, rushed through the apartment door. On the second-floor landing, he stopped abruptly knowing there had been yet another intruder, but more recently.

A thick envelope lay on Rosa's welcome mat. *Somewhere in the middle of all of this horror my son's documents arrived, and Miles will need them for...* He closed his eyes and shook his head. *Nothing is left to protect here. No. No more waiting.* Tucking the envelope into his jacket pocket he walked down the last flight of stairs.

At the outside door of the building, he had to take a moment. Although he had always been fearless, now his legs were unsteady. But he grabbed the doorknob and turned it.

The streets were still asleep as he rounded the corner. Lukas's scent came at him full force and he followed it up to the church. He now knew *exactly* where his son had been taken. *His kidnappers are humans. A good sign. I've not taken an innocent's life in over a century. But these are not innocent men and snapping their necks will bring me great pleasure.*

The small white church stood against a backdrop of pale-pink shades that hinted a new morning. As he climbed its stone steps, the door opened. An old priest stood waiting. Michael hesitated, but the priest stepped aside and motioned him to come in.

****

Valetta Russo threw a thick wad of Euros at the prostitute as he buttoned his shirt. She had needed a night of pampering after what that sadistic bastard had done to her in Portofino. Here in Rome, she had many connections. The docile lover had bathed, massaged, and serviced her with tenderness. She didn't need to know his name; she hadn't bothered to ask.

Intermittent beeps came from her cell phone and brought her mind back to business. The text-message from hours ago was fantastic news. She showered, dressed for the day carefully choosing her ensemble. A power dresser, the suit and shoes clearly stated *this* liaison is the one in charge. In a few minutes, she and her driver would be on their way.

The vampire won't be able to get to the villa till after sundown, but by then, I will have dealt with Clayton Mails. The lab's ready for the boy; the tomb's ready for the Guardian. Eventually, Michael's ashes will sit in the rat-infested subbasement, just as he deserves. Carlo will receive a nice bonus and then I'll have him killed.

Because it's always better to tie up loose ends.

Chapter 38

Mercy

Michael's assumption was correct. The hand extended in greeting belonged to Father Giovanni, and although his palm shook and was coated with sweat he extended it. The grip was tight, and Father clasped his shoulder. "Welcome, *Campione*, we've been expecting you." His voice was weathered and aged, but his eyes shone youthful. "Please follow. There is much to be done."

Once in the small church, he stopped. He had seen it before. The carved crosses on the pews were in his dreams. The altar and gilded altar rail as well. Expecting his skin to sizzle, he traced the Christian symbol on the nearest pew. The only sensation was of the wood's smoothness. "How is this possible?"

"Many things are possible, *Signore*. Ours is not to question why."

Seven nuns stood at the altar. In long, dark-brown habits and standing shoulder to shoulder like a barrier between vampire and sacred table. *So here is where I meet my end.* He fully expected his ashes to coat the incensed air. But he wasn't ready yet. He had to get to them. To bring them home. The anxiety churning within didn't lessen when he saw Rosa come from the sacristy to join the nuns.

Father took his arm. It steadied him for the short walk to the holy women. "We have prayed, and an answer has been given: Death cannot win against itself. Only in life will you triumph." It was as if he were led by someone who had looked into the eyes of God. "Ah, no, *Signore*, I am but a humble servant, as are we all."

His gait swayed. Father steadied him once more. When they reached the sisters, he could barely stand. Rosa's hand slipped into his right hand, the priest's in his left. The sisters joined them as well and a circle was formed.

Visions of his son and his eternal love were like a tornado swirling through his mind. Please destroy me and save them, he prayed in a panic. He'd bargain and beg if it could happen. A chant rose from the nuns, soft yet steady. He was afraid to think. Afraid to speak.

Michael saw his sisters as if in a vision joining the prayerful song.

Suddenly his eyes shot wide as a tremendous jolt shot through to his chest. Blessed blood raced through his starved veins pumping through his useless heart. He gasped a full breath of incensed air into his lungs while his skin tingled. His hands warmed. The necessity for breath fell into its natural rhythm. The sense of his chest rising and falling at a healthy pace—as with every throb of his heart. It terrified him.

But then true panic set in, and he tried to break free of their grips. His eyes raised to the crucifix, and he shouted full of fear, "Oh God, I cannot do this as a man!" Then there was a whisper in his soul. *The choice is not yours, son of my bloodline. It never was."* The voice of Helena…

His heightened senses quivered. They were intact as

if his existence as a vampire had not been purged. He heard the heartbeats of all in the circle. Each rhythm slightly different. He heard Mile's whispering encouraging words to sweet Celia, asking her to open her eyes. Then he met Father Giovanni's piercing gaze as his hands slipped free.

"Now you are ready, *Campione*. You will know the Georgian at the villa." When the priest's hand extended there was a worn calf's skin pouch placed in his hand. "This has been in the Council's possession for centuries. Place it in your left pocket… you are left-handed, *si*?"

"Yes," he whispered, yet he was hesitant.

"Once you fill the pouch, they will be out of danger." The priest began to walk, but Michael didn't move, and he turned back adding, "Ah, perhaps first you see your friends. *Andiamo*." And he followed. Full of doubt. Full of wonder.

****

Sconces lit their way. Stone steps led down to an open room. One sister sat at Celia's side on the cot. Miles sat in a chair on the other side of his daughter. Another sister handed him a warm cup of beef broth. Its aroma nudged awake human hunger. He simply stared at her when it was placed in his hand, gave a humble "*grazzi*" and drank it down. But she looked familiar, as if he'd seen her before. His gaze lit on Celia as Miles stood and approached. "Thank God you made it before sunrise."

"How is she?"

"She hasn't awakened, but—" the researcher narrowed his eyes. "Michael?" he looked about to fall, but a trace of a grin appeared, a gleam of astonishment in his eyes. "Good Lord, of course… Did Giovanni give you any cryptic words of wisdom?"

"Yeah, but I don't understand—"

Miles clasped his shoulder. "You will. Have faith."

"Wait… Take this. Here," he said reaching into his right pocket for the thick envelope and handing it over. "It's self-explanatory." He looked over Miles's shoulder. "Celia, oh my God… Thorn truly loved her." All the man did was give a grave nod.

Rosa came over. At her side, the sister who handed him the broth took the empty mug from his hand as he embraced Rosa. *All she has done this past week for me and my son. Words of wisdom, the aromatic soup, a puzzling legend… the healing.* He was at a loss for words but sure she sensed deep gratitude.

"Excuse me," he said to the sister at her side, "Have we met before?"

"No, *Signore,*" she softly replied.

Rosa patted his shoulders and then ran her hands over the lapels of his jacket. "Magdalena is a gifted surgeon. She'll tend to Alana and Lukas when you free them. An ex-Guardian will also accompany you. There is no more time, *Signore. Subito!*"

Rosa was pulling him towards the stone step. The ones that led upstairs and into daylight.

"But, *Signora,* the sun—"

She clicked her tongue but kept pulling him by the arm. "This is not a magic spell that will reverse at any random moment! You must accept your destiny, *Campione.*"

****

Michael stepped into daylight and immediately squinted and blinked. Something he had not experienced in centuries. His body warmed in the leather jacket, and it felt wonderful. *Everything happens for a reason* came to mind. He took the sea air into his lungs and blew out slowly.

A white van idled in front of the church. He walked down the weathered stone steps, a bit cautious yet curious. Two healing sisters wished him Godspeed. As he had been taught hundreds of years ago as a young man in the 1600's, he gave a gracious bow with his right hand over his heart.

"Good morning, Mister Malone. Isn't it a lovely day?" The nun, perched on the driver's side step, drummed her fingers on the van's roof and wore a quirky grin. "I'm Gabriella. I'll be doing the driving, and I've got a plan," she cheerfully stated in perfect English. "I guess you've already met Magdalena. She's one pretty nifty doctor. We know where they are and we'll be your back-up."

He simply stared at her. She appeared well-built and self-assured. But this wasn't working for him. Not in the least and his arrogance ramped up. "Excuse me, Sister, but exactly *how*— I mean no disrespect, but this isn't a hockey game we're going to... Angels-1, Devils-0. I don't care if you have a plan or not. Just get me there."

Her head tilted, her blue-eyes widened. "Gosh, golly, wow... I guess I really didn't think to, you know, run it by you first, *sir.* I mean, with all the praying and healing before, that testy ego of yours just didn't figure in." And she's a feisty one, he thought. "You know, Malone, keep that thought in your head because the sisterhood has changed. Some of us actually lead exciting lives before we answer, "the—call."" *Plus, she does air quotes!* "Does ten years as a Guardian on the forgotten back streets of San Francisco do it for you? You think it'll help any, taking out those nasty SOBs?"

She folded her body into the driver's seat and revved the engine.

Total disbelief had him glued to the ground. She called through the open window, "Now get in so I can tell you how I see this going down. And put on your seat belt. My brothers took me drag racing." She slapped the seat, and very cautious, he got in.

Sister Magdalena settled in the middle row of seats with a doctor's satchel. There were folded blankets next to her. Then, another nun walked out of the church and came towards them. Does she even belong in this impure world, he thought, recalling her beautiful brown eyes from the healing circle. Her hands were invisible, tucked into the habit's wide cuffs and stiff at her waist. Serene strength radiated from her. It was as clear as the day.

"*Bon Giorno, Signore*. I am Rosalinda," she said, not very proficient in English. "It is determined I go." Her gentle voice could calm any anxious heart.

The good sister didn't appear comfortable around him, but he sensed a world of history behind a quick glance, which came at him through thick, long lashes. Hope swelled within him. And like a dancer, spry and sure-footed, she got in and sat next to Magdalena, never touching the vehicle, never revealing her hands.

The van door slid shut and Gabriella tossed a pair of sunglasses over, which he caught midair. "Super! Mystical vamp speed intact. Seeing as you haven't been in heavenly morning sunshine for a *really* long time, I think you're gonna need them more than me. Put them on, and there's no need to say thanks out loud, either. Healer…holy girl…psychic… ex-Guardian all rolled into one. Some of us just seem to have all the luck," she added with a touch of sarcasm.

"And talkative, too," he muttered under his breath.

The van sped down the empty streets with him gripping the dashboard.

"Relax, Malone. The color's already draining from your face, and I don't have any yummy yogurt bars hidden up my sleeve to sop up those wicked tummy acids you're about to experience."

As his stomach growled, he shot her a glare. She reminded him of Alana but didn't look old enough to be released from the mystical mission.

"I'll be thirty-two in October. I did my ten years, packed up my weapons and came here to get ready—just for you," she replied, taking treacherous mountain turns on two wheels. When they were almost to the top of the mountain, she pulled the van off the road into a dense patch of trees. She cut the engine and turned to him. She outlined what would happen. It was a very simple plan, and she answered every one of his questions before he could ask it. Then she said with a devilish grin, "Okay, are we ready to rumble, Malone?"

His answer? "Absolutely."

Chapter 39

The Villa

"There are two of them in the circular drive," Gabriella whispered. Her habit was tucked up into a cinch at her waist for the hike up the hill. A pouch hung from it, containing items she'd need. Unlike the other healers in black sandals, Gabriella wore sturdy work boots as well as thick, black leggings under her habit.

"You must like carrots," he whispered with a sardonic smile.

"Nah, I'm an old burger and fries girl. I'm using my *other* set of eyes. The one on the left is built like a bull, don't ya think? We'll make sure he does the carrying." Sister Magdalena nodded, but he was confused. *Where is the third sister?* "Rosalinda is going in the other direction. Her mission is different. Don't worry, Malone. She grew up here…she can walk the mountain blindfolded," she replied to his unanswered question—again.

He shrugged, not about to question *this* one. Sister Magdalena waited, silent behind him. He couldn't imagine how this shy doctor was going to pull it off. The ex-Guardian smoothed her habit back in place, and both nuns smudged earth on their hands and faces. Gabriella signaled. Magdalena started to whimper. They stumbled toward the skinny guard. In perfect Italian, Gabriella cried, "*Scussa, Signore, scussa.*" She held up Magdalena, who sobbed between coughs.

The guard eyed the villa but let them approach. Gabriella spoke rapidly, pointing at the trees, gesturing wild with her hands, frantically describing how the van had "broken down". Michael heard the translation in his mind: *"Please, sir, can we use your phone to call our convent and a towing service? We don't wish to impose, but this is the closest villa."* Gabriella started to cry, and Magdalena swooned into the guard's arms.

"Vincenzo," he called loudly, "*Vieni qua!*" The beefy guard came running, completely forgetting his evil mission.

"*Grazzi, mille grazzi,*" Gabriella said, swiping away her tears. Then they were led into the villa where Alana and Lukas were being held.

****

Michael stayed low and followed the tree line around the back. Outside, a broad disfigured woman was hanging clothes. When she turned in his direction with clothespin in hand, he knew she was the Georgian and her name was Sofia. He followed her sightline to his right. A window yawned open. He crawled through tall weeds, climbed into a small bedroom, and moved in silence stopping behind the open door to the kitchen.

Two guards were eating breakfast. Michael smelled his son's blood on them. He sensed Lukas was directly under the kitchen and heard his boy's shallow breaths. *Unconscious. Irregular heartbeat.* He swallowed his rage. *But not time to kill. Not yet.* Gabriella's animated voice came at him, talking rapid Italian on the foyer's phone.

The beefy guard brought Magdalena into the kitchen

and sat her down carefully trying to revive her. "Hey, old cow," he yelled in Italian, waving his arms over his bald head, "get your ugly face in here." Again, he understood every word watching from the slim space where the bedroom door met its frame. Sophia trudged in and saw the pale nun, blessed herself, then brought her a glass of water. No emotion animated her scarred face even though he sensed she knew Magdalena.

As soon as Gabriella entered the kitchen they sprang into action. Magdalena slumped to the floor and the guard dove for her. Sophia dumped the pot of hot coffee on one eating breakfast. His howls of pain erupted, and Michael burst in to snap his neck. Gabriella knocked the wind out of the other guard with a hard, fast punch to his chest. Michael snapped his neck as well. When the third one cornered Gabriella, Michael killed him swiftly by crushing his windpipe and then, he did the same to the fourth guard before he could shout.

"Four down, two to go," he said as Sophia looked at Gabriella.

"Okay, she says they're upstairs not feeling too well. She served them spoiled food an hour ago. What do you say, Malone? Are you ready to kick a couple of sore butts?" she asked, with tight fists on her waist.

"You know, Sister, you're some piece of work," Michael whispered with a smirk. "Remind me never to get on *your* testy side."

She gave a quick shrug and signaled him to slip silently up the wrought-iron staircase in the foyer, and he had no trouble following her lead. At the top landing, they detected two beating hearts. The men were located in the smaller bedrooms, both on the villa's right side. Michael started to speak, but Gabriella held a finger to her lips. She pointed to her forehead, instantly conferencing him without words. Each took a bedroom and waited by the bathroom doors for their unsuspecting victims.

Alana's scent was on a shirt lying on the floor by the bed. A toilet flushed and then water ran in the bathroom sink. Fifteen seconds later, a man staggered out moaning, holding his stomach. Michael grabbed the sweating perpetrator by the throat, held him high off the ground and glared murderous.

"You touched her, didn't you?"

Choking, the wiry bastard eyes popped wild. When released he collapsed on the floor, coughing and grunting.

Rage stood in his eyes. *This one is evil, devoid of anything except vain stupidity.* He grabbed the shirt off the floor and bound his mouth, and then stood on each hand. Bones broke when he ground a heavy heel into each of them. One at a time. And slow. His muffled screams were useless as Michael pulled him up by the hair. "You will *never* lay your filthy hands on an innocent again." He kneed the guard's chest, sent him careening across the room to land in a broken heap. "And just in case you feel like running," he added, bringing down the heel of his boot on one kneecap, then the other, which rendered the man unconscious.

"A little bit of overkill, ya think?" His gaze lit on Gabriella dragging the other guard gagged and trussed with nylon cords behind her.

"Pent up aggression, Sister, or payback?" he asked noticing the guard's broken jaw.

"Well, he kept cursing at me, so I taught him a lesson. There's hope for this one's soul." Michael took over, flinging the guard across the bedroom, which landed him in the bathroom tub.

She suddenly stilled. "You need to hurry. I'll get the van up the driveway." Adding with respect, "This is as far as we can help, Champion. The rest is up to you." Without a sound, she left, and he followed her down the staircase. As she sprinted through the foyer he turned and stared at the open basement door. The time had come.

Like angelic sentinels the two sisters were standing silent and still. Sophia walked over to Rosalinda with a kitchen knife in hand. Her head bowed and Rosalinda placed her hands on the Georgian's wispy-thin hair and blessed her. With tears in her eyes, Magdalena embraced Sophia.

Sophia looked down the stairs. Something close to resolve echoed through his soul.

"No, *Signora*," he whispered, "this is my fight— mine alone," but she put her right hand over her heart and bowed her head.

The angelic sentinels moved away, and he approached just as she grabbed a broomstick which was wedged between the wall and the first stair. More than ready, he followed her down. She stood by a door. Alana's scent came at him, but she shook her head and pointed to the opposite door. He jerked his head toward it. The scent of his son wafted strong, and his heartbeat was erratic. As the Georgian entered the room with Alana, he entered the other.

Chapter 40

Rescue

The room was dark and reeked of spoiled wine. *Lukas. Barely breathing.* He choked down rage and taking a firm hold on his son's bleeding wrists he pulled them up and over the meat hook. Tiny ribbons of old scars covered his son's back and chest, which amped up his fury. He slashed the rope that bound his boy with his pearl-handled knife. Weighing nothing in his arms he flew up the stairs with Lukas cradled close. Immediately he handed him over to the two waiting sisters.

A deep breath refocused his fury as he walked back down. He entered the room with Alana without a sound.

Nothing could have prepared him for what he saw. To his left, Sophia's body had been gutted down the center. To his right, the love of his life. Her expression was pure terror, but she was alive. Shallow slashes covered Alana's naked body. Her limbs tied with ropes and spreadeagle on the dirt floor. Her lifeblood smeared like a morbid second skin. Tall black candles burning high and bright stood at the five points of a pentagram painted on the dirt with animal blood as if in preparation for some perverted ritual.

Standing over her? Clayton Mails, barefoot and shirtless. "You fucking. Miserable. Little. Bastard," he hissed.

Clayton turned. The look was pure shock, but then his mouth curled into a wicked smile. Carved symbols bled down his chest and arms. His fly was open, and one hand was reaching in. Clayton's beady eyes narrowed as he blew a foul wind toward him, which sent his body flying across the room like a piece of paper.

Hitting the wall, air deserted his lungs. He winced in human pain and tried to breath.

"Your vampire's here, whore. And I didn't expect him until sunset." Clayton sneered, glowering at him. "How'd ya manage *this* one? Let me guess… You went groveling to the Georgians. I figured that old bitch was one of them when she came at me with a fucking kitchen knife and a broken broomstick; with that pathetically "holier than thou" look on her hideous face. Never send a religious fanatic to do a dead man's job."

Clayton's hand stretched toward him. He hit the ceiling and then crashed to the dirt floor. Blood dripped from his nose, the copper taste coating the back of his throat. Something sinister like dark magic pulled at his soul, which made him nauseous enough to vomit.

"I have powerful abilities that far exceed one *mystically enhanced* vampire's. You can watch my final human act before I descend. Satan's son will burst forth from her womb. My gift to the sorcerers will destroy Guardians, one by one. Not like your insane brat! He'll be dead within minutes. *Mine* will thrive!"

A quick glance slid to Alana. Unexpectedly she rolled her eyes as if bored by the creep. *"In life you will triumph"* echoed through his brain. Whatever dark spell held him in place had to be broken. And his body should have been wracked with pain, but it wasn't. Something came to mind. Clayton had always been too stupid to be witty, so he took a chance.

"What is this, your awful audition for a scary movie? How long did it take to practice those spooky lines? Jeez, couldn't you pick something with more pizzazz and a bit less speechy?" Alana nodded and he kept going. "Do you think your twisted little sperm will be able to swim far enough? You've got that little thing out and look how you're pumping yourself. Nothing's rising. Just a flaccid piece of flesh. But let's get a ruler. We could measure. I mean, I'm just guessing, but I'd say I have *more* than a few inches on you." The crushing sensation against him was still unmovable. "You know, you need to learn a thing or two about lusty sex. There's a trick to it you're sorely missing. I've never had to tie a woman down to do her. You can pump and thrust all you want, but you'll never get that pathetic excuse for a dick as far as I have."

The liaison's face reddened with rage. He whispered words and with a thrust of his hands, the Champion went sliding into the corner of the stone room. His head split open, and blood trickled down his forehead. "You miserable *little* vampire, now you don't get to watch and listen!"

"Oh, come on, Clayton, let's play fair…just this once. I promise I won't cheat," he whined, like this was a game of checkers. But his arms released from the dark magic grip. And the little egomaniac had become distracted, needing to pump his "prized possession."

"Isn't it a fucking pain when that happens. Look. Your hands are shaking." He propped himself up on an elbow. "Look at all that pumping and pulling. I've had a little experience. Three hundred years of hand jobs makes me an expert. I could give you a few tips. It's all in the way you—"

"Shut up! Shut up! Shut up!" Clayton yelled and turned to face him.

Michael stretched one leg far enough to kick over a candle. Its tall flame extinguished. He was free. "*Death cannot win against itself. Only in life will you triumph.*" He finally understanding the priest's cryptic words.

When Clayton rushed him, he rolled his body and got another candle down. But it wasn't time for the liaison to touch him. Yet. Swiftly skirting the pentagram, Michael swiped at a third with an outstretched hand and kicked at the fourth. One candle remained—at Alana's head. With super speed, he grabbed for its base and flung it in the direction of the liaison.

Clayton took his hands off himself, raised his arms high and swiped the candle away. Michael clicked his tongue and sympathetically shook his head, staring at the pitiful penis. "Oh well," he said in a matter-of-fact way, "all gone." The demented liaison made the mistake of looking down at it, and Michael leapt to his feet.

Taking one long stride forward he slammed his boot into Clayton's carved chest. The puny man sailed into the wall. Out of nowhere, it was as if Clayton rallied more sinister power shrieking, "You think you can take me, vampire? Think again!" Both fists balled. Levelled at his groin. Like a massive shot of hot energy had hit him, he dropped to his knees unable to breathe, which he needed to do now.

Clayton picked up the knife. "I used this on the empath and the Georgian. I used it on that Helena, the meddling angel who raised your brat. I cut your whore with it, too. I'll be killing you with it as well." He strutted over and sliced Michael's left cheek, cackling when his new victim winced in pain.

"Ah, now boy-o, did I finally shut ya up," he asked, smearing the blood off the blade and down Michael's leather-clad shoulder. "I want it clean when it goes through your neck. Silver will do the trick, right vampire? But then again, it's ancient *and* mystical. They'll be screaming at their end. They will suffer, vampire. But for you it only takes a second… swoosh across your neck! Oooh—and this blade will send you home to Hell."

He stood over him gloating, far too talkative and far too confident.

"Only in life will you triumph…"

"Clayton. You have me. Please. Let them go," he managed to whisper with measured humility.

"What's this, lad, you'll be beggin' me now? Ah, Michael, Michael, Michael—tis not like ya, boy-o! Suffering's what ya need, hero. It's what you do best. I'm not sensing the brat's heartbeat. I think we've already lost him, Daddy!" He had slipped out of the phony brogue like a bad actor, came in front of him and sneered.

Michael let a dramatic sob escape. He bent low, aware the maniac was eating this up.

"I win! You're defeated!" The liaison howled with excitement, closing in for the kill. "Now that's more like it, you wayward freak. Kiss my feet and beg me more!"

Death cannot win against itself…Only in life will you triumph— He steadied himself.

"Look at me, vampire, I want to see blood tears drip as I send you to my master!"

Slowly, he knelt up straight and defiantly raised his head. The sacrificial blade was positioned at his neck.

But when Clayton grabbed a fistful of his hair, a loud shriek sounded and Clayton staggered back.

Boldly, he stood leering. Screams filled the room as the liaison's hand burned. Charred bone took its place as Clayton whimpered and howled. "What did you do to me, you miserable traitor! Why the sorcerers wanted you in the first place is a mystery to me!"

Michael steadily strode toward him. His eyes filled with pure hatred. "I told you years ago that the sorcerers would never own me," he said, now dangerously calm. "They could never own my soul. You screwed with my head, used my innocent son as bait, but you did not win."

The liaison lunged with the charmed knife in his other hand. Michael grabbed his wrist, which went up in flames as well. Screaming, the liaison scurried back against the wall, and he followed with slow, sure steps.

"Then you have the *nerve* to sic that poisonous beast on me…instead of turning away and doing the right thing." He touched Clayton's shoulders and both arms went up in flames. Howling and crazed, his beady eyes bulged.

"You tortured my son within a breath of his life. You destroyed my loyal empath, and you murdered another pure soul today."

Clayton cowered and slid down the stone wall as Michael sank down on his haunches. He laid his hands on Clayton's legs, which burned and blazed. Standing up slow, he looked at Alana and unmerciful rage swelled pointing at her, shouting, "This woman is mine and mine alone! I'd walk through the fires of Hell for her! You took them from me, you miserable maniac. No one touches my son. No one touches my Guardian. *No one* takes them from me!" His words thundered off the thick,

343

stone walls piercing the screams and screeches of the liaison to the North American sorcerers.

Then he turned to rescue the love of his live.

With a steady hand on the pearl-handled knife he sliced the ropes holding Alana prone. He peeled off the leather jacket, removed his shirt, and tenderly guided his Guardian's arms through soft, dark silk to cover in modesty her slashed body. After a reverent kiss to her lips, he cradled her to his chest, nuzzling her matted hair. "I've got you, my love," he gently whispered.

He raced up the stairs. Although the internal struggle to release her from his arms was real, he gave her over to Gabriella. *His* Guardian. *His* son.

They were safe. They were out of this miserable place.

With resolve he turned to the basement stairs and didn't look back. In a split-second he jumped the staircase and then came face to face with the moaning torso. He booted what remained of Clayton to the center of the pentagram, got all five candles upright and reset. They ignited, as if by mystical command.

Clayton's mouth began to form a word, but his tone sank low. "Don't ruin this moment, Clayton. I'm way past the forgiving thing. The fact that you *didn't* get the chance to kill my son and my soul mate doesn't matter. You were always the sorcerers' twisted sycophant…a pathetic excuse for a human being. There's only one thing keeping you alive—in a manner of speaking."

He stared down at Clayton's face and stated with controlled rage, "You've ripped my heart out with every torturous act committed on those I love. Now it's time for me to do the same. This is over. Let God forgive your miserable soul, because, as sure as there is a Hell, I won't."

The liaison's beady eyes stayed wide—no more heartbeats, no more breaths. With cold calculation, Michael pulled on the brown leather jacket. He knelt. Then he tore into Clayton's chest and pulled out his heart. As he stood up, the torso burned to a crisp, but Clayton's head remained with a look of infinite agony written across it.

He pulled out the ancient pouch and shoved the heart inside, knotting then replacing it in his pocket. He strode out of the room and raced up the stairs.

****

Michael jumped into the middle seat of the van and closed the door. Gabriella revved the engine. Rosalinda sat in the front with her, and Magdalena tended to both his son and Alana in the back.

Alana gave him a weary smile. Tears spilled down her cheeks without a sound. His eyes misted as well. "She will be fine, *Signore*," Magdalena whispered. Alana's eyes closed. Then, swallowing hard, he studied is son. *Pale. Still unconscious...* Helplessness invaded every fiber of his being. Magdalena gave a soft, *"Signore"* beginning to lift his boy. Michael changed his position and reached for his son getting him over the seat and cradled on his lap with his bloodied blond curls on the center of his chest. *Do you hear my heartbeat? Do you know you are safe and in my arms, little boy?* He memorized every mark that had been beaten into his little boy's body years ago as his nostrils flared. As he swallowed his rage. A white cotton blanket was handed over the seat, which he took and tenderly tucked around his child.

He cleared his throat and with a catch in his voice

ordered, "Let's fly, Sister. Gun it, floor it... Give it all you've got." Tears swam in his eyes. He didn't care. Couldn't stop them. Wouldn't try to. Terror ripped at his heart for his precious child.

The van pulled out of the driveway passing a black limo pulling in.

Chapter 41

Outcomes

Valetta Russo stared at a white van leaving the driveway. It kicked up small, gray pebbles as its wide tires connected with the narrow road. The liaison straightened her suit and licked her lips as she stepped out. The driver closed the limo's door and followed. Confidently, she entered the villa's quiet foyer. The only sounds were the click-click-clicks of black Stilettos on a marble floor.

"I smell coffee. Check the kitchen," she ordered the driver, somewhat suspicious. "Something happened here, something unexpected." She eyed the second-floor landing and climbed the stairs, holding the wrought-iron rail. Carlo was the first one she saw. His eyes stared up at her in terror. She recoiled and screamed with disgust.

Moans came from the bathroom and stepping over him she followed the sound. With a curse, she took a small knife from her purse, cut the nylon cords that bound the guard's hands and feet. The man's jaw hung out of position on his face. Grabbing his shirt collar, she hissed, "What happened?" The guard pointed toward the floor, and when she let go he slumped over the rim of the tub.

"*Basta!*" she screamed and returned to Carlo. Without a second thought, she placed a pointy heel over

347

his trachea and punctured his throat. Life slipped away, but it was the gurgling sound that made her stomach turn. The guard from the bathroom suddenly burst out of the bathroom and ran through the bedroom door. She heard his squeals while tumbling down the stairs. "I'll find you later and put an end to your misery as well," she vowed. She pulled her heel out of Carlos's throat and sashayed down the stairs, just as her driver and the broken-jawed guard sped away in the limo.

It didn't matter. She'd take care of the little double-crossing pervert herself. There would be literal Hell to pay. The basement's stairs were steep and old, made with two boards nailed together, uneven spaces between them. Descending with care, it'd be a shame to get a heal caught and ruined because she planned a haughty entrance.

She peered into the wine cellar. Empty.

"The vampire's brat is supposed to be in here. Carlo wouldn't have lied." She hissed with a sneer and went across the narrow hallway. An immediate stench of burned flesh made her cover her nose with both hands and cough.

The body of an old woman was in a far corner, gutted and in a pool of blood. Then Valetta walked to the pentagram and found what was left of Clayton. She locked her hands on her hips and grinned widely. She spit on his hideous face. "Serves you right, you fucking prick!"

A new wickedness filled her. Throwing her head back, staring at the expression on Clayton's face. Her eyes widened, full of fire as she imagined her just reward. As if talking to what was left of him, she stated rather proudly, "I will use this and bring them your head.

Make it beneficial. I had *nothing* to do with this *at all,* you miserable sadist. No vampire, no Guardian, no boy to take apart piece by piece. I'll make sure they know you failed because I am the most-worthy liaison! Your head will be my proof, you inconsequential fool."

An icy wind blew through the windowless room. The door slammed shut. She heard rumbling begin. Strutting to the door her evil glower turned to terror. But she pulled on the latch. Nothing happened. She banged on the door, pushed and pulled again as the room began to shake.

She cursed and screamed with her hands in the air and brimming with terror as cracks raced up the walls— as the villa collapsed on her. The entire structure was sucked deep into the bowels of the earth, along with the surrounding perimeter owned by the NWT.

In the solitude of the mountains, jagged black stone appeared to cover the property. No contractor would ever build here again. Excavation instruments would indicate this was solid rock, hundreds of miles deep.

Hell had opened and swallowed Valetta's soul.

****

"This isn't the same way we came," Michael said, almost in a panic.

"We aren't going to Portofino, *Signore*. We're bringing you to our Motherhouse. Lukas and Alana will heal there," Magdalena whispered calmly. "The researcher will meet you there. His daughter stayed behind with my mother."

Michael had leaned against the window with Lukas tight to him so he could see Alana. Then it clicked. "Your gray eyes are a mystical trait, I'm guessing," and caught her half-grin. "And Rosa is your mother."

She offered a nod. Turning to Alana who tried to reposition herself, Magdalena said, "Try to stay still or you'll experience a very severe migraine for days. She will be fine in a few hours, *Signore,* when the numbing agent wears off."

But Alana locked her eyes to his. "Do what your cousin says. She knows best," he whispered in agreement.

"We will tend to you as well, *Signore.*"

He didn't care about his own issues. He could sense bruised ribs and the cuts were superficial. Blood dripped from his cheek and a gash on his forehead. His nose wasn't broken. Battling human exhaustion, his eyes watered. But his greatest concern, his greatest fear was for his son.

"*Signore,* the child has been through an ordeal. We will care for him."

He swallowed hard and finally said, "Thank you, Sister," It didn't stop him from worrying any less.

Silence surrounded him as the van sped down the autostrada, which was fine with him. He'd never been loquacious nor a conversationalist, neither in life nor undeath. Except with Alana. They are probably all praying, he thought.

"We pray all the time. Rosalinda isn't a conversationalist, either. Let Alana rest and I'll tell you her thoughts." Gabriella looked in the rearview mirror capturing his gaze. "She's very worried about Lukas. She knew you'd come for them. Pain's not a problem but the numbness is annoying. She can't wait to feel your beating heart, and no, he didn't get a chance to. In her words exactly: You are the only one...my love."

He gave a nod and looked out the window watching

her pass car after car. *God, she drives like a bat out of Hell.*

"Oooh...love that song. Meatloaf—right? Rosalinda's an oldies diva. And I'm going to stop now because she's praying extra hard for your son. Close your eyes, Malone. Get some rest." Lukas moaned and the quiet nun turned and climbed into the seat next to him. "She'd like to hold him for you," Gabriella said.

He couldn't say "no" carefully placing Lukas in her arms, oddly aware he should not touch the skin of her hands. Rosalinda nodded. A shiver ran down his spine.

"Please sit in the front. We will both be more comfortable." A powerful soul, he realized because she spoke as Helena...without words. Gingerly he maneuvered around her and when in the front, Gabriella shot him a look. "She wants you to put this to your cheek so the bleeding will stop." Gabriella reached a hand back and produced a white handkerchief fragrant with lavender.

Dabbing the cut, it stung. *Human pain is a long-forgotten experience. So is feeling stubble on my cheek and chin. Another human experience I haven't had to deal with in centuries.* Awhile later the sign for Sienna came into view, and Gabriella took the turn-off.

Minutes passed before the van screeched to a halt in front of tall gates that stood open. He saw Alana's car in the circular drive. Two gurneys stood side by side. Two sisters in white took Lukas from Rosalinda and Alana from Magdalena. Gabriella matched his long strides with brisk ones of her own. "Our infirmary is better equipped than some Italian hospitals."

They took turn after turn, down quiet corridors until reaching the hospital wing of the convent. He saw Miles pacing the floor as Gabriella said, "Take a seat. I'll come back for you," before she left.

Miles walked over to him. "How are they? How are you?"

"Alana's pretty strong," and his eyes turned brutal adding, "that bastard beat my boy." He palmed an eye and sniffed back the moisture in his nose.

"I hope you ripped his heart out," Miles said, speaking figuratively, of course, to which he replied with his hand over his left pocket, "I've got it right here. How's Celia?"

"She woke up saying you killed Clayton. And the mark on her abdomen faded. She said the villa would descend into Hell."

"Where it belongs," he bit out. Gentler he added, "That's Thorn's gift, allowing her to see as he did. God, he loved her—in the purest sense of the word."

He rubbed his warm chest. How his heart brimmed with love and worry. Sweaty and hot, he shrugged out of the leather jacket, laid it on an empty chair. A nursing sister came over to say, "*Scussa, Signore*, please…to put on." She handed him a black shirt, which he did with a respectful "*Mille grazzi, Sorella.*" It hung on him very loose. He rolled up the sleeves saying to Miles, "I guess this isn't the kind of place you walk around bare-chested, right, researcher?"

Miles tilted his head asking, "And how are you."

He blew out a long breath. "I'm tired and achy, and my ribs hurt like hell. And I'm worried for my boy."

A nursing sister motioned him over to an empty examination room. He raised an eyebrow and looked at Miles. "That's not a demon specialist, so watch your language," the researcher whispered.

"W-what's she going to do to me?"

"Probably take your blood pressure and clean your face. Let her butterfly the cuts and tape your ribs. You may not be able to heal as quickly as before, but you're not quite a-a normal man, Michael. You've never been a normal anything."

Very reluctant to oblige, he got as far as "Miles, I don't want to—"

"Of course, I'll come along if it makes you feel better. Come on."

They both stood at the same time, but he let Miles lead.

Chapter 42

Sacrifice

Leaving the examination room and somewhat humbled, Michael buttoned his shirt as Miles said, "That wasn't so bad, was it?"

His eyes took a slow slide to the researcher. "I didn't need a tetanus shot. You made her give me that." He stared at the leather jacket lying where he'd left it. A thought came to him and as nun passed, he quietly asked, "*Sorella, posso vedere … il*, uh, *Superiore?*"

She looked puzzled at first. "Ah—" as she motioned him to follow with a soft, "*Vieni con me, Signore.*"

****

The architecture was serene. The wooden floors a dark chestnut. It was a short walk to the Mother Superior's Office, which smelled of fresh-cut lemons. Every paper and book had its place.

Gabriella came in. "You'll need a translator. Mother Aurea speaks very little English.."

Mother Aurea stood. "*Benvenuto, Signore?*"

He touched his left pocket and lowered his gaze. She simply nodded. *An Old One on earth, gentle yet wise.* Sister Gabriella took hold of her arm. "Mother wants you to go with her, Michael." He followed them down different corridors until they came to a chapel. "Wait here with me," she told him as the elderly nun went into the sacristy. When she came back, what she held sent shivers down his spine. "Mother believes this belongs to you," she whispered.

As she held it out to him, he hesitated as a memory unraveled—the last Christmas he spent with his sisters. "How is this possible?" he asked in disbelief.

Mother Aurea placed the forgotten treasure in his hands. "*Andiamo*," she said, and led the way.

He held the silver jewelry box with care. It looked as it had in 1677. Not a spot of tarnish marred the forgotten heirloom. Its tiny key lay still intact in a hidden compartment underneath. They walked through the convent's cemetery. Marble crucifixes, old and worn, marking the graves. They stopped at the one tucked in the far corner. It was beneath the high, brick wall lined with lilacs. Reading the names, his jaw tightened as his eyes misted—and his heart skipped a beat.

Sister Gabriella translated as Mother spoke: "Three sisters arrived from England—in 1678…all gifted seers. They presented the Mother Superior with this ornate box. It remained in our office, untouched and preserved until the day I became the leader of this community. I sensed it had survived the centuries for a special purpose. When I became Mother to our order, I had it placed in the chapel's vault. It is yours, *Signore*. Do with it as you must. We will leave you alone."

Only the rustle of their habits broke the sacred silence surrounding him.

Stunned, he knelt to touch their names carved in stone. His hand slid over the monogram on this lost treasure, which had been etched by his grandfather. An ornate "M" in the middle, with four letters inscribed at compass points: A, R, P, and M—one for each of

Rebecca's children, his proud heritage. The vision came back with such clarity that he held his breath.

Running back to my room as you settled into the carriage on that foggy August day. How I begged you to stay. Anne hugged me tight, Priscilla took the silver box from my hands, Rosalind kissed me on the forehead...and you were gone forever.

Gripping the key, he twisted it in the lock, opened the lid. Anne's gold locket... inscribed with an exquisite "A", it had once contained an ink drawing of him as a little boy. He swiped at his eyes with the back of his hand.

Perhaps no one had ever thought to look inside— perhaps her locket had been waiting for him. His gaze lifted to the cloudless sky. Radiant mid-day sun shone bright. Fragrant purple lilacs shaded their grave offering privacy and tender coolness. He slipped the locket into his breast pocket and then reached into his jacket. After placing the ancient pouch in the silver heirloom, Michael locked it and replaced its hidden key.

At the foot of the cross, he pulled fistfuls of earth out of the ground. This burial was closure. What Clayton had done to Alana, to his son, and to countless other innocents. Furiously, he clawed out the dirt until he could reach no deeper.

He placed the silver box in consecrated earth. After filling its grave, he packed it down with a boot-heel. Task complete. He kissed his sisters' headstone. Allowed their memories to hold him one last time. It had taken centuries, but he had finally found them.

****

Getting back to the infirmary had not been as difficult as imagined. He stayed close to the building and at its main entrance retraced his way to Alana's room. Her face lit up when she saw him. "I've missed you," she said, her voice hoarse yet thick with emotion.

He kissed her and brought her palm to his chest. As his heart quickened, he whispered, "My Guardian, my love." She appeared about to cry. "Are you sure you're okay?"

"I refuse to take my hand from the center of your warm chest. I just want to experience every precious beat, my love." Her expression became serious. "How's Lukas?"

As soon as she said his son's name, he shook his head. "I came to you first. I... I—"

"Go... If I could, I'd be right there with you. Give him a big hug for me." His kiss was tender. "Hurry. Go," she whispered again. He broke the capture of her gaze and left.

****

Michael stood outside Lukas's room. Fear filled his heart. He took a deep breath, blew it out slow and walked in. A circle of white habits surrounded the bed. Machines beeped. Each step forward quickened his fear. Each second passing could have been a year.

The white around his son parted. Rosalinda stood next to Lukas holding his hand. When their eyes met his heart sank. Lukas had never regained consciousness. An intravenous bag dripped liquid into his vein at a rapid speed. His beaten body had been washed, yet every welt and cut still appeared bright-red and angry. *Just a frail little boy. My cherished gift.* It was as if his entire world had come to a sudden stop, but he was still running—and then the motion reversed itself.

The other sisters left. He sank into a chair near the

bed as Sister Rosalinda softly said, "We make him comfortable. Hold on to hope, *Signore*. It is simply a matter of time." Her accent was heavy, but he understood every word.

Almost numb, he whispered, "*Mille grazie*," but an overwhelming sense of futility descended upon his soul. He took his son's hand in his. *So small. So still.*

"Talk to me, Lukas. I love you, little boy. Please wake up," became his private chant. As the hours dragged on, he must have said it a thousand times. Eventually, Michael placed his elbows on the bed and his head in his hands. He closed his eyes…

I stand before the Old Ones with terror in my beating heart. "Please, send him back to me." My eyes cloud… And I am contrite, heavy in my heart.

They are unmoved.

I fall to my knees, penitent and full of remorse. Centuries of killing, of self-absorbed willfulness are shown to me, once again.

"I confess to Almighty God." This Act of Contrition is an apology. Tiny droplets blur my vision. I yearn for comfort. "Must I suffer for eternity?"

They give no answer.

"Our Father, who art in heaven," I cry—filled with regret as I recall the love of my son, my flesh and blood. A gift that something like me does not deserve. "I promised I would never leave him. Must I break this bond to my child?"

They give no answer.

"Hail Mary, full of grace," I plead. My eternal love set me on a righteous path. "I would walk through the fires of Hell for Alana. Why must I leave her?"

They give no answer.

"Eternal rest, grant unto them," I pray. All those I cherish are now in the path of death. Save them. Take me... An eternity of penance cannot absolve my guilt.

I quake with fear at their silence.

Yet... So be it. I acquiesce to your will. My death is their life. My death is their survival.

My son will learn from the researcher. He will grow up strong and good.

My Guardian will find love with a man who does not bring danger to her door.

Warm air swirls rapidly as I tumble through time, free-falling through the portal. I land in the passageway, a creature of the night with a regretful soul...alone forever.

Let the blood tears drip from my eyes. I step silent into the shadows of an empty street. My solitary path lay before me. Nothing has changed—it never could.

****

The last thin thread of sanity was gone. So was the ability to dream of survival or the desire to spin a detailed fantasy of love and redemption. No trace of hope. Bled dry for days—how many, he was no longer sure. The stark reality of the situation finally claimed him. In the dark, dirty cell five floors below the New World Technologies building on a street in Manhattan, the vampire's last thought was, *"Let me die."* Michael Malone gave in to the poison.

Chapter 43

Stark Reality

Eight days of snaking through Michael's twisted dreams thanks to an angel, Thorn thought. In the basement of Kendrick House, he opened his eyes somewhat startled, somewhat pissed. "No! Damnit! Do *not* give up." The silent solitude of the basement bedroom had been a Godsend. Fasting and meditation had kept his mind clear of everything except for a mystically enhanced vampire who took on a heroic task.

He opened his mind to his soulmate, just ten city blocks away. Sweet Celia had flown back to Manhattan days ago. They hadn't spoken… well, not in the verbal sense of the word. In this enclosed refuge, and with the help of the Kendrick witches' good magic, he'd been off evil's radar—specifically the dark seers at NWT or, of course, Clayton's cronies.

The Servant of Souls had the privilege of joining Helena's guide of Michael's mind. For that, he was truly grateful. He stood and stretched, still shocked about seeing it all like an out-of-body experience. He had no idea why. Or maybe he did. *The dreams would need to be documented for the Georgians. But writing is Celia's forte, not mine.*

He began to pace. Not exactly buff like in that surreal fantasy but pounds had been shed. Nerves and necessity could do that to a person. A frustrated sigh escaped. "You lost hope, damnit. But I didn't. And you, my friend, didn't listen to *all* of the angel's whispers to your soul."

Physical help was on the way. They wouldn't leave him there.

They would get Michael Malone out of captivity.

****

Celia Bookman stood up and moved away from the desk in her room. The Georgian penthouse in a Manhattan high-rise had always been home. But a shiver of panic ran up her spine like a slithering snake. She caught Thorn's mind-message. She rubbed her forehead, began to wring her hands and pace the spacious bedroom. *Ally is already on a flight. Our trusted friend Philip will be on the inside as of midnight. Lukas is fully protected by good magic, thanks to the Kendrick Witches, to keep him safe and off of NWT's evil radar.* Michael's son was terrified, locked into himself in a really bad way.

But as soon as her adopted sister landed, the plan would be shared and put in to motion. *Tomorrow night. Michael has to hang on because soon he'll be out of that disgusting cell five floors below-ground.* Georgians around the world were sending protection and prayers.

"One more day, Michael, hang on just one more day," she whispered.

****

On Sub-Level Five of NWT Denny Kim handed Philip the clipboard with a grumpy look on his face. "Ya know? I hate being given the greenest of the green to train. In ten years on the dead man's shift it's only been me and Big J." He motioned Philip to follow so he could show off the cells. "Ya got your demons. Ya got your humans who bargained their souls and then reneged. And, of course, one special case. Every once in a while we get to haul a demon to the incineration chambers up two levels. I mean, the job's got perks. Doped up—They can't howl or fight, ya know? Pluck out an eye or a demon claw souvenir... the real pleasures in life." He snorted with a laugh. "We got a vampire going on day nine and no sign of mold or worms." Denny stopped in the aisle. His eyes narrowed. "What'd you say your name was again?"

"Philip Segallo, Mister Kim."

"How do you know Big J?"

"He lives in my mother's building. Jamal had me put in an application months ago, but this was the first opening," the ex-Guardian replied with a quirky lisp—one of Celia B's funnier details in creating this persona. "It's, uh, pronounced fill-leap say-guy-oh." *Add vacant grin and a flick of the wrist.* "Thanks for taking me on. Jamal said you're very smart." Of course, Jamal Storm had briefed him on the overweight and under-enthusiastic floor manager.

A wide grin began. "The night they dragged that vampire in... shit, the shift was awesome! Me and Big J watched them. I chose it. Cell 5027: played those four numbers straight and boxed and it hit big. I bought me a wide-screen plasma TV and a brand new cell phone."

As Celia had shown him, he gave an excited, "Oooh...Congrats!"

"That pathetic bastard of a vampire...took one helluva beating. Tricia, uh, my friend in Records? She has all the office gossip. Says Mister Mails wants to keep it like a trophy for all the trouble it caused him." Kim looked around and leaned close. "You stay clear if Clayton Mails comes down here…a nasty little mother-fucker. He's got lots of voodoo know-how."

"Sure, Mister Kim… I totally defer to your expertise," he answered, respectful-like.

"Yeah… It's a shame about Big J. Breaking his foot shooting hoops with his son. Out for *eight* weeks, so you better learn quick, newbie." He nodded with two "uh-huhs." "Say… You go cruising around those Village bars, Phil?"

"Um, no sir…uh, I don't."

Denny turned around as if to get a better look at him under the stark florescent overheads and tucked the clipboard under a flabby arm. "Do what I tell ya and our shift flies. Two passes a night, an hour dinner-break in between, and then it's home sweet home."

"Do we get to eat together? I make the most *divine* seafood salad on the planet, and I brought enough for two," he said as animated as possible.

"Nah…it's a staggered dinner hour. Someone's always got to keep his eyes open in case one of the things decides to pull an *Escape from New York* move, but it ain't possible," Kim whispered with a snort. "Fifty cells, twenty-five and twenty-five lined side-by-side. You read out the numbers and I do the systems check. If ya don't fuck this up, tomorrow I'll show ya how to look for worms."

The ex-Guardian scanned the clipboard quickly, kept the eager grin. He had memorized a specific entry door's code already. Numbers were his specialty, as was his penchant for speeding. It took an hour to get to Michael's cell. "All right, read it just like ya been doing. To open this here cell, ya start with 7-2-9-6 plus—"

"The cell number," he replied. The glass door unsealed. The exhaust system swooped up the odor of decay. *Oh Lord above, he's in a horrible state. Caked with dried blood everywhere. Cuts and slashes and his right thigh looks shattered. He's practically bled out. What a mess.*

Denny stated like a pro, "Good. No worms. Name."

"Michael Malone."

"Date of internment."

"Ummm—Saturday, 6:35 a.m., May 20. 2005."

"Demonology?" Denny said in a business-like manner.

"Vampire?"

"Status: same or deterioration?" Denny waited.

"Um, um… Oh, here it is!" he replied in a proud way. "What's tonight's status, sir," asking as if he'd finally got it.

"Same. Did you check the right box?"

"Yes, just like you showed me." He watched Denny punch in a second series of numbers, and the cell went dark.

"Each of these things is different. But as soon as skin starts to drop off, that's when we get to burn em because of the worms. Ya gotta bleach the cells because those damn things squirm all over the place." He moved across the aisle to Cell 5028.

The ex-Guardian had memorized every aspect of the captured Champion.

****

Alana passed through heightened security at Newark Airport in the middle of the night without incident. She had no luggage—anything she needed Celia would have. *Nervous much*, she thought while trying to secure her carry-on over a shoulder for the third time. But this was no time for nerves. Her mission was sanctioned and specific. Her mystical senses would stay on high alert until it was accomplished. Her step quickened walking out of the terminal. A car was waiting, and she recognized the driver, an ex-Guardian. Tears threatened to undo her because now the reality of the situation hit like a gut punch. Without a word, she settled into the passenger side seat.

****

Traffic is minimal tonight. Thank God, she thought as they slowed down and pulled over in front of a familiar brownstone. No lights could be seen, yet she steeled herself against a flood of memories. All of them good except one. She stepped out of the ex-Guardian's car and stood motionless. Seconds later she was hugging Celia. She stayed in her adopted father's arms longer than expected. He was an honorable man, a respected one.

"You look good, honey," he said to her.

"I came as soon as I could. The Sovereign Council had one heck of a time getting everyone to agree, Dad. Then it was days before they approved my plan." More immediate worry took hold. "What's Lukas like?"

"He's in a really bad place, Ally. It took Dad days to convince him we'd go in for Michael...that we weren't just screwing with his brain. He's super scared. Torn up inside his heart like he's unsure what to feel. Guardians have been on 24/7 shifts staking out the place in case he decides to bolt."

"What about Phil?"

Her head bobbed in a nod. "He started tonight. Poor Jamal—Doc Chamberlain broke his foot to throw any

365

suspicion off. It's way too dangerous for him to get anywhere near this. He's been Dad's best contact, you know. After all of this is over with, he'll go back when his foot heals, and no one will be the wiser."

She had to ask. She had to know. "How is Michael?"

The slow shake of her sister's head said it all. Her heart fluttered. Her stomach clenched. "Not good," Celia whispered. "Thorn and I, well, we can't be sure he'll survive because of everything they did and then *didn't* do."

"And the city... what have you sensed? What's happening?"

"He put a major dent in the sorcerers' playland. Clients leaving, plus no portals equals no dark magic, and they've got zilch. I'm hearing Clayton's scrawny chest is all puffed out like he won, but there's so much chaos he didn't even put extra security on NWT... and smart employees are taking vacations or calling out sick."

"What about Thorn? You said he was in Michael's mind. I need to know."

"He-he thinks Michael is pretty, you know, devastated mentally and physically." Celia wore her classic what-can-you-do look. "Thorn sends me Michael's dreams to journal—for Dad to study. Michael has one *very* active imagination. Who'd have thought—" Alana glared with a raised eyebrow. "You and Lukas—are all he cares about."

And I still love him, too, she thought, but kept it to herself. Her adopted father took her elbow. "Put Michael out of mind, honey, because we must reassure Lukas. Get him to come with us where he'll be safe and cared for. We cannot leave him here. They will kill him. Ready?"

She took a deep breath and blew it out slow. Then they started up the brownstone's steps.

The door was unlocked, the apartment dark. She stepped in to the small foyer and then flicked a switch on the living room wall. A broken Tiffany lamp with a dim bulb came to life. The meticulously decorated brownstone had been thoroughly trashed. Miles had told her how Lukas watched from the top of a tree while Clayton's men searched both floors. She grabbed a sofa cushion off the floor and settling it back in its proper place—and that's when she saw him. Huddled in a narrow space between couch and wall.

Lukas looked younger than fifteen, although all this mayhem started on his birthday so technically, he was still closer to fourteen. *But his small stature, such boney arms. You would think him younger by maybe two or three years*. His sand-colored hair was full of disheveled curls. But his face… like in a classic portrait of an angel. His face and clothes were dirty. He maneuvered as quick as a Guardian and stood at the sofa's edge by the lamp with his fists balled and ready to strike. *But such a vivid dark-blue of his eyes… a color she'd never seen before*.

"Lukas," her father said in a soft, sure tone, "This is Alana. I told you about her. She is a very close friend of your father's. Come. Sit on the sofa. No one's here to hurt you. She and Celia can help. I promise."

Her mystical senses vibrated like a taut violin string. *Unmistakable sadness. Something close to rage barely manageable, yet he smells of tears and fear*. She sat down slowly. *How have my father and Celia kept him under control? Celia had said one more day and he'd probably fight his way into NWT and go looking for Michael himself. And I could see it happening. A suicide mission because Clayton probably wants this boy as much as he had wanted his father.*

Lukas recognized her right away. When he was thirteen…*Michael following her, but always at a distance on many nights.* He moved slow and steady not taking his focus off the new visitor. Miles had said his father loved her. Did she love him back? *Yeah, she was pretty…* Just a couple of inches taller than he. He knew she had wicked Guardian skills. Nevertheless, he decided to uncurl his fists. Approaching the couch slow, he sank down and put his feet on the couch, keeping his arms hooked around his knees.

"We have a common bond," she said softly. And he didn't flinch or pull away when she touched his knee. Her heart was racing, and she smelled nice, too. She looked sincere. And sad.

"He watched you—from a distance. But I never saw him talk to you."

"We have a complicated history," she said with a half-smile. He felt edgy enough to bolt. "First, I want to you relax. Your dad is *very* important to me. Second, when we get to the penthouse you've got to tell me everything you saw that night… Agreed?" He gave a tight nod. "I… I know what NWT is capable of, so when we go for Michael, you have to trust me. You can't make a mistake." *The look on Miles's face. Serious and resolute…just like hers.*

"I hear you," he replied.

"We need your promise, young man," Miles said, sounding calm, but almost stern. "This is the real world, real danger. Your father hit NWT where it hurts."

"I get it. Shit, I'm not stupid."

Alana's hand pat his knee. "You're a big part of this.

We need you on our team."

He studied her before saying. "Okay. I just want him out of there."

"Good, because what I feel for your father... I can't even put it into words." Her expression turned cold as ice. "Nobody does this to someone I-I ...We won't leave this city without him. I'll get both of you to a safe place. Ready?" She stood; hands on her hips looking like nothing could stop her. "In twenty-four hours, this will be behind you."

Lukas pulled himself off the couch. His feelings were all over the place. But he wanted to trust her. He really did.

****

An hour before dawn, Miles parked in the underground garage beneath his building. Four vastly different individuals took the elevator to the penthouse. He turned on the lights and went into the kitchen to make a pot of coffee. Alana followed. "Where's Mamma B?"

"I sent her to the Georgian Estate in Hampton Hill. Deepa Chandra, my counterpart in Europe and she go way back. In the event our rescue backfires, I want her as far away as possible."

"We can do this; you know we can, Dad. The Georgians are backing us. Michael's done them a major favor. The Sovereign Council has agreed to heal him, whatever that means."

"Alana, nothing's changed. He still is what he is."

"He's a mystically enhanced vampire. He has a soul and a conscience."

"He is still a vampire."

"There's no such thing as a dumb Italian brunette, Daddy B." She gave a thin smile. "And what he is and what he's done won't change my mind or my heart." Her bright hazel eyes flared. "I'll get him out. Cesar has a private plane waiting at Teterboro. We'll all be in Italy this time tomorrow." He nodded a few times. "Look. I didn't fully understand this healing ritual *Zia* talked about. Which reminds me. She sent something. Doc Chamberlain has to use it on him as soon as we're over the Atlantic Ocean. This is all going to work out. I feel it in my bones."

"That's good enough for me, honey." He hugged her tight. "I've missed you, Alana. Celia begged us to join the two of you for Easter, but neither Laura nor I could get away, and you know how I hate to fly. How's Rosa doing? Still cooking up a storm?"

"Ugh… I think I've gained five pounds since September," she said as he poured her a cup of coffee. He hoped to God she was right about this plan working. Because Michael's son looked beyond terrified.

****

Celia beamed when they entered the living room. "I'm so relieved that Dad got him to eat, I mean, he practically inhaled that turkey sandwich. Oooh.. and he even took a shower. Thank God my visions are accurate. He said the jeans and the T-shirt fit perfectly!"

"So, where's the dream journal?" her sister quickly inquired.

"I-I don't have it all sequential yet. There's nothing in it that'll help get him out. Michael knows he's been poisoned." She had to stop the twenty questions Ally was known for because they would lead to the content of Michael's dreams, which couldn't happen. "Philip's shift is almost over. We created a great persona that he balked about, but I'm sure it worked."

"You're holding out on me, Celia B, I know you are. But you're going to hand it over, *sooner* instead of later."

"As sure as the sun sets while we're sipping some sweet red wine in Portofino!"

Lukas walked into the living room. His blond curls dripping wet, and just as she planted the thought, he flopped down right next to her on the sofa. "You've got to feel a teeny bit better now, right?"

The pout turned into an angelic smile complete with the deepest dimples Celia had ever seen. "Yeah. Neat T-shirt."

Her sister took a sip of coffee and placed it down on the glass table next to the recliner. "Okay—tell me everything."

With a little psychic assistance from her, he started to talk. Seated at the dining table her father, the consummate researcher, began to take notes. Incredible, Celia thought as he spoke.

His explanation is almost word for word in Michael's fantasy about what happened to the Hell-beasts in the passageway. Chills danced down her spine. She couldn't wait to tell Thorn how accurate this part of his dream had been. As for her sister? Sitting in a living room chair across the coffee table—she picked up strong vibes of terror and fascination at the same time as Lukas told his story. And when Lukas reached the end, Ally looked speechless.

He gave a slight shrug and kept his arms hugging his knees. "When do I get to, like, talk to him?"

She nudged his shoulder with hers, saying, "Soon, sweetie. Very soon." But his edginess came at her like a monster wave. He was fully uncomfortable talking about what happened nine nights ago. *He didn't use "father" or "dad" ...just Michael. Ally had to have noticed.* Maybe he'd be more comfortable talking alone with her father.

No one spoke for a full minute. And then Lukas said, "I did what you told me to do. I didn't leave the place." She gently bumped his shoulder again giving two thumbs up and a proud smile. But his attention slid back to her sister. "Miles says you were, like, Michael's special Guardian or something."

Ally opened her mouth to speak just as she blurted out, "Philip's out and on his way, Dad."

Her father put down his pen. "Perhaps we can give my daughters some time alone to talk. Come help me prepare breakfast and I'll explain who Philip is and how he'll help us."

With a slow, "Yeah…sure," he followed her father out and the kitchen door swung closed.

The smile faded from her face. Ally's as well. Her sister was suddenly sitting next to her on the couch whispering, "Want to hear the plan—or have you already plucked it out of my mind?"

Her reply was an open look of admiration. "I think it's so simple, Ally, that it's ingenious!"

Chapter 44

Rescue

"You did good, Phil, and half the night's over." Denny Kim laughed, "Jeez, for all that fluff in your head, you really got this down faster than even Big J did—and he's one hell of a smart guy!"

"Thanks a whole bunch, Mister Kim." He gave a huge grin. "I went home, and my friend helped me study. We just moved to this fab condo in Fort Lee. Oh, I almost forgot, I brought you a slice of cherry cheesecake." He pointed to the plastic container on Denny's desk.

Denny scratched his head. "It's my favorite. Isn't that something?"

Denny ate it at 3 AM, got up from his desk, and Philip caught him before he hit the floor, down for the count. At the same time, the "temporary" security supervisor checked his watch. At 3:15 there'd be a pre-recorded CD confirming how everything had been routine during the dead man's shift. Philip would have three minutes before the back-up alarm showed an elevator door open.

He scanned down the clipboard charting statuses and times until he got to Number 5027. Next to "Second Rotation" he noted: Rapid Deterioration. He replaced the clipboard on the desk and got the metal gurney. After unsealing 5027, the ex-Guardian lifted Michael onto it and wheeled it down the hall. He didn't think he'd ever get what the mystically enhanced vampire looked like out of his mind.

As the elevator reached the loading dock, he placed a piece of duct tape over the motion sensor. When the doors opened, Philip started the countdown.

A delivery truck had come from the food service company to refill the vending machines. Of course, they were an NWT subsidiary. Not so tonight.

Miles waved to the guard after he backed the truck to the dock's freight elevator, conveniently blocking the man's view from his station. He climbed down from the cab and slid up the back door of the truck. As the elevator doors opened, the researcher stood to the side looking at a clip board and scratching his head.

Lukas had to wait patiently until he heard the elevator motor. It was his job to jump onto the back platform and take the gurney from the ex-Guardian and get it to the truck where Alana waited. As she lifted Michael into the open back, Lukas pulled a body bag containing a sedated vampire and placed it on the gurney, then ran it back to Philip. As the elevators closed, he sprinted into the back of the truck. Pulled the heavy backdoor down.

No one said a word. No one deviated from the plan.

Miles made a show of going to the back of the truck and securing the back, even though it was already down. He scratched his head again, climbed into the cab and started the engine. Slow to pull away, he reached the guard station some fifty feet away.

He threw the truck into park, saying to the guard in a perfect Staten Island drawl, "Wouldn't ya know it? Just my rotten luck tonight. They loaded the wrong order. But

I called and Dispatch has another truck on its way, okay? Hey, sorry, my man. Listen don't let them know about this screw up, okay? I've got a sick wife at home and a bitchin' pile of bills, ya know?"

A look of disgust swept across the guard's face. "Things are fuckin' nuts here. A friggin' mix up like this might get me fired, too. You sure? Cause I got two kids in college."

"Nah...we just keep this between you and me. I swear on my dead mother's grave, man, may she rest in peace. Another truck's on the way. He put the truck in gear and drove out the gates. As he signaled a right turn by the light, another company truck had its left turn signal on. The two drivers waved to each other.

****

Hours later, Philip roused Denny from his sleep. He had the chubby man sitting at his desk. The drug had allowed him to plant vivid images in Denny's head. Taking Number 5027 to the incineration room, doing what Denny liked best, feeding him to the fire...and of course, cleaning out worms from the cell. All Clayton would find was a pile of fine dust which would be unidentifiable.

"Shit, Mister Kim, that was some kind of high!" He held a look of admiration. "The way you just stuck your fingers in his eye sockets to gouge them out! You are just so strong. And the way you used the pliers to yank out that fang you got in your pocket. Wow. Just wicked." Denny's eyes latched onto the empty gurney behind him in the hall. "Oops. I'll get that back in a few. Boy, this shift really flew!"

Denny shook his head, checked the fang in his breast pocket, and then smiled proudly. "What'd I tell you,

Phil? I bet you don't get to have fun like that in those Village bars, right?"

"No sir, I sure as hell don't. And the way you cleaned out that cell. I hope I was enough of a help," he added with a good stroke to Denny's ego.

Scratching his head, Denny replied, "Oh yeah, sure-sure, you caught the worms. The lazy bastards on dayshift, they don't like to clean up so fast. I see it differently. Wash the worms, then see them burn!" Denny gave a snort. "You know, Big J says I could be a star with my rhyming. Maybe there's a market for a half-Asian rapper who sees this kind of shit, ya know?"

Philip Segallo had played his part like a pro. When he finished his shift the morning sun streaked the spring sky. Alana's strategy was flawless. The Champion was safe.

Chapter 45

Salvation

The luxurious jet, owned by Medico Research Labs, was over the Atlantic Ocean. It had two bedrooms, each with their own bathroom, and a gorgeous sitting area with plush couches and chairs that reclined. Thorn sat with Celia, engaged in quiet conversation, the majority of it non-verbal. His smile lit her heart. *"I like your idea better. Leave it all in but slide over the sex in a clean way. The Council doesn't need to know that part. Give it the "I need you; I want you" old-fashioned voice of his, even though it has drama queen written all over it. Besides, if we share those sex scenes, he'll come after both of us."*

"All right, I'll help you do this, but it'll cost you," she replied to his thoughts with a devoted grin. She rested her head on his beefy shoulder. True, he had dropped more than a few pounds, but the auburn curls she loved to run her fingers through were still there. She asked another question.

"No, he won't walk away from her again. Her mission's over. Alana's free to live her life. I'd also say he's scored big with the Sovereign Council because of what he did. That slip-up with her almost seven years ago shouldn't figure into their decision to protect him and the kid. I don't see any problems. Adding to it...

Closed portals on an entire continent? Ruining NWT? Clayton is crab meat for the other continents' sorcerers, once they think he had this bad boy vampire barbequed. That's another plus."

"What if they won't let Alana be with him? What if they just see the vampire part…without consideration for the mystically enhanced—" Celia whispered.

"Sovereign Council members are the purest souls that still walk this good earth. They'll be fairer than fair. He could have avoided all this by just humbling himself in front of the Council. Instead, the arrogant thick-head took a wrong turn. I swear I can't wait to get my hands on him."

Her stomach flipped seeing such uncharacteristic irritation in the man she loved. *"And poor Lukas… So much pain and confusion in him. He just needs time to heal."*

"I'm glad someone can read that kid, because I can't get a glimmer." Their conversation wasn't meant for Lukas's ears. *"You think it's going to end for the kid like it did in his father's dream?"* He shook his head. *"No, dearest, but Michael's going to have to do some serious soul searching. He'll be good with the kid."*

"I'm totally curious. What parts of Michael's dream of survival were truths?"

"I honestly don't know." He gave a long moan. "Let's try to separate his sensual fiction from what we know is reality. Helena let Michael see many things, and I doubt an angel tells lies. But this dream wasn't your every-night variety. It was one incredible, mystical mind-trip. The poison jacked it up a bit—like his punishing mini-scenes. That was guilt talking. They creeped me out, especially the rats." They both shivered.

"But is everything going to unfold the way he dreamt it? Can't happen... The inconsistencies are obvious. Lukas didn't get to him in the alleyway, and I'd never cut my hair short and lose the curls because you love them." She positively loved his shy smile. "Plus, as we both know, I'm *not* a demon." But his expression turned grim. "All right, let's say there are grains of real-world thrown in. Helena chose him for this "I'll let you see your soul" experiment because there's an ancestral connection, a bloodline to regenerate. A lineage link exists. But as for healers making him human again? I do not think so... Only God alone could pull that one off. The fact that I was able to see every thought is definitely a Heaven-sent intervention. I usually grab one and then I'm out...but so many days of melodrama? I guess my mission includes going wherever he goes."

"You picked up some pretty out of the ordinary stuff, by the way."

Thorn shrugged. "Helena helped him keep his mind intact as long as possible. Even going back to the battle... It's a miracle one of those Hell-beasts didn't go for his heart." He kissed the top of her head.

"His fantasy was picture-perfect, but it did have many flaws."

"Your entire family has known for a long time how much we love each other. Michael never saw my feelings for you."

"So what he didn't know about Lukas, Alana, or any of us, his imagination filled in the blanks."

"There you go," he whispered switching to non-verbal. *"I still can't get over the fact that he actually believes I am a demon. It just hurts! Definitely a drama queen...and a bad one. He may look young, but he thinks with a centuries-old mind like he's stuck in the Romantic Era—Chopin, Liszt, Browning, Dickinson. Long live that kind of passion."*

Thorn shook his head, addressing her silent question. "I don't see any heart-gouging showdown coming. Clayton will be dead in days. Michael made it out, well, I won't say alive, but very undead and still sort of kicking." He paused. "I know you're feeling just how really annoyed with him I am. I'm sorry… It's too strong to shield. He's got a lot to answer for with me. Just to put the fear of God in him, I should sling him over my shoulder and smack his ass good and hard. That arrogant son of a bitch pulled the wool over my eyes and drugged me! I never saw it coming."

"You wouldn't have been able to help him in the battle. It's not your mission."

"Yeah, but believe me, I'd have stopped him from doing something so unbelievably stupid. I'd have pulled the plug on his plan before *anyone* got hurt. Michael's in trouble—and I don't mean the physical kind." He wasn't playful anymore, pulling her close, both of them thinking about two friends who were gone. "Clayton could have let them go. He killed Rob and Dan, you know… after they took out the Summoned Six. At least the Guardians got their bodies back for a proper burial."

Tears began to well in her eyes. "Please stop. I can't talk about them yet." She swiped at the corners of her eyes. "But Michael does respect you, Thorn."

"I know. The good sisters will heal him, I'm sure. Michael will help the kid put his life together the right way, without magic tricks. That was his *biggest* mistake." Then his eyes drifted down.

"What about Ally?"

"Alana, ah…dearest Alana… She has a lot of soul searching to do." That was all he said but she sensed some kind of internal conflict as well. What amazed her was the amount Michael had figured out. Many details were twisted, but solid facts were there. This would be a challenge and it'd be interesting to see which parts were fantasies, which parts premonitions.

****

Miles sat across from Lukas Malone, who was sprawled across the leather sofa, watching him click away on a laptop. He looked innocent enough, but anything could set him off. With such unnatural strength, talking him out of doing something rash was always his first thought.

"What are you writing about me? That can't all be about my…about Michael."

He let it slide that the word 'father' hadn't come out of the boy's mouth yet. "Why don't you have a look?" Lukas moved next to him and started to read.

"That's what happened at the brownstone."

"Yes. Did I get it all down correctly?" he asked hoping to engage.

"Looks good to me. Creative Writing is my favorite class in high school." Then Lukas paused, turned away, and mumbled, "I'm not going back to my school. I'm not going back to my happy life."

He came off lonely, with no connection to anyone. Watching his shoulders slump forward and the way he lowered his head… He put a gentle hand over the boy's.

"Don't do this to yourself, young man. Your father will find you a great school, and you've already made new friends. Why don't you start a journal of your own? It might help you understand some of what has happened. When you write it down, oftentimes it helps clear your mind. I'd like to close my eyes for a little while. Here. I've opened a new file." Handing over his prized possession, he hoped the boy would open up a bit because he was seriously concerned.

"Maybe I can get a laptop my own, you know?"

"It's a definite possibility. We'll see when we arrive in Italy."

This was good. He was talking. Then he noticed a quick eye-slide at Thorn. It appeared hostile. Angry. He felt too tired to address the issue right now. It had been a long tense ten days. He still didn't know how to journal all he'd been told about. Reclining the plush seat, he tried to relax. I detest flying, he thought to himself, no matter how comfortable the plane. Touchdown in La Spezia couldn't come fast enough.

****

The bedroom had been turned into an air vac emergency room. Doctor Chamberlain and Doctor John Baker cleaned Michael's body as well as the many wounds and pumped him full of human blood. Careful to stitch every cut and slash, they had disinfected the vampire's shoulder as well as the deep claw marks with a strong organic solution sent by her *Zia* Rosa.

His skin tone was a dull gray. His eyelids like black, hollow holes.

Alana sat off to the side while the demon specialist documented every festering contusion. She knew Michael was a mess…especially his right leg. He hadn't stirred. In over ten years, she'd never seen the mystically enhanced vampire this badly injured. *We've had almost seven years apart because I couldn't trust myself. Turning my back on you was the only way I could handle*

382

my feelings.

Doc Chamberlain came to her side. "There's nothing more we can do for him now, Alana. So many days in such a state, you need to be patient. We'll be right outside if you need us."

She watched them leave and close the door. She walked over to the bed and sat on its edge. "After so many years of avoiding each other we're finally alone." Careful yet hesitant, she lay down beside him. Seeing him again brought back so many memories. She had buried them deep, prayed day and night to keep them far from her heart. She had questions. Many questions. *Where would loving him lead to? Why had he done this?*

Because he is a Champion. Commanding and strong. Seeing him this way shredded her heart. And yes, he was her destiny. Her soulmate. She kissed his pale lips; stroked his sutured cheek full of tender affection. "Michael, my love," she whispered in his ear and pressed his cold hand to her beating heart. "You're safe. I've got you."

A tiny bead of crimson tear escaped from beneath an eyelash. Alana was next to him. He knew her scent. This wasn't a dream. She was real. He felt her strong heartbeat rhythmically pulsing against his hand. How he craved her touch. The only words Michael Malone could clearly think were etched deep in his soul for an eternity. *My Guardian...my love.*

A word about the author...

Always an avid reader, the realm of paranormal fiction continues to be the perfect landing point for M. Flagg. After a successful career as a music teacher and an urban school administrator, she continues to spin stories of passion, love and redemption. Along with published paranormal fiction, she has been a contributor in a book on urban music education and has also authored an article for Still Standing, a web-magazine about loss and healing. Her Action Research Project was recognized for Outstanding Writing in 2006 and she was named a Distinguished Music Educator at the Yale Music Symposium in 2010. A life-long New Jersey resident, M. Flagg is a member of Liberty States Fiction Writers and currently serves as a Professor in Residence at a local university.